...at they say about Kate Atkinson:

'An exceptionally **funny**, quirky and **bold** writer' *Independent on Sunday*

'One of the country's most **innovative**, **exciting** and **intelligent** authors' *Scotsman*

'Kate Atkinson is **brilliantly**, defiantly **playful** with the stuff of fiction' *New Statesman*

'A **brilliant** and **profoundly original** writer' *Daily Express*

'**Funny**, bracingly **intelligent** . . . a genuinely **surprising** novelist' *Guardian*

What the critics wrote about
Emotionally Weird

'The lustre, energy and panache of her writing are as striking as ever in this, her third novel . . . Funny, bold and memorable'
Helen Dunmore, *The Times*

'Lively . . . very funny' *Sunday Telegraph*

'Complex, multi-layered and beautifully written . . . brimming with quirky characters and original storytelling . . . Kate Atkinson has struck gold with this unique offering' *Time Out*

'A truly comic novel – achingly funny in parts – challenging and executed with wit and mischief . . . an hilarious and magical trip'
Meera Syal, *Daily Express*

'Her novels are remarkable both in and of themselves, and as evidence of an important emerging body of work from a brilliant and profoundly original writer' *Daily Telegraph*

'A challenging work of fiction . . . brilliantly original' *Mirror*

'Kate Atkinson's strength as a writer lies in her talent for observational humour' *Guardian*

'Sends jolts of pleasure off the page . . . capable of causing loud and involuntary cackling on public transport. Kate Atkinson's funniest foray yet . . . a novel for people who love novels . . . eccentric, unstoppably entertaining, it is a work of Dickensian or even Shakespearean plenty . . . will be enjoyed hugely by both literary and non-literary readers' *Scotsman*

'Kate Atkinson is brilliantly, defiantly playful with the stuff of fiction'
New Statesman

'Her descriptive powers are striking. She is also witty . . . thought-provoking and nonconformist' *Sunday Times*

'A novel purely for fun . . . entirely to be recommended' *Independent*

'Really comic, really tragic, bracingly unsentimental' *Boston Sunday Globe*

'Her enigmatic and comic flair rise to greater heights in this *reductio ad absurdum*' *Sunday Tribune*

'Her inventive energy, unfettered by realism, make this roller coaster of a novel a highly entertaining read' *Mail on Sunday*

'A sparkling comic meditation on how authors choose to tell their stories' *Entertainment Weekly*

'Kate Atkinson writes with the most finely tuned literary instincts . . . funny, clever and strangely moving' *Caledonian*

'Fairly crackles with energy, wit and the pleasure of writing' Lesley Glaister, *Literary Review*

'A full-bore, old-fashioned yarn – the kind that keeps you turning pages, hurrying toward the denouement long after you've told yourself you're going to bed' *Washington Post*

'Subtle, evocative and wonderfully funny' *Glasgow Herald*

'A brilliant and gripping piece of fiction that not only proves Kate Atkinson's adeptness as a storyteller but also firmly establishes her as one of the most remarkable writers of recent times' *Yorkshire Post*

'Kate Atkinson has found her best subject, thereby letting out the secret to writing a truly funny comic novel' *Newsday*

By KATE ATKINSON

Behind the Scenes at the Museum

A surprising, tragicomic and subversive family saga
set in York, Kate Atkinson's prizewinning first novel,
like all her novels, has a mystery at its heart.

'Little short of a masterpiece'
Daily Mail

Human Croquet

A multilayered, moving novel about the forest
of Arden, a girl who drops in and out of time,
and the heartrending mystery of a lost mother.

'Brilliant and engrossing'
Penelope Fitzgerald

Emotionally Weird

Set in Dundee, this clever, comic novel depicts student life
in all its wild chaos, and a girl's poignant quest for her father.

'Achingly funny . . . executed with wit and mischief'
Meera Syal

Not the End of the World

Kate Atkinson's first collection of short
stories – playful and profound.

'Moving and funny, and crammed with incidental wisdom'
Sunday Times

Life After Life

What if you had the chance to live your life again
and again, until you finally got it right?

'Grips the reader's imagination on the first page and never
lets go. If you wish to be moved and astonished, read it'
Hilary Mantel

A God in Ruins

A masterful companion to *Life After Life*. For all Teddy – would-be poet,
RAF bomber pilot, husband and father – endures in battle, his greatest
challenge will be to face living in a future he never expected to have.

Featuring Jackson Brodie:

Case Histories

The first novel to feature Jackson Brodie, the
former police detective, who finds himself investigating
three separate cold murder cases in Cambridge,
while still haunted by a tragedy in his own past.

'The best mystery of the decade'
Stephen King

One Good Turn

Jackson Brodie, in Edinburgh during the Festival,
is drawn into a vortex of crimes and mysteries,
each containing a kernel of the next,
like a set of nesting Russian dolls.

'The most fun I've had with a novel this year'
Ian Rankin

When Will There Be Good News?

A six-year-old girl witnesses an appalling crime.
Thirty years later, Jackson Brodie is on a fatal journey
that will hurtle him into its aftermath.

'Genius . . . insightful, often funny, life-affirming'
Sunday Telegraph

Started Early, Took My Dog

Jackson Brodie returns to Yorkshire, in search of
someone else's roots, while shopping mall security chief
Tracy Waterhouse makes an impulse purchase that will
turn her life upside down.

'The best British crime novel of the year'
Heat

EMOTIONALLY WEIRD

A COMIC NOVEL

Kate Atkinson

BLACK SWAN

TRANSWORLD PUBLISHERS
61–63 Uxbridge Road, London W5 5SA
www.transworldbooks.co.uk

Transworld is part of the Penguin Random House group of companies
whose addresses can be found at global.penguinrandomhouse.com

Penguin
Random House
UK

First published in Great Britain in 2000 by Doubleday
an imprint of Transworld Publishers
Black Swan edition published 2001
Black Swan edition reissued 2015

A CIP catalogue record for this book
is available from the British Library.

ISBN
9780552997348

Typeset in 11/15pt Giovanni.

Penguin Random House is committed to a sustainable future for
our business, our readers and our planet. This book is made from
Forest Stewardship Council® certified paper.

MIX
Paper from
responsible sources
FSC
www.fsc.org   FSC® C018179

Printed and bound in Great Britain by Clays Ltd, St Ives plc

37 39 40 38 36

For Lesley Denby, née Allison, with love

With thanks to:
Helen Clyne, Lesley Denby, Helen How,
the Howard Hotel (Edinburgh), Maureen
Lenehan, Gareth McLean, David Mattock,
Martin Myers, Ali Smith, Sarah Wood.

'That's a great deal to make one word mean,' Alice said in a thoughtful tone.

'When I make a word do a lot of work like that,' said Humpty Dumpty, 'I always pay it extra.'

'Oh!' said Alice. She was much too puzzled to make any other remark.

'Ah, you should see 'em come round me of a Saturday night,' Humpty Dumpty went on, wagging his head gravely from side to side: 'for to get their wages, you know.'

(Through the Looking-Glass, Lewis Carroll)

The Hand of Fate

(First Draft)

Inspector Jack Gannet drove into Saltsea-on-Sea along the coast road. Today's sun (not that he believed it to be a new one every day) was already climbing merrily in the sky. It was a beautiful morning. Shame it was about to be spoilt by the *Lucky Lady* and her cargo – one very unlucky lady. One very dead lady. Jack Gannet sighed, this job didn't get any easier. Jack Gannet had been in the force longer than he cared to remember. He was a straightforward, old-fashioned kind of detective. He had no strange tics or eccentricities – he didn't do cross-words, he wasn't Belgian, he certainly wasn't a woman. He was a man suited to his profession. What he wasn't, was happy. He didn't want to be dealing with a dead body on a glorious morning like this. Especially not on an empty stomach.

Madame Astarti didn't know about the dead body yet. She was having some trouble opening her eyes. They were glued shut by sleep and mascara and one too many gins in The Crab and Bucket last night with Sandra and Brian. Madame Astarti sighed and groped blindly around on her bedside table for her lighter and a packet of Player's No.6 and inhaled deeply on a cigarette. She loved the smell of nicotine in the morning.

Seagulls were clog-dancing on the roof above her head, heralding a brand new day in Saltsea-on-Sea. Through a gap in the curtains she could see that the sun was the colour of egg-yolks. Sunrise, she thought to herself, a little daily miracle. It would be funny, wouldn't it, if it didn't happen one morning? Well, probably not very funny at all really because everything on earth would die. The really big sleep.

1972

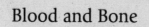

Blood and Bone

MY MOTHER IS A VIRGIN. (TRUST ME.) MY MOTHER, NORA — A FIERY Caledonian beacon – says she is untouched by the hand of man and is as pure as Joan of Arc or the snow on the Grampians. If you were asked to pick out the maiden in a police line-up of women (an unlikely scenario, I know) you would never, ever, choose Nora.

Am I then a child of miracle and magic? Were there signs and portents in the sky on the night I was born? Is Nora the Mother of God? Surely not.

On my birth certificate it states that I was born in Oban, which seems an unlikely place for the second coming. My beginning was always swaddled in such mist and mystery by Nora that I grew up thinking I must be a clandestine princess of the blood royal (true and blue), awaiting the day when I could come safely into my inheritance. Now it turns out that things are more complicated than that.

I am twenty-one years old and I am (as far as I know, for we can be sure of nothing it seems), Euphemia Stuart-Murray. Effie, for Nora's sister, who drowned in a river on the day that I was born. Nora herself was just seventeen when I entered the material world. A child looking after a child, she says.

These Stuart-Murrays are strangers to me, of course. As a child I had no kindly grandfather or playful uncles. Nora has never visited a brother nor spoken wistfully of a mother. Even their name is new to me, for all of my life Nora and I have gone by the more prosaic 'Andrews'. And if you cannot trust your name to be true then what can you trust? For all she has acknowledged her family – or vice versa – my mother may as well have washed ashore on a scallop shell, or sprung fully formed from some wrathful god's head, her veins running with ichor.

The closest Nora ever came to talking about any family until now was to claim that we were descended from the same line as Mary Stuart herself and the dead Scottish queen's flaws had followed us down the generations, particularly, Nora said, her bad judgement where men were concerned. But then, I doubt that this is a trait exclusive to Mary Queen of Scots, or even the Stuart-Murrays.

I have come home – if you can call it that, for I have never lived here. My life is all conundrums. I am as far west as I can be – between here and America there is only ocean. I am on an island in that ocean – a speck of peat and heather pricked with thistles, not visible from the moon. My mother's island. Nora says it is not her island, that the idea of land ownership is absurd, not to mention politically incorrect. But, whether she likes it or not, she is empress of all she surveys. Although that is mostly water.

We are not alone. The place is overrun with hardy Scottish wildlife, the thick-coated mammals and vicious birds that have reclaimed the island now that the people have all left it for the comfort of the mainland. Nora, ever a widdershins kind of woman, has made the journey in reverse and left the comfort of the mainland to settle on this abandoned isle. When we say the mainland we do not always mean the mainland, we often mean the next biggest island to this one. Thus is our world shrunk.

Nora, a perpetual déracineé, the Wandering Scot, a diaspora of one (two if you count me), spent the years of my childhood in exile from her native land, flitting from one English seaside town to the next as if she was in the grip of some strange cartographical compulsion to trace the coastline step by step. Anyone observing us would have thought we were on some kind of permanent holiday.

I used to wonder if, long ago, Nora began her journey in Land's End and was trying to get to John o'Groats, although for what reason I couldn't imagine – unless it was because she was Scottish, but then many Scots live their whole lives without ever finding it necessary to go to John o'Groats.

Now she says she will die here, but she is only thirty-eight years old, surely she is not ready to die yet? Nora says that it doesn't matter when you die, that this life is nothing but an illusion. Maybe that's true, but it doesn't stop the cold rain from soaking us to the skin or the gales blowing in our hair. (We are truly weathered here.) Anyway, I don't believe that Nora will ever die, I think she will merely change state. It has begun already, she is being transformed into an elemental creature, with tidal blood and limestone bones. She is unevolving, retiring into the ancient, fishy regions of her brain. Perhaps soon she will crawl back into the watery realm of Poseidon and reclaim her Saurian ancestry. Or metamorphose into something monumental – an ice-capped ben, littered with granite boulders, or a tumbling, peat-brown burn, bubbling to the sea with its cargo of elvers and fry and frothy green weed.

I am bound to the unknown and neglected Stuart-Murrays by spiralling tapeworms of genetic material. We are, dead and alive (but mostly dead, it seems), the glowing molecular dust of stars, a galactic debris of bacteria and germs. Our veins are the colour of delphiniums and lupins, our arterial blood a febrile brew of crushed geranium petals and hot-house roses, thinned with plasma like catarrh and—

~ Wheesht, says Nora, talk sense, our bloodline is that of ancient warriors, of berserkers and invaders. Our blood tastes of rusted weapons and hammered-out coins. We are not the sort, she says, who stoically slit their thin veins like reeds, and slip away quietly down their own bloodstream, we don our breast-plates and hack and hew and rive at our enemies.

The Stuart-Murrays, it seems, are even-handed – they have fought against the English and also stood shoulder to shoulder with them in support of Empire and exploitation. We are num-bered amongst those wha' bled wi' Wallace and have been present at nearly every rammy, stushie and stramash in Scotland's tortured history.

And where are they now, these feckless Stuart-Murrays? The line, Nora says, will end in daughters. Or, to be more precise – me. I am, it seems, the last daughter of the house of Stuart-Murray.

I am a young woman composed of blood and flesh, sugar and spice, all things nice and the recycled molecules of the dead. I have thin bones that snap and shatter too easily for my liking. I have Nora's narrow insteps and broad toes, her love of senti-mental music, her hatred of Brussels sprouts. I have my mother's temperamental hair – hair that usually exists only in the imagin-ation of artists and can be disturbing to see on the head of a real woman. On Nora it is the colour of nuclear sunsets and of over-spiced gingerbread, but on me, unfortunately, the same corkscrewing curls are more clownish and inclined to be carroty.

I also have my mother's native tongue, for we led such an iso-lated life when I was a child that I speak with her accent, even though I never set foot in her country until I was eighteen years old.

Some people spend their whole lives looking for themselves, yet our self is the one thing we surely cannot lose (how like a cheap philosopher I am become, staying in this benighted place). From the moment we are conceived it is the pattern in our blood and our bones are printed through with it like sticks of seaside rock. Nora, on the other hand, says that she's surprised anyone knows who they are, considering that every cell and molecule in our bodies has been replaced many times over since we were born.

Some people say that we are nothing more than a bundle of perceptions, others claim that we are composed entirely out of our memories. My earliest memory is of drowning – like my mother, I am clearly drawn to the dark side. Perhaps I am a living, breathing example of reincarnation – perhaps the drowning Effie's spirit leapt out of her body and into my newborn one?

~ Let's hope not, Nora says.

Memory is a capricious thing, of course, belonging not in the world of reason and logic, but in the realm of dreams and photographs – places where truth and reality are tantalizingly out of reach. For all I know I have imagined this aquatic memory, as insubstantial as water itself – or remembered a nightmare and thought it real. But then, what is a nightmare if it isn't real?

Before she had a purpose (turning into landscape) Nora herself was always a distracted and absent-minded person. Mnemosyne's forgotten daughter. How else can you explain the obliteration of the Stuart-Murrays, not to mention the terrible circumstances of my birth?

We are walking along the puffin-populated cliffs that fall away into cold-boiling sea. Above our heads a succession of wheeling, screeching birds – kittiwakes, guillemots, gannets – are creating complex and unreadable auguries.

We can see almost the whole island from here – the big house where we stay, the bracken and heather and boggy peat and beyond, on the far side, the yellowing machair, home to rabbit and feral cat, the latter the terrifyingly ugly product of genetic isolation – animals descended from a pair of pet Siamese brought on holiday by some long-gone Stuart-Murrays. For this island, according to Nora, is the holiday home of our ancestors.

I have no reason to dispute this fact with her, although why anyone would want to holiday in this blighted place I cannot imagine. Even in high summer I expect there is an air of autumnal desolation about it. In winter, it is like a place that has been long-forgotten or never discovered at all. Nora says she remembers holidays here, remembers being a small child, dipping in and out of rock pools for little brown crabs and tiny tinsilver fish and eating windswept picnics on the impoverished sea-salted grass of the lawn.

Nora is a woman with a past, a past she has always resolutely

28

refused to speak about, and you cannot imagine how strange it is to hear her talk about it now. It disturbs me more than it disturbs her, for she has carried it in her head all these years, whereas for me it is a newly opened box of frights and wonders.

Nora says that we shall wrap ourselves in shawls and blankets like a pair of old, cold-boned spinsters (Euphemia and Eleanora) and sit by the cracking flames of a driftwood fire and spin our stories. When she spills her own tale into the silence for me, she says, it will be a tale so strange and tragic that I shall think it wrought from a lurid and overactive imagination rather than a real life.

~ Hurry, hurry, Nora urges, we must get on, we must tell our tales. How will you begin? she asks. *A lone fisherman up early looking for sea trout . . . ?* And will it be real? Or will you make it up as you go along?

~ Will you excise the tedium of everyday life – the humdrum of kettles boiled, toilets flushed, curtains drawn, doorbells rung, telephones answered, the skin shed, the nails grown, and so on (ad infinitum, ad nauseam)? Do we really, she asks, want to listen to the prolixity of petty marital disputes over the cat, the lawnmower, the bottle of blood red wine?

~ Nor, says Nora, do we want commonplace tales of *Hausfrau Angst*, of the woman heroically making over her life with a handsome new lover, a beautiful child, a happy ending. Instead, we shall have murder and mayhem, plots and sub-plots, a mad woman in the attic, purloined diamonds, lost birthrights, heroic dogs, a soupçon of sex, a suspicion of philosophy.

29

Very well. I shall begin at an arbitrary moment just over a month ago (how much longer it seems). The season is winter, it is always winter. Nora is the very queen of winter.

The place is the land of cakes, the city of the three Js, the home of the Broons, the schoolyard of the Bash Street Kids and William Wallace, the kailyard of Scottish journalism, Juteopolis – Dundee!

Dundee. A place far, far away in the magical north country, whence I got my nature but not my nurture. 'The North' – that magic road sign with its promise of ice floes and Eskimos, polar bears and the aurora borealis. Dundee – land of outlandish street names – Strawberrybank, Peep o'Day Lane, Shepherd's Loan, Magdalen Yard Green, Small's Wynd, Brown Constable Street, Bonnybank Road.

Dundee – built on the solidified magma and lava of an extinct volcano, Dundee with its crumbling, muddy-sandstone tenements, impenetrable accent, appalling diet and its big, big estuary sky. Bonny Dundee, where the great Tay broadens into the firth, carrying with it salmon, sewage, the molecules of the watery dead, perhaps even of Nora's sister, beautiful Effie, who drowned on the day that I was born, swept downstream like a dead fish.

~ Just get a move on, Nora says.

Chez Bob

A MONDAY MORNING AND MY DREAMS WERE INTERRUPTED AT some unearthly hour by the doorbell ringing with a shrill urgency that implied death, tragedy or a sudden, unexpected inheritance. It was none of those things (not yet anyway), it was Terri. It was only seven o'clock and it seemed likely therefore that rather than being up early she hadn't actually been to bed at all.

Small and thin, Terri was dressed, as usual, in the manner of a deranged Victorian governess. She had the pale pallor of a three-day-old corpse on her cheek and, despite the dark on the unlit stair, was wearing Wayfarer Ray-Bans.

Although I had opened the door, Terri's finger remained on the doorbell, as if she had been struck by *rigor mortis* while pressing it. I forcibly removed the finger, almost having to break it in the process. She held out a hand, palm up, and said, 'Give me your George Eliot essay,' her face as expressionless as an assassin's.

'Or what – die?'

'Fuck off,' she said succinctly and lit up a cigarette in the manner of a *film noir* villainess. I shut the door on her and went back to bed and the warm, slack body of Bob with whom I lived in urban squalor in a festering tenement attic in Paton's Lane, former residence of Dundee's reviled yet noble-hearted poet, William Topaz McGonagall. Bob rolled over and muttered some of his usual sleep gibberish ('The leopard's going to miss the train!' 'Got to find that radish,' and so on).

Bob, known by some people as 'Magic Bob', but for reasons which were obscure and not based on any sleight-of-hand on Bob's part, was in fact an unmagic Essex boy, Ilford born and bred, although when he remembered, he affected a monotonous, vaguely northern accent to give himself more credibility with his peers.

Like me, Bob was a student at Dundee University but said that if he had been in charge of the university he would have thrown himself out. He seldom handed in an essay and considered it a point of honour never to go to a lecture and instead lived the slow life of a nocturnal sloth, smoking dope, watching television and listening to Led Zeppelin on his headphones.

Bob had recently discovered that he was in his final year of university, he had already repeated second year twice – a university record – and for a long time had presumed that somehow he would remain a student for ever, a misconception that had only recently been cleared up. He was supposed to be studying for a joint degree in English and Philosophy. If people asked him what his degree was in he always said 'Joints,' which he thought was a brilliant joke. Bob's sense of humour, such as it was, had been developed by the Goons and honed by The

Monkees. Bob's screen hero was Mickey Dolenz, right back to Mickey's early days as Corky in *Circus Boy*.

Bob was an unreconstructed kind of person, his other hero was Fritz the Cat and he had a complete lack of interest in anything that involved a sustained attention span. Nor was he political in any way, despite the three unopened volumes of *Das Kapital* on his bookshelf – which he never could explain, although he had a vague memory of joining a radical Marxist splinter group after seeing *If* . . . at the cinema. He was prone to the usual obsessions and delusions of boys his age – the Klingons, for example, were as real for Bob as the French or the Germans, more real certainly than, say, Luxemburgers.

The doorbell rang again, less insistently this time, and when I opened the door Terri was still there. 'Let me in,' she said weakly. 'I think I've got frostbite.'

Terri was a little mid-western princess, a cheerleader gone bad. She may have once had corn-fed kin back in the heartland (although it was easier to imagine her being hatched in the nest of a prehistoric bird) but in time they had all either died or abandoned her. Her father, an executive with Ford, had enrolled her in an English Quaker boarding-school during a brief secondment to Britain and had carelessly left her there on his return to Michigan.

Terri liked to keep her ethnic origins chameleon, sometimes hinting at Italian, sometimes pogrom-fleeing Russian, a touch of the Orient, a hint of the Hebrew. Only I knew the dull mongrel mix of Irish navvies, Dutch dairymen and Belgian coalminers who by mere genetic chance had given her the appearance of an exotic houri or a handmaiden of Poe. We were the best of friends, we were the worst of friends. We were the sisters we'd never had. I felt sorry for someone so at odds with the mainstream of humanity. Sometimes I wondered if my role in Terri's life wasn't to mediate between her and the living, like a vampire's assistant.

Although she hated staying in it, Terri did have her own ruffled lair in Cleghorn Street – an unappealing cold-water flat that wasn't good for much other than storing her coffin of earth. In a rare fit of activity she had painted it purple throughout, a colour-scheme that did nothing to alleviate her own darkness. At least Terri, unlike myself, had worked out her future destiny – she was going to marry a very old, very rich man and then 'screw him to death'. She wouldn't be the first, but I doubted whether she would find a suitable candidate in Dundee.

I fumbled around in the dark for a candle. We were in the midst of a discontented winter of strikes and three-day weeks which meant there was no electricity this morning. If I had been capable of forethought, which I feared I never would be, I would have bought a torch by now. I would also have managed to acquire a Thermos flask. And a hot-water bottle. And batteries. I wondered how many three-day weeks it would take before civilization began to break down. Sooner for some than others, I supposed.

From the window I could see that across the water

in Fife they had electricity. The houses of Newport and Wormit were studded with cheerful lights as more purposeful people than us embarked on their day. If it had been daylight we would have had a magnificent view of the rail bridge and its freight of trains, the black iron lacework curving lazily across a Tay that was sometimes silvery, often not, and which in today's dark dawnlight was like a ribbon of tar running past the city.

In the bedroom, Bob was still fast asleep. In these night-like days of hibernation his waking hours were even more severely curtailed than usual.

'The butterfly's got the cornflakes,' a sleepfaring Bob warned us in a loud voice.

'I don't know what you see in him,' Terri said.

'Neither do I,' I said gloomily.

It couldn't have been his looks that attracted me, as Bob looked much like everyone else did – the Zapata moustache, the gold hoop earring, the greasy Royalist locks curling over badly deported shoulders. He looked, if anything, like a tramp – an impression reinforced by the second-hand army boots and the oversized air-force greatcoat he habitually wore.

Bob had recently discovered the meaning of life, a discovery that seemed to have made no difference whatsoever to his everyday existence.

I met Bob the first week I was at university. I was already eighteen years old and thought that I could discern a certain librarian caste to my features and was afraid I would end up a lonely figure, forever wandering a spinster wasteland, and it was mere chance that Bob was the first person to cross my path the morning I decided to lose my virginity.

I met him when he ran me over. Bob was on a bicycle and I was on a pavement, which perhaps gives an indication of whose fault the accident was. I broke my wrist (or rather, Bob broke my wrist), and the exciting combination of circumstances – drama, blood and a brown-eyed man – all served to make me think that destiny had spoken and therefore I should listen.

Bob hit me because he swerved to miss a dog. The man who would sooner run over a woman than a dog introduced himself by bending over me where I lay on the pavement, staring at me in amazement, as if he'd never seen a woman before, and saying, 'Wow, what a bummer.'

The dog came out of the accident unscathed, if a little surprised, and was returned to its tearful owner. Bob rode to the Dundee Royal Infirmary in the ambulance with me and had to be physically stopped from inhaling the gas and air.

Terri had finally taken her sunglasses off after tripping over Bob's boots left carelessly in the middle of the floor. There were many drawbacks to living with Bob, not the least of which was the way he created a mysterious amount of self-replicating debris that constantly threatened to engulf him.

With no power and the cupboard bare, we had to imagine breakfast. Hot chocolate and cinnamon toast for Terri, while I preferred Braithwaites' 'Household' blend tea with one of Cuthbert's well-fired white rolls, its outside crisp and blackened, its inside filled with doughy white air. We remained hungry, however, for you cannot really eat your own words.

'Well, at least being up at this hour means we'll make it to Archie's tutorial on time for once,' I said, without any great enthusiasm, but when I looked at Terri closely I realized she had fallen asleep. She should take more care, she had just the kind of sluggish metabolism that gets people buried alive in family crypts and glass coffins. In some ways (but not in others) Terri would have made the perfect wife for Bob – they could have simply slept their way through married life. Rip van Winkle and Duchess Anaesthesia, the lost, sleepy daughter of the Romanovs.

I gave her a little pinch and said, 'You know you shouldn't—' but then I came under the sleep spell as well.

Sometimes I wondered if we weren't all unwittingly taking part in drug trials being conducted covertly by a pharmaceutical company, perhaps for a drug with the opposite effects of speed. They could just call it *Slow* when it hit the market. Perhaps that was who was watching me – an undercover research assistant observing the effects of *Slow* on his unsuspecting guinea-pig. Because I was sure someone *was* watching me. ('Well, you know what they say,' Bob said, in what I think was a misguided effort to comfort me, 'just because you're paranoid it doesn't mean they're not out to get you.')

For several days now I had been aware of the unseen eyes on me, of the inaudible feet dogging my every footstep. I hoped it was merely the projection of a heated imagination rather than the beginnings of some paranoid delusional breakdown that would end on a locked ward in Liff, the village where the local mental hospital was located. ('Take more drugs,' was the advice of Bob's best friend, Shug.)

I woke up with a jolt. My head had been pillowed uncomfortably on the edge of Wittgenstein's *Tractatus* and the book had left a painful gouge in my cheek. Terri was making little whimpering noises, dreaming about chasing rabbits again.

I shook her awake, 'Come on, we're going to be late.'

My new resolution, rather late in my final year I realized, was to attend all the lectures, tutorials and seminars that I was supposed to. This was in a vain bid to curry favour with as many of the English department staff as possible because I was now so behind with my work that it was becoming increasingly unlikely that I would even be able to sit my degree, let alone pass it. I didn't understand how I'd got so behind with everything, especially when I was trying so hard to keep up.

Terri was even more behind than I was, if that was possible. The George Eliot essay ('Middlemarch *is a treasure house of detail, but an indifferent whole.' Can* Middlemarch *be defended against this criticism by Henry James?*) was just one of the many pieces of work that we hadn't managed to do.

I dressed as if for a polar expedition in as many clothes as I could find – woollen tights, a long needlecord pinafore dress, several reject men's golfing sweaters that had been acquired in a St Andrews Woollen Mill sale, scarf, gloves, knitted hat, and, lastly, an old beaver coat, bought for ten shillings in the pawn shop at the West Port, a coat that still had a comforting old lady smell of camphor and violet cachous about it.

'Ontological proof,' Bob shouted mysteriously in his sleep – a concept he wouldn't even know the meaning of if he was awake.

Terri grimaced and replaced her sunglasses and pulled on a black beret so that now she looked like a deranged governess engaged in guerrilla warfare. A Weathergirl.

'Let's do it,' she said, and we slipped out into the shock of a morning that crackled with cold so that every time we spoke our breath came out in cold white clouds like the speech bubbles in the *Beano*. We trudged up Paton's Lane and as we turned onto the Perth Road, the invisible, ever-watchful pair of eyes monitored our progress.

'Maybe it's the eye of God,' Terri said. I was sure God, if he existed at all, which was highly unlikely, would have better things to do with his time than watch me.

'Maybe he doesn't,' Terri said. 'Maybe he's like a really . . . trivial guy. Who knows?' Who indeed.

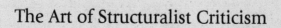

The Art of Structuralist Criticism

'*BLAH, BLAH, BLAH,*' ARCHIE SAID. (OR SOMETHING LIKE that.) Ten minutes after eleven in Archie McCue's room on the third floor of the extension to Robert Matthews' soaring sixties' Tower – the Queen's Tower, although no queen was ever likely to live in it. The gloomy atmosphere was made gloomier by the absence of electricity. A candle, stuck in an empty Blue Nun bottle, burned at the window like a signal. The university was still managing to run its heating although no-one knew how – perhaps they were burning books, or (more likely) students. The room was hot and airless and I had to peel off my layers of reject golfing sweaters, one by one.

Archie was talking. Nothing will stop Archie talking, not even death probably, he will rumble on from the inside of his large coffin until the worms get fed up with the noise and eat his tongue –

'*When words no longer strive for mimesis they become dislocated and disconnected. They illustrate <u>in themselves</u> the exhaustion of forms. Writers who eschew mimesis, looking for new ways of approaching the fiction construct, are disruptivist – challenging what Robbe-Grillet refers to as the "intelligibility* *of the world".'* Archie paused. 'What do you think of that statement? Anyone?' No-one answered. No-one ever had any idea what Archie was talking about.

Archie's blimpish body strained to escape from his dark green polyester shirt, a shirt stained at the armpits with large damp triangles of sweat. He was also attired in brown trousers and a tan-coloured knitted tie that sported a different quality of stain – dried boiled egg-yolk, or custard.

He spun round in his tweedy, executive chair, so much more comfortable than the chairs assigned to his tutees – the little *faux* wood tables attached to our chairs seemed to be specifically designed to restrain us, like a cross between a baby's high chair and an asylum straitjacket. The chairs were made from some artificial material – a hard grey plastic substance that the university seemed over fond of. It was only possible to be even remotely comfortable in these chairs for a maximum of ten minutes. An unfettered Archie, on the other hand, was free to birl and twirl around like a fairground ride on his Easy-glide castors.

'The act of writing itself comes to occupy the centre of the stage as the author is no longer concerned to invoke some a priori meaning or truth. Jacques Derrida reinforces the point . . .'

Archie McCue was an argumentative Marxist who claimed to be the progeny of a Glaswegian shipbuilder, although, in fact, he had been brought up by his widowed mother who owned a sweetshop in Largs. This long-suffering woman was now 'dottled' according to

46

Archie and had therefore recently been transported across the river to Newport-on-Tay and an old people's home called The Anchorage with a 'view of the water'.

'Valéry claims that literature is, and can be nothing else than, a kind of extension and application of certain properties of language . . .'

Archie lived in a big house in Windsor Place with Philippa, his bossy English wife. I knew that because I was the most recent in a long line of McCue babysitters – Philippa and Archie, both nearing fifty now, had been breeding, at spaced-out intervals, since the end of the war. They had four grown-and-gone offspring – Crispin ('Cambridge'), Orsino ('Oxford'), Freya ('year out in France') and their eldest son, the mysterious Ferdinand ('Saughton Prison, unfortunately'). Only one child, nine-year-old Maisie ('a mistake'), was now left at home.

'. . . and in its multiplicity and plurality it cries out for a new hermeneutics . . .'

We were a shrinking tutorial group. At the moment there were four of us – myself, Terri, Andrea and Olivia. Andrea was a grammar-school girl from the middle echelons of North Yorkshire society. Today, reeking of patchouli, she was wearing a flouncy, flowery dress, all buttons and bows and intricate bodice seaming, that looked as if it had been made for an amateur dramatic production of *Oklahoma!*

Andrea had recently converted from the Church of Scotland to paganism and was studying to be a witch. To this end she had apprenticed herself to a warlock in Forfar. Few things were more worrying than the idea of

Andrea with magic powers. Not that I have anything against witches, *per se*, of course – I am only too aware that my own mother is a wizardess of some kind – or wizardina, or wizardelle, for there appears to be no feminine form for the word. Perhaps I can just start making words up. Why not? How else do words come into being?

Andrea said that she wanted to be a famous writer and accordingly had done an evening shorthand-and-typing course run by a man in Union Street who turned out to be more interested in his female students' sweatered chests than he was in their Pitman short forms. So far, all Andrea had written were flimsy stories about a girl called Anthea who came from Northallerton and was studying English literature at university. Andrea's most interesting story to date was about a strange sexual encounter her *alter ego* Anthea had with a teacher at secretarial college. I thought that *The Adventures of Anthea* would be a good title for an English pornographic film – the kind that involves a lot of window cleaners and innuendo but not much actual sex.

Anthea was always having poignant moments sparked off by mundane experiences – going to lectures, finding spiders, buying A4 narrow-ruled with margins. Personally I think that reading the details of other people's domesticity is almost as tiresome as listening to them recount their dreams – *and then the fork-lift truck turned into a giant red squirrel that crushed my father's head like a nut* – fascinating to the dreamer, but tiresome for the indifferent listener.

Archie himself, of course, was famously writing a novel

– an experimental and epic tome that had now reached seven hundred pages. It was, reportedly (for no-one had actually seen it), an *Angst*-ridden, labyrinthine fiction about the metaphysical *Sturm und Drang* of the self called *The Expanding Prism of J.*

'. . . *a technique which might be considered emblematic of the essential arbitrariness of all linguistic signifiers . . .*'

Olivia politely stifled a yawn. A fair, willowy girl, Olivia was a doctor's daughter from Edinburgh, a St George's girl and a clever, methodical student, the kind who write up their notes every night, underlining everything in three different-coloured inks. Olivia was clearly a student who belonged at St Andrews or Warwick, or even East Anglia, rather than Dundee but she'd had 'some kind of a breakdown' during her A-Levels and had ended up with Es instead of As.

For the last year, Olivia had been having an affair with a lecturer in the Politics department called Roger Lake (generally known as 'Roger the Dodger' naturally) who was always trying to be trendy and hang out with students. Roger had a wife called Sheila and a clutch of small, blond daughters ('Just like Goebbels,' Terri said), aged from almost nothing to nine years old.

Although sex between staff and students was rife at the university, it was nonetheless forbidden by the Dean who took 'a dim view' of it. Roger Lake worried constantly that he was going to be caught in a scandalous situation and insisted that he and Olivia behave in a cloak-and-dagger fashion, exiting buildings separately and ignoring each other in public (and sometimes in private, she reported).

Having an affair with Roger Lake would have provided a good training for secret agents.

Terri was trapped in the chair next to me. She was already in a state of suspended animation – NASA could have used Terri for space exploration, they could have sent her beyond the final frontier, on long journeys that lasted for decades, and she would probably have arrived as fresh as when she was launched. Although an alien civilization might get the wrong idea about us if Terri was Earth's envoy.

'Derrida says, and here I quote,' Archie droned on, *' "it is when that which is written is deceased as a sign-signal that it is born as language."* Anyone?' The question hung invisibly in the stale air before fluttering around the room looking for somewhere to land. Kevin, reluctantly coming through the door at that moment, ducked to avoid it.

'Good of you to join us,' Archie said, and Kevin blushed and mumbled something indecipherable in his thick West Country accent, an accent which made everything he said sound either vaguely lewd or rather stupid. Like many of us at Dundee, in the so-called Arts and Social Sciences faculty, Kevin Riley had arrived, not through achieving good exam grades, but via the medium of the UCCA clearing-house, for, sadly, we were the students no-one else wanted.

Kevin was a plump, whey-faced boy, with a great frizz of bird's nest hair, a kind of Englishboy's Afro, and a pair of small penny rounders wedged on his nose. He had a rash of pimples on his chin which he'd misguidedly daubed with peachy-coloured Rimmel concealer. Kevin, shunned by the more robust members of his sex, had obviously spent a solitary childhood playing with Meccano and train sets, arranging and rearranging the postage stamps of the world and standing at the end of a draughty station platform with a flask and a small, ruled notebook.

These autistically boyish pursuits had now been replaced by writing – the true solipsistic disease. At some point in his drawn-out adolescence Kevin had created an alternative universe for himself – a lower-middle earth otherworld called Edrakonia, a fantastic kingdom from which the dragon queen Feurillia (who for some reason reminded me of Nora) had been exiled and the plot of which could probably be summed up in a sentence: (*And the Murk will fall on the land. And the Beast Griddlebart will roam the land and the dragons will flee.*)

Kevin crammed his big bumble-bee body into a chair, leftover flesh spilling out as he attempted to get comfortable. To cheer himself up, he took out a crumpled paper bag of lemon bon-bons and offered them round the class. Andrea recoiled in horror, she was one of those girls who wasn't entirely convinced that food was necessary for survival – anything more robust than a strawberry yoghurt made her anxious.

The question, which had been hovering indecisively all this time, finally made up its mind and decided to ignore Kevin, for it had spotted the slim charms of Andrea, on whom it alighted like an unwanted insect.

'Andrea?' Archie asked encouragingly. 'Derrida? [Not a

rhyme you'll find in many rhyming dictionaries.] Any thoughts?'

None, apparently, for, chewing suggestively on the end of her Biro, Andrea hitched up her pioneer-woman skirt and slowly crossed her legs. Andrea had her life all plotted out – she was going to graduate, get married, buy nothing on hire purchase, rear children, have a successful career as a famous writer, retire and die. She seemed to have no inkling that life wasn't as orderly as her pencil case and that everything is chance and at any moment any number of remarkable things can happen that are totally beyond our control, events that rip up our maps and re-polarize our compasses – the madwoman walking towards us, the train falling off the bridge, the boy on the bicycle.

Archie, still spellbound by the sight of Andrea's knees – and heaven knows what else she was covertly flaunting – seemed to have momentarily lost his train of thought. We all waited for him to re-board. It was one of those tutorial groups where no-one really had an opinion about anything, except for Archie, who had an opinion about everything. We were all relieved when he started up again and absolved us from the trachle of having to think for ourselves –

'. . . *made by several structuralist critics that it is only at the moment that the written word in literature ceases to refer to external "objective" data, that is, to referents in the "real" world, that it can begin to exist as language within the text . . .'*

Olivia chewed a strand of her long blond hair and looked thoughtful, although it seemed unlikely that she was thinking about anything Archie was saying. Kevin, who was in painful thrall to Olivia, stared aggressively at her feet, which were about the only part of her anatomy that he could look at without blushing. Olivia tended to dress like a down-at-heel medieval princess and today she was clad in a crushed velvet jacket over a second-hand satin nightdress and a pair of knee-high red leather boots that were a fetishist's dream.

Olivia had once mildly voiced the opinion to Archie that it was wrong to dissect books as if they were cadavers because you could never put them back together in the same way. 'Split the lark and so on,' she murmured, but Archie grew contemptuous and said that the next person to quote Emily Dickinson in his tutorial would be taken out to the Geddes Quadrangle and publicly flogged. ('Harsh but fair,' was Andrea's judgement.)

'*What the new fiction reminds us,*' Archie yakked on, '*is that signs need only refer to imaginary constructs – that perhaps that is all they do refer to, for perhaps it's not the job of fiction to make sense of the world . . .*'

We were a hedonistic and self-absorbed group – vague, lop-sided people, not fleshed out with definite beliefs and opinions, for whom the greatest achievement was probably getting out of bed in the morning. We had lost one of our original members – The Boy With No Name, a frail, pallid youth from Wester Ross, so called by the rest of the group because no matter how hard we might (or might not) try, none of us could ever remember his name. Of course, he didn't help matters much by habitually introducing himself by saying, 'Hello, I'm nobody, who are you?'

I was sure his name was something fairly ordinary – a Peter or a Paul – but I could never come up with anything more certain. It was almost as if he was under some kind of strange, existential hex, as though somebody – a tenderfoot witch, for example – had been practising from *The Book of Spells* ('a guid cantrip for disappearing'). What happened, I wondered, to someone who couldn't be named? Did they lose their identity? Did they forget who they were?

At first it had been a mere glimmering around the edges, a certain lack of definition, but before long he was almost completely erased and was no more than a breath on the air. Very occasionally, there was a certain slant of light that revealed his ectoplasmic form, like half-cooked, poached egg-whites. Perhaps if we could remember his name we could conjure him back.

'Maybe he just got pissed off and went home to Wester Ross?' Andrea speculated when he finally disappeared.

The Boy With No Name had been constantly working on a laboriously hand-written, heavily corrected manuscript that proved to be a far-fetched tale of alien invasion, the plot of which revolved around the imposition on Earth dwellers by aliens from the planet Tara-Zanthia (or something similarly debutante-like) of an economy based on domestic cats and dogs. It was a simple fiscal equation – the more cats and dogs you possessed the wealthier you were. Pedigree breeds became a kind of *über*-currency and puppy farms grew to be the backbone of the black economy.

Much of this writing fever (for it is an illness) had been

precipitated by the inauguration of a degree paper in creative writing the previous year. Archie had lobbied strongly for the paper, because he thought it would give the English department the avant-garde edge that it so obviously lacked. A great many students had enthusiastically signed up for the course, not because they were necessarily interested in writing, but because the creative writing paper didn't involve an exam.*

Archie, still tutoring the class in those days before the advent of Martha Sewell, dismissed the Tara-Zanthian tale as 'pathetic shite' and, mortified, The Boy With No Name had fled the room. He had always had some difficulty occupying all three dimensions at once, but it was from that day onwards he began to fade.

Archie, scooting around the room in his chair like the glass on a Ouija board, came to a sudden stop in front of Kevin. He looked at him vaguely as if he thought he recognized him from somewhere and then asked him an impenetrable question about Gramsci's concept of hegemony. Kevin squirmed in his chair but still couldn't take his eyes off Olivia's seven-league boots. He had begun to sweat in the clammy atmosphere and the concealer on his chin had taken on a strange consistency so that it looked as if his skin was melting.

---

* To fulfil the requirements of this class you must attend one seminar per week and two individual tutorials per term. The course work for this paper comprises one major assignment which must be a piece of individual, original work – a play, a novella, a collection of short stories, the first five chapters of a novel, a portfolio of poems, or some other work agreed with the course tutor.

55

Kevin was saved from Gramsci by Professor Cousins, who wandered into the room at that moment. He caught sight of Archie and seemed confused.

'Looking for something?' Archie asked, rather impolitely, and under his breath muttered, 'like your brain perhaps?' Professor Cousins appeared to be even more puzzled. 'I don't know how I ended up here,' he laughed. 'I was looking for the toilet.'

'You found it,' Terri murmured, without apparently opening her mouth, or even waking up.

Professor Cousins was English – an affable, rather eccentric person who had recently taken his first tottering steps into dotage. Sometimes Professor Cousins was lucid, sometimes he wasn't, and, as with anyone in the department, it wasn't always easy to distinguish between the two states. The university's strict laws of tenure dictated that he had to be dead at least three months before he could be removed from behind his desk. The crown may still have been perched precariously on the incumbent cranium of Professor Cousins, but the various faculty members were already deep in the throes of a momentous power struggle over the imminent possession of it. The sixties' breeze-block walls echoed with machination and intrigue, plot and counterplot, as pretenders and contenders jostled for position.

Unnatural selection had already taken care of the main challenger for the post. The members of the English department were a notoriously accident-prone lot and the favourite – a statesmanlike Canadian called Christopher Pike – had eliminated himself by mysteriously falling down a flight of stairs in the Tower. Now that he was strung up in complex traction on the men's orthopaedic ward of the DRI, the English department had witnessed a sharp escalation in hostilities between Archie and his two main rivals – Dr Dick and Maggie Mackenzie.

'Well,' Professor Cousins said, scratching his nose and hitching up his spectacles, 'well, well.' His almost bald head was covered in age spots; only a pale fringe of hair remained, like a friar's tonsure or a ghostly atoll. He reminded me of an old animal – a sagging carthorse or an arthritic Great Dane, and I had an impulse to reach out and stroke his bald freckled pate and search in my pocket for an apple or a dog biscuit.

Suddenly, spying the empty chair next to me, he teetered over and sat down, squeezing his bag of bones behind the little wooden table from where he smiled benignly at us, raising his hand in a papal kind of gesture. 'Do go on,' he said amiably to Archie. 'I'll be out of the way here.'

Archie, after visibly struggling over how to deal with this bewildering behaviour, finally seemed to decide to simply ignore it and set off again. '*By asserting itself* as a piece of fiction, *the non-mimetic novel is in a position to negate both Sontag's vision of an aesthetics of silence and John Barth's prescription for formal regeneration.* What do you think? Someone?'

'Well, it's got me flummoxed, Archie,' Professor Cousins laughed. Archie glared at him. Professor Cousins was an old-fashioned Shakespearean by trade and somewhat baffled by Archie's approach to literature. As we all were.

The new question was batted silently around the room, a room that was growing increasingly hot and airless. We all found different ways of distracting ourselves – I looked out of the third-floor window as if I'd just seen something interesting (which I had actually, but I'll come to that later) while Kevin stared at Olivia's feet and made little goldfish moues of distress with his fat blown-rose mouth and Olivia herself inspected her fingernails, one by one, very carefully. At first I thought Andrea was incanting a spell to ward off Archie but then I realized she was quietly humming a Crosby, Stills, Nash and Young song, which probably had much the same effect. Terri, meanwhile, as enigmatic as an egg, maintained an eerie silence, apparently occupying some mental space denied to the rest of us.

The door opened and Shug strolled into the room, carrying a purple velvet shoulder-bag embroidered with tiny mirrors and eclectically dressed in a pair of jeans which were composed almost entirely of patches, a black and white Palestinian shawl round his neck and an Afghan coat. Shug – who was our vertical neighbour in Paton's Lane – claimed to have bought this coat, which was considerably superior to the dirty, matted fleeces possessed by most students, in the 'Amir Kabir' in down-town Tehran.

Shug, lithe and lanky amongst a stunted population, liked to think he was the epitome of cool. He was one of the few native Dundonians at a university awash with English drop-outs. The first time I encountered Shug he was walking along the Nethergate, with Bob bob bobbing along beside him, holding a haddock in his hand like a lollipop – 'Arbroath Smokie,' he explained in his own kippered voice. I thought he was talking about some kind of hashish – although many people, of course, consider it to be a kind of red herring.

He sat in his usual place – on the floor with his back against the wall, facing Archie. Archie looked at his watch and said, 'Why bother, Mr Scobie?' and Shug raised an eyebrow and said gruffly, 'You tell me, Archie.' An enigmatic sort of an encounter but nonetheless containing the emotional charge of two rutting stags clacking antlers.

'You never know, you might learn something,' Professor Cousins said, smiling encouragingly at Shug and then, to no-one in particular, 'Dr McCue knows all kinds of things that no-one else does.'

Shug was older than everyone else in the tutorial group. He had already been thrown out of Duncan of Jordanstone Art College (something that was previously thought to be impossible) and had worked on several real jobs in between times – as a road mender, a bus conductor, even in a chicken factory ('Where the chickens are made,' Terri told Bob who believed her for all of a minute). Shug had also 'taken off' to India and all points east to 'find himself', not that I could imagine Shug being particularly lost to begin with. If only Bob would go away and find himself. What would he find? Essence of Bob, perhaps.

Andrea came over all moon and whimsy at the sight of Shug. (A girl in love is a frightening sight.) Since leaving behind the decorous ways of the Church of Scotland,

Andrea had, like many before her, developed a crush on Shug and seemed to be under the delusion that she was the woman for whom he would change his ways. If she was hoping to tidy him up and settle him down she was going to be sorely disappointed.

I myself had once had an unexpected, but not un-welcome, burst of sexual activity with Shug, down in the carrels in the basement of the library, next to the period-icals section. We had got as far as some enthusiastic kissing when I was shaken out of my Shug-induced reverie by his voice saying ruefully, 'You know I cannae shag you, hen, Bob's ma pal.' Still, it was an experience I remem-bered fondly every time I went in search of the *Shakespeare Quarterly* or *Atlantic Monthly*.

'*With reference to Proust*,' Archie said, pressing on hero-ically, '*Walter Benjamin reminds us that the Latin word* textum *means web; he further suggests* . . .'

The room sank into a state of settled ennui. I couldn't keep my eyes open, I felt as if I was suffocating in a warm fug of words. I tried to stay awake because it was import-ant to keep in Archie's good books as I was several weeks late handing in my dissertation to him. My dissertation (*Henry James – Man or Maze?*) was a degree paper and was supposed to be twenty thousand words long. So far I had fifty-one of them – *A great part of the struggle for James is caused by his desire both to master his subject matter through a rigorous process of fictionalization, and at the same time offer the appearance of reality. The author must never be apparent because his intrusion into the text destroys the care-fully wrought—*

The hum of Archie's words carried on in the background of my brain but it could no longer make any sense of them '. . . *by enregistering speech, blah, inscription has its essential object, blah, and indeed, takes this fatal risk, blah, blah, the emancipation of meaning . . . as concerns any actual field of perception, blah, from the natural disposition of a contingent situation, blah, blah, blah . . .*'

I tried to keep myself awake by thinking about Bob. More specifically, by thinking about leaving Bob. It was more than three years now since I had woken up that first morning in a tangle of his toast-filled sheets. I had been puzzled as to how to proceed. Bob's general passivity and iguana-like demeanour didn't give me any clues, or even encouragement. He grunted when I asked him if he wanted me to stay and grunted when I asked him if he wanted me to go. In the end, I decided to compromise and go, but come back later. I slipped out from beneath his sheets, dyed a streaky purple, wincing quietly at the ache in my plaster-of-Paris wrist, and went breakfastless back to women-only Chalmers Hall and fell asleep in my cell-like single bed.

When I returned at six o'clock, Bob was exactly where I had left him – the bicycling Bob had given me a misleading impression of activity, Bob was merely borrowing the bike from someone else so he could stuff the saddle-bags with home-grown grass and transport them across town.

I shrugged my clothes off and got back between the sheets. Bob rolled over, opened his eyes and said, 'Wow – who are you?'

For reasons which I didn't quite understand, my first night with Bob had been enough to leave me strangely attached to him. Later, I wondered if I had lost free will, as if in some strange way I'd merged with Bob's own (limited) persona. ('Like a mind-meld?' Bob mused, quite animated for once by this idea.)

After the bicycle incident, I had moved in stealthily, book by book, shoe by shoe, so that by the time he noticed that I didn't go home any more, he had got used to the idea of me and I was no longer a surprise when he woke up. I wondered if I could move out the same way. Remove myself bit by bit until there was nothing left to dismember and only the more intangible and enigmatic components remained (the smile, for example, and even that would fade eventually). Finally, nothing would be left but a space where I used to be. How much kinder that would be than walking out the door suddenly and all in one piece. Or dying abruptly.

'. . . *the autonomous work of art brings into question—*'

'But don't you think, Archie,' Professor Cousins said mildly, 'that really all literature is about the search for *identity*?' He made an expansive gesture, 'From *Oedipus Rex* onwards it's about the search of man –' he reached out and patted my hand '– and the fairer sex, of course, for the true understanding of himself – or herself – and his – or her – place in the universe, in the whole scheme of things. The *meaning* of life. And God,' he added, 'does He – or She – exist and if so why does He – or She – leave us bereft in a cold and lonely world, spinning endlessly through the black infinity of space, whipped by the icy interstellar winds? And what happens when we reach the end of infinity? And what colour is it? That's the question. What do we see when we stand on the terrace of infinity?'

Everyone sat in silence, staring at Professor Cousins. He smiled and shrugged and said, 'Just a thought, do carry on, dear boy.'

Archie ignored him. '*Not only the role of the creator of the fiction but also his relationship to the work itself—*'

'Excuse me,' Kevin said to Professor Cousins, 'did you mean "What is the colour of infinity"? Or did you mean "What is the colour of the *end* of infinity"?'

'Is there a difference, do you think?' Professor Cousins said eagerly. 'How intriguing.'

'*End* of infinity?' Andrea puzzled.

'Oh, everything has an end,' Professor Cousins said reassuringly, 'even infinity.'

Infinity, I happen to know, is the colour of sludge and dead seals, of sunken battleships and their crews, the dregs of Monday mornings and the lees of Saturday nights and of small harbours on the north-east coast in January. But I kept that knowledge to myself.

'. . . *represents the distance between the world and phenomena, not to mention the—*'

Archie was interrupted again, this time by a neat rapping at the door and Martha Sewell walked in without waiting for an answer. Martha was the recently appointed tutor in creative writing. After one year, Archie had declared the creative writing paper such a success that he had persuaded the department, for the sake of prestige, to appoint 'a real writer' to the post of tutor. Bostonian Martha, an Amherst type, was a poet in her forties whom no-one in the department had ever heard of. She wrote poetry with impenetrable syntax about a life where nothing ever happened. Her poems had titles like 'Abstraction Or [#3]' (and your hair, blurred with/rain makes me think/of the obliquity of existence) and had just published a new collection called *Cherry-Picking in Vermont*, which she carried around with her everywhere like a passport, as if she might be asked to prove who she was.

Martha was still in culture shock, having come to Dundee thinking that it was part of a Scotland that was built out of lochs and mountains and decorated with moorland and waterfalls, and every so often you could see a pained look cross her face when she had to negotiate a piece of shoddy modern architecture, a gas-lit close, or a hollow-eyed and abandoned jute mill. She was not convinced when Dundee's many good points were pointed out to her – the glorious parks; the municipal observatory; the view from the Law; the beautiful bridges; the Tay; a radical and seditious history; the almost unnatural friendliness of Dundonians, their concomitant violence; the curiously Dundeecentric press; the inhabitants' benign indifference to idiosyncratic behaviour (the way, for example, that you could walk down the street in nothing but a pair of baffies with a budgerigar on your head and no-one would think twice of it).

Tall and thin and as sensual as a cod, Martha had large beloafered feet that were designed for pounding the paths and trails of New England. She gave the impression of being extraordinarily clean and groomed, as though she curried herself thoroughly every morning. Her smooth hair, somewhere between blond and grey, a colourless colour, was worn in a tidy bob, kept in order by a black velvet Alice band.

Martha had been accompanied to Scotland by her husband, Jay – a professor at Ann Arbor and a Whitman specialist – who had taken a sabbatical to accompany his wife. The Sewells spent a lot of time – certainly more than the average Dundonian – visiting Edinburgh, where they purchased cashmere tartan travel rugs, Caithness crystal, and rare malt whiskies and daydreamed about renting a house in Ramsey Gardens.

Martha and Jay belonged to the class of people who run economies and design legislation, who arrive alive in the polar regions and survive in the equatorial, who invent chronometers and barometers, and mend clothes and darn stockings and never run out of milk or clean underwear. They led the kind of life I could never hope to, especially if I stayed with Bob.

Today Martha was wearing black courts, a grey flannel skirt and a rat-coloured woollen wrap that came down almost to her feet and was carrying a heavy, serious-minded, leather briefcase. Although not directly involved in the war of the departmental succession, Martha seemed to have become a trophy figure and the various candidates vied to have her on their side.

'You're busy,' she said to Archie. Archie denied this self-evident fact, waving his hand dismissively at his students as if we were a figment of Martha's imagination. Andrea made a gagging gesture as if she was about to throw up.

'Are you looking for the toilet?' I asked Martha kindly, but she had caught sight of Professor Cousins in the corner and a shadow of confusion passed across her granite-smooth forehead.

'He's sitting in,' Archie said, making Professor Cousins sound like a student protester. Professor Cousins leant so far towards me that he nearly toppled over in the chair. He jabbed a finger in Martha's direction. 'Remind me who she is again,' he said, in a loud whisper.

I shrugged. 'Some woman.'

'Ah,' he said as if that made everything clear. He folded his hands over his old man's soft belly and nodded benignly at Martha and said, 'Sit down, sit down,' gesturing towards a chair next to Terri. 'You might learn something,' he laughed. 'I know I have.' Martha looked to Archie for guidance but he just raised his eyebrows as if to say it was nothing to do with him and so Martha reluctantly folded up her awkward grasshopper limbs into the chair, all the while keeping a wary eye on Terri.

Seeing Martha was a blow, I was hoping to avoid her for some time. The creative writing assignment I owed her was another degree paper I was probably going to fail, and to make matters worse my assignment, *The Hand of Fate*, was a crime novel, the least reputable genre there was, according to Martha ('Why? Why? Why?') and I had to pretend to her that crimewriting was a postmodernist kind of thing these days, but I could tell that she wasn't convinced. Things would have been going better with

Martha if I'd had more words on the page, rather than in my head. (How much easier life would be for the poor writers if they didn't actually have to write their books.) So far I'd got little further than a rudimentary character introduction and a hint of plot –

'Well, time and tide wait for no woman,' Madame Astarti said out loud as she heaved her portly shape off the bed. Madame Astarti's torso would have fitted quite snugly inside a barrel. The only thing she could find to eat in the kitchen was half a packet of stale chocolate digestives. She wondered if there would be any point in going on a diet. She had lost her figure sometime in the sixties and had been unable to find it ever since. She lost it before she arrived in Saltsea. She'd never intended to come here; it was one of those haphazard kinds of decisions (which means no decision at all, merely circumstance). She'd arrived in 1964 with her then husband Gordon McKinnon on a cheap-day return from Cleveland when they'd both been in a rather tired and emotional state. They'd had a long-running argument which had culminated in a nasty moment on top of the Ferris Wheel with Gordon telling her about his personal interpretation of reincarnation - a theory which centred on Madame Astarti's imminent return as a seagull - but which eventually resolved itself with Gordon returning to Cleveland and Madame Astarti staying in Saltsea. The last she had heard of Gordon

67

McKinnon was in 1968 when he was on the run from the RSPCA. He could be dead for all she knew – an ambivalent state occupied by many people Madame Astarti had once been acquainted with. The could-be-deads, as she thought of them.

After several more cigarettes, and a rather prolonged toilette which included Madame Astarti's constant struggle with one of the world's eternal dilemmas – how to apply mascara when she couldn't even see her face without her spectacles on – she was finally ready.

The telephone rang but when Madame Astarti answered it the line went dead with a purposeful click. 'Went dead' – that was a curious phrase, wasn't it? she mused thoughtfully. Things that go dead, in their various tenses. Electricity, telephones, not people, they didn't go dead they just were dead. Things that go dead in the night – no, that wasn't right, was it? Sometimes she wondered if she wasn't in the early stages of dementia. But how do you tell?

She locked up carefully behind her, reasoning it was better to be safe than sorry, even though Madame Astarti had lived most of her life according to the opposite philosophy. 'Time to go,' she said to no-one, although—

Professor Cousins startled me by leaning over towards me again and producing a Nuttall's Minto from his pocket which he pressed into my hand, saying, 'You're a good girl,' as if he had been told otherwise by someone.

I wondered if Professor Cousins was as old as he looked. I was a kind of magnet to old people – at bus-stops and in shop queues they flocked around me, desperate to chat about bus timetables and weather. Andrea, who was frightened of old people (in case she became one, one day, I suppose), said that every time she looked at a baby she thought that one day that baby would be an old person. Personally, I prefer to look at an old person and remember they were once someone's baby. Perhaps there are two personality types (a half-full, half-empty kind of thing), on the one hand the people who can discern traces of the baby in the senescent and, on the other hand, the depressives that look at the fresh baby and see the demented old crone.

~ Wise, Nora amends, wise old crone.

Archie was beginning to get a slightly mad look in his eye. The overheated room and the number of people in it were making him increasingly dishevelled – he had loosened his tie and unbuttoned his collar and the damp patches of sweat were spreading further and further across his chest like two oceans determined on confluence.

'. . . or as the transition from one existent to another, from a signifier to a signified . . .'

'Excuse me, Archie,' Professor Cousins was waving his hand around in the air to catch Archie's eye.

'Yes?' Archie said stoically.

'Could you just go back a bit,' Professor Cousins said genially. 'I seem to be losing the thread of all this. I'm afraid –' he turned to Archie's students with a conspiratorial smile – 'I'm afraid I don't have Dr McCue's brilliant mind.'

Archie trundled his chair across the carpet, a mode of locomotion that made him resemble a particularly inept Dalek, but then stopped abruptly in front of the Professor and started doing strange breathing exercises, presumably to calm himself down, although he gave the impression of someone who was trying to inflate himself.

'Realism,' Martha intervened patiently on Archie's behalf, speaking very loudly and slowly to Professor Cousins, 'Dr McCue's talking about realism.'

'Ah,' Professor Cousins smiled at Martha, 'Trollope!'

Archie retreated back across the brown contract carpeting and snapped, *The mimetic form can no longer convince us of its validity in the post-industrial age, true or false? Someone? Anyone? Kevin?*'

Kevin shook his head miserably at the wall.

'Effie?'

'Well, I suppose these days,' I said, wriggling uncomfortably in my chair, 'there's an epistemological shift in fiction-writing, whereby second-order verisimilitude won't suffice any more when trying to form a transcendentally coherent view of the world.' I had absolutely no idea what I was talking about, but Archie seemed to.

'That seems to imply that achieving a transcendentally coherent view of the world might still be a good thing, doesn't it? Anybody?' There was another knock on the door.

'It's like Waterloo Station in here,' Professor Cousins said cheerfully. 'I don't know when you get any teaching

70

done, Archie.' Archie gave him a doubtful look. Professor Cousins may be on his way out but he hadn't gone yet and still had hiring and firing power. The knock on the door was repeated.

'Come in,' Archie said querulously. The candle wavered and flickered wildly.

'Oh, it's you,' he said to—

~ No, no, enough, Nora says wearily, that's far too many people already.

I sleep in a back room, a servant's room, that smells of mildew and wet soot. The thin paisley eiderdown feels damp to the touch. I have settled on this room because the larger bedrooms all have water coming in the roof, collecting *drip-drip-drip* into buckets like Scottish water torture. I have tried to build a fire in the tiny cast-iron corner grate but the chimney is blocked, most likely by a dead bird.

On the bedside table there still sits a pocket Bible covered in cheap black leather that has blistered with the damp. The pages are freckled with age, the paper as thin as old skin. It is not a family Bible but is inscribed on the flyleaf in the utility hand of a servant. I imagine some poor put-upon maid of the holidaying Stuart-Murrays waking in the morning here to the sound of the thrumming rain and looking out across the dreich wet view from her little window and wishing she belonged to a sensible family that spent their summers in Deauville or Capri.

I can hardly sleep because of the unearthly yawling and yowling of the feral cats, like feline banshees. They have startled me awake most nights since I arrived – dropped off by a passing friendly fishing-boat, the owner of which regretted that he could not return for me because the island was full of strange noises that made him 'feart'. He was not to be persuaded that they were merely Siamese cats gone horribly wrong.

I am convalescing. I have been sick with a virus, a strange influenza that has left me as weak as a kindle of kittens. I have come here to recuperate although, sadly, my atavistic mother's island does not provide the usual invalid comforts – warm bedrooms, soft blankets, coddled eggs, tinned soup, and so on – but I must make do, for Nora is all I have.

Nora herself washed up here a couple of years ago, in her little boat, the *Sea-Adventure*. She lives like a castaway in the 'big house', which is indeed bigger than all the other ruined crofts and roofless cottages that litter the island, themselves slowly eroding into landscape like the ruins of a Minoan palace. Nora says that her great-grandfather had the house built in the last century, imagining that generations of Stuart-Murrays, stretching out to the crack of doom, would wish to vacation here.

The house gives the impression of having been abandoned suddenly, in anticipation of some great disaster. Set up on the hill overlooking the Sound, and beyond that to the wide Atlantic, the winter winds are so fierce here that they cast up pebbles from the beach to rattle and knock against the windows, as if the ghosts of homesick mariners are asking to be let in.

The house is falling down around our ears. A house that was once grand and orderly is now reduced to little more than a stone shell. The roof leaks dreadfully so you cannot move for falling over old galvanized buckets of rainwater. The sandstone of the sills has been worn away by the sea air, the floorboards are rotten and the main staircase so eaten by worm and fly that you must walk at the edge of the stair for fear of falling right through to the mosaic-tiled floor of the hall below.

The house still has its heavy, moth-eaten drapes and cold, fireless grates, the big Belfast sinks, the monstrous Eagle cast-iron range, the Glass Queen washboards and a full set of bells for summoning servants who have long since ceased to respond. The walls are hung with gloomy oil-paintings, so in need of cleaning that you can barely make out the stags and liver-spotted spaniels and heathery vistas that form their subjects. There is even a plant that has survived, a dry old palm with papery brown leaves, struggling on from another era without benefit of water or warmth.

The house is full of the mouldering relics of a more complex, more opulent life – the huge silk umbrellas like marquees that rot in the outsized yellow dragon Chinese vases in the vestibule, the complicated deckchairs with canopies and footrests whose green canvas is worn so pale and thin that they can barely take the weight of a field mouse. In cupboards and trunks and out-houses there lurk decaying galoshes, sou'westers and rubberized macs, ancient shotguns and fishing-rods and nets. On disintegrating dressing-tables the bristles of enamel-backed brushes have caught the hair of people who are all now dead.

The cellar appears to have been used as a storehouse for the whole island and contains cargoes of mysterious objects – lengths of net and twine, old fish boxes and lobster pots, racing-pigeon hampers, shrivelled seed potatoes and, perhaps strangest of all, the figurehead from the prow of an old sailing-ship – a seafaring sailor's fantasy of a mermaid, with yellow hair and naked torso, she must have once flown beneath the bowsprit of some brave ship, her breasts jutting into the winds and her mad blue eyes looking on the wonders of the world – the Baltic ice and London fog, the tempests of the Capes, the soft yellow sands of the Pacific and the strange savages of Bermuda.

Everything is turning to dust before our eyes. Nothing escapes the hand of time, neither the cities of the Sumerian plain nor the holiday home of our ancestors.

Nora makes a supper of groats and curly kale. She lives like a peasant. But under the skin I suppose we are all peasants.

~ No, no, no, Nora says, striking her breastbone savagely, we are all kings and queens.

~ And now, she says, yawning – in what I consider to be a rather theatrical way – I'm going to go and get some sleep. Carry on without me, why don't you.

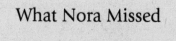

What Nora Missed

—WATSON GRANT.

'Ah, Dr Watson, I presume.' Professor Cousins beamed, as if he had made a great joke.

'Come in, why don't you,' Archie said, 'everyone else has.'

Watson Grant was one of the no-hope challengers for the departmental crown. His speciality was Scottish Studies, a strangely old-fashioned subject which occupied a country somewhere between Brigadoon and the White Heather Club, a landscape of burns and banks and braes where people danced strathspeys and reels while Moira Anderson and Kenneth McKellar sang duets in the background. Martha Sewell would have understood this version of Scotland.

Grant Watson always wore a Harris tweed jacket and came from somewhere remote that either began with 'Inver' or ended in 'ness' and was strangely asexual, like a mole, although he did have a wife and two children tucked away in Fife somewhere. He was a keen hill-walker, sometimes even turning up to teach in his clumpy leather walking-boots, still caked in Monro mud,

77

as if there was something virtuous about climbing a hill when you didn't need to.

Professor Cousins contributed to Watson Grant's usual air of nervousness by shooing him away with a good-natured smile and an absurd attempt at a Scottish accent, 'Ochhhh,' he said, as if trying to cough up a gobbet of phlegm, 'awa' ye gae, ma guid man.' Grant Watson hovered uncertainly on the threshold of Archie's room, not wanting to stay but not wanting to go either – in case Professor Cousins' presence there signalled an inclination towards bequeathing Archie his regalia. His little jog of indecisiveness was halted abruptly by Archie saying, 'The toilet's down the other end of the corridor.' He was saved from finding a reply by the bell which rang to signal the end of the hour.

Archie ignored the bell and continued talking but everyone stopped listening and started worming their way free of the hard plastic chairs. For a deluded second I thought I saw the flimsy form of The Boy With No Name spiralling like smoke out of his chair. I blinked and there was nothing there but the greasy soot of the guttering candle at the window.

Archie suddenly loomed over me, his bloated Zeppelin figure blocking out what little light there was. I thought for sure he was going to say something about the whereabouts of my dissertation but he just frowned vaguely at the garbled notes I'd been taking and said, 'Can you babysit for us tonight?' I agreed in a half-hearted kind of way; the non-existent *Man or Maze* put me in a difficult position *vis-à-vis* Archie. I just hoped he wouldn't start wanting to barter sexual favours instead of babysitting ones.

I helped Professor Cousins extricate himself from his chair. Everyone was slightly stir-crazy by this time and heading for the door like passengers evacuating an aircraft on fire. I had to reach out and grab at the worn brown corduroy of Professor Cousins' jacket to prevent him being swept away by the stream of students leaving the room in full spate.

Working his way upstream I spotted Martha's husband, Jay Sewell. He was a tall man with a big jaw and a shock of silver hair which Martha thought 'leonine' but which no lion in its right mind would envy. Jay had the manners and demeanour of a southern plantation owner and did indeed originate in the deep south, a fact that Martha seemed to find both politically challenging and sexually attractive.

Jay Sewell greeted Professor Cousins but ignored the students as if they were a lesser life form. He greeted Martha with a cool kiss on the cheek and said that he had Buddy in the car and that he'd been sick all morning.

'Oh, poor baby,' Martha said. I was eager to hear more about Buddy (A dog? A child? A friend? A dead rock and roll legend?), but Jay closed the door and Professor Cousins and I were shut out in the murky corridor.

'Where now?' he asked me cheerfully.

'Well, *I* have to go and write an essay about George Eliot,' I said, the very idea making me feel as weary as an inhabitant of Hades, 'but you don't. You're not a student,' I reminded him. 'You can do what you want.'

Professor Cousins frowned and said, 'Well, only within certain social, physical and ethical parameters,' a surprisingly coherent statement, only slightly undermined by a sudden lunatic outbreak of tap dancing from his feet. 'I dreamt of going on the stage once,' he said, looking crestfallen.

'It's never too late,' I said vaguely. A lie, of course, as often, unfortunately, it is much too late.

We navigated the Stygian gloom of the corridor arm in arm like a quaint, old-fashioned couple. Professor Cousins was very polite, always scurrying to get on the outside of women on pavements (in case they were knocked flying into the road by a hansom-cab presumably), proffering seats and opening doors and generally treating the female sex as if we were very delicate and made of glass, or something equally fragile and breakable, which, of course, we are, for we are made of bones and flesh.

His gentlemanly presence was rather reassuring especially as the doghairs on the back of my neck were standing to attention. Perhaps it was The Boy With No Name, lurking around his old haunts.

'Oh, we're all being watched,' Professor Cousins said blithely. 'We just don't know it.'

Archie, of course, had long held the conviction that Special Branch were watching him, although he never elucidated why that should be so. ('Perhaps because he's special,' Andrea said in one of her less intelligent moments.)

'Oh yes, but Archie's mad,' Professor Cousins said cheerfully. 'We're all mad here. I'm mad. You're mad.'

'How do you know I'm mad?'

'You must be,' Professor Cousins said, 'or you wouldn't have come here.'

Professor Cousins' room was at the other end of the English department corridor – always a perilous place fraught with danger but infinitely more so these days as the struggle for succession hotted up. Getting from one end of the corridor to the other was rather like being on a Ghost Train, ducking the spooks and spectres as they jumped out unexpectedly trying to frighten you.

Today, however, they all seemed to be absent. Dr Dick's door was firmly closed, while Maggie Mackenzie's was wide open as if to show she had nothing to be ashamed of although she herself was missing. Watson Grant seemed to have left the building. I was held captive by Professor Cousins' ancient mariner anecdotage as he embarked on a rambling story about his days as a spry young doctoral student at Cambridge and some girl he had seduced at a May Ball long ago, so that we didn't notice Maggie Mackenzie storming through the Murk, as thrawn as a Fury, until she was almost upon us.

Her shapeless, funebral garments billowed and her kirby grips scattered as she progressed. Maggie Mackenzie's long iron-grey hair began each day anchored or plaited or rolled in a variety of vaguely Victorian styles but by lunchtime it had begun to work its way free of restraints and encumbrances and by mid-afternoon she had the appearance of someone leading a tribe of ancient Britons into battle, a gnarled warrior queen bearing grudges.

'Dr Mackenzie, Maggie.' Professor Cousins nodded pleasantly at her. She glared back at him. Maggie Mackenzie, who taught the nineteenth-century novel (*Why Women Write*) harboured a bitter resentment against the male of the species, resentment precipitated by her ex-husband, also a Dr Mackenzie, for reasons which she never spoke about because 'some things went beyond language'.

'I believe you owe me an essay?' she said to me tersely by way of greeting, and added, 'Where *is* your George Eliot?' in a way that suggested there might be several George Eliots wandering the world and that I was the owner of one of them.

'I left it at home,' (or perhaps 'I left her at home'), I said with a helpless shrug at the way life was an entity apparently beyond my control.

Dr Dick opened the door of his room suddenly as if he was trying to catch someone out. He frowned when he saw the three of us and gave the impression that he would have liked to give us lines for loitering near his territory. Dr Dick, whose speciality was the eighteenth century (*1709–1821 – Rhyme or Reason?*), believed he should be made head of department because he was the only person in it who could construct a timetable properly. He was probably right.

Beardless and rather weedy, Dr Dick was a tall, anaemic-looking man who gave the impression of someone who had outgrown his strength. He was a peculiar Anglo-Scots hybrid. His father had apparently come from the same strain as the great veterinary Dicks but his mother was from a less pedigree brand of Kentish haber-dashers, and when the marriage failed she returned to the bosom of her family taking young Dr Dick with her, so although Edinburgh born, he was Canterbury bred. This cross-border fertilization had not, however, produced a more robust species.

At times, in fact, Dr Dick seemed more English than an Englishman. He had attended a minor Home Counties public school before progressing to Oxford, where he had helped to found a real ale society. He could recite, in his fruity accent, every member of the English cricket team since time began. ('What a wanker,' was Bob's laconic verdict.)

Maggie Mackenzie and Dr Dick looked as if they were squaring up for a fight. I supposed that would be one way of deciding who should be head of department.

'Hand-to-hand combat,' Professor Cousins murmured in my ear. 'It would save a lot of time, you know.'

Dr Dick backed down and turned his aggression on me. 'Your essay's late,' he said curtly. 'I want it immediately.'

Dr Dick was a man who revelled in his hypochondria, although he wanted to be head of department so much that it did seem to be making him sick. He forgot about me now, distracted by a sudden need to feel his pulse. 'I think I'd better sit down for a while,' he said limply and retreated to his room again.

'The man's perfectly idiotic,' Maggie Mackenzie said

and then turned to me and said irascibly, 'Tomorrow will do for me. I want your George Eliot on my desk by five o'clock,' she beetled her brows threateningly, 'or else,' and stomped off abruptly down the corridor.

'Such a frightening woman,' Professor Cousins said when she was out of hearing.

I was surprised that the university women's liberation group hadn't co-opted Maggie Mackenzie now that it had entered a new militant phase. Hitherto a peaceful refuge for students who wanted to drink coffee and moan about their boyfriends, the group had been hijacked recently by a girl called Heather, a junior honours politics student with a round face and owlish spectacles who was determined to teach us the finer points of dialectical materialism before she died, which was probably going to be sooner than she expected.

'Well, well,' Professor Cousins said, finally meandering to a halt at the door of his room. 'I think I'll have a little nap now. How about you?'

I was unsure as to whether he was asking me to join him in a nap or just generally enquiring about my plans; either way, I shook my head sadly and said, 'I've got to go home and do some work.'

'Give my regards to that boyfriend of yours.'

'Bob?'

'If that's his name.'

Professor Cousins caught sight of Joan, the departmental secretary, a middle-aged, big-breasted woman fond of mohair so that I always had to stifle an instinct to go to sleep on her furry bosom. Professor Cousins

84

made an elaborate pantomime of drinking a cup of tea and with a long-suffering sigh Joan went into the cupboard where she kept her kettle. For times of emergency – such as we were in – she had set up a little camping gas stove as well (which is probably how dreadful accidents happen).

'Got to keep my strength up,' Professor Cousins laughed. 'Someone's trying to kill me, you know.'

'I'm sorry?' I said, thinking I must have mis-heard, but he had shut the door of his room, although I could still hear him chuckling to himself on the other side of the flushed wooden door.

In the basement that served as the Students' Union all kinds of health and safety laws were being flouted. It was unusually crowded, the air thick with condensation and the flickering candles on the tables giving the place an air of subterranean gloom, especially when they illuminated the Breughel-like paintings which for some reason adorned the walls.

If you can imagine a place somewhere between a stone-age cave and a wartime air-raid shelter then you have imagined the Students' Union. A new union was currently under construction – all plate glass and open spaces – but I suspected that it wouldn't be occupied for long before it had acquired the same rank atmosphere, its new carpets marinated in beer and cigarette ash.

The Union was divided into two areas, a kind of self-service café and a bar, in which currently a group of rugby players, almost certainly an unholy alliance of medical and engineering students, were having a noisy lunchtime pint or ten. They were behaving as though it was Friday night rather than Monday lunchtime, downing pints of heavy in one draught and singing simplistic songs about bizarre sexual acts that they had almost certainly never indulged in and probably didn't even understand.

I found Terri cornered at a table, smoking intensely and trying to ignore Robin, who was breaching the perimeter fence of her personal space. Terri's personal space occupied an area roughly the size of Mull and therefore required vigorous defences.

Robin looked like Roy Wood from Wizzard with a touch of Rasputin in his last days, if Rasputin had worn burgundy-coloured loons and a rainbow tie-dyed T-shirt. He was ostentatiously reading *The Glass Bead Game*. Robin had the capacity to be extraordinarily tedious. His creative writing paper for Martha was a one-act play called *Life Sentence* ('post-Beckettian') in which disaffected young men sat around on packing cases and talked in unfinished sentences about how boring everything was and, in my opinion, was too true to life to be art.

Andrea was delicately eating a Golden Delicious – peeling it and cutting it up into careful segments – and frowning with distaste at the sight of Kevin opposite her who was stuffing a huge Forfar bridie into his mouth, greasy flakes of pastry adhering to his puffy lips. He sighed miserably when he finished chewing the last mouthful and said, 'Two's never enough, is it?' Kevin was feeling disgruntled because the cafeteria was only serving cold food.

A big girl called Kara was making a great performance out of sitting down at the table. Kara was laden with a tray of food, a heavy rucksack, a woven Greek shoulder-bag and, finally, a fat, pneumatic baby, strapped to her back with a shawl.

Kara lived with other students – Robin was one of them – in an old farmhouse called Wester Balniddrie out in the wilds of rural Angus. They kept goats and chickens and pretended to be self-sufficient but they were not really the kind of people to hang out with in the after-math of a disaster; they needed all the accoutrements of civilization to survive. Anything that involved a tool, for example, sent them into a panic. If the inhabitants of Balniddrie had been in charge of man's technical evolu-tion, people would still be storing things in hammocks slung from trees.

Kara finally managed to get settled and started wolfing a large bridge roll that was fraying at the seams with grated cheese and cress. Kara's main fashion influence was peasantry. Today she was wearing an Indian cotton skirt, a pair of big workman's boots, a huge, hairy sweater that looked as if it had been knitted on tent poles and some kind of cloth wrapped round her head, Russian serf-style. Her skin looked as if it had been rubbed with walnut juice.

Kara was from Kent originally although she looked like

a tinker, and was planning to do teacher-training after she graduated and be released into the world of primary school infants in the guise of 'Miss Jones'. The baby, whose paternity was almost as vague as mine, was called Proteus and was lugged around everywhere by Kara, much to the annoyance of the university staff who had discovered, rather late in the day, that there were no rules about not bringing babies into lectures and tutorials.

Robin grew tired of pretending to read *The Glass Bead Game* and took out a pack of giant Rizlas and started rolling a joint under the table. Robin had recently decided to become a Buddhist, which made him even more boring.

'What's it all about? The meaning of Liff,' Robin said, laughing in a stupid way that made his shoulders shake, like a cartoon dog. For some reason all Dundee students found this hilariously funny.

'What goes around comes around, eh?' Shug said, sliding into the seat next to Robin. Andrea smiled, rather pathetically, at him but Shug was more intent on eating his cold, round pie (or 'peh' in the Dundee patois). Nora has only ever given me two pieces of advice in my life, both of them on the station platform in Newcastle, when I boarded the train to come to Dundee for the first time:

1. Beware of people with blue eyes.
2. Don't eat the pies.

I have tried my best to heed this maternal counsel – despite its having been given in a rather unsatisfactory rhyming couplet – as I am unlikely to receive any more.

'So, I've decided to become a vegetarian,' Robin said staring fascinated at the pale, fatty innards of Shug's pie.

Proteus started to cry and Kara disentangled him from his makeshift pouch. He was still wound tightly in a grubby white Aircell blanket that made him look like a large maggot. His little fists waved angrily in the air until Kara fumbled inside her shirt for a breast and attached him to it. Kevin blushed in horror and stared fixedly at something fascinating on the ceiling until he noticed Olivia sitting at a neighbouring table and stared at her red boots instead.

Olivia was sitting with a group of social admin people, who were all ignoring her. She was reading *Gormenghast*, very slowly and deliberately in the way that lone diners in restaurants read. She put her hand to her cheek and revealed a slender wrist circled by a gold bracelet. Several months ago, in an unusual moment of intimacy in the cafeteria queue, Olivia told me that this bracelet had belonged to her mother.

'Dead?' I queried, in the rather off-hand manner of the semi-orphan (for my father, you will have noticed, is absent from my own story), and Olivia said, yes, dead and by her own hand, inconveniently gassing herself on Olivia's tenth birthday.

Andrea suddenly ducked under the table to avoid Heather. Heather – the priggish, rather frightening girl who had hijacked the women's liberation group – shared a flat with Andrea, one of those university places where no-one knows each other at the beginning of the year and no-one likes each other by the end. It was also one of those flats where everyone had their own provisions so that their rather small Hotpoint fridge contained, for example, five pints of individually labelled milk and there were constant arguments over purloined butter and pilfered cornflakes. Heather went so far as to mark the levels of her tomato sauce bottles and weigh her blocks of margarine.

Heather, making a beeline for the hapless Andrea, was wearing a skinny-rib, polo-necked sweater that made a feature of her small unrestrained breasts and surprisingly prominent nipples which bounced hypnotically as she walked.

'She thinks I ate one of her Dairylea,' Andrea sniffed, 'as if. One triangle has a million calories.' Luckily for Andrea, Heather was distracted by a drunken rugby player committing unspeakable practices and unnatural acts.

I noticed Olivia staring at Proteus, very intently, as if she was trying to work out a particularly knotty Logic problem. Like Bob, Olivia was doing a joint degree in English and Philosophy. Unlike Bob, she was set to get a first. Her preoccupation with Proteus allowed Kevin's tormented gaze to creep up as far as her knees. He was clutching a bit of *The Chronicles of Edrakonia*, now entering its fourth volume, which was very much the same as the previous three volumes.

'The Lady Agaruitha,' he said in a low voice to me, because for some reason I had been singled out a long time ago as his audience, 'has been imprisoned in a tower by—'

'The lady who?' Kara interrupted, looking up from a piece of dun-coloured fabric she had taken out and begun to smock, despite the hindrance of a suckling baby.

'A-g-a-r-u-i-t-h-a,' Kevin spelled out crossly, blushing because Agaruitha was based on Olivia, although I don't suppose Olivia was the goddaughter of a dragon queen, but she did sometimes have the look of someone imprisoned in a tower by 'the evil Lord Lebaron, known as Dragonscourge—'

Proteus unplugged himself from Kara's breast with a popping noise and looked abstractedly at the ceiling as if he was trying to remember something. Kara took the opportunity to root once more in her rucksack and this time produce some mis-shapen candles in dull plasticine colours. Some of them had been set with what were supposed to be decorations – beans and lentils, little pebbles and the odd leaf. Most of them looked as if they had been moulded in empty cat food tins. The candles were Balniddrie's response to the current state of emergency.

'We've had to put the price up,' Kara said, 'because of demand.'

'Capitalist profiteer,' Shug said.

I bought a candle out of necessity. It was very heavy, you could easily have bashed someone's skull in with it.

'And then burnt the evidence,' Kevin said, 'that's brilliant.'

Olivia hadn't noticed Roger Lake lurking in the doorway trying to make surreptitious gestures to attract her attention without attracting any to himself.

There was a sudden surge of renewed raucousness from

the rugby players at the bar, one of whom was standing on a table doing a slow, unattractive striptease. Then the power came back on causing a lot of people to flinch and cower like nocturnal animals suddenly caught in the beam of a headlight. The engineers rushed to the jukebox to put on 'Maggie May' and the noise level in the basement was cranked up a further notch.

When Olivia finally noticed Roger a little frown disturbed her perfection. But then she smiled at him and slipped away quickly, following him at a discreet distance.

The rugby players had used up most of the oxygen by now and I thought it was probably a good time to leave before people started dying.

'I'm going,' I said to Terri.

She followed me out, saying she was going to the Howff for a while. The Howff was Terri's favourite graveyard, although any cemetery would do when she was in the right mood, which was always. Where other students might knit or read or hillwalk, Terri's hobby was studying graveyards, exploring the topography of the cities of the dead – the Howff, Balgay, the Eastern Necropolis. Death was never going to have to worry about Terri not stopping for him.

At the entrance to the Union we passed a short, bland girl called Janice Rand. Janice was in Martha's creative writing class and wrote short, bland poetry that resembled vapid Anglican hymns. Janice had set up a table containing a handful of blue, badly printed leaflets and on which a hand-made banner was tacked, proclaiming quietly, 'Don't forget old people'.

Janice smelt of piety and coal tar soap. She had recently become a Christian, a neophyte of a student Christian fellowship whose members roamed the corridors of Airlie, Belmont and Chalmers Halls looking for likely converts (the afraid, the alone, the abandoned) and those who needed to use the Bible to fill in the spaces where their personalities should have been.

The student Christians ran some kind of volunteer service, visiting the elderly and the housebound. Janice was trying to sign up more volunteers.

'Don't forget old people what?' I asked, drawn by curiosity. 'That they fought in the war, that they know more than you do? That they feel afraid and alone and abandoned?'

Janice made a face. 'Not *what*,' she replied scornfully, 'just don't forget them. In general.'

We turned to go and Janice shouted after us, 'Jesus can save you!' She looked rather doubtful as if He might draw the line at us. 'Jesus is the Son of God,' she added, in case we didn't know. 'He came once to save us,' she said, rather stroppily, 'and He'll come again. He might even be here now.'

A blast of cold air swung the front door open with a loud crash and we all jumped, but especially Janice who looked as if – just for a fraction of a second – she believed that Jesus had walked into Dundee University's Student Union. She should warn Him about the lack of hot food. It wasn't Jesus, unless He had chosen to return as a scruffy student from the Socialist Society, carrying a box of newly printed leaflets – small pink ones as opposed to Janice's small blue ones.

'Because blue is the colour of heaven?' I asked her but she just scowled at me. The boy from the Socialist Society pushed one of his leaflets into my hand. It said, 'Stop the War Now'. He tried to give one to Janice but she wouldn't take it unless he in turn took one of her leaflets and when we hurried out of the door they were still having a stand-off, thrusting leaflets aggressively at each other.

Nora, who has been snoring gently by the cold ashes of the kitchen grate, wakes up and yawns.

~ Did I miss anything? she asks.

'A certain amount of fear and loathing, a little paranoia, acres of boredom, the Lady Agaruitha in a tower. A lot of new charac-ters that you'll just have to catch up with as best as you can.'

~ No dragons?

'Not yet.'

Nora has sea-change eyes. Today they are a murky rock-pool brown because the gulls are being chased inland by a deter-mined south-westerly. The wind on the cliffs is so strong that sometimes we find ourselves walking backwards.

I am strangely at home in this salty air, I am in my element.

~ The sea's in your blood, Nora says, the call of the sea.

Did the Stuart-Murrays – luckless landlubbers who farmed the rolled and folded landscape of Perthshire – have the salty, sea-going blood of sailors?

~ Quite the opposite, says Nora.

For it seems that the Stuart-Murrays, whilst mysteriously

94

drawn to the water – witness our ancestral holiday home, or Nora's peregrinations – are nonetheless incapable of keeping afloat on it. There was a Stuart-Murray sank at Trafalgar, according to Nora, and one aboard the *Mary Rose*, one outward bound on the *Titanic*, one homeward bound on the *Lusitania*, and one long forgotten Stuart-Murray who is said to have lost the king's treasure in the Forth, although which king and which treasure seems unclear.

I am surprised that Nora ever ventures out in her little *Sea-Adventure*. But it seems the Stuart-Murrays do not even have to be in boats to be drowned at sea, one of Nora's uncles was believed lost in the great and horrible Tay Bridge disaster, sneaking onto the train at Wormit, the last stop before the bridge, in a fit of youthful high spirits and alcohol. Ticketless, he remained unaccounted for in the lists of the dead.

~ Not your blood in particular, she says, it's in everyone's blood, where else does the salt come from?

Nora is watching the sea, through a huge pair of First World War binoculars that she is toting. She says they once belonged to her eldest brother. A brother? She has never mentioned a brother.

~ Oh yes, Nora says nonchalantly, she had a lot of brothers and sisters.

'Imaginary ones perhaps?'

~ Real, she says, and counts on her fingers, Douglas, Torquil, Murdo, Honoria, Elspeth . . . and those are just the ones who died before she was born. What an unlucky family the Stuart-Murrays seem to be.

~ Oh, that's nothing, Nora says glumly, not compared with what happened later.

There Are Places Between Edinburgh
and Dundee

I HAVE A STONE HOT-WATER BOTTLE, WRAPPED IN AN OLD SWEATER, that I hug to my body in a vain effort to keep warm at nights. It is difficult to sleep when the darkness is so absolute, the only illumination provided by the occasional chink of starlight or a faint moonbeam.

I remember the countless nights of my childhood during which Nora left me alone while she went to her work in some pub or hotel that had taken her on for the season. I can conjure her up now, smell her cheap lily-of-the-valley cologne as she bent to kiss me goodnight, her extravagant hair piled on top of her head like a seafront ice-cream and her figure sculpted by her barmaid's dress or baffled by a severe waitress habit. I can still hear her whispering in my ear, entreating me to be a good girl – not to get out of bed, not to play with matches, not to choke on sweets, to scream if I was attacked by a stranger or a strangler or a rapist climbing in through the bedroom window. Nora always feared the worst.

~ From experience, she says darkly.

We drifted on, in and out with the tide, like flotsam, spending our time departing and arriving (or arriving and departing, depending on how you look at it). I grew up a connoisseur of pavilions and winter gardens and miniature golf courses. I may have been mystified by the conjugation of foreign verbs and the complex lives of fractions but I always knew my tide-tables. Nora's talents (piano, French, Scottish country dancing) qualified her for nothing useful, but she never had trouble finding work in some Sailor's Rest pub or Crow's Nest café.

Nora usually lived in wherever she was working so that 'home' was some cold hotel attic or a ramshackle room over a public bar where the two of us slept in rooms where the smell of mass catering and stale beer seeped up through the floorboards to join the aroma of wet hand-washed laundry drying dangerously on an Ascot water heater. We lived off other people's leftovers – salted nuts and olives and maraschino cherries from gin palaces and lounge bars, or restaurant scrapings – wedding trifle from the bottom of catering bowls and stale canapés from dinner-dances. And endless fish and chips, eaten in vinegary haste straight from the newspaper before Nora rushed to work.

No wonder, therefore, that wherever we went I sought out friends with families of a larger and more conventional composition – girls who lived in ordinary houses (thirties semi-detached, good-sized garden), had a stay-at-home, homespun mother, a known father (an accountant, a grocer), at least one sibling, a grandmother, a dog, an aunt or two. Families who spent their lives boiling kettles, flushing toilets, answering phones (ad infinitum, ad nauseam).

Always, just when I had established myself as a cheerful, eager-to-please fixture in the homes of these families, Nora would uproot us again and we would be on a bus to the next small seaside town that looked very like the one we had just left. You would almost have thought that we were on the run from something. And we were, of course.

★　　★　　★

I wake up in the dead of night and find that I can't remember who I am. Is that normal? Almost certainly not. The feral Siamese have been holding a cats' concert in the night, a maniacal caterwauling that sends a shiver down the spine of every vertebrate on the island, whether quick or dead. Perhaps they're engendering more of their own consanguineous kind.

~ Spawn of the devil, Nora says cheerfully next morning, stirring watery breakfast oatmeal with an ancient wooden spurtle. Go on then, she says, dolloping out this gruel in a bowl in front of me. What happened next?

A faint, defiant cry of 'Jesus Saves' followed us as we set off listlessly down the Nethergate. A harsh wind was whipping litter and grit off the street and the occasional pink or blue leaflet. A fine Highland rain, like the spray from a plant mister, was falling in the wrong meteorological zone.

Terri wanted to go to the Morgan Tower pharmacy for a bottle of Collis Brown to boil down messily and opiate herself further with, while I was planning to buy a copy of Coles' *Notes* on *Middlemarch* from Frank Russell's University Bookshop.

At that moment a dog appeared from nowhere (as they do) on the pavement opposite. Catching our eye, it assumed a sociable expression and lolloped towards us as if it was crossing a field rather than a road. At that same moment, a 1963 Ford Cortina hurtled into view (in as much as a 1963 Cortina can hurtle), heading inexorably towards the same spot on the road as the dog. Seeing this,

101

Terri darted into the road to save the dog from the Cortina.

Narrative destiny (a powerful force) took charge at that point. The car-dog-girl scenario – lolloping dog, hurtling car, foolish girl – could only end in tears and although the Cortina swerved at the last minute and avoided Terri, it couldn't help but find the dog. I closed my eyes—

—when I opened them again the car was up on the pavement and Terri was sitting on the kerb with the dog's head in her lap. Although generally unattached to the human race, Terri was surprisingly fond of animals, particularly dogs – she was more or less brought up by the family pet (a large Dobermann called Max).

The dog which now lay limply in her arms was a big yellow mongrel with fur the colour of an old teddy-bear or a half-dead camel. The man who would sooner run over a dog than a woman got out of the car and lumbered over to this canine pietà, giving his front bumper a cursory inspection on the way. He had the stocky build of a cheap discotheque bouncer and hair that carpeted the backs of his hands so that you might have thought he was wearing a chimpanzee outfit beneath his crumpled suit. He bent down stiffly to observe the dog, revealing a dreadfully hairy shin. The cheap material of his suit, the colour of Maltesers, stretched tightly over his beefy thighs when he bent down.

'I haven't got time for this,' he said, 'bloody dog, why didn't it look where it was going? I'm late,' he added in a very agitated voice, 'very late.'

The dog, meanwhile, wasn't agitated at all, indeed so still and lifeless that it could have been demonstrating the taxidermist's art to the crowd that had begun to gather. Terri started to give the dog the kiss of life, breathing into its big Alsatian-derived muzzle with unusual determination.

'Oh dear,' a rather feeble voice said behind me, 'is there anything I can do to help?' The voice turned out to belong to Professor Cousins, waving a large duck-handled umbrella about, like a man in danger of becoming a caricature of himself.

With much creaking and straining he bent down next to the dog and tried to encourage its recovery by scratching the coarse hair on its sugar-pink belly while the onlookers susurrated in the background, earnestly discussing the best method of resuscitating a dead dog – recommendations varying from 'gie it a sweetie' to 'gie it a skelping'.

However, having Terri's vampire breath in its lungs seemed to be doing wonders for the yellow dog. It began to come slowly back to life, starting at the far end with its big tail – like a giant rat's – which started to thump heavily on the tarmac. Next it stretched its back legs, flexing the abnormally long toes that ended in big lizard-like nails. Finally, with a little sigh, it opened its eyes, lifted its head and looked around. It seemed agreeably surprised by the number of interested bystanders it had attracted and whacked its tail more vigorously so that its audience broke into a spontaneous round of applause at this Lazarus-like recovery. The dog got to its feet unsteadily, like a newborn wildebeest. I wondered if it might take a bow, but it didn't.

Terri regarded this recovery with a certain suspicion. 'He's probably in shock,' she said, her little white face pinched with worry. 'We still need to get him to a vet.'

'You're joking,' the Cortina driver said. 'I had to be somewhere else half an hour ago.' Terri began to hiss like a malevolent kettle, showing her little pointy teeth. Looking more surprised than shocked, the dog waited expectantly for its fate to be decided between the two warring parties. It was the Cortina driver who eventually backed down. 'Oh all right then,' he relented, 'but quickly then, I'm very late,' and started ushering us all urgently into the car.

The car – which didn't look as if it had ever seen better days – was a rusted white, more rust than white. I got in the back, followed by Terri and the dog which scrambled in awkwardly and insisted on sitting between us. Professor Cousins climbed gingerly into the front, behaving as if motor cars were a new and untested invention.

'A jaunt. This is fun,' he remarked and held out his hand towards the driver. 'Professor Cousins,' he said, 'lovely to meet you. And you are?'

The Cortina driver answered reluctantly, as if the information might be used against him at a later date, 'Chick. Chick Petrie.'

'Call me Gabriel,' Professor Cousins said, smiling and nodding his head.

'But that's not your name, is it?' I asked, puzzled by this sudden alteration of Professor Cousins' usual Christian names of Edward and Neville, but he just smiled cheerfully and said, 'Why not?' and Chick said, 'What's in a name and all that, eh, Prof?'

Professor Cousins beamed. 'Exactly! A man after my own heart, Chick.'

'A professor, eh?' Chick said. 'Me, of course, I was educated in the School of Hard Knocks and the University of Life.'

'And I'm sure it was a very broad and interesting education, Chick,' Professor Cousins said.

'It's a dog-eat-dog world out there,' Chick observed darkly. Terri clapped her hands over the dog's ears. Chick started the engine and a strange smell immediately began to fill the car, the smell of something sweet but dead –

rotting strawberries and decaying rat. Before anyone could comment on this assault to our olfactory sensibilities, Chick drove off the pavement with a jolt and into the traffic with a jerk, without looking to see if anything was coming, resulting in a cacophony of hooting horns following us down the Nethergate.

Professor Cousins gestured vaguely behind us saying something about there being a vet at the top of South Tay Street, but before the words had left his lips we had passed the turning and were accelerating round the Angus roundabout as if we were on the Dodgems. Within seconds we were roaring along the approach to the road bridge. Terri shouted at Chick that he was going the wrong way and he shouted back, 'Wrong way for you maybe, but the right way for me.' He didn't even stop at the toll-booth, merely slowing down in what appeared to be a practised manoeuvre and thrusting the toll money into the hand of the collector as he passed, before speeding onto the long, straight stretch of the bridge. I supposed we were in the hands of a madman. Terri leant forward and prodded Chick sharply in the back of the neck. 'What about the vet?'

'There's nothing wrong with the mutt,' Chick grumbled, glancing at the dog in his rear-view mirror. It was true, the dog did now look the picture of health, sitting up on the seat and as alert as any back-seat driver. But the smell in the car had grown much worse – a foul stench getting fouler the further we drove. 'What is that?' Professor Cousins asked.

'What's what?' Chick asked.

'That smell.'

Chick inhaled as if he was taking the sea-air. 'Vindaloo,' he said. He thought for a few seconds before adding 'and cat.'

'Cat?' I queried in alarm.

'Don't panic,' Chick said, 'it's dead.'

'None of us want to go with you,' Terri said sullenly to Chick.

'Kidnapped?' Professor Cousins said, growing quite merry. 'How exciting. Won't we have a tale to tell.'

Terri, clutching a handful of dirty yellow fur in one hand, was beginning to look a little green around the gills. 'It's a crime, you know,' she persisted, 'taking people against their will. You can go to jail.'

Chick snorted dismissively and said, with a certain personal bitterness, that the people who had committed the really serious crimes (murder, mayhem, et cetera) were not to be found behind prison walls but were roaming free in Brazil, or Argentina, 'or even Fife'.

'Yeah, well, I don't care,' Terri said, 'I want out.'

'Suit yourself,' Chick shrugged, 'on you go,' and he reached over behind to open the rear door, temporarily losing control of the car as he did so.

'Fucking creep,' Terri snarled at him and bit his arm. (Which is definitely how accidents happen.)

Chick seemed unperturbed, he had the air of a man who was used to being physically and verbally abused on a regular basis. He simply accelerated even more, patting the dashboard affectionately. 'The good old Mark 1,' he said, 'standard model, 1200ccs of effort, top speed seventy-six miles an hour.'

We reached the other end of the road bridge. 'The Kingdom of Fife,' Professor Cousins announced, as if we were entering a fairy-tale country.

'Heuchter-teuchter land,' Chick sneered.

'St Andrews,' Professor Cousins carried on dreamily, 'my old alma mater.'

'I thought you said that was Cambridge,' I puzzled. It was only a couple of hours ago that he had been deliriously describing May Balls and punting and porters and all those other remote activities of academia that were unknown in Dundee.

'Did I?' he said.

'We're not going to St Andrews,' Chick said hastily. 'I'm not a taxi. And I'm bloody late.'

'Late for what?' I asked.

'Surveillance,' he said, enunciating the word with a certain distaste.

'Surveillance?' I queried.

'Watching people.'

'I know what it means,' I said. 'I just can't imagine you doing it.'

He took a card from an inside pocket and handed it to me. Grubby and badly printed, it read 'Premier Investigations – all work undertaken, no questions asked'. Chick, it turned out, was (of all unlikely things) a private detective.

'A private eye,' Professor Cousins said thoughtfully.

Chick ignored him and looked at his watch agitatedly. 'I'm going to bloody miss her.'

'Who exactly are you watching?' Professor Cousins asked.

'Some woman,' Chick said, 'jealous spouse, usual thing.' He lit a cigarette (terrifying to observe at speed). 'Husband's a nutter, of course,' he said; 'they always are.'

'You don't have any qualms then,' Professor Cousins asked Chick, 'about doing this sort of work, I mean, ethical qualms.'

'Qualms?' Chick echoed. 'Qualms? How?'

Professor Cousins laughed. 'The more you say it the more ridiculous it sounds. It's often the way with words, isn't it? Qualms comes from the Old English, Chick – murder, torment, death.'

'Fascinating, Gabriel,' Chick said in such a neutral tone that I couldn't tell whether he meant it or not.

I leant forward to speak to him and got a whiff of his middle-aged aroma – Old Spice, sweat and stale eighty-shilling ale. Professor Cousins, I couldn't help but notice, smelt vaguely of attar of roses.

'Are you following *me*?' I asked Chick.

He raised a pair of amazed eyebrows so that his forehead made a rubbery concertina and said dismissively, 'Why on earth would I be following *you*?'

'The poor girl thinks someone's following her,' Professor Cousins said helpfully.

Chick cast a speculative glance at me in his rear-view mirror and said, 'Do you?'

'I'm just imagining it,' I said because I really didn't want to think otherwise.

109

'Poor Christopher – Dr Pike – thought he was being followed,' Professor Cousins sighed, 'and look what happened to him.'

'What happened to him?' Chick asked after a while when Professor Cousins didn't elaborate.

'He had an accident, like our friend here,' Professor Cousins said, indicating the dog in the back seat who cocked an ear to show he knew he was being talked about.

'And you don't think it was an accident?' Chick said; and Professor Cousins laughed and said, 'Oh, I'm sure it *was*, the members of my department are notoriously accident-prone. At any one time half of them are in hospital. There won't be anyone left in the actual university soon.'

'Professor Cousins thinks someone is trying to kill him,' I told Chick.

'You make a great pair,' Chick said sarcastically, 'the man who thinks someone's trying to kill him and the girl who thinks someone's watching her. And as for Little Miss Sunshine back there . . . You know what they say, don't you?' he said to Professor Cousins.

'No, what do they say, Chick?'

'Just because you're paranoid doesn't mean they're not out to get you.'

'A private dick,' Professor Cousins said gleefully. 'There once was a private dick/Who went by the name of Chick—'

'Is it far?' Terri murmured. 'Is it far to where we're going?'

'Far enough,' Chick said enigmatically.

We finally arrived wherever it was we'd been going – which might have been Cupar but I hadn't been paying much attention to road signs; it was certainly a place very *like* Cupar. The lights were on in Fife, the windows of the houses glowing with precious artificial daylight in an effort to illuminate the Murk of a dark afternoon. We parked in a pleasant street, lined with trees and filled with detached and semi-detached suburban villas. Chick turned the engine off, settled back in his seat and lit up another cigarette.

'So, Chick,' Professor Cousins said, rubbing his hands in anticipation, 'this is a stakeout? What happens now – you just sit here and watch her front door, then follow her if she comes out?'

'More or less,' Chick said.

'How do you know you haven't missed her?' Terri asked, reviving a little now that we were stationary.

'I don't,' Chick said.

'Aren't you supposed to have flasks of hot soup?' I said to him, 'and crossword puzzles, and tapes of classical music?'

'How about a camera?' Professor Cousins asked him eagerly, then added, 'Or binoculars? A notepad? What about a newspaper to hide behind?'

Chick wrestled a *Racing Post* out of his pocket and waved it in the air. 'It's not like that, Gabriel,' he said; 'you've seen too many films.'

'On the contrary, Chick,' Professor Cousins said, rather sadly, 'I haven't seen enough.'

'Mind you,' Chick said, after a few minutes' contemplative silence, 'you come across some rum things in this job, Gabriel. I expect I could write a novel about what I've seen.'

'I'm sure you could,' Professor Cousins said, with more encouragement than was strictly necessary.

'They say everyone has a novel inside them, don't they?' Chick said, warming to the subject now.

'Yeah, and maybe that's where it should stay,' Terri growled. Chick responded with something derogatory about students, something to the effect that he was paying his taxes so that we could lie around all day having sex and taking drugs.

'Don't think I'm not grateful,' Terri snapped, and Chick snapped back, 'Awa' and bile yer heid.' The car was too cramped for this kind of behaviour, something the dog understood if no-one else did. It suddenly gave a huge walrus sigh of boredom, turned round and round in an effort to dislodge myself and Terri from the back seat, then flopped down heavily and closed its eyes.

'It didn't just die, did it?' Terri asked, giving the dog an anxious poke. It opened one eye and gave her a thoughtful look.

'Keep still, will you?' Chick said tetchily. 'You're drawing attention to us.'

'Married, Chick?' Professor Cousins asked conversationally after a while.

Chick scowled and said, 'Who wants to know?'

'Just asking.'

'Man about town, that's me,' Chick said airily.

'Oh, absolutely, aren't we all,' Professor Cousins laughed.

After a pause Chick said, 'Bloody woman, bloody Moira, bloody cow. Took everything – the house, the furniture, the kids – not that I mind her taking *them*, mingin' little bastards,' he said reflectively. I was reminded of Dr Dick, whose ex-wife was also a Moira, a self-contained Aberdonian – a research chemist – who had summoned just enough emotion to petition for divorce. That, apart from assonance, must surely be the only thing that Chick and Dick could ever have in common.

With an exasperated sigh Chick put his *Racing Post* away, stubbed out his cigarette and settled back in his seat, closed his eyes and said, 'Don't let me go to sleep.' Who was it that Chick reminded me of? I wondered.

'You're looking at me,' he said, without opening his eyes.

'I was just trying to think who you reminded me of.'

'I'm a one-off,' Chick said. 'They broke the mould when they made me.' It began to rain, heavy drops thudding on the roof of the car.

'Goodness, it's raining cats and dogs,' Professor Cousins commented. The dog's ears gave an interested twitch but it didn't bother waking up. I wondered what happened to the Tara-Zanthian stock market when this particular weather phenomenon occurred.

The rain streamed down the windscreen, obscuring the view of the street. Terri asked Chick why he didn't put the windscreen wipers on. Moving himself as little as possible, Chick leant forward and pressed a button. The

113

wipers creaked into life, moving slowly across the windscreen, with a horrible fingernails-on-a-blackboard kind of noise.

'That's why,' he said and turned them off and closed his eyes again. 'Now how about we keep our mouths shut and our eyes peeled?'

'What a horrible idea,' Professor Cousins murmured to himself. The air in the car was damp and didn't sit well with the rank smell of the dog nor with the original awful odour which had now changed quality into something woolly and fungoid. I suppose it was a good thing there was no heating in Chick's car or else new life forms might have been incubated, but nonetheless it was freezing cold and I was glad of the proximity of the dog's big, warm, smelly body.

'I don't suppose you've got any of that waccy-baccy, have you?' Chick asked me suddenly.

'No, sorry.'

'Pity.'

'We could play a game,' Professor Cousins said hopefully.

'A game?' Chick said suspiciously. 'How?'

'How not?' Professor Cousins said, showing an unexpected command of the Scottish tongue.

'You mean poker?' Chick said.

'Well, I was thinking more of a word game, Chick,' Professor Cousins said, 'like "Doublets", say – that's where you turn one word into another, "Head" into "Tail" for example.' Everyone looked at him blankly and he said encouragingly, 'It's easy – head–heal–

114

teal–tell–tall–tail. See? You try – turn "Dog" into "Cat".'
The dog looked up in alarm. Terri stroked it back into
sleep. Professor Cousins was puzzled by our inability to
understand 'Doublets'.

'It was invented by Lewis Carroll, you know,' he said
rather sadly.

'Wasn't he the one who liked little girls?' Chick asked.

'I am going to Alyth where I shall advertise abominable
alcohol,' Professor Cousins said.

Chick gave him a wary look. 'We're *not* going to Alyth.'

Professor Cousins laughed. 'No, no, it's another game;
you see you go somewhere and you have to do something using the same letter of the alphabet – I am going
to Blairgowrie where I shall brave the braying beasts.'
Professor Cousins tried again, 'I am going to Cupar where
I shall cut cheap cabbages.'

'Maybe we could just go to Dundee,' Terri muttered.

'And do what?' Professor Cousins smiled encouragingly. Everyone – apart from the dog and Professor
Cousins – turned rather nasty at this point, especially
when Chick suggested that Terri might like to fuck off to
Forfar and do something illegal with a ferret.

Which put an end to the conversation for a good ten
minutes, at which point Terri said, 'I'm hungry,' and
Professor Cousins said, 'And I wouldn't mind going to
the little boys' room.'

'Little boys?' Chick queried, giving him a sideways
look.

'And it's uncomfortable back here,' Terri complained. I
imagined that this was what it was like being on a family

outing in a car (there were so many aspects of normal family life I seemed to have missed out on). But instead of a regular family – mother, father, sister, grandmother, Golden Retriever in a Vauxhall Victor – I had to make do with this strange patched-up affair with neither blood nor love in common.

'Anything to eat in here?' Professor Cousins asked hopefully, opening the glove compartment and bringing out an assortment of objects – a deck of dog-eared playing-cards adorned with photographs of big women in various states of undress ('Fascinating,' Professor Cousins murmured), a pair of handcuffs, a paper bag of squashed fern cakes from Goodfellow and Steven, a length of washing-rope, a large kitchen knife and a police warrant-card that displayed a photograph of Chick with more hair and less flesh.

'Don't ask me how I managed to hang onto that,' Chick said.

'How did you manage to hang onto that?' Terri asked.

'Piss off.' Chick stuffed all the items back in the glove compartment except for the fern cakes, which he distrib-uted amongst the Cortina's occupants.

'So you were on the force then, Chick?' Professor Cousins asked and then turned round to us in the back seat and grinned and said, 'A "pig", isn't it?' as if we needed a translation. According to Chick, who didn't seem the most reliable of narrators, he had been a detective inspector until there had been some misunder-standing over a holiday in Lanzarote that had landed him 'in the doghouse'.

116

'If the cow had kept her big mouth shut it would have been all right,' Chick said.

The 'cow' was now resident in Errol, in a new house, and said house was serving as a love nest for the cow and her new 'bidie-in', a gigolo, Chick claimed, whose day job was an insurance claims loss adjuster – a man, Chick reported vituperatively, who possessed a full head of hair and a brand new yellow Ford Capri 3000 and thought he was the cat's pyjamas. The cow, the gigolo and the mingin' little bastards had formed an economic conspiracy to bring about the financial ruin of Chick, Chick said.

'It's a dog's life, Chick,' Professor Cousins said, giving him a comforting pat on his hairy hand. Chick snatched the hand away, muttering something about ginger beer. Chick's eyebrows, I couldn't help but notice, almost met in the middle – a sure sign of a werewolf. Or so Nora had told me.

Chick said, 'Tell me if anything catches your eye' (Professor Cousins shuddered), and then appeared to fall asleep. Soon Professor Cousins himself was snoring in the front seat. When I glanced at Terri, I saw that she too had given in to her customary narcoleptic state. I amused myself by watching the sedate suburban activity of mothers pushing prams and old ladies sweeping paths. After half an hour, a woman came out of the house we were supposed to be watching. She had nothing of the Jezebel about her, in fact she seemed remarkable, if anything, for her ordinariness. In her thirties, with short brown hair, she wore a nondescript mac and carried a shopping-bag. She looked as if she was off to collect her

117

messages rather than conduct an adulterous liaison. She smiled and said hello to a woman walking past with a Labrador and then got into a Hillman Imp parked at the kerb and drove off. I didn't wake Chick up. It seemed to me the woman had a perfect right to go about her business unmolested by complete strangers. (Although is there any such thing as a partial stranger?)

Chick snorted suddenly, looked at his watch and said, 'That's enough of that. Fish supper, anyone?' and I realized who he reminded me of. Like the ghost of Christmas Future Chick was a picture of what Bob was going to be like in his middle age.

Chick started the engine and Terri assumed the tense position of a crash test dummy. We stopped at the first chip shop we came to and Professor Cousins said, 'Oh my treat, please, it's been such a lovely day out.'

'Very good of you, Gabriel,' Chick said, full of bonhomie at the sight of someone else's wallet. 'I'll have an extra single fish in that case.'

'As opposed to . . . a married fish?' Professor Cousins said vaguely.

'Ha bloody ha,' Chick said, popping a whole pickled egg in his mouth.

I thought we would be on our way home now but as we neared the bridge Chick took a sudden turning and drove down into Newport-on-Tay and then parked the car again on the opposite side of the road from a driveway that curved away into a thick screen of laurel bushes. After a short while a car emerged from the driveway – the very

118

same Hillman Imp as before, still being driven by the nondescript woman. Perhaps Chick was using some kind of sixth sense to follow her rather than simple powers of observation. The woman drove off in the direction of Wormit and another vehicle emerged from the driveway, a slow-moving hearse this time laden with a coffin. It was followed by a solitary car. Terri perked up considerably at the sight of the hearse.

'Anyone you know?' said Professor Cousins, giving an affectionate kind of nod in the direction of the coffin.

'Not personally,' Chick said impassively.

We drove off, slowly as if we were following the hearse, and I caught sight of a sign at the bottom of the driveway, *The Anchorage – a home from home for the elderly*, and told Professor Cousins that The Anchorage was currently home to Archie's mother and he said, 'Really? I never think of him as someone who has a mother.'

As we drove around the roundabout on the approach road to the bridge I saw a hooded figure by the side of the road, thumb stuck out into the rain.

'There's no room,' Terri protested to Chick as he slowed down. The hooded hitchhiker ran towards the back door of the Cortina. He looked like one of those sinister figures from urban myths, the ones who end up killing everyone in the car and then drive off with a boot-load of bodies and pick up a pretty young girl who's been ditched by her boyfriend and is looking for a ride home, blah, blah, blah. I was surprised that Chick, not overflowing with the milk of human kindness, had stopped but perhaps he recognized his younger more innocent self as the

119

hitchhiker turned out to be none other than—

'Bob!' I exclaimed.

'Put him in the boot,' Terri said hastily to Chick, but to no avail as Bob was already squeezing himself in beside me, to the particular annoyance of the dog, who could see that there wasn't enough room for this many bodies in a Cortina. The dog finally ended up sitting on Terri's knee, although it would probably have been easier the other way round as the dog had a slightly larger volume.

'What on earth are you doing here?' I asked Bob.

'I could ask the same of you,' he said, unhelpfully, although it turned out that Bob had accidentally taken the wrong bus, believing himself to be on the way out to Balniddrie for a mellow afternoon in the country with Robin and had found himself instead in the more foreign reaches of Fife.

'Transporter malfunction,' he said, delving deep into the pocket of his greatcoat and discovering a Caramac bar.

We were nearly over the bridge, the Tay beneath us was the colour of wet slate. Dundee grew nearer and nearer and Professor Cousins sighed with satisfaction and said, 'Well, what a day.'

'It's not over yet,' Chick said.

The funeral-paced hearse easily got the lead on us as Chick was a man who had obviously never watched a crow fly and executed several more detours once we arrived in Dundee – betting shops, The Golden Fry for a deep-fried pizza and so on – before finally bringing

120

the Cortina to a halt, parked half on and off the pavement outside the Phoenix bar, not far from where he had run into the dog. Professor Cousins looked at the Phoenix and its solicitation to 'Drink and be whole again beyond confusion' (an unlikely outcome, you would think) and said wistfully to Chick, 'Time for a wee doch-an-dorris, Chick, my man?' in his strangled dog-Scots. But Chick had already exited the car and was running up the street and dashing up the steps of the Catholic church on the Nethergate.

'Where's he gone?' Professor Cousins asked, peering through the rain-smeared window.

'Church, I think he's gone to church,' I ventured.

'He didn't seem the religious sort,' Professor Cousins mused, 'although a philosophical chap, don't you think?'

A hearse was parked outside the church; of course they all look alike, but it seemed likely that it was the one from The Anchorage.

'I think he's gone to a funeral,' I said.

'Do you think he's all right?' Terri asked after ten minutes of waiting. 'Not like I care or anything.'

'Who is he anyway?' Bob asked, his curiosity typically slow to be aroused.

'A gumshoe,' Professor Cousins said with relish.

'Uh?'

'A private investigator,' I explained.

'Wow.'

Some desultory conversation followed during which Bob accidentally revealed that he was, to a certain extent, an English student. Professor Cousins was bewildered by this information, never having encountered Bob before.

'Well, I'm a kind of . . . underground student,' Bob said, rather unsatisfactorily. We waited another ten minutes and then Terri and I decided to go and find out what had happened to Chick.

The church was Tardis-like, much bigger inside than it was outside, and was full of noises the sources of which were invisible – echoing footfalls and discreet coughing – as if there were people hiding behind screens and in the hollow crypts of the building. The coffin was miles away at the far end of an aisle that was like an airport runway. There was only a handful of mourners, scattered strategically around an ocean of pews, and they all turned to look at us as we entered. We sat down at the back and Terri gave me a little nudge to indicate how happy she was with the venue.

In the absence of electricity the church was lit by dozens of candles. The priest presiding over the funeral was old and bulky, his black priest's frock stained and strained over a big housekeeper-fed belly. The funeral service was complex and mysterious and seemed to have little to do with the corpse, who appeared to be called 'Senga'.

On the distaff side of the church I spotted Janice Rand. She was with a Christian friend – an unattractive girl with the beginnings of alopecia and thick-rimmed spectacles. You could tell just by looking at her that she'd spent her adolescence in a church youth-club playing table-tennis and 'Kumbayah' on acoustic guitar. Janice was carrying a handbag that looked as if it must have once belonged to her mother. It had a peeling Lifeboat sticker on the side.

There was a knot of old ladies at the front of the church – Senga's friends presumably – some of whom were clutching shopping-bags as though they'd stepped into the church by accident while out picking up their messages in Littlewoods.

There was an air of palpable gloom which seemed to centre on the coffin. Perhaps when unhappy people die they release an effluvium of depression, like marsh gas. What happened, I wondered, to the molecules of the dead? Do they wait around, to be absorbed into any passer-by? I put my hand over my nose and mouth like a surgical mask just in case I inhaled any of Senga.

The funeral service seemed suddenly to dwindle away into nothing and the mourners shuffled out of their seats and left the coffin to its fate. Janice Rand passed us by without acknowledgement. The electricity came back on, the harsh light rendering the church less attractive.

'What are *you* doing here?' Chick said when he saw us and then looked at his watch and said, 'Shite – that's never the time, is it?' then looked heavenward and mumbled an apology for his language. He made a hasty sign of the cross and rushed out of the church.

Surprised by the haste of his departure, we were rather slow to follow and by the time we got outside Bob and Professor Cousins had been decanted from the Cortina which was already pulling away from the kerb and nosing its way bullishly into the traffic. The dog's sleepy face appeared in the back window. I almost expected it to raise a paw in farewell but instead it gave an enormous yawn, exposing surprisingly wolfish teeth.

'I'm off,' Bob said, and was gone before I had time to say I would go with him.

'Me too,' Terri said, hastily setting off in the direction of the Cortina and its canine hostage to fortune.

Professor Cousins and I hung around on the pavement like people who'd been unexpectedly thrown out of a party and were wondering what to do next.

'Well, I suppose that's the end of the excitement for today,' Professor Cousins said, rather dolefully.

I accompanied him back to the university. I watched him walking up the path to the Tower, his back stooped and his legs bowed. He seemed too fragile and ancient to battle the biting winds that howled perpetually around the base of the Tower. He struggled to open the big doors of the building until a janitor finally took pity on him and yanked them open for him.

I trudged home, an icy interstellar wind at my back and a shadow on my shoulder all the way. ('We know we are sought,' Archie told me, 'and expect to be found,' which I thought sounded quite biblical but Olivia said it was from *Dangling Man* by Saul Bellow.)

Chez Bob

I FOUGHT MY WAY INTO THE FLAT IN PATON'S LANE. THE hallway was currently being blocked by a variety of objects – four tyres from a 1957 Riley 1.5 saloon, which was all that was left of Bob's disastrous attempt at car ownership (a long story that does not need telling); an art deco standard lamp that we had never got to work, and a stuffed King Emperor penguin that Bob had been unable to resist bidding for at the Ward Road auction rooms but which had been relegated to the hall because of the strange scent it gave off of death and badly digested fish.

Despite my best efforts the flat remained a filthy place, smelling of curry powder and incense with a strange undertone of asafoetida. Bob never dusted or tidied ('Why fight entropy?') and rubbish of all kinds seemed to be attracted to him as if he was some kind of living dustbin.

An important part of my leaving-Bob daydream was the place I would live in without him – an uncluttered white space full of nothing but me. And perhaps a coffee table. And a bowl of perfect green apples. Joni Mitchell on the stereo. A white rug.

For all of this time I had been expecting Bob to change, change into somebody more energetic, more interesting – into someone else, in fact. It had dawned on me, only very slowly, that this was never going to happen. In the beginning I had liked Bob because he was Bob (although heaven knows why); now I was beginning to dislike him for the same reason. I was living with someone whose hobby was playing air guitar and who sincerely thought he was going to be a Time Lord when he grew up.

'Hey,' Bob said when he saw me. He was wearing a tank-top knitted by his mother for the larger version of Bob that she kindly held in her mind's eye, and straight jeans which I had turned into massive flares for him by inserting pieces of old flannelette sheeting the colour of Germolene.

He was sprawled on the floor, watching the innocent little girl on the test card with a touching devotion. The rays from television sets were vital to Bob's continued existence on this planet, in the way that oxygen is for other people. He claimed that the three-day week was having an adverse effect on his metabolism. Bob had bought his small black-and-white portable set with the proceeds from his one and only summer job – counting trees in Camperdown for the parks department. Bob didn't actually count the trees individually but looked at 'a whole bunch' of them and calculated how many there were, as in, 'That looks like about twenty trees.' As you can imagine, he usually got it completely wrong.

'Where've you been?' Bob asked.

'With you, don't you remember?'

'No.' Bob was eating the remains of a two-day-old biryani from the Lahore on the Perth Road. The chicken in the biryani bore a worrying anatomical resemblance to cat. Bob's idea of a balanced diet left something to be desired. When I first met him he lived off fish suppers from The Deep Sea, the occasional tin of dog food ('Why not?') and jars of cold baby food, the latter a particularly sensible way of eating in Bob's opinion – no cooking, no washing-up, no thought at all beyond whether to have 'Lamb and Vegetables' or 'Pears and Custard'. Or both. It was wasted on babies, Bob said, and his only complaint was that Heinz didn't do fish and chips in toddler-sized jars.

I spent some time weaning him onto more regular student meals – sausage and chips, egg and beans, mince and anything and fish pie – the latter a concept that Bob found particularly bizarre for some reason and he kept repeating, 'Wow, *fish* pie,' until I had to ask him to stop. I took him shopping in Betty White's on the High Street once and he couldn't get over the idea that a shop could sell both fish and vegetables – 'That's not . . . natural,' he said. Although not as unnatural, in Bob's opinion, as fish farms.

What if I didn't leave Bob? What if our slouch towards commitment ended at the altar? What would it be like if I occupied the wife-shaped space next to Bob? My life as a wife. In a Barratt's starter-home, with an avocado bathroom and a three-piece suite in leather. If we ever had a child (a curious idea) I thought we should call it Inertia. Although our occasional dull missionary encounters didn't seem passionate enough to produce anything as real and lasting as a child, even one called Inertia, and Bob (more likely to consult Mr Spock than Dr Spock) wasn't fit to be in charge of a push-and-pull lawnmower let alone a baby in a pram.

I did so hope that Bob was a dress rehearsal, a kind of mock-relationship, like a mock-exam, to prepare me for the real thing, because if I tried to imagine Bob in a grown-up life I could only visualize him slumped on the leather sofa, watching *Jackanory* with a huge joint in his hand.

'Somebody just phoned for you,' he said, spilling grains of cold yellow rice onto the carpet.

'Who?'

'Dunno. Some woman.'

'My mother?'

'Don't think so.'

Of course not, what was I thinking, Nora didn't have a phone. Nora didn't even have electricity.

'She sounded . . . weird,' Bob said.

'Weird? You mean weird accent?'

'Quite correct, Captain.'

No-one ever phoned me. The only reason we had a phone was because it was paid for by Bob's father and mother – Bob Senior and Sylvia – so that Sylvia could remind Bob to have a wash occasionally and not eat Angel Delight at breakfast.

Although you would never think it to look at him, Bob had a more than adequate family back in Essex, a fact that he usually denied because they were such models of suburban decorum. I found Bob's family – Bob Senior, his mother Sylvia and his sister Cherry and a buxom black Labrador called Sadie – strangely charismatic; they lived the kind of banal, tediously quotidian lives that I'd always longed for – eating roast chicken, changing sheets, going for boring Sunday outings in the family car, treading on fitted wool carpets, taking holidays in Spain, entertaining from a full drinks cabinet. For me, they were the most attractive thing about Bob.

We spent nearly every vacation with them in the pleasantly anodyne atmosphere of their house in Ilford, so much more normal than Nora's wrack and insular home. Bob, on these visits, was his usual self, sleeping most of the day and then hanging around all evening, waiting for his parents to go to bed so that he could skin up a joint and watch *Come Dancing*.

Bob slept in his boyhood room, which, despite Sylvia's best cleaning efforts, had never been purged of the smell of the teenage Bob – a heady perfume of sweaty socks and unwashed foreskins, of night emissions and illicit lager. It was decorated with football-themed wallpaper and still contained his old Dinky cars and the grotesquely misshapen soft toys that Sylvia had lovingly knitted for him.

I was always sequestered in the guest room, to prevent any 'shenanigans' – as Bob Senior put it – taking place. ('As if,' Bob Junior said.) The guest room provided an antiseptic yet pleasant environment, with its decor of overblown wallpaper roses, the rag rug on the floor, the clean magnolia paintwork and the flimsy flowered curtain that let in the orange glow of sodium street lights. I spent long hours in there, reading my way through the miscellany of guest-room reading matter (old *National Geographics*, dog-eared Agatha Christies, *Reader's Digests*) and listening to the sounds of a well-ordered house. I couldn't help thinking how much better off I would have been as a child with Sylvia as my mother – in fact, I would have been a different person altogether. Instead, I had been subjected in my formative years to Nora's sloppy habits and laissez-faire philosophies ('Well, don't go to school if you don't want to.')

~ I was teaching you free will, Nora says grumpily.

It was surprising I got an education at all, scraping through seaside secondary schools – Whitley Bay being the last town in our coastal odyssey. Only after Nora had waved me off on the train from Newcastle did she leave her job in a dingy hotel and set off back to the land of her birth and to the Stuart-Murrays' holiday home.

'And what did this mysterious woman say?' I asked Bob.

He shrugged. 'Nothing.'

'Well, she must have said something. You can't say nothing.'

'She said,' Bob said, with theatrical patience, '"is there someone called Euphemia there?"'

'And you said?'

'No, of course.'

Bob was amazed when I explained to him that 'Effie' was short for Euphemia ('You know, Bob – Robert?') and seemed rather put out that I hadn't taken the time to clarify this before. Of course, this was the person who for

132

the first few weeks of our relationship thought I was called 'F.E.' like some kind of college or an abbreviated swear word.

No-one ever called me Euphemia, no-one ever had. Who could know me by that name? Who other than someone calling from the obliterated past? Nora's memory was like history itself – partial, fallible, inclined to oblivion – but surely there were other people somewhere who remembered – a best friend, a cousin, a school-teacher.

The doorbell rang. It was Shug, who mooched into the flat and settled down on the sofa, burying himself in a *Spiderman* comic.

'Can't stay long,' he said, 'things to do, people to see.'

'Yeah, well I have to go to the bog,' Bob said as if this was a meaningful rejoinder.

Shug, unlike Bob, always had things to do and people to see. He spent his life disappearing off on mysterious trips and errands – off to Whitfield to see 'the man', out to the country to 'get his head straight' (which usually resulted in the exact opposite happening) or down south to some festival or other. Or at least that's what he *said* – I had once spotted Shug in town, dressed (bizarrely) in a Territorial Army uniform, and on another occasion I had seen him pushing a toddler on the swings in Magdalen Yard Green. Perhaps he was leading a double life – per-haps I should warn Andrea before she found herself committing bigamy. On the other hand, it would give her something to write about.

'I've got an essay to do,' I said and took myself off to

the bedroom because it was obvious I wasn't going to get any peace if I stayed with Bob and Shug.

The bedroom was an icebox and I had to wear gloves, which made typing rather laborious. I worked on an ancient little Underwood that had a misaligned 't' which made everything I wrote seem perpetually jaunty and surprised, which was rarely the way it was. I had a deadline, so to speak. Martha wanted the first draft of *The Hand of Fate* by the coming Friday, 'or else'. I typed one-fingered and with difficulty.

Madame Astarti walked along the prom to her booth. The sea this morning was an expanse of blue, you couldn't see the join between sea and sky. It was like standing on the edge of infinity.

'Morning, Rita,' Frank the fishman said as Madame Astarti unlocked her booth. Frank's stall was a work of art - kippers in herringbone patterns and wheels of dead-eyed haddock. This morning's centrepiece was a big silver salmon, a lemon stuck in its mouth and a wreath of parsley about its neck. 'Rita' was what most people called Madame Astarti, a fact she always found intriguing because it wasn't actually her name.

Madame Astarti's stall was in a prime position, between the fish stall and the bomb. The bomb was a Second World War torpedo set in concrete and bore a plaque remembering the men of Saltsea who died in the war. It was de-

activated, of course, but just occasionally as
Madame Astarti sat in her booth a few feet away
from its hulking metal she did wonder - how did
you know for sure if it was dead? If it had gone
dead.

'Hear about the body?' Frank asked cheerfully.

The sound of the music coming from the other room was
loud and indistinct. It sounded like Deep Purple but it
could have been anything with a drummer really. I could
hear Bob and Shug descending slowly into reefer madness; they were talking about their fantasy future in which
they co-owned a vastly successful head shop and spent all
day discussing the finer points of the Fabulous Furry
Freak Brothers. They were reciting some kind of dope
mantra to each other – 'Red Leb, blue dots, Paki black,
Moroccan zero zero, THC.' I put on a pair of ear-muffs
made, sadly, from rabbit fur.

'A penny for them, Madame Astarti,' a silky
voice said in her ear and Madame Astarti gave a
little scream and jumped.

'You frightened the life out of me,' she said,
patting her fluttering heart (or where Madame
Astarti thought of her fluttering heart - which
was actually her left lung). Lou Rigatoni
laughed and doffed his hat, which Madame Astarti
thought was a fedora but wasn't sure.

Lou Rigatoni was the nearest thing Saltsea had to the Mafia, which wasn't very near, it was true, but near enough for most people. The Rigatonis had begun the ice-cream empire ('The Best Scoop in the North!') which now dominated the north-east stretch of coastline (or 'The Yorkshire Riviera' as Vic Leggat, the leader of the local council, would have it known) and had now expanded to include amusement arcades and fish and chip shops and anything that could turn a profit.

'Heard the news?' Lou Rigatoni asked. 'They've found a body in the sea, some woman.' He was lingering in a way that was making Madame Astarti nervous.

'Yes, well, must be getting on,' she said, fiddling with the padlock on her booth; 'things to do, people to see - you know how it is.'

'Yes indeed,' Lou Rigatoni laughed, 'I myself have to see a man about a dog.' And with that he doffed his hat again and was gone.

'Poor dog,' thought Madame Astarti.

I must have fallen asleep, for the next thing I knew I was woken by the ringing of the telephone. I seemed to be alone in the flat. I picked my way through the remains of the cat biryani strewed across the floor. When I picked up the receiver I found only silence on the line - a condensed absence of noise that seemed to contain unspoken words and unasked questions. Then I heard the click of the receiver being replaced at the other end and the line went dead.

I discovered a note written in Bob's primary-school hand informing me that he and Shug had gone to see John Martyn in New Dines. The phone rang again and I snatched at the receiver this time. Philippa McCue's compelling tones echoed in my ear reminding me that I was supposed to be babysitting.

'You hadn't forgotten, had you?' she said.

'No,' I sighed, 'I hadn't forgotten.' Although I had, of course.

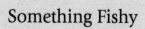

Something Fishy

THE SEA AROUND THE POINT IS A CURDLED YELLOW BREW, AND THE sun is an anaemic and watery thing that has struggled all day to crawl up its daily arc in a white squall of a sky.

I have borrowed dead Douglas's binoculars and am keeping watch on the cliffs, although there is nothing to see except for the seals treading water in the Sound, their black heads bobbing on the water like rubber balls. Occasionally, far away on the cloudy blur of water and sky that passes for the horizon around here, the shape of a ship glides by, like a theatrical illusion – a cardboard silhouette being moved across a painted sea. Perhaps we are on an *insula ex machina*, an artificial place not in the real world at all – a backdrop for the stories we must tell.

I feel as if I am waiting for something but I have no idea what that might be. I think I have been waiting all my life, waiting for someone to find me – a grandfather to claim me as his kin or the ghost of my father to appear and tell me his story. On the Oban birth certificate (a forgery, Nora confesses blithely) he is 'unknown', an anonymous person who seemed to have some-how slipped from Nora's memory, a man who made so little impression on her that she couldn't always be sure of his name and when I asked about him as a child she would say he was

141

called Jimmy, sometimes Jack, occasionally even 'Ernie'. Any Tom, Dick or Harry would do apparently.

~ He could have been anyone, she says stoutly.

'He must have been someone.'

The dead sometimes forget the living but the living rarely forget the dead. Not, however, in the case of my father. Half of what made me is completely missing – the forensics of my father a mystery. In their absence I am free to imagine him, but, unfortunately, even in my imagination he is leaving – on the deck of a ship, at the wheel of a car or leaning out of the window of a train carriage, his face obscured by clouds of steam from the engine.

From the occasional careless remark on Nora's part during my childhood, I deduced that our moneyless, itinerant existence in the Sea Views and Sailor's Rests of the English seaside was not the life that Nora had been born to. I wondered if perhaps Nora had got with child through a secret passion – impregnated by some black-hearted scoundrel, a passing vagabond perhaps, a groom in the stables or a gypsy in a wood – and that her angry father had thrown her out of the family home to find her own way in the world. I imagined her locked out in the cold and the driven snow, giving birth to me – her bastard daughter – in some freezing hovel.

'Was it like that?' I ask her, as I have asked her many times before.

Nora looks at me thoughtfully.

~ Not exactly, she says.

I dreamt that one day Nora's father – chastened and forgiving – would find me and claim me as granddaughter and heir, and I would be restored to my rightful place in a world where people

142

stay in one place and sleep in their own beds at night and avoid unnecessary journeys. Of course, life is composed almost entirely of journeys, necessary and unnecessary, but mostly unnecessary in my opinion.

I am waiting for Nora to give myself to me, to tell me about the time before my memory began, before I myself began.

'Perhaps you could start with Douglas,' I prompt her.

~ Who?

'Your brother.'

But she's already gone, striding across the cliff-top towards the house.

My babysitting services were required because Philippa and Archie were going to a dinner party at the home of the Dean. When I arrived at their house in Windsor Place I found Archie standing at the kitchen sink, stoking up beforehand in case there might not be enough food and drink on offer at the Dean's table – desperately quaffing the dregs of an old bottle of Bordeaux – a leftover from a French holiday *en famille* – between mouthfuls of a cold shepherd's pie that he'd foraged from the depths of the fridge.

'Politics,' he said to me, 'that's the name of the game – Maggie Mackenzie hasn't been invited, you'll notice. Nor Dr Clever-Dick. And as for Grant Watson, or whatever his name is – what a no-hoper.'

'What about the Professor?'

'The who?'

Archie finished off the shepherd's pie and started truffling around in the fridge again, finally retrieving a plate

143

of leftover roast chicken and Brussels sprouts. I never ate anything from the McCues' fridge when I was babysitting, there were things lurking in there that I recognized from two years ago – rancid dairy products and strange life forms blooming and reproducing in old Mason jars. Philippa, a Girton old girl and a part-time lecturer in the Philosophy department, was the slapdash sort and kept a remarkably filthy house.

Philippa had also recently become infected with the writing sickness and had embarked on her own novel – a doctor/nurse romance (*The Wards of Love*) in which the heroine bore the unlikely name of 'Flick' and which Philippa was intending to send to Mills & Boon. The large farmhouse table in the kitchen seemed to be acting as Philippa's desk – it was littered with papers, unmarked essays and textbooks. Philippa's surprisingly neat philosopher's hand was much in evidence, particularly on a great sheaf of narrow-lined foolscap, the aguish aura of which suggested it must be her novel.

Words peeled off the page – *hair the colour of a field of ripe wheat . . . eyes like drops from the bottomless depths of an azure ocean* – and rained onto the Nairn cushion vinyl. The McCues' dog, Duke, pattered into the kitchen. Duke was a burly, barrel-shaped Rottweiler made up of muscle and solid fat and built like a wrestler, a dog that looked like it was permanently on the verge of dying of boredom. He shook his weighty head as if he was being plagued by ear-mites and dislodged a scatter of small romantic words like a broken rope of pearls.

Duke sniffed around the floor looking for something

to eat other than words; the kitchen floor usually rendered up any number of food deposits. Today there was a raw egg that someone had dropped and not bothered to clean up. Duke licked up the egg with one sweep of his tongue, skilfully avoiding the broken shell, and then sat down heavily as if his legs had given way and drooled at the chicken drumstick that Archie was gnawing on like a caveman.

Adding to the general air of disarray in the McCue household were a number of animals. In descending order of size after Duke these were: a hefty cat called Goneril; a Dutch rabbit (Dorothea); a guinea-pig (Bramwell); and, finally, a hamster called McFluffy who was replaced by a new McFluffy every few months whenever the old McFluffy was either eaten by Goneril, trodden on by Philippa or sat on by Duke (or vice versa). A considerable number of McFluffies had simply packed their pouches and escaped from prison, disappearing into the innards of the house, so that behind the wainscoting and under the floorboards there now lived a tribe of feral hamsters conducting guerrilla warfare against the McCue household.

The current McFluffy was sleeping in a nest of shredded *Evening Telegraph*s, in a cage in the corner of the kitchen. The cage was precariously balanced on top of a Christmas-sized tin of Quality Street, containing five years of unfiled household receipts, and a copy of Kierkegaard's *Fear and Trembling*.

Goneril slunk into the kitchen and wound her body like a fat skein of wool around my feet. A piebald queen whose

145

white patches had grown a urine-yellow, like the pelt of an old polar bear, Goneril was an unattractive cat with dead fish breath and slovenly habits that she'd probably caught off Philippa. She was a cat who liked no-one, especially not Crispin, not after an unfortunate accident involving a tab of acid and a tin of Kit-E-Kat during his last long vacation.

Archie put his plate in the sink, already overloaded with dirty plates, burnt baking trays and Pyrex dishes that had acquired an unsavoury patina from years of McCue cooking. On the dull stainless-steel draining-board a huge raw salmon was laid out as if waiting for a post mortem.

'We're having a party,' Archie said, indicating the salmon, rather morosely. It didn't look like a party-going sort of fish; its silver-lamé scales may have gleamed under the kitchen lights but its dead eye was lustreless and fixed and it had leaked blood onto the draining board. The cat made a great pretence of not seeing the fish.

'Yes,' Philippa shouted suddenly from the hallway, 'Effie should come to the party.' She appeared in person in the kitchen doorway a few seconds later, carrying a giant-sized tin of dog food. She smelt vaguely of lard. At the sight of the dog food, Duke changed his dribbling allegiance from one spouse to the other, worshipping at Philippa's big feet like a slavering Sphinx.

'A few students at the party would be a good idea,' Philippa said to Archie.

'Why?' he asked doubtfully.

'Because,' Philippa said impatiently, 'being popular with students looks good.'

146

'Does it?' Archie said, looking even more doubtful.

'Bring a friend,' Philippa said imperiously to me. She would have made a good wife for Macbeth; she certainly wouldn't have fretted about a few blood spots.

Philippa's physique was remarkably similar to Duke's, although, unlike Duke, Philippa was wearing a kaftan. She hadn't got round to buttoning up the front properly and her jaded, wrinkled bra was visible as well as quite a lot of jaded, wrinkled breast. The hem of the kaftan ended mid-calf, thus revealing Philippa's unshaven legs, bare despite the inclement weather, growing stoutly out of a pair of red leather clogs that looked as if they were on the run from something Grimm. Philippa had dramatic badger hair – black with a swathe of white through it – which tonight she was wearing in a long squaw braid.

She was quite an embarrassing sort of person really, constantly referring to menstruation and sponge tampons and vaginal examinations so that she made women's health sound like car maintenance. A stalwart of the university women's liberation group, she was always urging us to examine our genitals in hand mirrors and stop shaving our body hair.

'Right,' Philippa said, making her way to the front door with Archie, myself and assorted animals tailing after her, 'there's food in the fridge if you get hungry, Effie, no sweets for Maisie, make her do homework, remember no television – except *Tomorrow's World* because that's educational, sort of, but she has to go to bed straight afterwards – the Dean's phone number's on the table if you have an emergency.' Finally rattling to a stop,

Philippa shrugged herself into an enormous Mexican-style poncho. She was still clutching the tin of dog food and I wondered if she was taking it with her to the party instead of a bottle of wine. Or just trying to drive Duke to the brink of insanity – a state of mind you had to judge, not from his expression of terminal canine ennui, but from the amount of dog slobber he was producing.

Archie, meanwhile, was admiring himself in the hall mirror, smoothing his hair and adjusting his tasteless kipper tie. Despite having a physical resemblance to a large sea-mammal, Archie was under the impression that he was attractive to women, which, for reasons beyond my comprehension, he was. ('Maybe you're not a woman?' Andrea suggested.)

'Of course,' Archie said to me, via the medium of the mirror, 'I don't believe in bourgeois crap like dinner parties, it's just a means to an end. Right,' he said, finally satisfied with his appearance, 'I'll be off. Don't take any nonsense from you know who.'

'Who?'

'You know,' Philippa said. 'The old mare.' (Or at least, that was what it sounded like.) She was halfway down the path by now and she turned and shouted, 'Catch!' and bowled the tin of dog food underarm to me. Philippa had once been captain of Cheltenham Ladies' College cricket team. And somehow she still was.

I found Maisie in the living-room watching a Monty Python re-run. I retrieved a bar of Cadbury's Fruit and

Nut from my bag and broke it into two and shared it with her. It covered several of the major food groups and hadn't been contaminated by the McCues' kitchen.

'Thanks,' she said, cramming most of the chocolate into her mouth at once. Nine-year-old Maisie was the most normal of the McCues (in some ways anyway). She was a plain girl, with straight hair and thin limbs and a mathematical turn of mind. Photographs of a newlaid Maisie in the overheated maternity ward of the DRI, showed her lying in a plastic cot like lidless Tupperware, looking like a small, skinned mammal, apart from a little thatch of mouse hair on her head. Even at six hours old, she seemed unaccountably old.

Maisie's full name was Maisie Ophelia. I can't help but think that it's an unfortunate custom to name children after people who come to sticky ends. Even if they are fictional characters, it doesn't bode well for the poor things. There are too many Judes and Tesses and Clarissas and Cordelias around. If we must name our children after literary figures then we should search out happy ones, although it's true they are much harder to find. ('Ratty' and 'Mole' are Maisie's suggestions.)

'Do you have homework?' I asked her.

'Not really,' she said, without taking her eyes off the television.

'I do,' I said gloomily, taking George Eliot out of my bag. I commenced to write very slowly – *James's judgement that* Middlemarch *is an 'indifferent whole' is refuted by even a superficial reading of the novel, when we cannot help but be struck by the highly wrought nature of the writing, the function*

149

of character, the careful thematic structuring and the balancing and illusion of autogenesis, something for which the paralleling of action and moral consequence – but then I must have fallen asleep again because the next thing I knew I was being rudely awoken by a scream and it was a little while before I understood that the scream had come from the television set, rather than one of the various inhabitants of the house.

Maisie was deeply engrossed in a black-and-white horror film of some kind. The woman who was screaming – tall and blond with her hair in a perfect French pleat and apparently called Irma – seemed to have realized (rather late in the day) that she had stopped for the night at a bed and breakfast run by a vampire, even though you would have thought, as B and B names go, 'Castle Vlad' wasn't exactly 'Sea View' or 'The Pines'.

'She's really thick,' Maisie said admiringly.

I tried to shift position; I was incredibly uncomfortable – Duke was slumped heavily on my feet while curled up in my lap, like a large evil netsuke, was Goneril. Not only that, but Maisie's bony body was sticking into me on one side, while on my other side, an old woman I had never seen before was fast asleep, her head lolling uncomfortably on my shoulder.

The old woman had skin that was the texture and colour of white marshmallows and in a poor light (which was always) you might have mistaken her hair for a cloud of slightly rotten candyfloss. Although fast asleep, she was still clutching a pair of knitting needles on which hung a strange shapeless thing, like a web woven by a

150

spider on drugs. She looked so peaceful it seemed a shame to wake her up.

'Maisie?' I said quietly.

'Mm?'

'There's an old woman on the sofa with us.'

Maisie tore her eyes away from the television to lean over and look and said, 'It's just Granny.'

'Granny?'

'My dad's mum.' (How strangely complicated that sounded.)

Surely she was supposed to be in The Anchorage in Newport-on-Tay, looking at the water?

'She escaped,' Maisie said.

Now that I looked at her I could see that Mrs McCue looked vaguely familiar. Despite Andrea's belief that 'all old people look alike' I thought I recognized her from the shoal of mourners at 'Senga's' funeral that afternoon. Mrs McCue woke up and automatically began to knit. After a while she stopped and sighed and, looking at me with yellowing rheumy eyes, said wistfully, 'I'm dying for a cup of tea.' She seemed to be altogether from the jaundiced end of the spectrum – the whites of her eyes were the colour of Milky Bars and her horsy teeth resembled blank Scrabble tiles.

It seemed churlish not to comply with her heartfelt request and so I levered Duke off my feet – no easy task – shoogled Goneril off my knee as gently as I could to avoid being bitten, and finally struggled free of the bookending bodies of Maisie and the dowager Mrs McCue, who both immediately shifted to fill the space I'd vacated.

151

While the kettle was coming to the boil I went to the toilet—

~ In the same sentence? Nora objects, it's been nothing but ringing phones and boiling kettles, doorbells and toilets, since you began.

Ignore her, she is in a bad mood today. She is avoiding telling her story.

—a journey that took me past the open door of the spare bedroom that Archie used as a study. A strange noise wafted out of the room, a faint little *purp-purp* noise like a kitten snoring, and I peered in the room, curious to find the source.

It turned out to be a boy – more a man really – who was lying on the bed, as still as a corpse. He was a very fine specimen of his sex – just the right shape and size, with no strange features or disturbing blemishes, only a rather fetching scar on his left cheekbone as if he had been raked delicately by a tiger's talon. If it hadn't been for the snoring you would have thought him dead.

I wondered who he was (how helpful it would be if people were labelled). His hair was dark, his skin pale, his lashes long, and you might have thought that his lips – carved into a curving pout by Cupid himself and slightly damp from sleep – were waiting to be kissed. But I didn't do that, because that would have been like asking for trouble instead of simply waiting for it to arrive in its own good time.

He was lying on top of the covers and although his feet were naked, the rest of him was fully clothed in a pair of Levi's, an old sweater and a battered leather biker's jacket that indicated a darker and more interesting personality than Bob's army greatcoat or Shug's Afghan ever could. I sniffed the lanolin of his rough wool sweater and the slaughtered smell of his jacket. I inspected his ears (clean, shell-like), his fingernails (dirty, bitten), the faint tide-mark of grime on his neck, the ingrained oil on his mechanic's hands, inhaled the faint aroma of marijuana on his breath.

He smelt like a Platonic ideal of a man would smell. Compared to the slugs and snails and puppy dogs' tails that composed Bob's biodynamic, he seemed to be made up of entirely testosterone-based ingredients – leather car seats, cut-throat razors, ropes and knots and binding cords, salt, mud and blood. He was all . . . other.

I wondered what colour his eyes were beneath those gorgeous sleepy lids. Of course, for all I knew he was squint and cross-eyed, or worse – a blue-eyed man. I thought about prising open one of his semi-comatose eyelids but decided against it. Was it possible to tell his character from his appearance? He looked sublime but he might have been any one of a hundred undesirable things. A university lecturer, for example. Perhaps he was a thief who had come in through the window and had grown tired in the middle of his thieving and lain down for a rest. More unlikely things happen every day, after all.

The window was wide open and the temperature in the room must have been near freezing. The unknown man's feet were turning blue and felt icy to the touch, more like cold corpse flesh than the appendages of a warm and breathing man. Hastily, I pulled a blanket over his motionless form. He was sleeping on his back with his arms and legs flung out like a dead starfish – although with fewer legs. (Or arms, or whatever it is that starfish have.) He didn't look as if he was on a harmless date with the Sandman, but more as if he was stranded in the Land of Nod for ever with no map and compass of return and I wondered if I shouldn't keep watch over him for a while, but, sadly, there is only so much pleasure to be got from observing a sleeping man – even a handsome one – and I was soon distracted by the sight of a very fat manuscript poking out from under the bed.

The edges of many of the pages appeared to have been nibbled by small animals – clan McFluffy, I presumed – and the title page announced it to be Archie's great novel, *The Expanding Prism of J.*

'Well,' I said to the sleeping man, 'I don't see what harm there can be in just taking a *look*.' Words which, as we know, everyone lives to regret (Pandora, curious cats, Lot's wife, all of Bluebeard's wives, and so many, many others).

The Expanding Prism of J appeared to be a novel with neither plot nor character (and certainly no pictures). Even the simplest details were cloaked in a claggy syntax, and reading Archie's prose was like trying to make sense of glue. As far as I could gather, the eponymous J was a university lecturer employed in an institution more tortuous than a Borgesian labyrinth. J himself had no fixed or true character but was a man made up of layer upon layer of impenetrable metaphor and alienated asides.

Struggling through the dense language of the first few pages, it took me some time to realize that J was not riding through a Mitteleuropean city on a tram but was indulging in something quite perverse with his mistress's lapdog. I began to feel slightly nauseous and wondered if Archie's words might be having a toxic effect. Perhaps if I looked further under the bed I would find small dead animals.

Despite the number of words, nothing really seemed to happen, although after a while J's paranoia began to produce a kind of mirage of a plot, as if something was about to happen at every moment and yet never did. A typical paragraph (for there was little to choose between them) read like this –

J felt a tenuous uncertainty as to which of the several tenebrous passages his presumed tormentor had chosen to disappear into. He permitted his imagination a brief glance down into that darkness to find what it would, but recoiled from the sudden vista of – not despair and madness as he had expected, but rather the torpor and enervation to be found there. He was made fully aware now of the kind of horror that his mental games had led him to and speculated as to the –

And so on and so on. No wonder the sleeper on the bed was in such a sopor, breathing in Archie's somnifacient words all the time. A sudden gust of wind lifted the curtains and sent an icy blast into the room, ruffling the pages of Archie's novel and sending several of them flying through the air like autumn leaves. I jumped up and chased around the room after them and managed to retrieve all but one, which floated serenely out of the window like a birdless wing.

I tried to get the manuscript back into some semblance of order but the pages, for some annoying reason, were not numbered so that it was impossible to tell what sequence they should be in and the sense of the text gave me no clue whatsoever. At a loss, I skimmed the page in my hand and discovered J in the process of meeting a nasty death. He was at the top of a flight of stairs when a banister he was leaning against gave way and sent him plunging down into the dark depths of a stairwell –

Falling, falling, into the dark depths of the unknown and unknowable chasm, the abyss of his own imagination rushing to greet him, to enfold, to smother him, the darkness circumscribing him, obfuscating his senses and finally stilling even the faintest glimmerings of cognizance and speculation –

Which I think meant he was dead. There was no knowing where this particular page belonged as Archie was obviously the kind of writer who thought nothing of killing off his main protagonist within the first fifty pages. In the end I just put all the pages back together at random and stuck them as far under the bed as they would go.

Another gust of wind sent a sudden chill shudder through the sleeping body on the bed. I pulled the blanket up further and closed the window—

~ How much more sensible if you'd done that to begin with.

I don't think Nora should talk about sensible, not when she herself is standing on a rock that is being lapped by an incoming tide as if she is trying to command the sea.

—I could just see the bridge from the window – a train was crossing, one bright headlamp marking its passage from the black unlit banks of Fife across the even blacker water, like a messenger from somewhere else. I drew the curtains.

The water in the kettle had almost boiled away by the time I got back to the kitchen and I had to start the tea-making process all over again—

Nora makes a great display of boredom.

—closely observed by the current McFluffy, which was standing up on its hindlegs, holding the bars of its cage in its tiny pink hands. Its cheeks were bulging with food and it looked unusually alert, as if it was about to embark on the great escape. I noticed that the salmon, previously whole and unsullied by anything except death, now had a large bite taken out of its side. It really should be in the fridge, especially as it had another day to go before its party appearance. I could almost see the microbes con-gregating festively around its silvery corpse. When I turned away from the salmon I found another old woman sitting at the table. Were they breeding?

When this one saw me, she gave a little scream and clutched her breast. 'Wha' a fleg you gave me,' she said. She was as small as a dormouse and almost entirely spherical, you could probably have rolled her from one side of the kitchen to the other. She heaved herself up from the chair, with the help of a walking-aid, and intro-duced herself as 'Mrs Macbeth'. I gathered she was Mrs McCue's friend and a fellow escapee from The Anchorage.

157

Mrs Macbeth was being followed around by an old fat Westie which seemed almost as lame as its owner. Its fur was a Chinese yellow and it seemed to have gone rusty around the mouth. Its teeth were as yellow as Mrs McCue's and in some strange way it reminded me a little of her. Its aged eyes – one brown, one slightly wall-eyed – looked at me in a resigned kind of way when I addressed it.

'She's cried Janet,' Mrs Macbeth said. 'We're no allowed pets at The Anchorage, but I couldna get rid of her, she's been my wee pal all these years.' She sighed and Janet seemed to sigh too, her lungs wheezing like a tiny pair of accordions.

'So you hide her?' I asked, trying to imagine the complexities of keeping a small dog hidden.

'Aye, it's a rare carry-on,' Mrs Macbeth agreed. 'The keech's the worst thing, of course.'

The pair of them followed me back into the living-room, Mrs Macbeth insisting on carrying a box of Tunnock's Teacakes, despite being hampered by the walking-frame. The old dog hobbled after her and when Duke caught sight of her he struggled up from the dead dog position he'd adopted on the floor and sniffed poor Janet's rear end with bizarre enthusiasm.

'Who is the man in the spare bedroom?' I asked Maisie.

'Ferdinand.'

'Ferdinand? Your *brother* Ferdinand? I thought he was in prison?'

'Early release for good behaviour,' Maisie said, not taking her eyes off the television, which was now showing some kind of curling championship.

'Irma escaped from Castle Vlad and went home,' Mrs McCue said helpfully to me. 'Ferdinand's a good boy really,' she added, nodding her old sweetie-selling head at me. Mrs Macbeth's old dog flopped down heavily on its side and fell asleep immediately, making a strange creaking noise when it breathed.

Mrs McCue inspected the inside of her teacup and frowned. At her feet she had a large sack-like bag, made from some kind of chintzy material. The bag looked as if it contained a dead animal – a middle-sized one, a hyena perhaps – but when she turned it out, proved to contain everything imaginable except a hyena. Eventually she found what she was looking for – a handkerchief, a little lacy thing with bluebells embroidered all over it, and cleaned the cup, rubbing it vigorously with the handkerchief.

'That woman keeps a clarty house, there's stour every-where,' she said to Mrs Macbeth, who gave a little shiver and said, rather enigmatically, 'The flair.'

'I'm an affie tea-jenny,' Mrs McCue said, pouring the tea in an unsteady stream from the heavy brown pot.

'Me as well,' Mrs Macbeth agreed.

'Why was Ferdinand in prison if he was such a good boy?' I persisted.

Mrs McCue shrugged. 'Who knows? That's a rare cup-pie,' she said to Mrs Macbeth. Mrs McCue was managing to drink her tea, knit and read the *Sunday Post* all at the same time.

'Mistaken identity,' Maisie said through a mouthful of teacake.

Mrs McCue reached into her chintz sack again, and produced a large bag of Iced Gems which turned out to be soft but we ate them anyway. Then she produced a packet of Player's No.6 and offered them round. 'I only smoke for the coupons,' she told me, shaking a cigarette out of the packet for Mrs Macbeth.

'Don't mind if I do,' Mrs Macbeth said and they both lit up. Maisie coughed theatrically and Mrs McCue delved into the bag again and came up with a packet of Tyrozets for Maisie.

'A'thing but the kitchen sink,' Mrs Macbeth said, nodding approvingly at the bag.

As soon as I sat down Goneril leapt back onto me, kneading my chest with her claws. She was an extraordinarily heavy cat – if the Tara-Zanthians got hold of her they'd probably keep her in a safe deposit box. As soon as we were all nicely settled the doorbell rang suddenly (how else?), a simple enough event but one which set in motion an alarming amount of chaos – Duke barked his way to the door, a clumsy process which involved treading on Janet, knocking over the milk jug and sending Goneril in a death-defying leap from my lap to that of Archie's mother who gave a little scream of horror and dropped an entire needleful of stitches from her erratically woven web. Thank goodness there was no baby to wake up – the usual conclusion to this kind of chain of events.

After all that commotion it was irritating to discover that there was no-one there when I opened the front door. The entire street was hushed and deserted, not even

The Boy With No Name, just howling winds and freezing rain.

As soon as I sat down the doorbell rang again. How boring this was.

'Let me go,' Mrs Macbeth insisted, heaving herself out of her chair with enormous difficulty and zimmering to the front door. She hirpled back – looking smaller than ever – with a waterlogged Kevin, his hayseed hair plastered to his head by the rain. Since lunchtime he'd developed a huge pimple in the middle of his forehead, like an angry caste-mark.

'What are *you* doing here?' he asked by way of greeting.

'Babysitting,' I said, which wasn't, technically speaking, quite true, as I seemed to be sitting everything except a baby. He followed me into the living-room and sat down, looking awkward in the presence of so many women at different stages of their lives. He stared at Mrs McCue's feet, securely encased in bootee slippers with sturdy zips. Mrs McCue glanced down at her feet to see if there was anything interesting about them.

'That's some plook you've got, son,' Mrs Macbeth complimented him.

'Thank you,' Kevin said, slightly confused. He blew his nose to cover his awkwardness – a large trumpeting noise that unsettled the already too-twitchy cat – and then sat his acreage of flesh down heavily in an armchair (which is just how small rodents are unwittingly killed). Maisie strained to watch the progress of a curling-stone across a television screen that was being partly blocked by the bulk of Kevin's body.

'I came to talk to Dr McCue,' Kevin said, inspecting the contents of his handkerchief.

'He's not here.'

'I can see that.'

Like everyone else of my acquaintance, Kevin was looking for an extension on the deadline for his dissertation (on *The Lord of the Rings*, naturally). 'I've been spending too much time in Edrakonia,' Kevin said, a look of wistfulness passing over his face at the very mention of the place. The spot in the middle of his forehead glowed. 'The dragons have been mustering their forces for a spot of counter-insurgency.'

'The dragons?' Mrs Macbeth echoed, glancing warily around the room.

'Don't worry,' I reassured her, 'only Kevin can see them.' Kevin was eating Iced Gems by the handful, in a mindless way that would have disturbed Andrea.

'Explain something to me,' I said to him, because, to my irritation, I took a strange interest in Edrakonia. 'I can't understand whether the dragons are good or bad.'

'Well,' Kevin said earnestly, 'historically, the dragons of Edrakonia do have their own system of ethics, but you have to remember, of course, that it's a school of moral philosophy of an essentially *dragonish* nature and the ordinary mortal – you, for example – wouldn't recognize it as containing the simple tenets of "good" and "bad" which, for dragons, are—'

'OK, Kevin, that's enough.'

For some reason Mrs McCue and Mrs Macbeth got quite excited when Kevin told them he was 'a writer' and started urging him to read something to them. Kevin always carried his writing around with him, bits of papers like talismans.

'Well,' he said doubtfully, 'I'm in the middle of a chapter, and it's the fourth book, so I don't know if you'll understand what's going on.'

'It disnae matter,' Mrs Macbeth said, 'the beginning, the middle, the end – it makes no difference.' She would do well in Archie's class.

'Just fill us in quickly,' Mrs McCue encouraged, 'you know – characters, a wee bittie plot and we'll soon get the hang of it.'

'Is there going to be a moral to it?' Mrs Macbeth asked.

'Well, everything's got a moral,' I said, 'if only you can find it.'

Kevin hesitated.

'Just begin at the beginning,' Mrs McCue coaxed.

'And carry on until you've finished,' Mrs Macbeth added.

After a short resumé (*And the Murk will fall on the land. And the Beast Griddlebart will roam the land and the dragons will flee*), Kevin settled down and began to narrate in a portentous tone, undermined somewhat by the clotted cream of his accent: 'Duke Thar-Vint of Malkaron mounted his steed Demaal and prepared himself mentally for the long journey. His trusty steward Iart rode beside him on one of the sure-footed shaggy brown ponies bred by the horse breeders of the Mountains of Galinth –'

'Are the mountains a good place to breed horses?' Mrs McCue asked thoughtfully.

'Well, it's a good place to breed sure-footed ones,' Kevin said irritably. 'Can I continue?'

'Aye, on you go, son.'

'Lart had helped his master, Thar-Vint, to strap himself into the bronze armour that had been handed down, father to son, father to son, by the Lords of Malkaron—'

'Is that grammatical?' Maisie asked, although she had given no indication of listening at all, having now become absorbed in a late-night Gaelic teaching programme, silently mouthing the inscrutable vocabulary.

'I don't know,' Kevin said impatiently. 'Thar-Vint's thoughts strayed to the great palace of Calysveron and the Lady Agaruitha to whom he was secretly betrothed, despite the objections of her mother the Lady Tamarin—'

'Lady Agga who?' Mrs Macbeth said.

'Agaruitha – A-g-a-r-u-i-t-h-a.'

I wondered how much time Kevin devoted to making up these ridiculous names. Quite a lot, I suspected. (Or, on the other hand, not much time at all.)

'My lord,' gasped a man who had ridden up hastily by his side. Thar-Vint recognized him as the Lord Vega, whose lands stretched from the River Voloron to the provinces of Celentan and Ggadril. The Lord Vega doffed his velvet cap with the single plume of feather and spurred his steed away to—'

'Doffed,' Mrs McCue said, 'that's a strange word, eh?'

'It sounds . . . historical,' Mrs Macbeth said, 'it's not a word you hear often these days.'

'That's because men dinnae wear hats the way they used to,' Mrs McCue said. 'There were times,' she said to

Maisie, 'when hats had names – the trilby, the fedora—'

'Homburg,' Mrs Macbeth offered, 'the porkpie.'

'The porkpie?' Kevin queried doubtfully.

'Yes indeed,' Mrs McCue affirmed, 'the Glengarry, the bowler, a nice Panama in the summer.'

'Doff,' Mrs Macbeth said dreamily, 'doff, doff, doff. The more you say it the dafter it sounds.'

'It would be a good name for a dog,' Mrs McCue said, looking at Janet noisily asleep at Mrs Macbeth's feet.

'Do you mind . . .' Kevin said. '*And spurred his steed away to . . .*' I nodded off. I think I preferred it when Kevin was writing about the dragons.

When I woke up he had gone.

'What a tube,' Maisie said and Mrs McCue agreed. 'Aye a gey queer laddie,' she said.

Prompted by some innocent small talk on my part ('So did you always live in Largs, Mrs McCue?'), Archie's errant mother raided her spangled memory and embarked on her life story, a commonplace enough tale, I suppose – a broken heart, a lost child, death, abandonment, loneliness, fear. This was the condensed version of her life story, naturally, otherwise we would have been there for seventy-odd years. We came up to date with her current mooring at The Anchorage.

Before long Mrs Macbeth was unpicking her own life for me – she had been a jute spinner in the Dens Road Works and the first time she tried to get married she was 'jilted at the altar'. Why is it that everyone has had an interesting and dramatic life except for me?

~ Don't be so sure, Nora says.

Mrs Macbeth's fiancé was already on an émigré boat to Canada when she was stepping into the church in full bridal finery on her father's arm. Mrs Macbeth shook her head sadly and said that she had never quite recovered from this betrayal. 'Although I take comfort,' she said, contemplating an Iced Gem, 'from the fact that he's deid the noo. And I married Mr Macbeth and we were very happy together.'

'Mr Macbeth'. How odd that sounded, as if the Thane of Cawdor had decided to give up on ambition and settled in the suburbs and worked towards his pension.

'It all seems like yesterday,' she concluded sadly.

'Aye, you dinnae age inside,' Mrs McCue said; 'inside you're aye young.'

'How young?' Maisie asked.

'Twenty-one,' Mrs McCue said.

'Twenty-five,' Mrs Macbeth said.

~ Well, personally, Nora says, I feel a hundred years old.

But you must excuse my mother, she has led a very strange life.

Once started, neither Mrs Macbeth nor Mrs McCue seemed inclined to stop – I suppose that by the time you're old you have acquired quite a lot of things to talk about (your whole life, in fact) and after a while I just let their lullaby voices wash over me without really listening. They were talking about people in The Anchorage – Miss Anderson ('a crabbit wee wifie'), Mrs Robertson ('a nice wee wifie') and Billy ('a poor soul'). Many of these people appeared to be in the grip of strange notions. Miss

166

Anderson, for example, had a terrible fear of premature burial, while Billy was convinced that his dead body was going to be stolen for (unspecified) nefarious purposes. Mrs Macbeth herself seemed disturbed by the idea that no-one was going to check that it really was her body in the coffin and not one belonging to someone else (although you would think that might be a good thing).

'Mistaken identity,' she said. How grisly these pre-occupations seemed for people with a view of the water. Something, Mrs McCue said, was killing the old people. Not just old age then? I asked.

'No,' Mrs McCue said airily, waving her knitting needles about in a dangerous fashion, 'I know for a fact that someone's trying to kill me.'

'Oh aye,' Mrs Macbeth said cheerfully, 'me too.' I thought of Professor Cousins who had said exactly the same thing to me only this morning (what an incredibly long day it was turning out to be).

'Just because you're paranoid,' I said to Mrs McCue, 'it doesn't mean they're not out to get you.' She gave me a worried look.

'So who do you think's trying to kill you?' Maisie asked, finally finding a topic of conversation more interesting than television. 'Dad?'

Mrs McCue laughed and said fondly, 'Archie disnae have the balls for murder.'

'Look at poor Senga,' Mrs Macbeth said, shaking her head.

'Face like a tatti-howker, but a harmless wee wifie,' Mrs McCue said.

'Do you really think she was *murdered*?' Maisie asked, a thrill of excitement in her voice, but at that crucial dramatic moment we were interrupted (naturally) and the noise of the front door being unlocked set in train the usual commotion of barking dogs, hissing cats and dropped stitches. Mrs McCue cocked her head like a dog, behaviour that was mirrored by Janet, and said, 'That'll be them,' so that for a moment I thought perhaps she meant her imaginary assassins until reality took a grip and I realized it was Archie and Philippa, home from the Dean's.

Duke lumbered to the door to greet them, while Maisie fled and threw herself under her bedcovers, feigning a child who had been asleep for hours, watched no television, eaten no sweets and done all her homework. The rest of us conducted a charade of sober purposefulness – I took out a pen and furrowed my brow while Mrs McCue managed to add a stitch or two to her mysterious weaving and Mrs Macbeth produced a yellow duster from about her person and rubbed hard at a lamp on the small table next to her chair.

Philippa went straight upstairs while Archie, glassy-eyed with drink, fought to get himself through the door-frame of the living-room.

'Good to see you're finally getting down to some work at last,' he said to me. He frowned at his mother. 'Still here?' he said. 'You've missed the last bus, you know.'

'Aw, son,' Mrs McCue said affectionately.

Philippa clacked downstairs in her clogs. 'Sleeping like a baby,' she announced.

'Who is?' Archie asked, looking vaguely alarmed as if Philippa might have given birth to yet another McCue while she was upstairs.

'Ferdinand,' Philippa said, in the tone of voice she reserved for people incapable of doing compound-propositional logic. 'How was the old Ma?' she asked me, as though Mrs McCue wasn't in the room. 'And her friend,' she added, giving Mrs Macbeth a doubtful look. Mrs Macbeth spat on the duster and rubbed hard at the lamp as if she was conjuring up a genie.

'Must be going,' I said hastily. Much as I would have liked to learn more about the handsome jailbird sleeping upstairs I felt I'd had enough for one day somehow.

'Come and see us,' Mrs McCue said. Mrs Macbeth nodded vigorously in agreement with this invitation. 'In our jile,' Mrs McCue added with relish.

'The Anchorage is a very nice place,' Philippa said to me. 'It came highly recommended by Grant . . . or Watson . . . or whatever – the old Ma's friend over there is his mother-in-law.'

'Dozy wee bugger that he is,' Mrs Macbeth agreed cheerfully.

Mrs McCue and Mrs Macbeth seemed far too sprightly to be in an old people's home but as if she read my thoughts (a terrifying idea) Philippa said, 'They're not as capable as they look, you know. They're always having accidents. The old Ma's forever falling and breaking bits. We thought we'd get her in before she started to deteriorate.'

'Thanks,' Mrs McCue said.

Mrs Macbeth and Mrs McCue waved to me from the doorway of the living-room. After a struggle, Mrs Macbeth had hoisted Janet up in her arm and was now waving her paw for her like a puppeteer. Archie accompanied me down the hallway, taking up most of the space, so that I had to squeeze past him to get to the front door. He usually chose the hallway as the locale for the obligatory pass he made at all female students who strayed within the walls of his domain. Tonight it was a half-hearted affair that I managed to side-step quite easily due to the night-long transfusion of red wine into Archie's veins.

It was a relief to get into the outside air although an evil kind of sleet was now falling (which is a cold, hard rain by another name). The Perth Road was completely deserted but it was only a short distance home and I was comforting myself with the fact that at least there was electricity when all the street lamps went out. Then, all of a sudden, I began to feel apprehensive. I was all gooseflesh and was overcome by a strange sense of dread, as if something malevolent was about to befall me in the shape of apparitions or ghosts, mad people and axe-murderers. I quickened my pace.

A woman was walking towards me, carrying a long furled umbrella and wearing a red winter coat that had been leeched of most of its colour by the darkness. There was something about the woman that was both familiar and foreign, as if she reminded me of someone. There was something odd about her too – a slight stumble in her walk, a lopsided look to her face. As she drew near, she called out and asked me the time. She was close enough for me to smell the gin on her breath, almost doused by the strident perfume she was wearing.

My sense of foreboding had grown so strong that I hurried past her without looking in her face, mumbling that I didn't have a watch. I glanced anxiously behind me but the woman had disappeared. A sudden wink of light behind me made me think of The Boy With No Name until I realized it was a car, headlights extinguished, cruising very slowly along at a distance behind me. I quickened my pace and by the time I reached the top of Paton's Lane I was running. The car didn't turn to follow me and I paused for a moment in the doorway and watched it glide past the top of the street. It gave the distinct impression, I noticed, of being Cortina-shaped.

Heart thudding uncomfortably in my chest, I ran up the unlit stone stairs of the tenement. The darkness at each corner of the stair seemed to have a thicker quality, as if the shadow of a ghost was skulking there. There was a smell of fried food and something sweet and cloying. This was probably what it was like to be trapped in *The Expanding Prism of J*. Or a horror film. It was with an overwhelming sense of relief that I turned my key in the lock and achieved the safety of the inside.

Frozen to the bone, we are in the great cold kitchen where the lichen grows between the stone flags beneath our feet. The old oak barometer in the hall is indicating a curlicued 'Storm' and Nora, as salty as an old sea-dog, taps it and says, 'The glass is falling,' and I feel a melancholy tug inside me as if my body had its own tides and currents and can feel the pull of the moon. Which it can, I know.

Nora is boiling a copper kettle on the range, a complicated process that involves us first having to collect driftwood on the strand. Why does she live like this? I swear it's colder inside than out. We would be better off building an igloo. To help us with this idea it has begun to snow. Nora says, it never snows here, as if the snow had made a mistake.

I lay out the old chipped Spode cups and saucers. We drink our tea black for we have no milk cow, nor a good red hen, not even a single honey-bee.

We sit and drink our tea at a kitchen table where resentful servants must once have sat. Living here is like living in a folk-museum, actors in *A working kitchen, circa 1890*, except there is no-one to observe us. Or so we hope.

~ Is any of this going anywhere? Nora asks, staring into her teacup like a fortune teller.

'Well, it's leading here, eventually. As you know.'

~ It's a rather roundabout route.

'There aren't any maps. You see if you can do better then, tell me about Douglas.'

~ Who?

'Your brother.'

Nora closes her eyes, takes a breath, begins –

You have to remember this was long before I was born, so I have to imagine it. It started out well. Donald Stuart-Murray had a house in Eaton Square, one in Edinburgh's New Town and

172

endless ancestral pastures north of the border centred on his own glen – Glenkittrie – and a bloodline intimately entwined with the kings and queens of Scotland, and therefore England. He married the third daughter of an English earl, a plain, rather nervous girl, whose family were relieved to have her off their hands. The bride wore some exquisite family diamonds – a dowry-gift to mitigate her shortage of aristocratic qualities – and when she walked down the aisle the wedding-guests gasped in admiration so that the young bride, who was called Evangeline, blushed with joy, thinking they were silently applauding her efforts at beauty.

Evangeline soon fell pregnant and bravely gave birth every two years from then on until the end of the first decade of her marriage to Donald. Altogether they had five children, three boys (Douglas, Torquil and Murdo) followed by two girls. The first of these, Honoria, was dropped on her head from an upstairs window in the house in Eaton Square by a nursemaid who was later certified insane. Honoria was not exactly dead but neither was she exactly alive and after several months of dedicated nursing by her mother, Honoria finally gave up the struggle and died.

The second girl, Elspeth, followed her shortly afterwards, succumbing to an epidemic of diphtheria when she was one year old.

'As if,' Evangeline said, 'little Honoria just couldn't bear to play alone up there.' This was a little sentimental for Donald's taste. Donald was not, in truth, a very nice man. Bluff and blunt, he disassociated himself from emotion, believing it to be the territory of women, children and weak-brained idiots.

Evangeline, never particularly stable, became morbid. She was convinced that her remaining children were going to be plucked from her arms, one by one (she was right, of course), and eventually Donald gave in to her insistent wish that the remnant of her family be brought up back in Scotland away from metropolitan dangers.

The house – 'Woodhaven' at Kirkton of Craigie in the glen – was not the most hospitable of homes. Built from local stone and decorated with Alpine gables, it was little more than a glorified Victorian hunting lodge, erected by Donald's father, Roderick. It was a cold place and a succession of housekeepers and servants had failed to warm it up. Donald, however, was quite content with this move as he could spend all his time now shooting and fishing and generally destroying everything that ran or flew on his rainy estate.

Evangeline concentrated on keeping her sons alive, feeding them on oatmeal and potatoes and boiled chickens and keeping them well away from disease, immorality and nursemaids. She had to be particularly vigilant when it came to the large amounts of water threatening them at every turn. The river Kittrie flowed not a hundred yards from the house and had been partially diverted on the instruction of Roderick to feed a small, artificial loch he had created. This had been stocked with a great many young trout and, accidentally, a rogue baby pike which fed at leisure on its companions and grew to be legendary. Roderick devoted the rest of his life to trying to catch it.

The boys were all taught to swim in case of accident as well as being made to undertake regular walks and suffering annual bracing holidays at the island holiday home—

'You mean here?'

~ Yes, don't interrupt – and were forced to sleep for ten hours every night with their bedroom windows wide open, even in winter, so that they were sometimes woken by snow falling on their faces. By the time they were in their teens they were all in aston-ishingly good health with strong teeth, straight bones, good manners and clean habits and were, as everyone remarked, a great credit to their mother and their country.

When they went off to school, to Glenalmond, Evangeline wrote each of them a letter every week begging them to eat well, refrain from unhealthy thoughts and be vigilant around water, sharp objects and occupants of the sick bay.

When war was declared and the Hun were begging for a good thrashing Douglas was amongst the first to volunteer to give it to them. Feudalism still being a concept that was understood prop-erly in that part of Scotland at the time, his example was followed by a swathe of his father's tenants from the glen. Torquil crossed to France three months later and Murdo decided he wasn't going to be left out of their adventures. Although he had been brought up not to lie, he swore to a recruiting officer that he was eighteen years old – he was fifteen – and eager to fight the foe. The recruiting officer signed him up with a conspirator's wink.

They died in reverse order to that in which they'd been born. Murdo fell at Mons, neatly decapitated by a shell and six months later Torquil was lost for ever, drowning in the mud of no man's land. Donald and Evangeline were not told at first because Torquil's commanding officer thought he might eventually turn up but after a few weeks it became clear that those calcium-rich bones of his were going to secretly fertilize foreign soil for years to come.

A year later, Douglas was accidentally shot by his own side. He lived for several minutes after the bullet entered his brain and the snow that started falling on his face made him think that he was lying in his bed at home with the snow blowing off the hills through the window and that his brothers were safely asleep in their adjacent bedrooms (which in some ways they were), dreaming of their lives to come. Little Honoria had clearly been determined on her full complement of playmates.

Evangeline and Donald called their lost sons 'the boys', as if they were a single entity, rather than the individuals they had never really had the time to become. Donald comforted himself by imagining himself an unwilling Abraham, called upon to sacrifice his sons on the altar of patriotism. For a long time, Evangeline hung onto a secret hope that instead of drowning in mud, Torquil had deserted (she'd never been much of a patriot) and one day soon was going to walk up the long rhododendron-lined driveway, as jaunty as when he was alive. Time dulled this possibility and when the armistice was announced and there was still no sign of him, Evangeline decided that it was unlikely he would be coming home now and went down to the laundry room and hanged herself with a length of washing-rope from a large hook in the wall the purpose of which had always puzzled the laundrymaids but which now seemed only too clear. The end.

'Sorry?'

~ The end.

'Well, *that* was cheerful.'

~ Don't hold me responsible, Nora says with a careless shrug, blame the story, not the storyteller. Do you want more tea?

Chez Bob

BOB WAS FAST ASLEEP IN BED WHEN I ENTERED THE FLAT. THE bedroom curtains were open and when I went to draw them I was reminded of Ferdinand – a comparison that couldn't possibly work in Bob's favour, especially as he was now sleepmumbling something about herring ('They've got knives!').

Something caught my eye down on the street – a figure was standing in the doorway of a building. It was surely the woman who had asked me the time only a few minutes ago. She struck a match to light a cigarette and I could see her hair – the colour of old threepenny-bits – and her perfectly straight nose. I suddenly realized who it was that she had a look of – the height, her carriage, the way she stood with feet splayed – she was like a poor and scrawny version of my mother, a prototype of Nora that hadn't quite worked. The little flame of the match caught something else too – bitterness in the set of her features, disappointment etched in her skin.

~ What a good police witness you would make, Nora says, rather cynically.

179

The woman caught sight of me, turned away, and disappeared into the darkness.

I shivered with the cold and slid into bed beside Bob, who was clutching a blue rubber hot-water bottle in the shape of a small teddy-bear.

'Show by the use of reason,' he muttered, 'that reason itself is unreliable.'

I couldn't help but wonder if Bob really had been to a John Martin concert. On page 58 *I looked out of the third-floor window as if I'd just seen something interesting.* The thing I had seen was Bob, deep in conversation with one of Archie's postgraduate students, a young woman who was built like a pencil and whose doctoral thesis (*Losing the Plot*) was on *Finnegans Wake*, thus making her totally unsuitable for Bob. I would have thought it an innocent enough encounter if it hadn't been for the expression on Bob's face – bright and interested, almost, dare I say it, flirtatious. Had he looked at me like that once? If he had I could no longer remember. I hoped he wasn't planning on being unfaithful to me, at least not with such a very *plain* girl.

'Shagging Shug?' Bob said contemplatively when we were woken in the middle of the night by noises from Shug's flat below. 'Forever Changes' was seeping up through the floorboards, a sure sign that Shug was in a mellow mood. The strains of 'Andmoreagain' were counterpointed by the inarticulate grunts and troats of coition, with an occasional whinny that sounded suspiciously like Andrea.

It's impossible, as we all know, to fall asleep to the sounds of someone else's lovemaking (except possibly Bob's) and so we had to wait out the denouement. ('What are they *doing* for so long?' Bob puzzled.)

To pass the time, Bob suggested a game. I vetoed his usual choices – 'Animal, Vegetable, Mineral', the inevitable 'I-Spy' and Bob's favourite game, naming the Seven Dwarves; he had never yet managed to get all seven at one time. Eventually we settled on 'The Minister's Cat Went Shopping' ('The Minister's Cat went to town and bought an Aberdeen Angus cow,' and so on), and by the time our downstairs neighbours had finally finished fornicating, the poor cat was trying to man-oeuvre a large walnut wardrobe through the door of the manse.

Just as I was finally dropping off to sleep, Bob said, 'Oh yeah, that woman phoned again.'

'And?'

'I said you did live here, after all.'

'And?' I prompted.

'She said she'd be in touch.'

'And you didn't find out who she was?'

'Was I supposed to?'

Someone – Mother Nature, presumably – was hurling handfuls of sleet like wet sand at the window and I shivered and moved closer to Bob's unyielding body and thought about Ferdinand in the hope that I would dream about him – *I love my love with an F because he is Felicitous. I hate him with an F because he is Felonious. I fed him with Fern cakes and Forbidden fruit. His name is Ferdinand and he lives in the Far North* – but instead all night long I dreamt I was a seagull because Bob had put his copy of *Jonathan Livingston Seagull*, the only book he had actually read all year (apart from *The It Book of Drugs*), under my pillow.

I was awake at seven but it felt like the middle of the night. I tried and failed to go back to sleep. Bob was snoring with delirious abandon – a complex and apparently random pattern of snorts and dramatic gasps like a large carp drowning on air.

Reluctantly, I heaved myself out of bed. At least there was electricity, even though it made little impression on the morning Murk. I made myself a cup of instant coffee and draped myself in a blanket so that I resembled a tepee and with a heavy heart began to type.

Jack Gannet was a man who believed there was a logic that underpinned existence and if he couldn't find the logic then he had faith that it was unavailable rather than non-existent. Absence of evidence, he said, did not mean evidence was absent. One of the men he relied upon to back this belief up was Henry Machin, the pathologist.

Henry Machin picked up a scalpel and looked at it affectionately.

'What do you think – accident?' Jack Gannet asked hopefully.

The pathologist laughed, a hollow sound that

you could imagine came out of the same box as the noise of swishing scythes and hissing pendulums. 'Doubt it,' he said. He was one of those people who always saw the funny side of everything, Jack Gannet thought morosely.

He threw a tentative glance at the new constable - Collins - to see if he was the fainting sort, but so far he looked normal. Whatever that was. Constable Collins, pale and gently loitering in the background, had helped to bring the dead woman ashore and felt that it was his duty to see his charge through to the end. Traces of her red nail varnish, he noticed, could still be seen where her fingertips hadn't been eaten. He wondered what kind of sea-creatures did that. Shrimp? Constable Collins liked shrimp and often bought a tub of them when he was down on the Front. Did shrimp eat people? And if in turn you ate the shrimp did that technically make you into a cannibal? And what about scampi? His wife, who said she was dying of boredom - which would be a first for the medical world - was very fond of scampi. He couldn't imagine what scampi looked like swimming around in the sea.

'How long has she been in the water, do you think?' Jack Gannet asked Henry Machin.

'Hard to tell,' the pathologist said. 'At this time of year the water's warm; decomposition sets in quickly. She looks a bit of a mess.'

'So do I first thing in the morning,' Jack

183

Gannet said wearily. 'Five days maybe?' He kept his voice respectfully low when he was talking about the dead for sometimes he had this eerie feeling that they could hear him, that they hadn't quite . . . gone.

He knew this was no accident, he could feel it like a vibration, like an angry aura of wasps. Henry Machin slipped the scalpel into the dead mermaid flesh like a hot knife in butter and Constable Collins fainted quietly so as not to disturb anyone.

The morning post clattered through the letterbox. It contained a rather threatening note, signed by Joan, the departmental secretary, reminding me that my essay for Professor Cousins (*'Tragedy plus Time equals Comedy' Discuss*) was several weeks overdue. I wondered if it worked the other way round – *Comedy plus Time equals Tragedy*? Perhaps not.

The brusque, almost callous, tone of the note indicated that it had been penned by someone other than Professor Cousins, who, even if he remembered omissions and absences, never cared enough to reprimand people for them.

I decided that, rather than speak to him, I would leave him a letter, beseeching leniency, and plead a dying grandmother in mitigation. Is my grandmother dead? Or grandmothers in the plural, for surely there must have been two of them unless autogenesis runs in the family?

~ Dead, Nora says.

'And your grandmothers, what about them?'

~ Very dead, and I only had one.

But you can't have only one grandmother, that's illogical. Everyone has two. Don't they?

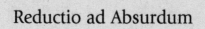

Reductio ad Absurdum

I HADN'T ACTUALLY EXPECTED TO FIND PROFESSOR COUSINS IN his room as he was supposed to be giving a lecture on revenge tragedy at that time of day. Instead he was rifling through the drawers of his filing-cabinet. He seemed to be even more skittish than usual, laughing away to himself as he pulled out, and then discarded on the floor, an endless cache of photocopied timetables and study guides. I reminded him that he was supposed to be giving a lecture and he looked at me in astonishment and said, 'Really?' as if he'd never given one before in his life.

I offered to help him find whatever it was he was looking for but this seemed to cause him even more amusement. 'I can't remember *what* I'm looking for,' he said, 'but, don't worry, I will when I find it.' He gave me a curious glance. 'Can I help you with something, did you want to see me?'

I told Professor Cousins that I'd come to write a note to him and he gestured wildly in the direction of his desk and said, 'On you go, my dear, on you go then.' It seemed the easiest thing to do somehow, so I slipped behind his desk and got out a pad of paper and started writing.

Professor Cousins' desk was very untidy, scattered with little bits of paper on which he had scrawled messages to himself in his spiky italic hand – 'Buy fish!' 'Find glove!' 'Send letter!'

''*Tis Pity She's a Whore*,' he exclaimed suddenly, just as Martha Sewell passed his open door. She gave him an unreadable look. Professor Cousins waved to her. 'That's what I'm supposed to be teaching, isn't it?' he said to me.

'Yes.'

He sighed, looking very downcast.

'I'm not in the lecture theatre either,' I said in a feeble effort to comfort him. He made a helpless gesture and returned to the filing-cabinet, muttering something to himself on the lines of 'Mummery flummery, mimsy whimsy, blah, blah, blah,' before wandering out into the corridor, bleating Joan's name in the ridiculous helpless tone he adopted in the belief that it endeared him to Joan, when in fact it drove her up the wall. When he'd gone I propped up my note for him between 'Go to Draffens!' and 'Joan's birthday!' and discreetly pocketed the one that said 'Mark Honours essays!'

Seeing Martha had been a blow as I had been hoping to avoid her two o'clock creative writing tutorial, but now that she'd seen me I supposed I was going to have to put in an appearance in her class. I looked up and was startled to see Watson Grant lowering in the doorway.

'Goodness, what happened to you?' I said to him, for his head was bandaged up and he was sporting a black eye that made him look more manly than he really was.

'Mugged,' he said miserably. 'I was concussed, I'm lucky I'm not dead.'

Professor Cousins came back at that moment, bearing aloft a cup of Joan-made tea. 'Good God, man,' he cried when he saw Grant Watson, 'what on earth happened to you?' When Watson Grant explained, Professor Cousins said, 'Laid low by some anonymous stranger in the dark, eh?' He proffered a Nuttall's Minto but Grant Watson declined. 'Concussion,' Professor Cousins reminisced dreamily, 'I was concussed once – during the war, or *a* war, certainly. Unconscious for the best part of an hour. When I came round I couldn't remember anything, had no idea who I was. I rather liked it, looking back,' he sighed regretfully; 'a *tabula rasa*, a blank sheet of paper. A fresh start.'

'And do you know who you are now?' Watson Grant asked him with a little more asperity than usual. Professor Cousins looked thoughtful. 'Well, I know who I *think* I am.'

Me, I am Euphemia Stuart-Murray. I am the last of my line. My mother is not my mother.

It does seem a little harsh of her to tell me this now, after twenty-one years. Although I always suspected there was something not quite right, some skeleton waiting to fall out of a cupboard. If she's not my mother how did she acquire me?

'Did you steal me? Did you find me?'

~ It wasn't quite like that.

'Well what is it like, for heaven's sake?' My mother stares into the empty hearth. Not my actual, factual mother, of course, for she – apparently – is dead. It turns out that I have been wrong all along – I am not a semi-orphan, I am a complete orphan, whole and entire. I belong to no-one.

I made my excuses and left before Grant Watson remembered I owed him an essay. As I was getting into the lift a voice shouted, 'Wait for me,' and a breathless Bob rushed in and said, 'Beam me up, Scottie. And be quick about it.'

'I'm going down not up, and what are you doing here anyway?'

'I've been to a philosophy tutorial,' Bob said, the unfamiliar word sitting uncomfortably on his tongue. Bob had no idea how he'd ended up taking five of his eight degree papers in philosophy and presumed it must be due to an administrative error somewhere. And, of course, philosophy attracted exactly the wrong kind of girls for Bob – earnest intellectual ones, for example, who wanted to discuss Foucault and Adorno and other people Bob had tried very hard not to hear of. If Bob could have designed a girl he would have started by getting rid of her vocal cords. In Bob's ideal world, Bob's girl would be, not me, but Lieutenant Uhura or Honeybunch Kaminski. Or – better still – Shug.

Bob frowned at a photocopied sheet he must have been given in the tutorial and started catechizing me. 'Have you ever heard of Secondary Rules of Inference?'

'No.'

'The Law of the Excluded Middle?'

'Sounds like something from Gilbert and Sullivan.'

'Is that a no?'

'Yes.'

He looked at me doubtfully. 'Monadic predicates?'

'No.'

'Hypothetical Syllogisms?'

'Not really.'

'Not really?' Bob said. 'What kind of an answer is that?'

'OK – no, then.'

'The Law of Identity?'

'Well . . .'

'Yes or no?'

'No,' I said irritably, 'this is boring.'

'You're telling me. Reductio ad Absurdum?'

'Endlessly.'

Bob waved a sheaf of past exam papers in my face and said, 'This stuff's unbelievable. Listen.' ('Stuff' was Bob's all-purpose word for everything.) He proceeded to read a question, in a ponderous tone, from the exam paper –

> *Symbolize the following propositions in the symbolism of Predicate Logic:*
>
> *(a) Cupar is north of Edinburgh.*
>
> *(b) Dundee is north of Edinburgh.*
>
> *(c) Cupar is not north of Dundee.*
>
> *(d) Cupar is between Edinburgh and Dundee.*
>
> *(e) There are places between Edinburgh and Dundee.*
>
> *(f) If one place is south of a second place, then the second is north of the first.*
>
> *(g) If one place is between two others, and is north of the first, it is south of the second.*

('Nxy' is 'x is north of y'; 'sxy' is 'x is south of y';
'bxyz' is 'x is between y and z'; 'c' is 'Cupar'; 'd' is
'Dundee'; 'e' is 'Edinburgh'; universe of discourse:
places). Show by formal derivation that (a), (d), (f)
and (g) together imply (b). You may need to supply
a further premise expressing one of the properties of
'is north of' referred to above.)

Bob shook his head in a fish farm sort of way. 'Wow, who thinks this stuff up? What are they on?' We had exited the lift by now, of course, as it only takes a sentence to travel the two floors to the ground, and then a longish paragraph to reach the Students' Union where, to a seemingly endless diet of 'American Pie' on the jukebox, I plied Bob with (Scotch) pie and beans in an effort to cheer him up. Terri was asleep at a table. She was wearing a long cloak and a pair of high-heeled black boots with a little astrakhan ankle-trim and had a moth-eaten black lace parasol clutched in her nerveless hand. She looked like someone Jack the Ripper would be attracted to. I told Bob to tell her to meet at two o'clock in the Tower and left him playing table football while I went to a women's liberation meeting.

'Liberated from what,' Bob said, rolling his eyes, 'that's what I don't understand.'

'Before we can produce a blueprint for praxis we have to understand the ideology behind the revolutionary consciousness—' Heather broke off her one-sided conversation to tell me I was late. 'You're late.'

'So?' I said.

Heather had recently declared that separatism was the way forward for women and the logical conclusion of this, she explained, was that we must all become lesbians. Heather was having some trouble finding anyone willing to take her up on this theory, let alone the praxis, although Philippa had volunteered ('Well, I'm willing to give it a go,') as if we were talking about playing a new rule in lacrosse.

Heather glared at me and then continued zealously, 'The subordination and oppression of women within capitalism is the real issue. We all know that male hegemony leads to the oppression and subjugation of women.' Kara nodded in vigorous agreement, without taking her eyes off the piece of petit-point she was absorbed in stitching.

~ Who's Kara? Nora asks.

'You were asleep.'

Proteus had been shucked from a Moses basket and was being dandled on Olivia's knee. He smelt like sour milk and he was drooling like a dog all over Olivia's velvet dress. Foolishly or ironically or riskily – almost any adverb would do for this situation, Olivia was sitting next to Sheila, Roger Lake's stay-at-home wife. Sheila had no idea that Roger was having an affair with Olivia, a fact that always added a certain frisson of tension to these meetings for everyone else. Heather, before becoming a lesbian separatist, had also had a fleeting affair with Roger Lake – an affair that Sheila Lake did know about – and which added even more of a frisson to the proceedings.

Olivia smelt of Miss Dior while Sheila was wearing babyscent, which is a perfume made from Milton fluid, curds and vomit. The newest little Lake was outside in the corridor in a handed-down Silver Cross pram built like a tank.

'Engels says that the emancipation of women remains impossible as long as women are excluded from socially productive work . . .' This was just like being in one of Archie's tutorials, except I could tell Heather to shut up when she got too overbearing.

'So you don't think being a housewife is socially productive work?' Sheila snapped at Heather. Proteus turned his head and gave her a surprised look.

'Well, Sheila,' Heather said carefully, 'in a society defined by the white, western, ruling-class male—'

'Exactly,' Kara said. Philippa barged into the room at that moment, lugging a mountain of student essays and a bag of hamster bedding and apologizing loudly for her lateness. 'I was doing the Cartesian Circle with first-years,' she said, making it sound like an exotic eastern European folk dance or a forgotten play by Brecht.

'We were talking about the sexual imperialism of housework,' Heather said.

'*You* were,' Sheila said tartly.

In my opinion, these meetings would have been much improved by the presence of a few men. Seeing Philippa reminded me of Ferdinand – I wondered if he was awake by now and if I could find the time to visit the McCue house today and come upon him as if by chance.

I was distracted suddenly from these pleasant thoughts

by noticing that, like the eyes in certain portraits, Heather's nipples seemed to have the uncanny ability to follow you round the room. This is the kind of observation that once made, cannot be unmade. Unfortunately.

'Some of us have to stay home and rear the children,' Sheila spat at Heather. 'If it was left up to you, the human race would die out.'

'It won't be long before men are relegated to a biological footnote anyway,' Philippa said breezily and then, apropos of nothing, 'We're having a party tonight, by the way, everyone's welcome.' In my experience, a party is simply an invitation to disaster but everyone in the room nodded and murmured enthusiastically. Everyone except Sheila who reared up like a cobra in front of Heather and said, 'You think that screwing anyone that takes your fancy is a gender equality issue.'

'Well, Sheila,' Heather said querulously, 'if you want to be the private property of some man, that's up to you.'

'Better to be private property than to be a public whore,' Sheila hissed triumphantly. Heather suddenly grabbed a chair and prodded it at Sheila like a lion tamer (this is how accidents happen) and screamed, 'At least I've worked out how to use birth control.'

I decided discretion was the better part of valour and made my apologies: 'I've got an essay to do.' Olivia followed me out, handing Proteus back to Kara who gestured vaguely at the Moses basket at her feet. Olivia replaced him in the basket and pushed it under Kara's chair as far out of harm's way as it would go.

The last thing I heard as she closed the door was a

high-pitched wail as if someone had jabbed a baby with a pin.

'I don't know why people bring children into the world,' Olivia said. 'They don't seem to love them and the world's so awful anyway.'

'Have you got an essay on George Eliot, Olivia?' I asked (rather callously, I can see now).

'Sorry,' she said, 'I didn't choose that one. I've got a Charlotte Brontë if that's any good to you?' She was going to say something else but then she started to look uncomfortable and fled towards the toilets. 'Sorry,' she said, 'I think I'm going to be sick.'

I followed her and held her lovely blond hair out of the way for her.

'Thank you,' she said politely.

'Do you want that coffee now?' I asked, but she shook her head and said she was going home. Olivia lived in a civilized flat on the Perth Road that she shared with three other girls. All four of them knew how to cook and use a sewing-machine and they held 'dinner parties' and shared Immac and Stergene and did each other's hair and cleaned up each other's vomit when necessary. Olivia had a pleasant room painted dark green, full of nice things like oil-lamps and healthy plants and old embroidered linen from Dens Road market. Olivia sat in her pleasant room and listened to Bach and Pachelbel and worked hard, waiting for Roger Lake to squeeze her into his timetable.

★   ★   ★

At the back of the Tower a student who sold the *Socialist Worker* on Saturdays thrust a yellow leaflet into my hand. In crude black letters it said, 'END THE FASCISM NOW! – All concerned meet in New Dines 6.00 p.m.' A sudden gust of wind caught it and whisked it out of my hands.

Terri was waiting inside, sitting on a sofa in the foyer of the Tower – a warm place panelled entirely in a lovely russet wood, polished to a lacquered finish.

'I've been to the pound,' she said, looking more downcast than usual.

'The pound?'

'The lost dogs' home. To look for the yellow dog. He wasn't there though.'

Perhaps Chick had taken the yellow dog to his own home, decided to make a pet of it, but that seemed unlikely somehow. I couldn't even imagine Chick having a home, much less keeping a dog in it.

We sat in the foyer discussing the dog's whereabouts right through the two o'clock bell and the general hubbub of people going to lectures and only at ten minutes past the hour could we finally bring ourselves to make our way to Martha's room.

We were delayed further by Dr Dick haranguing us in the English department corridor about unwritten work and unattended tutorials and only breaking off to declare himself ill. He did look rather sick – his skin as white and waxy as an arum lily – but no more than usual.

'Do you have symptoms?' I quizzed. 'Sore throat? Headache? Swollen glands?'

'Headache,' he said hopefully.

'Pounding, throbbing behind the eyes? Or dull ache at the back of the head?'

He looked unsure. 'Well, a sort of sharp, piercing pain at the temple.'

'Brain tumour, then,' Terri said.

'Go and lie down,' I suggested gently, 'and try not to think about marking essays.' Luckily he took this advice and went off, clutching his forehead and moaning quietly to himself.

'Ah, there you are,' Professor Cousins said, leaping out of his room and doing a little jig in front of me. 'I was hoping I would see you today,' he said. 'I was going to ask you about our mutual friend.' There seemed no point in telling Professor Cousins that it was only an hour or so since he had last seen me since time, as we all know, is a subjective kind of thing.

'Our mutual friend?' I queried.

'The dog of yesterday. And Chick, as well, of course,' Professor Cousins said fondly. 'Quite a wag, isn't he?'

'We have to go to Martha's creative writing class now,' I explained to him; 'we're already late.'

'I'll come with you,' Professor Cousins said. 'I've always wanted to know what creative writing really is. And does it have an opposite?' he laughed, manoeuvring himself between us and taking an arm of each as if we were about to do some complicated reel.

'Oh, it's you,' Martha said, 'you're so late you're almost early. It's now twenty minutes past the hour,' she said

200

sternly, 'that's twenty minutes late, if you can't manage the math. Sitting in again?' she added sharply to Professor Cousins.

'You don't mind, do you?' he said. 'I'm so terribly interested in what you're doing.'

Martha always bade us move our terminally uncomfortable chairs into a circle, as if we were in therapy or about to play one of those getting-to-know-you games – 'My name is Effie and if I was an animal I would be a . . .' But what would I choose to be? Not a domestic pet, surely, forever at the whim and behest of someone who thought they owned you, and certainly not a beast of the field useful only for its milk and meat and skin. Some shy creature perhaps, hidden deep in the untamed forest?

There was the usual roll-call of names – Andrea, Kevin, Robin, Kara, Janice Rand, Davina. Davina was a keen mature student from Kirkcaldy, a divorcee and one of the few grown-ups at the university. Shug didn't do the creative writing paper, saying that his mother's weekly Willie Low shopping-list was a more creative piece of writing than anything produced at the university. Bob did do the creative writing paper, he just didn't know it. For weeks, Martha had stood at the front of the class at the beginning of every hour and frowned at the class list in front of her, puzzling, 'Robert Sharpe? Does anyone know a Robert Sharpe?' I never spoke up, I didn't really want to admit to knowing Bob.

I was sitting next to Terri – a black wolf prowling the night. Terri's assignment for Martha was poetry. Terri's poems came under the collective title *My Favourite Suicide* and you can probably imagine the content matter. Some of them (although undoubtedly derivative) were surprisingly cheerful –

> I drank the glass of
> milk you left on the
> bedside table. it was
> sour. thank you

Martha was wearing a long cashmere plaid woven from the dull colours of infinity, that she had fixed, toga-style, with a brooch made – disturbingly – from the claw of some game bird, a grouse or a ptarmigan maybe, set with a purple amethyst.

Andrea was making a great show of sharpening her pencils and laying everything out on her little table while Kevin was staring at the space Olivia's feet would have occupied if she had been there.

'I think we should begin with a little exercise to flex our writing muscles,' Martha said, speaking very slowly as if she was on prescription drugs but I think it was just her way of trying to communicate with people less intelligent than she thought she was. How tedious this all seemed. I wasn't sure I could sit still for a whole hour.

'Write me a paragraph,' Martha enunciated clearly, 'in just ten minutes, which incorporates these three words – *bracteate, trowel* and *vilifies.*'

'That's four words,' objected Robin, sitting next to me in the circle. Robin was wearing a leather trench coat that had apparently once belonged to a member of the *Waffen SS*.

Martha gave him a considered look. 'Not the and,' she said finally.

'*Not the and*,' Professor Cousins chuckled, 'a strange sentence if ever there was one; it could only possibly make sense in context, couldn't it?' Martha made a resigned kind of noise and busied herself with the insides of her briefcase.

Professor Cousins was sitting between Kara and Davina. Davina was writing an historical thing about Shakespeare's mother, Wordsworth's sister or Emily Brontë's hitherto unmentioned illegitimate daughter – I could never quite remember which. Personally, I don't think it right to make up things about real people – although I suppose there's an argument for saying that once you're dead you're not real any more. But then we have to define what we mean by real and none of us wants to go down that tortuous path because we all know where it leads (madness or a first class honours, or both).

Martha turned back to the class and said sternly, 'A paragraph with structure to it, not abstract free-fall. No nonsense.'

I wrote down *bracteate, trowel* and *vilifies* and then sat staring at them. I seemed to remember doing this exercise in one of the many primary schools I had attended, although with more useful words (*sand, bucket, red,* or perhaps *porridge, bowl, hot*). I had no idea what *bracteate* meant. It sounded like a kind of seaweed. I doodled helplessly.

Professor Cousins meanwhile was labouring diligently over his work, making strange exploded diagrams with spidery connecting lines. He was too far away for me to copy anything from him; the light in Martha's room was scanty. Kara, on his other side, leant over surreptitiously to try and see what he was writing but Professor Cousins put his arm protectively around his scribblings, like a small boy. The Moses basket that contained Proteus had been shoved more or less into the middle of the circle of chairs, as if he was going to be the centrepiece of a voodoo ritual.

Kara was writing a Lawrentian kind of novella about a woman who goes back to the land to discover her emotional and sexual roots, a journey which seemed to involve unnecessarily large amounts of dung and mud and seed of all kinds, but mainly male. Strangely, the genteel Martha seemed to relate to this. At some previous point in her life she chose to suddenly 'share' with us, she had run a smallholding in upstate New York with her first husband, a famous playwright whom she couldn't believe none of us had heard of. Martha said she and this first husband had found 'the continuous juxtaposition of the cerebral and the bestial in country life very stimulating'. As she 'shared' she fingered the bird claw at her neck, a faraway look in her eyes.

Anyway, she concluded with a somewhat rueful sigh, the outcome of all this had been a return to urban living accompanied by (sadly) a divorce on account of the playwright's rampant adultery, but also (happily) Martha's first collection of poetry, Chicken Spirits, 'Critically acclaimed, but hardly a bestseller. But then which would you rather have, after all?'

'A bestseller?' Andrea suggested.

Martha was planning to break out of the ghetto of poetry. She had, she claimed, an unwritten novel, which seemed like a contradiction in terms to me (like the unspoken word). Martha's novel was about a female author getting over her writer's block by discovering that in a former life she had been Pliny the Elder – so probably not a bestseller.

'They say everyone has a novel inside them, don't they?' Janice Rand suddenly piped up.

'Not everyone can write it though, Janice,' Martha admonished gravely.

There was some kind of commotion going on outside, every so often a shout of 'Ho, Ho, Ho Chi Minh' went up and I wondered if the protesters knew he was dead, and if that made any difference. Martha glanced out of the window and frowned at what she saw.

I tried the words in a different order – *trowel*, *vilifies*, *bracteate* – but this didn't result in any inspiration. Martha was always urging us to 'Write what you know,' (how boring books would be if everyone adhered to that principle!) but although *vilifies* was a word I felt comfortable with, my knowledge of *bracteates* and *trowels* was limited. Oh, for a good etymological dictionary to be carried on one's person at all times.

Nora has no dictionary, there are no books on the island apart from the Bible by my bed. Nora appears to have banished books, except for the one she herself keeps, writing every day, her 'diary'. But how can you keep a diary when nothing ever happens, except the weather?

~ Yes, but there's so very much weather, Nora says.

The words didn't help matters at all, prising themselves off the printed page and hanging around like bored flies, adding further to the instability of the phenomenal world. Terri, in the twilight world of the zombie, was writing the three words over and over again. She looked quite content.

Martha wandered over to the window and leant with her forehead on the glass as if she was trying to absorb daylight. (I was surprised we didn't all have rickets.) Andrea used this opportunity to lean over and whisper to me that she thought a *bracteate* was a kind of animal, possibly a frog. Which sounded like wishful thinking to me. Nora, of course, believes that we all have a totem animal, a manifestation of our spiritual nature in the animal world. ('Your mother sounds kind of cool,' Andrea said. Misguidedly.)

Andrea whispered in my ear that she thought her spirit animal was a cat. How predictable. Why do girls always think of themselves as cats? I didn't suppose Andrea would much enjoy ripping the insides out of tiny helpless mammals or licking her own nether regions or being chased by mad dogs or eating cat food without the help of cutlery.

Kevin's glasses had slipped down his nose as he stared at *bracteate*, *trowel* and *vilifies*. If we were animals (which we are, I know), Kevin would be a sponge – a sea-cucumber perhaps or something rounder and squishier.

But what I might be I did not know. (I prefer monosyllables. They stick to the page better.)

'Surely sponges aren't animals?' Andrea puzzled.

'What do you think they are then?'

'Vegetables?' she hazarded.

This was a bit like playing 'Animal, Vegetable, Mineral' with Bob, or – worse – asking Bob general knowledge questions. (Question: 'What is Formosa now called? Bob's answer: 'Cheese?')

Andrea gave up and started colouring the words in instead.

'Right,' Martha said suddenly, 'ten minutes are up.' Only ten minutes had passed? What a nightmare. How long would it take before the hour was up? I calculated miserably – nearly three thousand words at this rate, more than ten pages. Time for some omission and reduction. Surely no-one would miss, for example, nine sentences on the theme of 'The man *vilifies* the *bracteate trowel*.' And so on.

'I didn't say a sentence,' Martha reprimanded irritably, 'I asked for a paragraph. I asked for *text*. Do you understand what *text* is?' You could tell that she wanted to slip the word 'morons' into this sentence somewhere.

'Well, according to Proust,' Professor Cousins said helpfully, 'it's a web.' Professor Cousins hadn't even managed a sentence, despite all his diagrams.

'Does this mean,' he asked Martha plaintively, 'that I should abandon all hope of becoming a writer?'

'Yes,' Martha said.

'Thank goodness for that,' Professor Cousins said.

'Let's turn to your assignments,' Martha said tetchily.

It was when the bell rang at five to twelve and no-one moved that a horrible realization dawned on me – this was a two-hour seminar. I thought about fainting but that was Andrea's usual ruse for getting out of sticky situations.

Martha had just singled out a passage in Kara's novella that she said she found particularly meaningful. The passage was an intimate description of killing a chicken. The poor bird had so far been chased, strangled and plucked and the Kara-like narrator currently had her hand inside the chicken's egg tube (or whatever the technical term is), rescuing unlaid eggs.

'Those last little yolks,' Martha said, nodding sagely, 'so good for an egg custard.'

The mewing noise that Proteus had been making throughout this critique suddenly escalated into a loud bawling and Kara hauled him out of his basket and slapped him carelessly on a breast. We moved on swiftly to Davina and everyone prepared for extreme boredom. It wasn't that Davina couldn't write it was just that she had nothing to say. Andrea wasn't much better. 'Anthea's not been doing much lately,' Andrea said, looking rather faint.

'Does she ever?' Robin said.

'All right, all right,' Andrea said and began to read reluctantly. 'The bees could be heard before they were seen.'

'Have you started?' Kara asked.

'Yes, of course I've started,' Andrea said peevishly. 'Shall I start again?' she asked Martha.

'If you must.'

'The bees could be heard before they were seen. The girl, leaning out of the window, thinking about what her father had said at breakfast, worried, irrationally, she knew, that the bees would fly into her hair –'

'The bees?' Martha checked. 'As in honey?' Perhaps like me she had been under the delusion that they were alphabet Bs, imagining them in a monoliteral swarm around Andrea's head.

'She preferred not to think about where her fears came from. She was, though she did not know it, on the brink of an unhappy discovery. Would she have cared if she had known? And yet in some way, she already knew everything.'

Martha stifled a yawn.

'Then she's omniscient?' Davina asked. 'But you have to be a narrator to be omniscient, don't you? She doesn't narrate, she's . . . narrated.'

I am narrated therefore I am. What would that be – a narratee? That can't be a word. It sounds like a sea-animal. The young narratees leapt and frolicked in the wake of the ship. The narratees swam in playful circles.

'Effie?' Martha said. 'Something you want to share with us?'

'No, not really.'

'Your assignment?'

'It's at a problematic stage, I need to work on the metastructure some more.'

Martha raised a perfect circumflex of an eyebrow and

gave me a pitying look. 'Try,' she said.

I sighed and started to read –

'Penny for them, Madame Astarti,' a voice boomed behind her.

'I should be a rich woman, Jack Gannet,' Madame Astarti said to him, 'for all the thoughts I'm having today.'

'Take a stroll along the prom?' Jack Gannet said, offering her his arm.

'Always the gentleman, Jack,' Madame Astarti murmured appreciatively. Indeed 'Gentleman Jack' had been his nickname during his days on the Met, on account of his good manners, but Jack Gannet didn't like that, he thought it made him sound too like a criminal. And Jack Gannet was perhaps one of the straightest coppers on the force. Jack Gannet and Madame Astarti went a long way back, almost as far as Sheffield and that was a very long way indeed. There had been a few occasions during his rise to Chief Inspector when he had been thankful for Madame Astarti's help, not that he liked to admit it.

'It's not the weather for murder,' Jack Gannet sighed, wiping his brow.

'Murder?' Madame Astarti queried sharply.

'The woman found in the sea, just had the pathologist's report back on the body. It was decomposing fast, of course, bodies don't last long in the sea, especially in this weather. Ice-cream?'

Madame Astarti felt confused. The woman was killed by ice-cream?

Jack Gannet stopped suddenly so that Madame Astarti, whose braking distance was quite long, slammed into him.

'Rigatoni's,' Jack said cheerfully, 'the best scoop in the north.' They were outside the big Rigatoni ice-cream parlour on the Prom, the flagship one, and he opened the door and gestured Madame Astarti inside and to a table in the window. A buxom waitress appeared and smiled warmly at Jack.

'Hello, Deirdre,' he said. 'I think we'd both like a Five-Scoop-Sundae-Special, please, even though it's a Saturday,' he added and Deirdre laughed, far too much, Madame Astarti thought, for such a feeble joke.

'How was she killed?' Madame Astarti asked eagerly, sticking her fan-shaped wafer into the heart of her sundae.

'Difficult to say for sure,' Jack Gannet frowned, 'but it looks like she was strangled.'

'Crime of passion, perhaps,' Madame Astarti said thoughtfully.

'Well,' Jack Gannet said. 'You know that frog—'

—The frog is large and green and cool to the touch.

~ It's not a frog, Nora says, it's a toad. She strokes it, a toad-wife, and kisses it gently on the top of its head, an indignity it suffers in silence. When she places it on the floor at her feet it contemplates her for a few seconds as if it's worshipping her, before hopping lazily out of the door.

211

~ I must pick nettles, she says, for soup.

'It's winter, there are no nettles.'

~ Well, I have to go and pick something, she says vaguely. She is avoiding telling me her story. I know why – it is not a pretty tale.

'If I were you,' Martha said to me, 'I would think seriously about doing a secretarial course so that you can get a job when you don't graduate.'

But if she was me she wouldn't say such nasty things.

Janice Rand read out a poem that was something to do with the sun in the sky and the birds flying by and no-one could think of a single thing to say about it.

'Robin?' Martha sighed.

'OK,' Robin said. 'I've been reworking a scene from *Life Sentence*. I wasn't really happy with it before. I'll just read all the parts, shall I? Unless someone else wants to read? No? Right, well this is the scene where Dod, Jed and Kenny are discussing whether Rick had been right to do what he did –' Robin took a deep breath and closed his eyes. There was silence for quite a long time and then he suddenly started reading:

DOD	Yes, but I mean –
JED	Look, there isn't any point.
DOD	I mean –
JED	It's all finished now anyway. It's over, we just don't know it.
DOD	If I thought for a minute that you were –
JED	Yeah.

DOD   I mean . . .

KENNY It's meaningless. Meaning less. Less and less. Why
       bother?

DOD   But do you know what I'm talking about (*shouts*)?
       Do you know what I mean?

And so on (ad infinitum, ad nauseam) until the
audience died, one by one, a death of a thousand small
words.

'What *did* Rick do?' Andrea puzzled but Robin's answer
was drowned out by the groans of those who didn't want
to remember. Kara patted Proteus vigorously on the back
and he burped obligingly, then she turned him round
and placed him on the other breast. Outside, I could hear
someone singing 'Where Have All The Flowers Gone' in
a flat voice, to the two-chord accompaniment of an
acoustic guitar.

I was just searching in my pocket for a handkerchief –
I was sure I was coming down with a cold, I was feeling
quite light-headed – when I discovered a crumpled piece
of paper. I spread it out on the little desk-table and discovered it was the page of *The Expanding Prism of J* where
J falls over the banister. I wished I'd found it earlier, I
could have handed it in to Martha and pretended I'd written it – I expected it was just the kind of writing she
would like.

'Do you think you could pay attention?' Martha said to
me so I screwed the piece of paper up in a ball and stuffed
it back in my pocket.

'And so, finally, to Kevin,' she said, turning her gaze

213

reluctantly on our fantasist. 'How is Edrakonia this week, Kevin?' Martha had tried to persuade Kevin that his *magnum opus* was not suitable for the course assignment and had indeed told him at one point she was going to fail him point blank if he didn't stop writing 'garbage', but lately she seemed to have become inured to Edrakonia. If nothing else, Kevin could be relied upon to have actually done some writing and there was something about the eager expression on his bovine face that made you feel so dreadfully sorry for him that you couldn't help but encourage his one pleasure in life. Kevin read in a kind of Benny Hill accent –

'Duke Thar-Vint and his trusty steward Iart, who himself was of a noble family through the blood of his mother, Martinella, daughter of Si-Jagdar–'

'Martinella – is that like the female form of "Martin"?' Robin asked.

'No,' Kevin said.

'Because if it is,' Robin persisted, 'it's a really crap name.'

'Shut up.'

'Duke Thar-Vint and his steward Iart–'

'Trusty steward,' Kara reminded him.

'Thank you,' Kevin said sarcastically, *'Trusty steward Iart, were journeying to the Vale of Tyra-Shakir for the great celebration of the feast of Joppa–'*

'That's in Edinburgh,' Andrea objected. 'They're hardly going to go on some great epic journey on their stupid shaggy mountain ponies to go to Edinburgh, are they?'

Kevin ignored her. *'It will be difficult travelling but the* feast must be observed—' Kevin interrupted himself for once to explain, 'Of course, parties really are a pre-Murk thing, the Murk is a bit like Cromwell's Protectorate,' he explained, 'no singing, no dancing, that kind of thing.'

Professor Cousins looked perplexed. 'And so . . . the dragons are Royalists?'

'No, no, no,' Kevin scowled, 'the dragons don't hold with *affiliation*.' His face took on a dreamy expression. 'Before the Murk, the Duke Thar-Vint was renowned for his parties – the food was wonderful, naturally—'

'Naturally,' Martha said.

'The entertainments were spectacular – the famous acrobats of Hartha-Melchior, the jugglers of Wei-Wan, the dressage horses from the plains of—'

'Kevin,' Martha said looking very pained, 'could you just get on?'

'If the Duke Thar-Vint hadn't stolen the treasure of Alsinelg to begin with he wouldn't be in this mess,' Kara said.

'Yes, but that's the whole point,' Kevin said crossly.

'Kevin,' Martha warned.

'The Duke Thar-Vint scanned the vast horizon for signs of danger. This journey would be perilous, he knew – the greatest test yet of his courage and ingenuity. It was spring, yet not a green bud was to be seen. In the old days before the Murk fell on the land the steppes of Chargap would have been ablaze with flowers, the Verduna plants like tiny blue stars and the Rykil which the wise women of the steppes plucked and used for their healing properties.

His faithful steed, Demaal, sniffed the air—

~ How long are you going to go on without stopping him? Nora asks, rather irritably. You're wasting words.

'There isn't a finite stock of them.'

~ How do you know? You might suddenly just run out and then you won't be able to finish the—

Chez Bob

FOR JAMES THE SPECTRE OF THE OMNISCIENT AUTHOR CANNOT *be dismissed lightly. He cannot sanction interference with the interior drama of the novel. Given historical perspective, I think it is easier for us to recognize this aspect of the book as a precondition of the type of realism to which George Eliot subscribed.*

I wasn't sure I actually understood that sentence. I had stolen it from a book, but that didn't necessarily mean it was any good. I tried it out on Andrea, who had come home with me instead of going to work on *Annasach*, the student newspaper, and was now hanging around disconsolately in Paton's Lane in the hope that Shug might turn up. She was laying out her Tarot pack amongst the clutter on the table.

'You couldn't just magic up an essay for me, could you?' I asked her.

'Magic isn't to be used for selfish purposes or personal gain,' she intoned solemnly as if she was reading from a necromancer's primer.

I still felt queasy from Martha's tutorial. Perhaps there

was a bug going around. It was extraordinarily cold in the flat, even though both bars of the electric fire were burning. The fire was giving off an unpleasant smell of molten dust and melting fuses.

'Damart,' Andrea said enigmatically when I queried the wisdom of wearing broderie-anglaise in this weather.

The Court of the Crimson King was playing very loudly on the stereo and every time I tried to turn it down Bob wandered back over to it and innocently turned it up again. He was eating Marmite straight from the jar and looking perplexed.

Bob had recently begun to make incoherent attempts at study and he was surrounded now by a chaotic sea of textbooks and essays. The textbooks – Descartes' *Discourse on Method*, Woozley's *Theory of Knowledge*, Ayer's *Foundation of Empirical Knowledge* – were mostly stolen – Bob didn't think that stealing books was actually a crime ('Thought's free, isn't it?') – and remained steadfastly unopened, as if he was hoping to absorb their contents by osmosis.

The guddle of essays had all been salvaged from people I'd never heard of – *'Could scientific advance show that we are never really free?'* by an unlikely-sounding Wendy Darling Brandy; *'Is there a Cartesian Circle?'* by someone called Gary Seven and *'What has Hume shown about our belief in miracles?'* by an Audrey Baxter.

Bob frowned at a list of English essays. 'You haven't got an essay on George Eliot, have you?' he asked me.

Bob's methodology for writing essays was straightforward: he simply cut up other people's essays and stuck them together again in a random way. Of course, we're all plagiarists and forgers of one kind or another, if only in our minds, and Bob's cut-up technique, although occasionally resulting in gibberish, generally passed muster with the somewhat dazed and confused members of staff.

Bob had a list of 'Senior Honours Essays, Session 1971–72' in his hand and read aloud in his monotone, '*Whenever Hume is aware of himself in any degree, he is aware of a perception, and when he is not aware of any perceptions he has no conception of himself. Discuss.*' He poked his ear in bewilderment. 'I mean what's that all about when it's at home?'

'It's life, Bob,' I said, 'but not as you know it.' He picked up Kant's *Impossibility of an Ontological Proof* and showed the cover to us as if it was something we might never have seen before.

'It's a book,' Andrea told Bob.

'I know,' Bob said, shaking his head wearily. '*Is the self just a bundle of perceptions?*' he read mournfully from a Philosophy past paper. '*If so, does anything hold the bundle together? Discuss.*' Bob ruminated on his Marmite. 'Who are you supposed to discuss it with? Yourself?'

'Yes.'

'You are going to travel a long way,' Andrea said to him indifferently, turning over a fan of Tarot cards, 'meet with much failure and die a horrible death.'

'Yeah, yeah,' Bob said.

Shug turned up with Robin. 'Where've you been?' Andrea said.

221

'Out and about,' Shug said carelessly, 'things to do, people to see.'

Andrea wanted to go and see a matinée of *Les Parapluies de Cherbourg* (which Bob had slept the whole way through), while Shug wanted to go to the film society to see *W. R. – Mysteries of the Organism*. Robin skinned up a joint and started reading aloud from the *Dandy*. Would I spend the rest of my life with these people?

James believes that Middlemarch *lacks an overall unity, that it is a mere string of disparate incidents which lack any true dramatic purpose . . .*

The doorbell rang and Andrea let Terri in. She was in an unusual state of agitation. 'I've seen him,' she said breathlessly to me.

'Seen who?' I asked.

'The dog, the yellow dog. He was following that weird girl, the medic that lives at Balniddrie.'

'Miranda,' Robin said.

'Robin,' Terri said, noticing him for the first time. She sat down next to him on the sofa and did something strange with her face. It took me a while to work out that she was trying to smile at him. He shrank away from her in fear. 'How are you, Robin?' Terri asked.

He stared at her like a panicked rabbit and stuttered, 'What do you want?'

'Well,' she said cajolingly, 'are you thinking of going home soon?'

'Yeah, why?' he said, shrinking even further away. 'You want to come home with me?'

'Yeah.'

222

'She just wants a lift,' I explained to him because he looked as if he was going to throw up or pass out.

'A trip to the country?' Shug said. 'That would be cool.'

'Listen to this,' Bob said, reading aloud, '*Symbolize the following argument in the symbolism of Compound-Proposition Logic, and show it valid by any means (construction of a formal derivation, complete truth table, or indirect truth-table method): If I exist, I exist as a sentient being; if I exist and don't know it, I don't exist as a sentient being. Now if I know I exist, I'm certain of that fact and I can prove it; but, although I can prove I exist, I still feel doubtful about it. So I don't exist. ("E", "S", "K", "C", "P")*'

Luckily, at that moment, Bob's brain exploded.

~ Plot development? Nora murmurs quietly, almost to herself.

'Is not necessary in this post-modern day and age,' I tell her firmly.

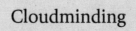

Cloudminding

'CAPTAIN'S LOG: STARDATE 5818.4,' BOB ANNOUNCED AS WE clambered awkwardly into the transport for our trip to the country.

Our chauffeur, Robin, had recently acquired new 'wheels'. Unfortunately, the wheels were attached not to his skinny body but to an old hearse. The hearse didn't appear to have been decommissioned in any way, I noticed – it still retained its bier, for example, thus making it rather difficult for people travelling in the back unless, like Bob, they were eager to lie horizontally and rehearse being a corpse. Terri settled for riding shotgun up front with Robin and brooding darkly for the entire journey. Now that she'd achieved her goal of a lift out to Balniddrie she had no intention of treating Robin like a human being.

As I squeezed myself reluctantly into the wreath-space at one side of Bob's prone carcass I suddenly thought of Senga, cabined in her coffin in the Catholic church and now, presumably, locked away for ever underground. Andrea and Shug crammed themselves in opposite me so that we might have been at an Irish wake, but with no drink and a corpse that occasionally said to itself things like, 'Can you repair the ship's engines in time, Mr Scott?'

Driving a hearse didn't worry him, Robin explained (although nobody had asked him to), because being a Buddhist he was phlegmatic about death, 'Because I know I'll come back.'

'What as?' Terri asked. 'A protozoa?'

'I think you'll find,' Robin said, 'that protozoa is a plural form, it would have to be protozo*on*.' Perhaps Robin was on such a tedious karmic journey that he would just come back as himself. I'm sure it was no coincidence that his name was almost an anagram of 'boring'.

'Reincarnation,' Shug said hoarsely. 'What goes around, comes around, eh?' He lit up a joint that immediately filled the all-too-small space with a fug of acrid smoke. If we crashed how would the circumstances of my death ever be explained to my mother? (Or, rather, the woman who has masqueraded as my mother for the last twenty-one years.) Perhaps it would be some comfort that I had eliminated the middle-man and saved her the undertaker's fees.

'If you can say what it is, then that is not it,' Robin said sententiously and apropos of nothing as far as I could see. Terri twirled her moth-eaten parasol menacingly in his direction.

'Things equal to the same thing are equal to each other,' a gnomic Bob contributed.

'Pythagoras?' Robin puzzled.

'James T. Kirk.'

Robin manoeuvred the hearse away from the kerb and

Bob shouted happily, 'Warp speed, Mr Sulu.' What a simple creature he was. If only my needs were as lacking in emotional complexity as Bob's.

'Eastern stuff,' Robin said bobbishly, 'it's like so much more in touch with what's really real. Stripped of materialism and intellectual bullshit. Look at the haiku.' Robin thumped the steering-wheel of the hearse enthusiastically. 'Compare that to the moribund structures of English poetry.'

'What's a haiku?' Andrea asked.

'It's a three-line poem of five, seven and five syllables,' Robin said, 'so simple, so essential. The plural of haiku is haikai,' Robin said, warming to his subject, 'or at least that refers to a related series of haiku. The haiku was originally—'

'The enormous dog stuck in a beautiful vase of white peonies,' Bob said.

'What?' Robin gave Bob a worried look in the rear-view mirror of the hearse.

Bob lifted his shaggy head off the veneer and metal of the bier and declared, in a ponderously poetic way:

'The enormous dog
stuck in a beautiful vase
of white peonies –

'That's a haiku. I'm a poet,' he laughed, 'and I know it.'

Bob himself had once tried to become a Buddhist – the sound of one hand clapping kept him occupied for days – but had given up in the end because he couldn't see the

229

point of it. Of course, much of Bob's behaviour had a curiously Zen quality to it and if you viewed some of the things he said as koans rather than nonsensical rubbish he might have almost seemed wise. Almost. Take slugs, for instance, a genus of the animal kingdom particularly despised by Bob's father, a keen vegetable grower. Wouldn't it be less hassle, Bob Junior suggested, on a home visit during which Bob Senior was setting out endless beer traps for his pesty foe, wouldn't it be less hassle if they simply bypassed the vegetables and ate the slugs?

'And meditation,' Bob said, staring at the ceiling of the hearse, 'that ought to be easy, it's just thinking about nothing, isn't it? But when you try to think about nothing . . .' Bob lapsed into a mystified silence, aided by the Curly-Wurly he'd just found in his greatcoat pocket.

We were accelerating along the Perth Road at a speed much faster than is normally associated with exequies and therefore causing considerable consternation amongst our fellow motorists, especially when we overtook them. A sedate Wolseley sedan containing an elderly couple mounted the pavement in distress and a rogue nun along Riverside crossed herself in horror. To make matters worse, we were in convoy with another of Balniddrie's inhabitants, a fey former Harrovian called Gilbert who was driving an old ambulance – so it seemed as though we were hurrying to the aftermath of some dreadful disaster, rather than going for a simple trip to the country – although Bob, for some reason, seemed to be under the impression that we were on a starfleet expedition to collect the element zienite.

'God,' he said, once the Curly-Wurly allowed him to speak again, 'do Buddhists believe in God? And what is God anyway? I mean, who's to say I'm not God?'

'There are standing stones at Balniddrie, you know,' Andrea said, ignoring this metaphysical prattle. 'They're supposed to be seven sisters who were dancing on top of this hill and were turned to stone by an angry wizard.'

'Why was he angry?' Shug asked.

'Oh, they always are,' she said glumly.

Considering they lived at Balniddrie, Robin and Gilbert seemed woefully lacking in any understanding of how to get there so that we crossed and re-crossed our own path several times, even finding ourselves at one point driving through the flatlands of the Carse of Gowrie (or the boundaries of the Romulan Neutral zone, depending on who you were). The occupants of the hearse were no help with navigation as it appeared that none of us had a sense of direction. Bob had once famously caught the circular bus and been trapped on it for hours and I, of course, have been lost all my life.

'Wow,' Bob said, peering like a curious cadaver through the window of the hearse, 'cows.'

Andrea frowned at him and said to me, 'He doesn't get out much, does he?'

Robin executed a death-defying U-turn at the Errol turn-off. Not long after that it began to hail, huge moth-balls of ice clattering against the windscreen. The hailstones began to accumulate, obscuring the view of the road because the windscreen wipers of the hearse had long since given up the ghost, as it were.

The purpose of two lengths of hitherto mysterious string was now revealed by Robin. One of the pieces of string came in through the driver's window of the hearse, the other through the passenger window. Robin tugged at his piece of string and one of the windscreen wipers jerked towards him.

'See?' Robin said hopefully to Terri. 'Your turn now.' Her reply was succinct and negative.

Robin eventually gave the hearse its head and it nosed patiently through the hinterland of the Carse and along the long straight avenues of trees that are the back roads of Angus.

'Wow, sheep,' Bob said.

Finally, the hearse made a left turn at a sign that said 'Wester Balniddrie', and progressed up a rough road to a boxy old farmhouse that was harled and painted a darker shade of sky, which is to say grey.

'Prepare to beam down, Dr McCoy,' Bob said, 'and investigate new life forms.'

We drove past a front lawn that looked as if it had once been a neat tapestry of box hedges and clipped yew but was now a wilderness of nettles and rusted objects. Robin parked the hearse in a cobbled yard at the back of the house where a range of dilapidated farm buildings were huddled together trying to shelter from the weather. When we were disinterred from the confines of the hearse and its lingering afterscent of embalming fluid and chrysanthemums, I discovered that it was even colder

232

than it had been in town. A frost had already begun to ice over the cobbles of the yard.

Bob had fallen asleep in the time it took to park and had to be winkled out of the back door of the hearse like a sleepy winter bear out of its cave.

'Magic Bob – how'ya doing?' Gilbert said when he caught sight of him. Gilbert was the scion of an ancient aristocratic family that had fallen somewhat into disrepute. His mother had obtained a scandalous divorce from his father which Gilbert always maintained was on account of bestiality although what I *think* he meant was that his father had been beastly to his mother. With his etiolated body and rather inbred eyes he gave the appearance of being slightly defective but he had lovely manners and was rather sweet, not to mention rich. If he hadn't borne such a close resemblance to a beansprout I would have been happy to leave Bob for him.

'Hey,' Bob said to Gilbert, and the two of them wandered off together.

Shug had already disappeared, Andrea trailing on his heels like a lovesick dog. Trying to avoid Robin, I followed Terri into the house, through a disintegrating weatherboarded porch and down a freezing stone-flagged passage which was littered with boots and wellingtons, bits of bicycles, the top half of a skeleton suspended on a stand (a relic of earlier medics who had once lived here), most of the engine from a small car, the stuffed and mounted head of a stag and a jumble of demijohns and carboys – some empty, some fermenting with risky things found in hedgerows. A rack of old Irn-Bru bottles,

233

home-corked and labelled 'Elderflower champagne', pointed at us in a threatening way like a broadside of light artillery. An accident waiting to happen, in my opinion.

The passage led to the kitchen, a vast room that must have once been full of warmth and farm-cooking but was now glacially cold and dominated by a huge Aga that Miranda, the current medic (a vocation that seemed to be driven more by the availability of drugs than any desire to heal the sick), was tending listlessly, like someone in a fairy story put under a spell of drudgery.

'The dog you were with this afternoon,' Terri said without preamble to her, 'where is he now?'

Miranda, who looked as though she was mainlining intravenous Valium, said, 'What dog?'

'The dog that was following you.'

'There was a dog following me?' Miranda said. 'Why?' Terri's interrogation of Miranda petered out eventually but not until she had completely exhausted every possibility on the Miranda/yellow dog axis: ('Maybe he's on your bed and you just haven't noticed?' 'Maybe you've hidden him in your wardrobe because you don't want anyone to see him?' and so on). If Miranda had had more energy – she looked as asthenic as a vampire's victim – I think she would have punched Terri.

She reluctantly offered us something to drink and Terri chose coffee which turned out to be made of oats or barley, or maybe beans, and she gagged impolitely on it. I didn't fare much better with the tea Miranda had stewing on the hob of the Aga; the tea leaves were like iron filings

234

and the milk in it was rank with the taste of goat.

Gilbert reappeared, *sans* Bob, but accompanied by Kevin who had materialized out of nowhere. I was surprised to see Kevin who, despite being born and bred in the countryside, was immune to its pastoral charms ('Green, green, green – what's the point?'). He was wearing a short brown anorak that looked as if it was left over from his trainspotting days.

Miranda had grown bored with her task now and abandoned the Aga to Gilbert's ministrations. She shrugged on a white coat and said, 'Obs and Gynie,' by way of explanation.

'Don't forget you're killing the goat tonight,' Gilbert reminded her in his terrifically posh accent as she went out the door.

'Why does it have to be me?' she asked sullenly.

'Because,' Gilbert said reasonably, 'you're the doctor.'

The occupants of Balniddrie took turns in cooking (although Miranda was generally excused as there was a paranoid house rumour that she was overly interested in toxicology), and today was Gilbert's day apparently.

'At home the servants do all the cooking,' he said, 'so this is terrific fun.' He opened one of the doors of the Aga to reveal a loaf of heavy dark bread proving lopsidedly. He took out a large pottery bowl and removed the rather dirty tea-towel that was covering it. 'Yoghurt,' he announced as if he was introducing it to us. The yoghurt smelt even more goatish than the milk and had separated into gelatinous curds and a thin wershy whey.

'Do you think that's what it's supposed to be like?' he

asked Terri, who almost fell off her chair in surprise as no-one had ever previously thought to ask her a question about cooking (or indeed about anything). Rather gratified, she did her best. 'Try jam,' she said.

'What a *fantastic* idea,' Gilbert said, retrieving a jar of jam from a damp and mouldering pantry that I never wanted to see the insides of. The jam was elderberry and had retained a lot of the little twiggy stalks. It also contrived, strangely for jam, to be sour. He stirred it enthusiastically into the yoghurt.

'I've got more yoghurt somewhere,' he said, yanking open another of the Aga's doors and finding, to his surprise, a pile of (we must hope) clean nappies.

'They're airing,' Kara said, appearing in the doorway, her body sagging with the weight of Proteus on her hip.

'Well, I didn't think they were cooking,' he murmured, but not so that she could hear. Gilbert's childhood nanny had inculcated a dreadful fear of women into him, a fear that Harrow had refined into an art.

Kara sat down at the kitchen table and started breast-feeding Proteus, currently encased in a grubby Babygro. She was followed into the kitchen by another of Balniddrie's residents, a woman called—

~ For heaven's sake, Nora objects grumpily, not another character. There are far too many already, and all these minor ones, what's the point? You introduce them, give them a trace of character and then abandon them.

'Who? Who have I done that to?' I can see she's having to rack her brain to come up with one but finally she says,

~ Davina.

236

'Who?'

~ In the creative writing class. I bet she doesn't appear again.

'How much?'

~ A pound.

'Anyway, life's full of minor characters – milkmen, newsagents, taxi drivers. Can I go on?'

~ And what about the boy with no name?

'No,' I correct her, 'it's The Boy With No Name.'

~ Whatever, I don't even see the point of introducing him – someone who doesn't even exist any more. You would be as best not giving any of them names, they last for such a short time.

'Be quiet.'

—a woman called *Jill*, who had a three-year-old daughter called by a Gaelic name that no-one was ever quite sure how to pronounce once they had seen it written down. Jill sat down next to Kara who had stopped breastfeeding in order to start rolling an enormous loose joint of home-grown grass.

'You don't have a George Eliot essay by any chance?' I asked Jill. She gave me a rather disparaging look and took out a tin of Golden Virginia, which she opened to reveal a layer of tiny neat joints packed in like sardines. 'I'm a Law student actually,' she said, prising one of the tiny joints out of the tin.

Gilbert had set about – with much banging and clattering of pans – to cook some kind of meal. This might have been lunch, it might have been dinner, I couldn't really say – it was so very dark outside that it was impossible to tell what time of day it was and I had lost all track of time by now.

Kara inhaled on her joint as if her life depended on it. Every so often a seed exploded like a tiny pistol-shot and sent a glowing red spark skittering across the table or onto an inflammable piece of child's clothing (which is also how accidents happen). Jill and Kara exchanged their joints. They had embarked on a heated discussion about the age at which you should stop breastfeeding. Jill favoured two years old while Kara thought you 'should let them decide for themselves'. A decision she might live to regret when Proteus was a thirty-year-old civil servant commuting daily from Tring.

At that moment a small child lunged into the room and gave a bloodcurdling scream. I jumped up in alarm – the cry was so ghastly that for a moment I thought it must be on fire and was searching for something to throw over it. No-one else in the kitchen seemed moved by the noise, all except for Terri who stuck a surreptitious foot out and tripped the child up. It ceased the noise abruptly and I recognized it as Jill's daughter.

'If you're hungry you'll have to wait,' Jill said to her. The child unearthed a plastic potty from under the table and threw it across the kitchen.

'Don't forget we've got to kill the goat,' Gilbert said, casting a doubtful look over a wrecked Kara. In the hierarchy of Balniddrie – although pecking-order might be a more accurate term – Kara was the unacknowledged leader. The goat to be killed, it transpired, was a little billy-kid because, Jill explained, 'Billy-kids are no use for anything.'

'I didn't know we got executed if we weren't of any use,'

Terri said. 'I didn't realize *usefulness* was the criterion by which we lived or died.' (Quite a long sentence for Terri.)

'We're not talking about people, we're talking about *goats*,' Kara said.

'Goats, people – what's the difference?' Terri said, looking as if she was about to stab Kara with her parasol.

'It'll be a humane killing,' Jill said in an attempt to mollify Terri. 'Miranda's going to do it, she's the—'

~ Excuse me, Nora says, but where is Kevin? Have you forgotten he's in the kitchen?

Kevin, who had been remarkably silent until now (unlike Nora), was helping Gilbert to peel potatoes and carrots in a slow, ham-fisted way. He popped the top of a can of McEwan's and said, 'That's what animals are *for*, they exist so we can eat them. In the great kitchens of the Palace of Calysveron there's always an animal roasting on a spit – hares and rabbits, capons, a fine hart, a wild boar, a great ox for the feasts.'

'That would be a real place, would it?' Jill scoffed. 'The Palace of Callyshite?'

'Calysveron,' Kevin corrected her. 'Real as anything else.'

'Real as this table?' Jill quizzed. Kevin scrutinized the table as if he was thinking of buying it and finally said, 'Yes, as real as this table.' This dialogue would have gone on longer and grown more tedious (although the premise was interesting) if the child hadn't set off round the kitchen again, at the same hectic pace as before and yet again screaming for dear life. This time it made a beeline for the Aga and was saved at the last minute from immolating itself by a modified rugby tackle from Gilbert. Perhaps they could substitute the girl for the goat in whatever Satanic ritual they were planning for later. A kid for a kid.

Before the Murk got any Murkier, and before we had to face whatever nightmarish repast Gilbert was preparing to serve to us, Terri and I decided to take a tour of the outside. Terri was still holding onto a lingering hope that the dog might be somewhere about. We visited the garden but there was little to see; the combination of endless winter and poor husbandry meant that nothing was growing in it apart from a large crop of dandelions, the few valiant remains of Jerusalem artichoke stems and some poisonous water hemlock that had colonized the burn at the bottom of the garden.

The chickens were free to roam this winter garden, although the sensible ones had gone to roost by now. Kara had said that some kind of fowl pest had been laying claim to the hens and the few stragglers that remained in the gloaming certainly looked rather lacklustre, their feathers dishevelled and their eyes dull. Terri cluck-clucked and chick-chick-chicked at them but they were indifferent to conversation.

Adjacent to the garden was a bumpy field full of some kind of mutant thistle that hadn't died down in the winter cold. This was where the goats lived when they weren't shut up for the night in a pig-pen. They were Anglo-Nubians, with floppy rabbit ears and devil-eyes – two nannies and two kids, a big one and a little one, this latter presumably the subject of tonight's sacrifice.

'Poor baby,' Terri said, attempting to kiss it.

Although a little downcast, the goats were quite friendly, certainly friendlier than the chickens, and so we spent some time petting and commiserating until a genuine kind of darkness fell and it grew too cold to be standing around in a field so we made our way back to the kitchen from which was emanating an unappetizing aroma.

Jill was setting the table, trying to make a space amongst the candles and candle-making equipment that were strewn everywhere.

'That's my *pièce de résistance*,' Gilbert said, pointing proudly to a particularly ugly candle – a pyramid of brown studded with lumps of mauve wax. 'We could light some of these candles,' he suggested to Kara; 'that would be nice.'

'They're to sell,' she snapped, 'and besides, we've got electricity, for heaven's sake.'

Robin emerged from 'the wine cellar', which was actually another pig-pen, carrying several bottles of home-made wine – rose-hip, elderberry and a rather lethal-looking parsnip.

'I'll just uncork the reds,' he said, 'so that they can breathe for a moment.' I had a sudden rather unnerving glimpse of the polite schoolboy lurking within the hairy chrysalis – of Robin helping out at parental cocktail parties, handing round salted nuts and topping up the tonic in large, middle-class gins.

'Yeah,' Robin admitted, shamefaced, 'Surrey. Dad owns a firm of estate agents.'

'Lucky you.'

Andrea and Shug had reappeared by now, their pupils dilated from either drugs or a bout of sexual activity or – more likely – both. Bob also turned up, although where he had been was less clear – another transporter malfunction, I suppose.

'I am not a number,' he whispered defiantly to me, casting about warily for a giant bubble that had apparently been chasing him.

Several people I'd never seen before made an appearance for the meal, all of them Balniddrians, presumably.

'Balniddrians,' Kevin said, writing the word down in a tiny little notebook. 'Good name.'

The meal was a strange primeval slop of semi-identifiable ingredients – brown rice, potatoes, carrots, something that might or might not have been a vegetable, all of it vaguely goat-smelling even though not a morsel of goat was in it, according to a vow on his mother's life that Terri made Gilbert swear on his knees.

'What did you do with that pan of wax that was on the stove?' Jill asked Gilbert, who pretended not to hear.

Proteus was 'asleep somewhere' according to a rather vague Kara but Jill's unpronounceable child was up long past her bedtime and had to be force-fed her rice-carrot-wax sludge before falling asleep with her head on the table, by which time she had acquired an almost feverish complexion.

'You should try Heinz toddler jars,' Bob said earnestly to Jill, who said, equally earnestly, 'Never.'

'Babies should eat what we eat,' Kara said.

'I think we should eat what babies eat,' Bob said.

'I think we should just eat babies,' Terri murmured, a remark which, luckily for her, went unheard.

Before long Bob found himself unwittingly taking part in the 'what age should you stop breastfeeding' argument, even at one point arguing vehemently against feeding on demand because it would lead to a generation of layabouts and slackers.

'Watch it, Bob,' Shug said, laying a reasonable hand on his arm, 'you're turning into a Klingon.' Perhaps there was another Bob inside Bob – a conventional person who would grow up to be a teacher and vote Liberal and worry about his pension. A Bob who would one day rip off the rubbery facemask of the false Bob and take his place in the world of alarm clocks, Burton suits and lunchtime bank queues.

'Is there a pudding?' Kevin asked, trying to ignore the whole unpalatable topic of conversation of infant nutrition.

'Absolutely,' Gilbert said. 'In fact here's one I made earlier, ha, ha.' He produced a plate of brownies which turned out to be surprisingly good.

'They're lovely,' I said to him.

'Oh, thank you,' he said, clasping my hand. 'It's so nice of you to say that.'

Miranda reappeared, more lethargic than ever but not so comatose that she couldn't eat Andrea's share of brownies.

'Well?' Kara said to her, and she made a face and took a long thin box out of her pocket and opened it to reveal a shiny surgical-steel scalpel.

'Whoa – phasers on stun, Mr Spock,' Bob said in alarm.

'I don't think Captain Kirk would say "Whoa"!' Shug said.

'It's not logical, Captain,' Bob agreed. (Bob, you will have noticed, tended to cast himself in his mind as the entire crew of the *Enterprise* rather than any one particular member.)

I don't know why, but I had presumed that we would be going home after we had eaten. No such luck, it seemed, as everyone was now extraordinarily mellow and laid back, especially for people so intent on goat-slaughtering.

'That woman's phoned again, this morning,' Bob said to me suddenly, 'while you were at the . . .'

'University?'

'Yeah.'

'And?' I asked him patiently.

'And . . . she said she was going to come round tonight. To see you.'

'And you've just thought to tell me now?'

'There's a bus,' Robin said indifferently. 'The road's just over the hill.'

No-one, it seemed, was coming with me. Robin had begun a game of Go with Kevin – possibly the most boring board game ever devised – and Terri was intent on staying to save the condemned goat by kidnapping it (naturally) although I couldn't imagine what she planned to do with a billy-goat in her fourth-floor Cleghorn Street flat. Andrea uncharacteristically offered to show me the way to the bus-stop but only, as I discovered to my cost, so she could talk endlessly about Shug.

Our route, apparently, took us past the standing stones which were 'Over there somewhere,' Andrea said, pointing vaguely into the darkness and tramping off before I could question her orienteering skills.

We tripped over brambles, fell into burns, slid on the thickly frosted grass and bumped into badly parked cows before finally encountering a steep hill that we had to haul each other up like funicular trains until we were sweating and freezing at the same time, all the time the air full of Andrea's Shug catechism – *Do you think he likes me? Do you think he really likes me? Do you think he loves me? Do you think he really loves me?* And so on.

By the time we reached the seven sisters, Balniddrie was no more than a couple of pinpricks of light in the distance. For a moment, I thought I heard a strange pagan chant of 'Kill the goat! Kill the goat!' followed by a scream but Andrea said I'd imagined it and I hoped she was right.

Careless of any bad-tempered wizardry that might be lurking, Andrea began dancing around the stones in an abandoned one-woman eightsome reel. 'Sky magic,' she said breathlessly.

The standing stones, although only four of them were still actually standing, were about the same height as Andrea, roughly hewn and pointed like the teeth of a gigantic cat. Andrea flung her arms around an upright one in a dramatic fashion and, hugging it, said, 'Feel the earth magic.' I gave the nearest stone a tentative embrace but experienced no thaumaturgy – the stone felt like a stone, clammy and napped with lichen. What was I doing cavorting with boulders in the middle of nowhere? I should have a pair of warm arms embracing me instead of the cold clasp of a megalith.

'Are you sure this is the way to the bus-stop?' I asked her, but before she could answer I noticed something astonishing. I was developing astronomical skin! The back of my hand was like a *réseau*, a perfect grid of lace waiting to be mapped by stars. Andrea was searching on the ground for agates and still wittering on about the mystical properties of rocks, but I was hypnotized by my hand – even as I watched it the skin was expanding and magnifying into a huge stretch of parchment. My pores were like tiny, distant stars and the lines on the surface of the skin were the ghostly paths of the heavenly bodies. My cosmic self was about to have a glimpse of immanence.

'Wow,' I whispered (I couldn't help myself). 'This is amazing, Andrea.'

'You ate the brownies, didn't you?' she said, rather wearily.

I don't know how much time passed while I was con-templating my celestial body but when I tore myself away there was no sign of Andrea. I called her name, but received no answer, only an echo ringing in the gelid air. I looked behind the stones, I looked *at* the stones – perhaps they really were accursed maidens. They gave no indication, however, of harbouring lapidified girls. I touched one cautiously but did not go so far as to whisper 'Andrea?' in its mossy ear.

The power must have gone off because there were no comforting lights from the farms and cottages spread around the hillside, no visible topography of any kind. It was so quiet I could have heard a mouse rustling through the stiff grass, or an owl's wing swooping, but no mouse rustled and no owl swooped.

Then the silence rumbled into unwelcome life with the sound of heavy breathing – a slack snorting that belonged to something teratoid and beastly. From behind the crest of the hill steam clouds of ogreish breath bellowed into the cold air and a phosphorescence rose like a nightmarish sunrise, fringing the stone sisters with an unearthly arc light. I didn't wait to find out the source of this strange incandescence but took off, stumbling down the hill as fast as I could.

The stertorous breathing, like a labouring steam engine, was following me, but I didn't look behind. It was accompanied now by a dreadful reek of foul-smelling stinkhorn and hard-boiled egg sandwiches. I tripped over a root and fell into something cold and plashy which I hoped was nothing worse than a burn, although I could feel oozing icy mud. For a second I thought I caught a glimpse of something gleaming in the dark – a flash of silver and bronze, something fishy and scaly and then in an instant it had gone and everything was quiet.

~ So is that magic realism? Nora asks.

'No, it's fiction.'

Or more like a kind of madness. When I got my breath back I noticed a bus shelter further up the road and hurried towards it. There was a timetable stuck up inside but it was too dark to make out the tiny print. I sat on the narrow, plank-like bench and waited, although the idea that a bus might come along any time soon seemed highly unlikely somehow.

A light appeared in the distance, less alien and monstrous than before but nonetheless bobbing across the darkened landscape like a will-o'-the-wisp. As the light got closer it started to resolve itself into not, as I'd hoped, a bus, but a car. The car slowed to a halt beside the bus-stop and the driver leant over and opened the passenger door.

'You've missed the bus,' a familiar voice said. 'Get in.'

I got into the car and slammed the door. 'You *are* following me, aren't you?'

'In your dreams,' Chick said.

Until very recently, time had been a slow slurry of nothingness for me; now the days were suddenly packed to overflowing, a turn of events that I found surprisingly unwelcome.

'A dragon?' Chick queried mildly, as if I'd said something as unremarkable as 'a door' or 'a Dandie Dinmont'.

* * *

To pass the time as we travelled the road and the miles to Dundee, Chick gave me a brief and reluctant rundown of his curriculum vitae: 'Tulliallan Police College, three years as a village policeman in teuchter land because the cow had a hankering for it, the birth of the bairns, the move back to Dundee when the cow got bored of teuchter land, joined the CID, Lanzarote, blah, blah, blah, the rest is history.'

'Blah, blah, blah?'

Chick took a half-bottle of Bell's from his pocket, took a large swig and then handed it to me. The whisky tasted sour and made me gag, but I kept it down.

'Good girl,' he said. We were silent for a long while and then Chick said reflectively, 'I was a good policeman, you know.'

'I believe you. Did you work on any famous cases?' I asked him, thinking about *The Hand of Fate*, wondering if Chick could be some help with police procedure, modes of detection, and so on.

He gave me a sideways look and after a while said, 'I worked on the Glenkittrie case. Ever hear of that?'

'No.'

'Famous in its day,' he said, draining the dregs of the whisky.

'Tell me about it.'

'Some other time,' he said and peered into the empty bottle as if he was trying to conjure up more whisky.

When I cast a glance at Nora I see she has grown pale as any corpse during the course of this innocuous tale.

249

~ You've got a party to go to, she reminds me, very like someone who is trying to change the subject.

I had completely forgotten about the McCue party and certainly had no intention of going.

I must have fallen asleep.

'You fell asleep,' Chick said when I woke up. I had been sitting uncomfortably with my head resting against the door of the car. I was numb with cold and the whisky had left a bad chemical taste in my mouth. Chick was reading the *Evening Telegraph* by the light of a torch. He lit a cigarette from the stub of the one in his mouth.

There was a familiar look to the street we were parked in but it took me a few sleepy seconds before I registered that we were in Windsor Place, parked right outside the McCue house.

The McCues were *en fête* – from where I was sitting I could see into the brightly lit living-room. I could just make out the faint vibrating *thum-thum* of rock music. Several people who looked as if they had last danced around the time of the Suez crisis were capering to the music – but in a constrained way, shuffling their feet and occasionally doing something daring with their elbows. Grant Watson was one of them, turning pink with exertion as he pushed his limbs around out of time to the music. I decided I would be in more jeopardy inside the McCue house than I had been in the hands (or whatever) of a rampant dragon.

The party looked dire, although I'm not sure that there

250

is such a thing as a good party. Perhaps there is a perfect form of merriment somewhere but what its constituents are I do not know and cannot imagine.

~ Fireworks, Nora says dreamily, and Chinese lanterns strung in trees and the moon reflected in the water.

I could see Philippa trying to encourage the Dean to dance. She was bouncing around in a tent-like dress, patterned in psychedelic swirls of purple and brown. The Dean was trying to pretend he was somewhere else – the Caird Hall perhaps, listening to the SNO in concert, or, preferably, lying in his bed fast asleep next to the flanneletted body of his wife, a large matronly woman called Gerda, currently in rayon and being propositioned by a swaying Archie.

A different tableau-vivant could be observed in the adjacent window, which looked into the dining-room. I could see Professor Cousins daintily sipping sherry while talking to Martha Sewell, who was wearing sober black. In the background I could just make out Dr Dick having a furious fight with Maggie Mackenzie.

'Why are we here?' I asked Chick.

He shrugged. 'Who knows.'

'No, I mean, why are we *here*?'

'Why not?' How annoying Chick was. How strangely Bobbish. When I informed him that I was supposed to be at the McCue party he tried to shoo me out of the car and into the house (to see if anything fishy was occurring, naturally). I steadfastly refused, even though I could see that there was much material for narrative there – the drunken *faux pas*, the misaligned relationships, the forbidden sex, even plot advancement – but none of that was enough to tempt me inside.

A woman appeared at the dining-room window, a glass of red wine in her hand. She gazed into the street, an abstracted expression on her face. For a moment I couldn't place her because she was so out of context and then I suddenly recognized her – it was the Hillman Imp woman, the woman we had been watching in Fife.

'It's the Hillman Imp woman,' I hissed at Chick and he said, 'I know,' from behind his *Evening Telegraph*.

'What's she doing here?' I said to him. 'I don't understand.'

I watched her move away from the window. The next moment she reappeared in the neighbouring room and walked up to Watson Grant. He paused in his inept dancing and lurched drunkenly towards her, pulled her into his arms and started kissing her neck – an unattractive activity that she endured with rather a long-suffering expression on her face.

'So she *is* having an affair,' I said, 'there's your proof. She's having an affair with Grant Watson. You should photograph them or something.'

'Nah,' Chick said, dragging hard on an Embassy, 'that's his wife.'

Chez Bob

UNBELIEVABLY, IT WAS ONLY EIGHT O'CLOCK WHEN I got home. I ate Cornish Wafers and Philadelphia cream cheese; I watched the news, although I turned it off when it showed trees being napalmed. I read *Me and Miss Mandible* and listened to *After the Gold Rush*; I washed out a pair of tights and sewed on a button. I ate more Cornish Wafers, but I had run out of Philadelphia. I wrote a half-hearted sentence of Henry James (*James's implication is not only that the novel is episodic and fragmented but also that it is a vehicle for far too much analytic and philosophical intrusion on the part of the author herself –*) until finally I went to bed only to be woken a couple of hours later by Shug and Bob rolling in with a couple of traffic cones and a clutch of warm rolls from Cuthbert's all-night bakery. Of my mysterious promised visitor there had been no sign at all.

~ Have you guessed who she is yet? I ask Nora, who is chewing on a Jacob's cream cracker from a packet she's found in a tin at the back of a cupboard. I can smell its staleness. Nora has coiled her hair up in a careless heap and I can see fiery little

255

tendrils curling at her neck. Today our hair is very red on account of the rain that is threatening us. For we live in a raincloud. Nora says she can feel the rheumaticky weather in her bones. She says she is a human barometer.

'Do you recognize her?'

~ Do you think that's a weevil? she asks, staring at the cream cracker.

Bob and Shug started playing a relentless, noisy game of Diplomacy until, overcome by an attack of the munchies, they went out into the darkness on a quest for Mars Bars. The clock by the bed said six o'clock. I wondered if it was morning or night. It didn't make any difference, I was wide awake anyway. There seemed to be nothing for it but to write.

Madame Astarti took an early lunch, ambling out to buy fish and chips from a little place down a side street called 'The Catch Of The Day'. It was off the tourist track and much frequented by the locals. It was a comfortable, old-fashioned kind of place with tiled pictures of fish and a back room with a coal fire. It took a minute or two for Madame Astarti to notice that it was no longer the chip shop it had been, but was now called 'The Codfather' and had been fitted out in stainless steel and pale blue plastic.

'One of each, please, Sharon,' she said, 'and perhaps an extra portion of chips,' she added as an afterthought.

'Scraps?' Sharon offered.

'Oh yes, scraps,' Madame Astarti agreed.

'Mushy peas?'

'Go on then,' Madame Astarti said.

'Pickled onion?'

'All right.' Madame Astarti drew the line at a pickled egg. You had to draw the line somewhere, after all.

The fish supper came on a cardboard tray with a plastic fork. 'What happened here?' Madame Astarti asked.

'Modern times,' Sharon said, 'that's what happened.' Shades of Lou Rigatoni, if Madame Astarti wasn't mistaken. Clearly, he was a man who wasn't going to be satisfied until he bought up everything on the coast.

Madame Astarti ate her fish and chips out of the tray, sitting on a bench on the pier, watched, from a discreet distance, by a yellow dog. She could see part of the harbour festooned with blue-and-white crime-scene tape like bunting, but there were few onlookers as there was no longer anything to see. The tide was now out as far as it could go and the exposed beach littered with bodies in various stages of pinkness, like boiled shrimp. They looked dead, although Madame Astarti presumed they weren't.

Over by the donkeys she spotted Councillor Vic Leggat deep in conversation with one of Lou Rigatoni's henchmen. What were they up to? she

wondered. No good, probably. She tossed the
yellow dog a chip.

'Captain's log supplemental,' Bob announced, rolling in
around dawn, 'subject has entered *pon farr*, the Vulcan
mating cycle. You are the lovely T'Pring – fancy a shag?'
An offer which I rebuffed rather swiftly and Bob was soon
sleeping the deep sleep of the innocent fool.

Madame Astarti waddled back along the pier.
My, my, she thought to herself (but who else do
you think to?), that was some sea-fret that was
rolling in. A great white wall of fog was moving inland, beyond it everything dark and
obscure and yet in front of it the sun shone
gloriously on the beach and the holidaymakers.
Some of them had noticed the sea-fret by now and
had jumped up in alarm. It looked like something
out of a horror film, a malevolent presence
swallowing everything before it. The fog horn
started booming, a deep, thrilling vibration
that Madame Astarti could feel resonate in her
bones. They called it haar in Scotland, didn't
they? It was a funny word. She had been up there
once with a Jock. A Jock called Jock. Haar Haar.

'Wet fish!' Bob shouted in his sleep and began to laugh
uncontrollably until I smothered him with a pillow.

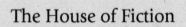

The House of Fiction

NO WOMAN IS AN ISLAND, EXCEPT FOR MY MOTHER. HER LEGS ARE growing into the rock, her head is surrounded by clouds, her skin is covered in barnacles and her breath holds the weather in it. Or perhaps that's just my imagination.

She is wearing ugly black wellingtons that she has found in a cupboard somewhere. The wellingtons are too big for her but she doesn't care. She has her face turned up towards the white fogged sky, she is smelling the weather, like an animal.

Fog is rolling in from the sea, wave after wave of whiteness. A sea-fret. I watch it coming. We walk like blind women along the fog-bound cliff-top path.

~ A fine haar, Nora says, as if it was something to admire. But it is obscuring the sound of her voice. She's dissolving in the white fog, melting into it.

~ I was thinking about the day you were born and how I killed –

Her voice dwindles, taken by the fog. It presses against my face like a cold, wet shroud. When I look again I can't tell what is Nora and what is haar. A strange keening noise rises above the muffled cushion of white.

~ Whales, Nora says, lost at sea.

'Do whales get lost at sea? What a strange idea.'

~ We get lost on land. Why shouldn't they get lost at sea?

I try and catch up with her. 'So,' I shout to her through the brumy air, 'everyone in your family died and then you were born?'

~ More or less, she says, a distant, disembodied voice.

'Go on.' I want to hear her voice as much as I want to hear her story. I don't know where the edge of the cliff is, don't know where I am. I am afraid of the fog, it's like something out of a horror story. Her voice is the thread that keeps me safe.

~ Well, Nora says thoughtfully, this is how it was:

Marjorie was a big raw-boned, red-haired woman from a Perthshire military family whose ancestors had fought everywhere, from the wrong side at Culloden to the right side at Corunna. She married Donald Stuart-Murray when she was thirty-five; no-one else wanted her and she couldn't think of anything else to do even though Donald's first wife was still warm in her coffin and his catalogue of personal disasters was long.

The Princess of Wales herself had been at Donald's first wedding to Evangeline, held in London way back in the previous century, but only a duke could be mustered the second time round for the rather less flamboyant nuptials at St Giles' in Edinburgh. Marjorie wore Evangeline's diamonds but, like the new bride, they failed to sparkle under a miserable Edinburgh sky.

Donald set about replacing his lost children, first with a girl, Deirdre, who went to be Honoria's playmate almost straight away, then a boy, Lachlan, followed swiftly by Effie and then, finally, fourteen long years later, the afterthought that was Eleanora—

'You mean you? I think you should tell this in the first person.'

~ Why?

262

'To make it more real.'

~ I would prefer it if it was less real.

Silence.

'That's *it*?' I call into the fog but receive no answer.

When I finally get back to the house Nora is boiling up a mish-mash of something unpalatable in an old cloth.

~ Clootie dumpling, she says. Carry on, do.

Philippa was in the kitchen, stirring a vast vat of soup, a hotchpotch made from anything she'd been able to find, not all of it necessarily edible.

'Everything but the kitchen sink,' she laughed. The soup was thin and rancid-looking and smelt of rotten cabbage leaves, and something living seemed to be swimming around in it.

'Taste?' Philippa offered, holding up a ladle.

Philippa was wearing a pair of Archie's trousers and a fisherman's smock in a thick brown moleskin material, and had tied an Indian silk scarf, Apache-style, around her hair. She trawled for something in the pocket of her smock and netted a new and very sleepy McFluffy. After trying in vain to rouse it, she stuffed it back in her pocket. Somewhere in the depths of the house I could hear the sound of energetic hoovering.

I was sitting at one end of the McCues' huge pine kitchen table sipping reluctantly at a cup of acrid coffee that Philippa had forced on me. Goneril, looking cross-eyed in the morning light, was slumped on an essay entitled, *'How can I tell whether what seems to be a memory of mine is in fact a genuine one?'* She was washing herself indolently, every now and then dislodging little feathery dandelion tufts of feline fur that floated through the air. I watched one of them land delicately in the soup.

'I think she's got some kind of mange,' Philippa said, chucking the cat under the chin.

The salmon, a little the worse for wear – indeed, only half of it now remained – occupied the centre of the table. It had been poached for the party and in an effort to restore it to life its silver-lamé skin had been replaced with cucumber slices and its dead eye with a stuffed olive. It wasn't fully dressed; many of its cucumber scales had fallen off, revealing pink flesh underneath. Here and there a few flakes of skin still lingered like the scurf of stars. A row of cooked shrimp had been placed along its back, perhaps as a garnish, perhaps as a misguided attempt to recreate its spinal cord.

'You didn't come to our party,' Philippa chided, throwing a huge handful of salt in the soup.

'Sorry. I had to write an essay.'

It was cold in the Windsor Place kitchen, that horrible damp cold that makes you feel suddenly melancholy. All the windows were misted up from the soup-making and from the rack of wet laundry that was hanging over the radiator. I cast a cursory glance over the clothes, wondering if any of them belonged to Ferdinand, some intimate garment perhaps that had touched his skin, but all I caught a glimpse of was a pair of Archie's huge, slightly grey Y-fronts and quickly looked away. No wonder all the

McCues always smelt faintly of cooking. Except for Ferdinand, of course.

'So, how's Ferdinand?' I asked Philippa, trying to sound off-hand.

'Oh, you know Ferdinand?' Philippa said. 'How nice.'

The sound of the vacuuming grew more insistent until finally Mrs McCue hoovered herself into the room on the end of a Goblin cylinder. She was followed by Mrs Macbeth, who had slung a net bag from her walking-frame to act as a container for cleaning materials – a tin of Mansion House polish, a box of Flash, a large bottle of Parozone, a pink bottle of Windolene – things that had probably never seen the inside of the McCue house before. Bringing up the rear, Duke shouldered his way into the kitchen. I almost expected to see a feather duster in his mouth.

Mrs McCue hoovered noisily over the vinyl, picking up anything in her path – egg-shells and cabbage stalks, broken pencils, assorted grit, bushels of cat fur, the odd Brussels sprout. Finally, to my relief, she switched the machine off and said, 'That's enough for now.'

Sensing the need for an explanation, Philippa said, 'Good old Ma's doing some cleaning for me. And her friend, too, of course,' she added.

'Just making ourselves useful,' Mrs McCue said.

'That bathroom,' Mrs Macbeth said *sotto voce* to me, shaking her head in disbelief. She waved the bottle of Parozone like a Molotov cocktail.

'They let you out again then?' I asked.

'They don't keep them under lock and key,' Philippa said irritably, 'it's not a *prison*. And anyway, they're always out. They're never *in*.'

Mrs McCue muttered something under her breath as she sat down next to me. Goneril opened one evil eye and assessed her fearlessly.

'Lunch,' Philippa said. I made a move to escape; I couldn't think of anything worse than eating Philippa's soup, but Mrs McCue laid a heavy hand on my arm and said, 'It *is* nice to see you.'

Philippa slopped soup into bowls and slung a large sliced Sunblest onto the table with a thud that made Goneril flinch but not move.

'Unhygienic,' Mrs McCue hissed, giving the cat a surreptitious pinch. Goneril ground her body further into the essay, as if digging in for the duration. Maisie flung herself into the kitchen, reporting that she was starving, and tore into the Sunblest's plastic wrapper and started stuffing soft doughy pieces of bread into her mouth. She was accompanied by a hollow-eyed, adenoidal girl – Lucy Lake, Roger and Sheila's eldest offspring, who was in Maisie's class at Park Place Primary. They both had the same neglected air about them with their unbrushed hair and unkempt uniforms. Mrs Macbeth couldn't resist the urge to spit on a handkerchief and give Lucy Lake a quick rub.

'We can have some of this salmon as well,' Philippa said, dishing out plates and cutlery; 'it needs eating up.'

Mrs McCue eyed the salmon doubtfully. The stuffed

olive eye of the fish returned her gaze with a certain inscrutability.

'Food poisoning,' Mrs McCue whispered when Philippa turned her attention back to the soup pot. 'It may as well have "salmonella" stamped on its forehead.'

'Such a bonny word that,' Mrs Macbeth said. 'It would make a lovely name for a girl. Salmonella.'

'Is that where the word comes from, from salmon?' Maisie asked the room in general, and Philippa said, 'No, it's the name of the man who discovered it.'

'Mr Salmon?' Maisie said sceptically.

'*Do* fish have foreheads?' Mrs Macbeth puzzled.

'Well, they have fingers,' Lucy Lake smirked.

'Really?' Mrs Macbeth said, looking worried.

Maisie picked the small naked body of a shrimp off the salmon and scrutinized it. 'What do shrimp eat?' she asked speculatively. 'Do you think they eat drowned people?'

'We'll make a philosopher of you yet,' Philippa said brightly.

Maisie braved a shrimp, biting it in half delicately, and reported it 'pure bowfing'. Mrs McCue said she couldn't imagine what shrimp looked like swimming around in the sea and Lucy Lake said, 'Like insects, probably.' Philippa clapped her hands and said, 'Stop it, before this goes any further,' because everyone had begun to look rather sick.

Philippa took the new McFluffy from her smock pocket and looked at it quizzically. It did seem rather limp and lifeless. She gave it a little shake and it woke up with a start. Maisie took it from her mother and placed it on her shoulder and crooked her head so that it could nestle into her neck.

'That looks very uncomfortable,' Mrs Macbeth said.

'It is,' Maisie said, eating her soup awkwardly.

~ I think you drink soup, Nora says. (But then she has had a correct upbringing, whereas I have been dragged up anyhow.)

We all chose a different adverb to sup with. Philippa consumed her soup hungrily, Mrs Macbeth decided on messily, Mrs McCue on recklessly, whereas I myself opted for cautiously. Lucy Lake opted for not at all.

'What's this?' Mrs Macbeth asked, poking at the manuscript on the table.

'I'm writing a novel,' Philippa said.

'Why?' Mrs Macbeth asked.

'Why not? It's a doctor/nurse romance, I'm going to send it to Mills & Boon. Archie thinks I'm prostituting my art, of course,' Philippa said cheerfully (a common cry, it seemed), 'but as far as I'm concerned that's a specious argument based on the premise that all art is didactic in origin. Don't you think?' she said, turning to Mrs Macbeth.

'Hmm,' Mrs Macbeth said, shuffling through the manuscript. As a diversion from answering unanswerable questions she began to read out loud: '*Flick's cornflower blue eyes sparkled with devilment. Jake McCrindle may think he was better than she was because he was a high-flying house doctor and she was a mere first-year student nurse but she would soon show him—*'

'Flick?' Mrs Macbeth queried. 'Flick? Are you sure?'

'Isn't Flick the name of a horse?' Lucy Lake asked.

'No, that's Flicka,' I told her. '*My Friend Flicka.*'

'You have a friend called Flicka?' Philippa asked, interested.

'A-hem [or something like that],' Mrs Macbeth said, *'Flick had been on the men's surgical ward only two days and already had clashed twice with the arrogant Dr McCrindle who seemed to think he was God's gift both to St Vernon's and to the nurses who worked there.'*

'Was there a St Vernon?' asked Mrs McCue, who was contriving to knit and eat soup at the same time.

'Perhaps you're thinking of the football pools,' Mrs Macbeth offered.

'It doesn't matter,' Philippa said dismissively, 'it's fiction.'

'"So, Dr McCrindle," Flick said, only too aware of the effect she was having on him. "What is your diagnosis?" He smiled wolfishly at her—'

'I don't think wolves *can* actually smile,' Maisie interrupted, but just then Mrs Macbeth began to splutter and cough, and started to turn as pink as the salmon. Her eyes began to water and her mouth formed a surprised oval as she fought for breath. Philippa barked out, 'Heimlich!' and grabbed her from behind and yanked at her tiny body until Mrs Macbeth spat out a wad of words – *smouldering, aching, throbbing* – along with a large fish bone.

'That was close,' Mrs Macbeth said hoarsely, sinking back into her seat – as if a brush with death was part of her daily routine. She examined the fish bone. 'A fish bone,' she said, shaking her head in a mystified way. 'Where did that come from?'

'A fish?' Lucy Lake (a sarcastic child) offered. The salmon was saying nothing. Mrs McCue gave Mrs Macbeth a cigarette to aid her recovery and lit one herself. 'I'm saving for a Philips toaster,' she said, 'that's a lot of cigarettes to smoke.'

A door closed and I heard water running upstairs. I wondered if this signalled the presence of Ferdinand somewhere in the house. I made my excuses and tip-toed up the litter-laden stairs. Sadly, the bathroom was empty of Ferdinand, although it did contain an unusual smell of male cleanliness – toothpaste, shaving foam and Lifebuoy soap – as if someone more used to regular institutional habits than the rest of the McCues had just vacated it. Beneath the smells of personal hygiene I could detect faint traces of Ferdinand's own animal scent and if I listened closely I could almost hear the fading echo of his heartbeat.

The bathroom was a paean to sixties' taste, from the sickly primrose yellow suite with transparent acrylic taps to the herringbone pine panelling which extended even to the ceiling where recessed lights glimmered darkly. There were mats of soapy hair in the plugholes and a deposit of slimy grey in the tub and another one of crusty brown in the toilet bowl, and an anaemic spider plant struggled for life on the windowsill, its leaves weighed down by a coating of talcum powder. The assorted reading matter of the different McCues was piled randomly on top of the cistern – *Rubber Monthly*, the *Beano*, and back issues of the *Philosophical Quarterly*.

Of Ferdinand himself, however, there was no sign. I looked in the upstairs rooms, hoped for his sleeping form in the spare bedroom where I had first encountered it, but could find nothing, only Mrs Macbeth's old dog, Janet, asleep on the bed. She was snoring noisily, her breath rumbling loosely in her chest, but woke up when I sat on the bed and pushed her dry black nose into my hand. ('Aye, she's a wee bittie wabbit,' Mrs Macbeth said mysteriously.)

I heard voices in the hall and peering over the banisters caught a glimpse of Ferdinand. Awake, he seemed more feral, with a hungry look about him as if he could happily eat raw meat and snap the spines of small animals if necessary. Unfortunately, he was just leaving the house, kissing Mrs McCue on the cheek and saying, 'Bye, Gran.'

~ Where do you suppose he's going? Nora asks.

'I don't know.' Who knows where characters go when they're not needed? Into some kind of limbo, I suppose. Like death or dreaming. Perhaps he was with the yellow dog which had slipped off the page with such ease.

~ Where could they be? Nora asks, keen on this idea. St Andrews, on the beach? That would be nice.

'What, like – "The yellow dog ran ahead of the man who was walking along the empty stretch of beach, his collar up against the biting wind, his hands thrust deep in the pockets of his leather jacket" – that kind of thing?'

~ Better weather.

' "The yellow dog frolicked in the waves ahead of a man strolling along the beach. His naked feet revelled in the warmth

271

of the sand and the seawater, his face soaking up the summer sun." How about that?'

~ You could give it some plot, Nora says. God knows you need some. Something could *happen*.

'Like?'

~ A plane could fall out of the sky, a woman could walk out of the water, a bomb could go off.

'I'm not writing that kind of book.'

~ You could.

'Right, I'm off,' Philippa said, digging her bicycle out from the midden of junk which occupied the McCues' hall. 'I've got a second-year tutorial on the existence of God. Who's coming down the road with me, maybe to the bus station?' She looked hopefully at Mrs McCue and Mrs Macbeth.

'Nae me,' Mrs McCue said, switching on the vacuum cleaner to prevent any further discussion.

'I'll just give the kitchen a wee going round,' Mrs Macbeth said, reaching for the Ajax.

'Careful what you read,' I advised her, retreating down the hallway as Mrs McCue tried to hoover me up.

Philippa scooted slowly down the Perth Road, one foot on her bike pedal and one on the pavement, while Maisie, Lucy Lake and I trotted smartly to keep up with her.

A swarm of people were buzzing around outside the

Tower, most of them looking rather aimless. Someone had made a placard which they were waving aloft like a centurion and on which was written END AMERICAN IMPERIALISM NOW! although it seemed unlikely that this was something within the remit of the university senate.

We paused for the parting of our ways opposite this scene, outside the undertakers.

'If only they'd bring the same enthusiasm to philosophical logic,' Philippa said, bending down absently to allow Maisie to plant a goodbye kiss on her cheek. 'They're late,' Philippa said fondly as we watched Maisie and Lucy Lake meander along Park Place back to school.

At the back of the Tower, where there was usually a constant ebb and flow of students, a logjam of bodies had built up. Some students were trying to get into the building so they could attend tutorials and lectures, while other students were intent on preventing them. I could see Heather wielding a placard which read SAY NO TO FASCISM!

A burly rugby player, with whom Andrea had once spent a hectic night, shouldered his way through the narrow passage that linked the Students' Union to the Tower and amid much scuffling and cries of 'Scab!' managed to gain access to the building and, like Moses parting the Red Sea, held open a passage for others.

'Well, goodbye,' Philippa said, giving me an encouraging pat on the back that nearly knocked me over. She mounted the bike and wobbled precariously for several yards before attaining a kind of equilibrium along Small's Wynd and disappearing.

I hurried along the Red Sea passage before the waters closed over it again.

'Thanks,' I said hastily to the rugby player, just as Heather jumped on his back with a kind of Sioux warrior scream and started biting his ear.

'The only way a woman can gain the respect or even the attention of the male protagonist is when she proves herself to be possessed of an absolute, childlike innocence . . .' Maggie Mackenzie was striding up and down at the front of the lecture theatre like a restless zoo animal, her hair already living a life of its own. '. . . a regression which, as in the case of Clarissa, for example, takes the extreme form of death . . .'

'What's she talking about?' Andrea whispered to me. I shrugged incomprehension. I'd been under the misapprehension that Maggie Mackenzie was going to be lecturing on *Middlemarch*, otherwise I would never have come.

'I thought she was going to be talking about *Middlemarch*,' Andrea hissed.

'Maybe she *is* talking about it and we just can't tell.'

Andrea was looking very prim in a Laura Ashley fantasy milkmaid ensemble that Marie Antoinette would have coveted. You couldn't tell that she had been thrashing around in paroxysms of lust just a few hours previously. ('Again?' an amazed Bob said as we tried to sleep between our purple passion-free sheets.)

'How is death a regression?' Kevin whispered in my other ear. 'I don't understand.' I was the meat in a Kevin and Andrea sandwich in the back row of the lecture theatre, where assorted loafers usually slept out the hour.

'I don't know.'

I reached in my pocket for a tissue. I definitely had a cold coming on, if not worse, but instead of a tissue I again found a crumpled-up piece of paper, which after some puzzling I recognized as yet another stray page of *The Expanding Prism of J*. How were they getting there? Was someone putting them in my pocket? Or maybe they were sticky, like flypaper.

J, I noticed, was still as paranoid as ever and seemed to have become entangled with some kind of angry mythical beast (a common enough occurrence, it was beginning to seem) – Snorting, snorting, and dire snuffling of something ponderous and male, the beast of his imagination made manifest in muscle and sinew and arching frame, scaled like the sinful snake, the bloodlust of ages in the great thrust of the –

I supposed the angry mythical beast was an allegory or a metaphor but who knows – perhaps it was real, in as much as fiction is real, which it must be because it exists, unless something can exist without being real. And even if it only exists in the form of words, words themselves must exist or we wouldn't be able to use them and Wittgenstein himself—

'Miss Andrews?' Maggie Mackenzie was climbing up and down the stairs looking for bad behaviour. 'I don't think you can afford to daydream, do you?'

Terri sidled into the lecture theatre. She was dressed in black fingerless gloves and a disintegrating taffeta cape and looked as if she'd been recently exhumed. From the look on her face I guessed she had not saved the goat last night. She was abruptly directed by Maggie Mackenzie to sit on the front row, 'So I can make sure you stay awake,' obviously unaware that Terri could sleep with her eyes open. Olivia, a natural front-row student, lent Terri pen and paper (which was never used) before returning to her assiduous note-taking.

'Roland Barthes,' Maggie Mackenzie, 'says—'

'Not him again,' Andrea sighed. A faint cry of distress went up from the heart of the student body, indicating the presence of Proteus. Kara was sitting on the far side of the lecture theatre, well away from the source of the cry. She was dressed in a rainbow-striped jumper that looked as if it had been crocheted for a gorilla by a gorilla.

'—claims that the classical narrative is based on the male Oedipal drama . . .'

Andrea leant across me and asked, 'Is that what Edrakonia's based on, Kevin?' presumably out of mischief rather than genuine curiosity.

Kevin rolled his eyes like a cow in an abattoir and said, 'Don't be stupid,' quite loudly, so that some people turned to stare, including Maggie Mackenzie, who tapped an impatient foot and said, in the words of teachers everywhere, 'Do you have something you would like to share with us, Mr Riley?' and then carried on without waiting for an answer –

'As Althusser says, we are all "inside" ideology . . .'

'What's she *talking* about?' Andrea muttered.

'I don't know. I don't know anything. Stop asking me questions.' I could feel the beginnings of a headache.

Janice Rand was sitting in front of us with her balding Christian friend. I had to suppress the desire to flick things at them. They occasionally passed notes to each other on tightly folded little pieces of paper.

'Freud . . . believing that women were less powerful because they know themselves to be castrated . . .'

'Come again?' Andrea said, looking alarmed.

'. . . and also possessed of a less developed superego.'

Janice and her friend were passing notes furiously to each other. I managed to read one that said. 'What's a superego?' Written down, it looked very odd, like a sauce for spaghetti or a musical tempo mark – *spiritoso*, *sforzando*, *superego*. My headache was growing worse. I wished I had an Anadin (a rather poetic cry of pain). I was too tired to concentrate.

'Of course,' Kevin said, to no-one in particular, 'research has shown that ten minutes is the absolute limit of anyone's concentration span, so the last twenty-five minutes have been pointless.'

'Mr Riley? Something to contribute?' Maggie Mackenzie said harshly. Kevin slid down in his seat and tried to look as if he was deaf and dumb.

'The passive heroine in the phallic-centred myth . . .'

I inadvertently started daydreaming about Ferdinand. I made a mental list of what I knew about him – he was kind to old ladies, he slept like the dead, he might have blue eyes (I still hadn't caught a glimpse of them), he was a convicted criminal. I was having trouble forming a whole character from these bits and pieces.

Andrea was doodling strange magic symbols on her

jotter – fylfots, Ing runes, caducei and so on. Perhaps it was homework her Forfar wizard had set her. Janice caught sight of the swastika-like fylfot and was so startled by it that she could remain mute no more and started chattering eagerly to her Christian friend about Andrea being 'a Nazi'.

Kevin, surreptitiously eating a banana, turned to me and, nodding in Maggie's direction, mumbled, 'Is she actually going to talk about George Eliot, do you think?'

An exasperated Maggie Mackenzie threw the blackboard eraser in the general direction of the back of the lecture theatre. It caught Janice a glancing blow on the temple and she screamed in an outraged martyr way.

'No, I don't think she is.'

Janice's scream set off Proteus, who embarked on a desperate kind of wailing as if he was about to fall over the edge of the world (well, who knows what babies think) and Kara had to make her way along a row of people like an annoying late theatregoer – 'Sorry, excuse me, sorry' – until she reached her infant. 'Nappy,' she announced to everyone.

'I think I'm going to faint,' Andrea murmured.

The lecture theatre disgorged its students. Kevin came trotting purposefully after Andrea and, tagging her by her milking sleeve, said breathlessly, 'I ought to clear something up, the dragons don't have psychological complexes, Oedipal or Electrical or any of that stupid stuff. The dragons are all female, you see.'

'How do they breed, then?'

Kara wandered out of the lecture theatre. She smelt earthy as if she'd just been dug up. Her long lank hair was corralled in a headscarf and she was wearing black wellingtons and a cotton dirndl skirt and had a streak of mud – or worse – on her cheek. She had the musty, un-appetizing scent of chicken feed and camomile flowers on her.

'Don't forget your baby,' I reminded her, although you wouldn't think you could, would you? Nor should you.

Terri caught up with me and said she was going to go and find Chick and ask him what he'd done with the yellow dog. She was followed out of the lecture theatre by Olivia, warily side-stepping Kevin with whom Andrea was still wrestling over the illogic of Edrakonia. 'But if the dragons are immortal and Griddlebart isn't, why don't they just wait until he dies and then take over again?'

'That's ridiculous.'

'Why?'

'Because,' Kevin said loudly as if Andrea was deaf, 'it's a matter of honour, not simple expediency. Honour amongst dragons is—'

'Do you want a coffee?' Olivia said to me. She was wearing a high-necked velvet dress that had little velvet-covered buttons that ran from throat to hem so that if you'd wanted to split her open you would have had a handy score mark to follow. She looked pale and other-worldly, like someone who usually lived in a ballad and was expecting to be accidentally locked in a kist on her wedding-day or abandon her goosefeather mattresses and run away with a band of gypsies—

'Effie?'

'Yeah, right, coffee—' but we'd failed to notice the bulky advance of Maggie Mackenzie until it was too late. Terri said, 'Got to see a man about a dog,' and disappeared with commendable alacrity.

'George Eliot?' Maggie barked at me like a sergeant-major.

'Nearly finished,' I lied.

'Don't lie, Miss Andrews. Where is it?' I gestured vaguely towards the world outside the walls of the English department, indicating that my George Eliot might have been working away in the library or playing table football in the Union.

'Come with me,' she said peremptorily and turned on her heel and raced off towards the lift so that I had to run to keep up with her.

'Later,' I gasped to Olivia. In the lift itself there was barely enough room for the two of us and I tried to shrink myself into a corner to avoid having to breathe in Maggie Mackenzie's inky scent.

I followed her into her room, where she paraded up and down her crowded bookshelves, swiftly pulling out books here and there and handing them to me, a *Casebook* series on *Middlemarch*, a *Literature in Perspective* on George Eliot. 'These are not difficult books,' she said, 'they won't task your brain *too* much.' She made a visible effort to be encouraging. 'You have to try, you're wasting your life.'

'No, I'm not,' I said without any conviction.

'You haven't produced a single piece of work all term,' she said harshly. Maggie Mackenzie was one of those

280

people who believe that there's nothing in the world that can't be done with the application of a little effort. (I suppose she was right.) I glanced down and noticed that the hem of my recycled-sari skirt was loose and torn, some of the little mirrors on it hanging by a thread. I was so clearly a girl who was never going to get her homework in on time.

'You hardly ever show your face in tutorials,' she continued. 'It's all very well enjoying yourself now, but in twenty years' time—'

A ragged and uncoordinated chant had started up outside:

'*What do we want?*'

'*Peace!*'

'*When do we want it?*'

'*Now!*'

'It's beginning,' Maggie said with some satisfaction.

'What is?'

'The end.'

~ Not yet, surely? Nora says. Nothing's *happened* yet.

'Well, I must get this essay finished,' I said, making a surreptitious move to leave the room, and Maggie Mackenzie startled me by suddenly shouting, 'For God's sake, pull yourself together, girl – before it's too late! What do you think's going to happen to you?'

I expected I was going to grow old and die, or, if I was unlucky, just die, but I didn't say that to her because it wasn't what she wanted to hear and instead I mumbled something inarticulate and she grabbed the nearest missile she could lay her hands on – a copy of *Cranford*, although I don't think the choice of book was significant – and threw it across the room at me. Her aim was, as usual, poor, the throw executed more in exasperation than aggression, and *Cranford* hit the back wall of her room, dislodging a rather frightening Frida Kahlo print. If it had been Philippa McCue throwing she would have hit me smack between the eyes and then caught the rebound off Frida.

'I want that essay on my desk at ten o'clock on Friday,' Maggie Mackenzie said sharply, 'or else. You'll thank me for this later, you know.'

I doubted that I would, but I kept quiet as there was no point in antagonizing her further, and at least she seemed to be giving some thought to my future which was more than anyone else was, including myself.

As I hurried away I heard an odd lowing sound coming from Martha Sewell's room. I paused to listen and detected more animal noises, followed by some distressed sobbing. I hesitated outside her door, and then knocked.

It was opened by Jay Sewell. Behind him I could see Martha sitting at her desk. She was wearing a grey poncho that seemed to have been made out of felted squirrel fur and was holding her hand to her forehead in an attitude of despairing grief.

'We lost Buddy,' Jay explained.

'I'm sorry,' I said politely. Buddy had been sick a couple of days ago and now he was dead. It seemed a rather sudden demise. I still didn't understand who Buddy was, of course.

'We have no children of our own,' Jay said, tears welling up in his eyes, 'and Buddy was like a son to us.' I didn't really want to be this intimate with the Sewells and the sight of a distraught Martha, not hitherto prone to any emotion at all, was unnerving. Jay had somehow manoeuvred me into the room by now and at the sight of me Martha started sobbing even more. I put out a reluctant hand and patted her on the shoulder and said solicitously, 'I'm sorry for your loss.'

She stood up suddenly, knocking me to one side, and shrieked at her husband, 'We have to find him, we have to find Buddy.'

'He's not dead, then?' I asked cautiously.

Martha looked at me in horror. 'What makes you say that?'

'What does Buddy look like?' I said hastily. 'Maybe I've seen him.'

'He's very handsome,' Jay said.

'And he has beautiful blue eyes,' Martha added, calming down a bit and dabbing delicately at her nose with a tissue.

'Well, green, really,' Jay corrected gently.

'Nonsense,' Martha said, 'they aren't green. Perhaps a hint of green,' she conceded. 'Aqua might be a more accurate word. I could compromise on aqua.'

Jay didn't seem willing to compromise. 'Not aqua exactly,' he said frowning, 'cerulean maybe.'

'Cyan,' Martha offered, like a bridge player making a last, rather outrageous, bid.

'Cyan?' Jay said contemplatively. 'How about

glaucous?' Whoever Buddy was, he was going to have crumbled into dust before Jay and Martha managed to decide on the colour of his eyes.

'Let's just say bluey-green, shall we?' I suggested helpfully.

'Greeny-blue,' Jay Sewell said, making a final stand.

Professor Cousins put his head round the door. 'I heard a commotion. Is there anything I can do?' He caught sight of me and smiled and said, 'I would introduce you, but I can't remember your name.' He laughed at Jay. 'I can't even remember my own name, let alone hers.'

'Cousins,' Jay said seriously, 'your name is Cousins.'

'I was joking,' Professor Cousins said, somewhat abashed.

'They've lost Buddy,' I explained. 'He's like a son to them. And he has bluey-green, greeny-blue eyes.'

'And a gorgeous coat,' Martha said.

'A Crombie? I had a Crombie once,' Professor Cousins said nostalgically. 'It *was* gorgeous.'

Martha wasn't listening, she was growing lyrical. 'It was like melted milk chocolate. We almost called him Hershey,' she added sadly.

'Really?' Professor Cousins said politely.

'A little light-hearted fun,' Jay said solemnly.

'You could ask the Salvation Army,' Professor Cousins said. 'I'm told they're very good with missing persons.'

Jay and Martha turned to look at him. 'Buddy's a dog [or dorg],' Jay said carefully.

'A pedigree Weimaraner,' Martha elaborated.

'Weimaraner,' Professor Cousins said, 'as in Weimar Republic?'

'I've got an essay to do,' I said, beating a quiet retreat.

'Keep an eye out for Buddy,' Jay shouted after me and I heard Professor Cousins murmur, 'Oh, what a horrible idea,' as I shut the door behind me.

Detour

I FINALLY MANAGED TO ESCAPE FROM THE ENGLISH DEPART-
ment and into the cold and inadequate daylight of the
real world. I had got as far as The Grosvenor pub on
the Perth Road when I realized that someone was kerb-
crawling me. When I stopped, a familiar rusting shape
drew to a halt alongside me and the passenger door of the
Cortina opened. 'Want to go for a hurl?' Chick asked.

I demurred; the Cortina looked as if it was actually
decomposing now. Chick, too, seemed to have deterior-
ated since I last saw him.

'Go on, get in,' he said in a way that he must have
thought persuasive. Getting in a car once with him was
foolishness, twice might have been from necessity, but to
get into the Cortina a third time was nothing short of
lunacy.

'I'm supposed to be doing an essay on George Eliot,' I
said, climbing into the cold, smelly car.

'Oh yeah, who's he?' Chick asked, pulling away from
the kerb in a nasty grinding of gears.

'*She*'s a woman.'

'Really?' Chick said. 'I knew a woman once called

Sidney, she worked as a stoker on the White Star line, can you believe that?'

A greasy fish supper sat on the dashboard. 'Chip?' Chick offered, holding up something cold and limp. 'Don't mind if I do,' he said to himself when I waved it away. He ate the chips as he drove. 'How's the Prof? Nice guy, that. And the Yank?'

'Terri.'

'That's a man's name,' Chick said.

'She's not a man.'

Chick finished his poke of chips, threw the paper out of the window and wiped his hands on the knees of his trousers. We were covering Dundee in an apparently random fashion on a route that took us along the Hawkhill and up the Hilltown and then back to the Sinderins and the Hawkhill again. This route took us to a newsagent, two different betting shops, a phone-box, an off-licence, a slow, mystifying drive past the Sheriff Court and a short tour of the docks. I noticed Watson Grant coming out of one of the betting shops. 'Look,' I said, giving Chick a dig in the ribs because he was absorbed in reading his *Sporting Life* (although, interestingly, still driving the Cortina), 'there's Grant Watson.'

'Who?'

'Watson Grant, you're working for him, remember? Following his wife?'

'Not any more,' Chick said, 'he couldn't pay his bloody bill. Mr middle-class university lecturer,' Chick said with some disgust, 'he's a bloody compulsive gambler.'

'No?'

'Yep.'

'Maybe that's why his wife's having an affair,' I said, remembering Aileen Grant's rather sorrowful features.

'Bet your bottom dollar she'll leave him,' Chick said, 'then he'll be in a *real* pickle.'

'Why?'

'Insurance policy,' Chick said, 'on his mother-in-law.'

'Mrs Macbeth?'

'You know her?' Chick said suspiciously.

'So, Grant Watson has an insurance policy on Mrs Macbeth?'

'No, his wife has one on her, what's-her-name?'

'Aileen.'

'Aileen, she's got the insurance policy, but it'll walk when she walks.'

'I *think* I see. If Mrs Macbeth died *now*, or indeed if Aileen Grant died now, Watson Grant would get the money. But if Aileen divorces him he won't get any money when Mrs Macbeth dies?'

~ I like this exposition, Nora says, everything being explained in black and white, you should do more of it.

'Yes, but,' Chick said, 'in black and white terms—' but we were interrupted by his dropping his burning cigarette into his lap and narrowly avoiding a lamp-post that was 'in the way'.

Everything Chick did seemed invested with suspicious intent, although much of his behaviour was probably

harmless. He stopped off for a 'pish' in the public con-
veniences in Castle Street. He went to Wallace's for the
classic Dundee take-away – a plain bridie and 'an inginin-
inaa' ('an onion one as well, if you would be so kind'). I
declined one. After driving through the Seagate Bus
Station – to the extreme irritation of a driver trying to
reverse a huge Bluebird bound for Perth – we paused near
the gates of the High School where a torrent of pupils was
emerging from its dark neo-classical portals.

A tall pretty girl separated herself from the mass and
walked towards the car. She had cropped dark hair
and was so very neat and tidy in her public school grey
that I felt I should offer to write out lines, 'First im-
pressions can never be made twice,' and so on. She was
carrying a huge briefcase of homework and wearing the
yellow hoops of a prefect on her blazer sleeve.

Chick rolled down the window as she drew nearer and
I wondered if I shouldn't shout out a warning, especially
when he took out a packet of Polos and offered one to
her. Chick looked exactly like the kind of person who
starred in public information films about not taking
sweets from strangers. The girl took the mint, bent down,
kissed Chick on the cheek and said, 'Thanks, Dad,' gave
him a little wave, and carried on walking.

I was astonished. '*That* was the "mingin' little
bastard"?'

'One of them,' he said gruffly, driving off in a horrible
grinding of gears. He drew level with the girl and said, 'I
suppose you want a lift?'

'No thanks,' she said, 'I'm fine.'

'Just as well,' Chick said, 'because I'm not a bloody taxi service.'

The girl laughed.

'You must have quite weak genes,' I said to Chick.

Our next port of call was a funeral parlour in Stobswell, where we settled into what I now recognized as surveillance mode, that is to say, Chick stubbed out his cigarette, folded his newspaper and closed his eyes.

'Is there anything you want me to keep an eye on?' I asked him, and felt an absent and invisible Professor Cousins give a little shiver of horror.

'Just anything fishy,' Chick said. Within seconds he was snoring.

No-one came or went and nothing fishy occurred, I reported when Chick woke up again.

'Right, we'd better go and have a look, then,' Chick said, heaving himself out of the car.

I followed him into the funeral parlour, where we were greeted by a businesslike undertaker. What a shame Terri wasn't with us, she would have thoroughly enjoyed this kind of visit. Undertaking was probably the perfect profession for her. The bland atmosphere in the funeral parlour would have disappointed her, though – it felt more like the Haze-freshened front office of a plumbers' supplies merchant than a house of death.

'Come to see the deceased,' Chick said to the undertaker.

It turned out that the funeral parlour was affording

temporary shelter to several deceased and Chick was unsure which one he was visiting. 'The one from The Anchorage,' he tried. The undertaker was polite but wary and it was only when Chick flashed his defunct warrant card that we were finally allowed to visit our chosen corpse.

'This had better not be anyone I know,' I warned Chick. I had never seen a dead body, never known anyone who had died—

Nora begins to count the dead on her fingers again, and I tell her to stop. She shrugs. She is drying the wet hanks of her hair in front of a fire made from sappy green wood salvaged from the beach.

We are waiting on a supper of potato soup to reach a semi-edible state and are passing the time by drinking some strange liquor which Nora has been concocting in a home-made still.

'From?' I ask dubiously. The drink looks and smells like the bottom of a stillwater pond.

~ Kelp.

The thin light of the fire is our only illumination tonight. There is no electricity here, of course. It went dead a long time ago. We are conserving our resources for we are down to our last few candles and have only one can of paraffin left. We need supplies but the seas are too heavy for the little *Sea-Adventure*. Nora's seamanship is extraordinary and unexpected – she can row the little boat for miles without tiring, she can navigate by the stars, she knows every eddy and tide and current of these her home waters. All the years we lived by the sea I never once saw her on the water. Where did she learn about boats?

~ From my sister, she says, she was a water-baby.

Beautiful Effie who drowned on the day I was born? How do water-babies drown?

294

~ With some difficulty, Nora says grimly. You're in the funeral parlour, she reminds me, like someone trying to change the subject, you're about to see your first dead body—

Thankfully, the room was not brightly lit. I hovered by the door, suddenly terrified by the idea of looking death in the face. My heart started to thud so loudly I felt it must have been audible even to the corpse. Chick gazed at the contents of the coffin as unperturbed as if he were viewing fish in an aquarium. Had Chick seen a lot of dead bodies?

'I've seen my share,' he said tersely as if there was a quota for each of us. 'Miss Anderson,' he said to me as though introducing me to the body. I advanced cautiously towards the coffin. 'She won't bite,' Chick said. One would very much hope not. Chick took me by the elbow to encourage me to move closer.

The coffin was lined with a kind of white ruff, like a soufflé dish, and the corpse of an old woman that nestled inside the ruff was, thankfully, unknown to me. The skin on the old woman's face was like tallow candlewax and her thin lips were pursed in a way that suggested she had died with a complaint on her lips. Miss Anderson, I recalled, was a 'crabbit wee wifie' according to Mrs McCue.

'So do you think someone killed her?' I whispered to Chick.

'Why would I think that?' Chick said.

'Well, why are you here then? And why were you at Senga's funeral?'

'She was my aunt,' Chick said. 'Aunt Senga.'

'Aunt Senga?' Maybe she was, but somehow nothing Chick said ever sounded as if it was true.

I told him that, according to Mrs Macbeth, Miss Anderson had a terrible fear of premature burial and Chick said, 'Is that so?' and took out a penknife from his jacket pocket and without any preamble jabbed Miss Anderson in the back of one of her hard veiny hands. I screamed, but quietly, given the hushed atmosphere of the funeral parlour and the undoubtedly illegal nature of the deed.

'She's definitely dead,' Chick said, as if he'd just done me a favour. But I had already left.

Next we spiralled up the slopes of the Law, the extinct volcano on whose ashy skirts Dundee was built. We parked, like tourists or lovers (and we were definitely neither), got out and walked round in a circle to view the full three-hundred-and-sixty-degree panorama on offer. There was snow on the Sidlaws and the Tay was the colour of polished tin.

'Aye, it's a bonny place,' Chick said, 'from this distance anyway.' He took another half-bottle of Bell's from his pocket – I had a vague, rather queasy recollection of having finished the last one.

'Go on,' Chick said, 'it'll put hairs on your chest. Just like Sidney,' he added and laughed – an odd phlegmy noise that ended in a hacking cough and an unpleasant choking that apparently could only be cured by lighting a cigarette.

'So do you think someone's killing the old people?' I persisted.

'Did I say that?'

'Maybe it's Watson Grant. Maybe he's hoping to kill Mrs Macbeth before Aileen leaves him and he's killing other old people to divert attention from his real victim – Mrs Macbeth.'

'You read too many books.'

It began to snow – cold wet stuff that melted as it fell. 'That's enough of the great outdoors,' Chick said, climbing quickly back in the car.

The snow grew thicker, whirling round in the eddies of wind at the top of the Law so that sitting in the car was like being inside a giant snowshaker. Dundee began to disappear behind a white veil while Chick drank his way steadily down the half-bottle. The odd thing about being with Chick – odd given the severe defects in his character – was that I felt safe with him, as if no harm could befall me in his presence. Maybe that was what it was like to have a father. But how could I know?

I tried to encourage him to tell me more of his own story. This request elicited a barrage of bad feeling, Chick again cursing the cow and the loss adjuster, particularly the loss adjuster's canary-yellow Capri.

~ How do you adjust a loss? Nora asks, ladling out potato soup, viscous with starch.

'Maybe you adjust *to* it,' I suggest.

~ I don't think so.

Nora is distinctly gloomy tonight – perhaps on account of the seaweed *aperitif*.

* * *

297

We set off back into town. 'You've wasted enough of my time,' Chick said. 'I've got other fish to fry, even if you haven't.'

'It's you that's wasting *my* time,' I said. 'I have an essay—'

~ Too much dialogue, Nora sighs. I prefer descriptive writing.

As we drove back along the Nethergate we were accompanied by a great winter sunset painted across the western sky in livid colours – blood-orange and vascular violet – as if somewhere up-river a terrible fiery massacre was taking place. The rays of the dying sun, reflected in the water, made the Tay appear (just for once) to be a river of molten gold. A hard frost was already falling and the smell of snow was in the air.

'Do you prefer that?'

~ Yes.

It must be a huge feat of celestial engineering to get the sun to come up and down every day. Of course, I do know it's not quite as mechanical as that. But I like to think it is. Within seconds the sun slipped out of sight, gone to the antipodes or wherever it goes, and we were left with a darker kind of darkness.

Nora frowns. Now you're just being whimsical.

'That was a braw sunset,' Chick said. 'Fancy a Chinky? We could go to the Gold Lucky.'

'Well . . . OK,' I said.

'Got any money on you?' Chick asked, when we'd finished our meal – including a second order of banana

298

fritters for him – 'I seem to have left my wallet at home.'

The sea in the sound is grey and choppy this morning and as uninviting as old bathwater. Even the playful narratees have deserted it for warmer waters. The wind has blown too much lately, ruffled our minds, decomposed our thoughts. The air holds moisture like a cloth.

We are in the kitchen, sitting by a fire made from damp drift-wood and bits of abandoned bird's nest. We are down to the last dustings at the bottom of the tea caddy. Perhaps we will die of starvation and thirst here.

~ There's plenty of water on the island, Nora says.

There's nothing *but* water, the rain has lashed the little rock for days now, the burns are overflowing, the little waterfalls have grown to cataracts, I expect that soon the sea-level will start to rise. My mother is a murderer. Or murderess. Did I mention that? Apparently we are caught up in some ghastly plot that we cannot escape.

~ There's a storm coming, Nora says, sniffing the air like a dog.

But she's always saying that.

'Your turn,' I tell her, throwing another inadequate log on the fire. 'Go on.'

~ Must I? Nora asks. Can't I go to the toilet or make a cup of tea, answer a ringing phone or commit any other number of tedious distractions?

'No. And we have no phone.' Even the postman doesn't knock here, not even once. 'Tell me about your beautiful sister who died on the day that I was born.'

299

Nora sighs a sigh so profound that it fathoms the bottom of the sound.

~ This is a very far-fetched tale, she warns, which you will find hard to believe. So . . . first there was Deirdre – who died – then Lachlan, then a year later came Effie, conceived in a thunderstorm, born during an earthquake.

'In *Scotland*?'

~ A small one. It happens. Occasionally.

'Very occasionally.'

~ She was born on the winter solstice when there is no light in the world and everything has shrunk back into the earth. Born when the earth sleeps, yet Effie never seemed to rest and had soon worn out a rather fragile Marjorie. To look at Effie you might have thought that she was possessed of a salamander nature, that her elements were air and fire or some insubstantial matter, but in truth she came from some dark underground place. A spiteful sprite, a malevolent kelpie. Only Lachlan could put up with her and that was because he was made from the same flawed clay. They were never more their true selves than when they were together.

The pair of them were wild, undisciplined creatures. Neither Marjorie nor Donald seemed to know what to do with them. Marjorie had never really recovered from having three children in as many years and soon resorted to the comfort of the gin bottle and Donald was, of course, quite old by then and he'd never been particularly interested in his children, so Lachlan and Effie's upbringing was left to a succession of nursemaids and nannies. These were all eventually driven away, there was even a rumour that one nanny had been hospitalized – something to do with flypapers and cocoa – and one of the downstairs maids had certainly

300

been paid off with her arm in a plaster. They were the sort of children who could always be found in the vicinity of an accident. Marjorie called it mischief and downed another gin.

They were sent away to school eventually, Lachlan to Glenalmond to follow in the family tradition, Effie to St Leonard's. Their behaviour improved a little once they were separated but nonetheless it was a wonder they were never expelled. And they still had the holidays to run wild together and torment every living thing.

They roamed the woods and fields like gypsies, sticking pins in caterpillars, cutting worms in half with their pocket penknives, catching fish and smashing them on rocks. There was some incident with the gamekeeper's cat, apparently – it was found hanging from a tree with its tail cut off—

'Are you sure you're not making this up?'

~ Why would I do that?

Their favourite place was the loch. No-one else ever went there any more. It was a gloomy place with its black water and its overhanging willows, surrounded on all sides by overgrown woodland. The man-made channels that had once fed and drained the loch had become clogged over the years so that it always had a rank, stagnant air about it. Occasionally, a long, dark pike-shaped shadow passed through the clouded water like a small enemy submarine.

When he was seven, Lachlan threw his sister into the loch – that was the kind of boy he was. By the time she dragged herself out amongst the half-rotten bulrushes she had learnt to swim. That was the kind of girl *she* was.

'That was when she became a water-baby?'

~ Yes.

301

'Then what?' My mother (who's not my mother) is not very good at this storytelling lark, is she? 'And she was beautiful?' I prompt, which gains a reluctant 'Yes' on Nora's part. 'In what way?'

~ The usual – blue eyes, Titian hair, round limbs, high breasts. Personally I always thought her eyes were too far apart. Made her rather frog-featured. She bit her fingernails down to the quick.

'What about her personality?' Nora shrugs. This is like pulling teeth. 'Incomplete sentences will do, single words if necessary,' I urge. 'Try adjectives, for example. Start with "A" if it helps.'

Nora takes a deep breath—

~ Abhorrent, blameworthy, catty, dreadful, empoverished (spiritually, obsolete usage), fearless (or fearsome), garrotted (should have been), histrionic, indolent, jadish, karmic (bad), left-handed, mean, negligent, oligarchic, psychopathic, quarrelsome, reckless, sly, tyrannical, ugly (inside), vain, xenoglossiac—

'Really?'

~ Might have been. (Quite a) yachtswoman, a zombie. The living dead.

'No redeeming features, then?'

~ No.

'No saving graces at all?'

~ No.

A bad case of sibling rivalry, it seems. But then Effie was four-teen years old when Nora was born and away at school, wasn't she? And how did a gin-sodden Marjorie and an ageing Donald manage to have another baby, even an 'afterthought'?

'Go on, carry on with your unlikely tale.'

~ Effie grew up, eventually. Got married, got divorced (twice), died. End of story.

'You can't do that.'

~ It's the post-modern day and age. I can do what I want.

My mother is not my mother. Her sister is not her sister. Lo, we are as jumbled as a box of biscuits.

Chez Bob

'You're back!' Brian's voice boomed out of the depths of The Crab and Bucket.

'I haven't been anywhere, you daft pillock,' Madame Astarti said, fighting her way past the draped fishing nets and glass floats that made up the interior decor of The Crab and Bucket - or The Crab as it was known affectionately by the locals. It was the kind of pub that holidaymakers went into thinking it looked authentic and interesting (it smelt of raw fish) and hurried out of again without even having put glass to lip. This was not so much on account of the gloomy green underwater lighting or the dead stuffed fish in glass cases around the wall, as the unwelcoming hostility of the natives. If Custer had had The Crab and Bucket's regulars on his side he would have lived to stand another day.

Madame Astarti did not even have to glance in the barman's direction - a melancholic man called Les (or Les Miserables, as the locals called him behind his back) – for him to put out a glass and start filling it with a large measure of gin and a token splash of tonic.

'I,' Brian said cheerfully, 'have been to hell and back.'

'Don't exaggerate, you've been shopping in Scarborough with Sandra,' Madame Astarti said, heaving herself onto a bar stool next to Brian. 'Where is she anyway?'

'On her way,' Brian said, plunging his face as far as he could into his glass and inhaling beer fumes. A little spasm of pain crossed his face and he said, 'Left my ruddy arch supports out.' Madame Astarti commiserated with him. 'Ah, Rita,' Brian said, 'why didn't I marry you instead?'

'Because I wouldn't have you,' Madame Astarti said and gave him a sharp rap on his knuckles with her—

—what? Her fan-shaped wafer-biscuit? Her crystal ball? Oh dear God, this was so tiring. I was developing some kind of fever, one of those hot and cold things. I took two paracetamol and went to bed with Bob's blue teddy-bear hot-water bottle and read *The Indian Uprising*. Then I must have dozed off because the next thing I knew Bob was lying in bed beside me, claiming to have spent the night in The Tavern – a particularly debauched student watering-hole – which was strange because Shug had telephoned from there an hour earlier asking if I knew where Bob was.

'If Alice comes,' Bob said earnestly to me, 'and either

308

Bernard or Charles comes, Dotty will show up. Bernard and Edward will either both come, or both stay away, and Alice will put in an appearance if and only if Charles and Edward are both going to be there. So Dotty won't be there if Alice isn't.'

'Bob, what are you talking about?'

'Don't ask me,' he said, 'given the premises of the above –

a) Could all five people come? Could only four come, and if so which four? Could three, and if so which three? Could two, and if so which two? Could one, and if so which one? Could none of them come?

b) In what circumstance will Alice come?

c) Whose absence will be sufficient to ensure the absence of Bernard?

d) Is it possible for Bernard to come without either Alice or Edward coming?'

I was asleep by then, of course.

Madame Astarti's head was throbbing. She peered into the dregs of her glass suspiciously. She had a hangover already and she hadn't even finished drinking. There was a man once, long ago, who had tried to spike her drink in an effort to sell her into the white slave trade and since then she had felt you should be as alert as possible when getting drunk. Not that it was likely that anyone was after her for the white slave trade any more.

'I've never really understood what that was,' Sandra said. It seemed to Madame Astarti that Sandra's thin red lips mouthed the words a second or two behind the sound and she leant forward to tell Sandra that she was out of synch with herself but lurched and nearly toppled from the stool.

'What is it exactly you don't understand, my darling?' Brian asked Sandra, 'the word "white", the word "slave" or the word "trade"?'

Sandra's neck and cleavage had grown scrawny over the years so that parts of her now resembled a chicken. She crossed one artificially tanned leg over the other and waved a gold strappy-sandalled foot around. 'Coming to see the show this season, Rita?'

'As if I would miss it,' Madame Astarti replied. Brian and Sandra weren't just Brian and Sandra, they were also 'The Great Pandini and his Lovely Assistant, Sabrina' – staple fodder for summer shows and holiday-camp seasons across the land. Every evening, Brian abandoned his British Home Stores pullover and polyester slacks and was transformed into a vampirish figure courtesy of a top-hat and a swirling black cape lined with scarlet satin 'from Remnant Kings at seventy-five pence a metre – that's fifteen shillings a yard to you and me,' Sandra said to Madame Astarti. Sandra herself donned fishnets and black satin and prepared herself for being sawn in half and vanished.

'Dickie Henderson,' Sandra said, 'now there was a great performer.'

'Is he dead?' Brian asked.

'Could be,' Madame Astarti said gloomily. The heat and the noise in The Crab and Bucket were beginning to make her feel quite ill.

'Another one?' Brian asked cheerfully, more to himself than anyone else.

'You've had too much already,' Sandra said. 'I'll have a port and lemon, you'll have a half, no more. Rita?'

'Don't mind if I do.'

'Fag?'

'Go on, then.'

'Did you hear about that woman?' Sandra asked, her face looming in and out of focus, 'the one in the sea. Dreadful thing.'

'Do they know who she is yet?' Brian asked, downing his half and then staring hopefully into the bottom of the glass as if he was expecting it to come back.

'*Was*, Brian, was,' Sandra corrected him. 'She *is* no more. Her name, I believe, was Anne-Marie Devine.'

'Was what?' Madame Astarti said, spilling her drink all over herself.

'Anne-Marie Devine,' Sandra repeated, 'a lady of the night. Rita, are you all right?'

'A lady of the night?' Brian said.

Sandra took another cigarette out of the packet. 'Give us a light,' she said to Brian.

Oh no, Madame Astarti thought, they were beginning to –

'Poor cow,' Brian said. 'I wonder what she looked like?'

'About my height,' Sandra said, 'not very bright.'

'I bet she's a sight.'

'Give you a fright.'

Madame Astarti moaned, the room was beginning to spin, she must get out of this nightmare.

The wind roars, the seas howl. Nora is standing on the headland like the figurehead on the prow of a ship. I think she is trying to conjure up a storm. It is a diversionary tactic – she will do anything rather than finish her tale.

My mother is not my mother. My father is not my father. Nora's father is not her father. Lo we are as jumbled as a box of biscuits.

The World Is Hollow

THE GROUND FLOOR OF THE TOWER WAS IN TURMOIL – A rowdy crowd of people milling about, uncertain as to what they were supposed to be doing. Many of them, naturally, were there simply on the off chance that something exciting might happen.

~ Excitement is very over-rated.

A few of them were heckling Roger Lake, who was in declamatory mode, standing on the stairs that led up to the library. Roger was preaching to an attentive group of militant students, most of them apparatchiks of the Socialist Society. A lot of them were sitting cross-legged on the floor so that Roger looked as if he was taking a primary school assembly. This inner sanctum looked as though they should all be waving little red books and were very vociferous. I was beginning to get a headache again.

I caught sight of Olivia, standing aside from the crowd. She looked oddly disengaged as if she had been hypnotized. Someone waved a placard behind Roger Lake's head that declared firmly INSURRECTION IS AN ART AND LIKE ALL ARTS IT HAS LAWS which I thought had probably been dreamt up by Heather, but Olivia said, 'No, Trotsky, actually.'

'What's going on?' I asked her.

'I think Roger's advocating overthrowing the establishment,' she said, looking rather weary, 'and setting up a "University of the Street" or something in its place.'

'The street? I thought we were protesting about the war? Or is it the government?'

Olivia shrugged indifferently and then – in an exemplary *non sequitur* – said, 'I'm pregnant.' Her skin was like milk.

'I'm sorry.' I hesitated. 'Or congratulations? Whichever.'

'Yeah,' she said ambivalently.

Roger shouted something that seemed to agitate his cohorts and Olivia said, 'I was wondering if I could talk to you?'

'Me?' But at that moment Robin bounded up, wearing red corduroy dungarees and a blue and white striped long-sleeved T-shirt, as if he was about to present *Playschool*. He had pinned a small shield-shaped badge onto one of his dungaree straps. The badge said 'School Prefect'.

'It's an ironic comment on the nature of power,' he said when I asked him if he actually had been a school prefect.

'Catch you later,' Olivia said to me and disappeared into the throng.

'This is real,' Robin exclaimed heatedly; 'this is important stuff.'

'I didn't know Buddhists were into politics,' I said.

316

'Buddhists?'

'You were a Buddhist yesterday,' I pointed out to him.

'Yeah, well maybe I'm a Maoist today. You know nothing,' he added. Which was true.

I spotted Shug and Bob strolling through the mêlée of bodies.

'Anarchy rules,' Shug said laconically. Bob had a brown paper poke in his hand from which he was eating magic mushrooms as if they were lemon drops. He offered one to Robin.

'Your sort doesn't have any kind of commitment to anything, do you?' Robin said, cramming a handful of psilocybin into his mouth. 'You're just lazy hedonists, all you care about is your own little lives.'

'He's been politicized,' I explained to Bob and Shug.

'Wow,' Bob said, 'did it hurt?'

Heather appeared at Robin's side. 'Direct action,' she said, nipples joggling feverishly, 'it's the only way we can make anything change.'

'Too right,' Robin said.

'You're so full of shite,' Shug said, rather concisely, I thought.

'Come the revolution,' Heather spat, 'you and your kind will be first against the wall.' Robespierre, Stalin, Heather – the line of descent was clear. She embarked on a polemical rant about how students were going to run the world and something I didn't quite grasp about the local Timex and Sunblest workers taking over the Faculty of Arts and Social Sciences (which might be a good thing).

'I thought this was about Vietnam? Or the miners?' I puzzled.

Robin sighed at my lack of enlightenment. 'It's about *everything*.'

'Everything? That's a lot of stuff.'

'You sound like your boyfriend,' Robin said petulantly.

Bob gave me a perplexed look.

'That's you,' I explained.

'We're having an *uprising*,' Robin said. 'We don't need frivolous people like you lot.'

'Nor fifth columnists,' Heather added, looking at me menacingly.

None of this was doing my headache any good. Added to which, my limbs had begun to ache and my tonsils felt as if someone had sandpapered them.

Bob and Shug declared they were going to 'hang out' and see what happened, but I fought my way through the flux and spill and out into the corridor, hoping that I wouldn't encounter Maggie Mackenzie.

As if the very thought of her very name had conjured her up, I suddenly heard her strident tones and dodged into the female toilets.

Where I found Terri. She was sitting on the ledge in front of the mirrors in the company of a surprise new dog. Silky-sleek and very elegant, it was clearly a pedigree of some kind and was an infinitely more sophisticated representative of dogdom than the elusive yellow dog Chick had run over. The new dog was sharing a packet of dog chocolate drops with Terri – one for the dog, one for Terri, and so on. The dog took the chocolate

318

drops from Terri's upturned palm like a fastidious horse.

'Meet Hank,' Terri said proudly, as if she'd just given birth. 'I found him,' she said, rubbing the dog's wet nose with her own slightly dryer one. 'Isn't he gorgeous?' The dog regarded me, rather mournfully, with a pair of beautiful sea-green eyes. A horrible thought occurred to me. 'What breed do you call that?' I asked her.

'Jesus, you're ignorant – it's a Weimaraner, of course.'

'I had a feeling it might be.' Somehow I couldn't quite bring myself to spoil her new-found happiness by telling her about Hank's suspect provenance, for who else could this be if not Buddy? Terri had tied a piece of clothes-line around the dog's neck and now stood up and gave it a gentle tug. 'We've got to go,' she said. 'We need to get stuff.'

'Stuff?'

'Yeah – dog stuff.'

'Do you want me to come with you?'

'No, it's OK.' Terri jumped down from the ledge, the dog following her like a shadow, and set off purposefully, an adverb I had never seen her utilize before. She'd even removed her Ray-Bans. Perhaps there was still an all-American girl lurking under that Lamian carapace, a cheerful, resourceful college kid (a babysitting, prom-queen type). One who didn't seem to need me any more.

Could I really be replaced so easily, I wondered as I left the toilets and wandered out into the corridor. And by a dog at that? Perhaps that was the answer to my problem with Bob – I could get him a dog as a substitute for me. And a dog would surely treat him better than I did. It might not cook, but it wouldn't judge.

I was so caught up in this idea – I'd got as far as picturing Bob in the company of a cheerful Border terrier that could do simple household tasks – that I failed to notice Maggie Mackenzie barrelling along through the Murk again and collided with her full on. I was winded but she appeared unmoved.

'Miss Andrews,' she said stiffly, 'I will extend my deadline for you as you are so incompetent. You have until ten o'clock on the day after tomorrow.'

My brain felt so addled that I could barely work out what that meant.

'If your George Eliot essay doesn't appear at the allotted time I shall have to inform the Dean that you are no longer eligible to sit your degree.'

The Students' Union was full of excited people talking about occupation and subversion and storming the library. Not Andrea and Kevin, however, who were sullenly enduring each other's company and having a protracted argument about some arcane Edrakonian law. Andrea was wearing a cheesecloth smock and agonizing over whether to eat a salt and vinegar crisp.

A scuffle broke out in the bar between a bunch of rugby players and some Revolutionary Communist Group cadres and Kevin said angrily, 'They're all so pathetic. Slogans and jargon, that's all it is. In Edrakonia when people believe in things they're willing to sacrifice their lives. They have real weapons – the rapier, the poniard, the Toledo. Weapons forged from finest steel, decorated with bronze and chased with gold and silver. The stiletto, the glaive, the falchion, the bombard, the falconet –'

I made my excuses. I finally found Olivia in the cafeteria queue, trying to juggle a tray of food with the unwieldy body of Proteus and a newfangled McLaren buggy, striped in blue and white and folded up like an umbrella. I offered to take the tray and she said, 'Thanks,' and handed me Proteus instead. He had an angry red teething rash on his cheeks and one small boxer's fist jammed in his mouth as if he was trying to eat himself.

'You haven't seen Kara, have you?' Olivia asked. 'Only she asked me to hold him for a minute and that was ages ago.'

'No, sorry.'

She was loading up her tray with cartons of milk and assorted Kellogg's Variety Packs. 'Do you think he can eat these?' she asked me. 'They don't have any baby food in the Union.'

We found a space at the corner of a table. Olivia sat Proteus on her knee and we tried pushing spoonfuls of cereal in his mouth, an idea which he seemed to find alarming and exciting at the same time. Every time the spoon approached him he opened his mouth like a giant baby bird and then went into a kind of delirious spasm, throwing his arms and legs out and squawking at the novelty of it all. Occasionally he spat out Ricicles or Coco Pops like grapeshot. 'I'm sure it's time he was weaned anyway,' Olivia said, rather sheepishly.

'Is that what we're doing?' I really did know nothing.

'Roger wants me to have the baby,' Olivia said.

'The baby?' I repeated, confused. I had forgotten she

was pregnant and for a moment thought she was talking about Proteus.

'He says I can move in with him and Sheila.' She shook her head in amazement. 'Can you imagine?'

I couldn't. 'Does Sheila know?'

'No. It doesn't matter anyway,' she said flatly. 'I'm going to have an abortion.'

'Are you sure? I mean, you're really good with babies.'

'I think it's wrong to bring babies into this awful world,' she said sadly. 'I mean, all you would want would be for them to be happy and that's the one thing that people aren't, isn't it? I couldn't bear the idea of knowing that my child was unhappy. Or that when they're old – a helpless old man, or a little old lady – you wouldn't be there to look after them because you'd be dead by then.' I wished I could think of something cheerful to say in response to this rather tragic outburst but at that moment Proteus gave a fractious cry and we both stared at him as if he might hold a key to some mystery, but he had jammed his fist back in his mouth and looked on the verge of tears.

'He's burning up, poor lamb,' Olivia said, putting one of her cool, pale hands on his forehead. 'I'd better take him out of here.' The Union was full of noise and smoke which probably wasn't good for a baby and certainly wasn't good for me so I followed her out.

'Thanks, anyway,' Olivia said, 'you're a real friend,' which made me feel suddenly guilty because I didn't really think of us as friends.

'See you,' she said.

*　*　*

Maisie was hanging around outside the main door of the Union in full school rig. 'There you are,' she said in the exasperated tone of a much older female.

'Why – had we arranged to meet? And shouldn't you be at school?' I asked as I followed her down the road.

'Yes to both questions. Come on, we'll be late.'

A feeble shout directed us to the slight figure of Professor Cousins, trotting towards us along the pavement as fast as he could. 'Hello there,' he gasped. I sat him down on a bench at Seabraes to recover and we contemplated the view of the railway goods yards and the Tay (which today was dull pewter) until he got his breath back.

'We have to go,' Maisie said.

'It's Dr Lake's daughter, isn't it?' Professor Cousins said to her. He started clicking his fingers. 'No, don't tell me, the name will come to me in a minute.' He twisted his whole body in an outlandish effort to remember.

'You mean Lucy,' Maisie said.

'That's it!' he exclaimed.

'We're going to be late,' Maisie said, growing more impatient.

'Are we going somewhere nice?' Professor Cousins asked hopefully.

'No.'

Chick gave me a cursory nod of acquaintance over Miss Anderson's open grave. He was in Balgay cemetery with his funeral face on – somewhere between a bloodhound and Vincent Price – solemnly witnessing Miss Anderson's interment. The grave was amongst the new ones at the foot of the hill and a bitterly chill wind was blowing so that the minister's garments billowed around him and I feared he would take off like a dandelion head if he wasn't careful. It began to spit with rain and the Tay dulled to a leaden colour.

'Wouldn't it be horrible if she wasn't dead?' Maisie whispered to me in a thrilled voice, after peering into Miss Anderson's new, rather muddy, home. 'Imagine waking up and finding yourself in a coffin. Buried alive,' she added with some relish, and made clawing motions with her hands, presumably in imitation of a corpse trying to escape although she looked like she was miming a demented cat. Several of the assembled mourners cast anxious glances in her direction.

'She is dead, trust me,' I hissed, remembering Chick's macabre penknife test.

'Dear Lucy,' Professor Cousins said affectionately, 'she's quite the little ghoul, isn't she?'

Mrs McCue, at whose invitation Maisie was present, although heaven knows why – some kind of initiation rite into womanhood, probably – put a restraining hand on the bony shoulder of her granddaughter who, in her enthusiasm, looked to be in danger of falling into the open grave. Mrs McCue was wearing her funeral hat – black felt with a brim – that she had tied onto her head with a Rainmate.

Professor Cousins gave Chick a cheery wave. He

seemed to be enjoying himself. There were quite a few other mourners, considering that Miss Anderson was supposedly a crabbit wee wifie. Mrs Macbeth, naturally, had accompanied Mrs McCue along with a minibus of Anchorage residents.

'Like a day-trip in a charabanc,' Mrs McCue said disapprovingly. 'It's not as if any of them liked her.'

'Neither did you,' Mrs Macbeth reminded her.

There was a small knot of relatives of the deceased who, unlike the residents of The Anchorage – all of whom were clearly veteran funeral-goers – did not possess mourning outfits and were self-consciously attired in plums and greys and navy blues. Some of them dabbed their eyes with handkerchiefs, others stared very seriously at the coffin lid. They all had the awkward look of over-rehearsed actors.

'Close family,' Mrs McCue scoffed, 'close not being the word I would choose. They weren't bothered about her when she was alive, I don't know why they're concerned now she's dead.' Mrs McCue seemed to have taken it on herself to recite the usual obsequial platitudes.

The rain was beginning to take itself seriously now and Professor Cousins opened up his duck-head handled umbrella (try saying *that* quickly) and gathered Maisie and myself beneath it.

Janice Rand had also remembered an old person, but only just, as she arrived rather late and breathless, but nonetheless had a spiritually superior air about her as if she was personally despatching Miss Anderson to her maker.

A sudden gust of wind lifted Professor Cousins off his feet so that I had to reach out and grab his arm to stop him being blown away. That was when I felt the eyes on my back ('Surely not?' Professor Cousins said, looking alarmed). My watcher had returned, it seemed. She was standing amongst the old graves of the cemetery, up on the hill, solemnly watching the funeral, like an outcast mourner or an unnoticed ghost. She was partially obscured by the umbrella she was holding but the red coat flared like a signal. This, surely, must be the person whom I felt dogging my footsteps at every turn – or did her life take her to the same unlikely places as mine did? Or perhaps I was being followed by two people – one I could see and one I couldn't.

My attention was diverted when Mrs McCue threw a handful of claggy soil onto the coffin lid, where it hit with a thud that made Professor Cousins wince (Maisie executed the clawing gesture again for my benefit), and when I looked again the woman had gone.

'Well, I dinnae ken about you,' Mrs Macbeth said as everyone started turning their backs on Miss Anderson, 'but I could do with a nice cuppie.' Mrs McCue rested on the ground a raffia shopping-basket that she was carrying. On the side of it the words 'A Present From Majorca' were worked in different-coloured raffia. It looked as though it weighed a ton and seemed to quiver every so often. An off-white ear poked out of one corner.

'Janet,' Mrs Macbeth whispered, 'aff her legs again.'

'*Achtung,*' Mrs McCue whispered as a tall, slim woman approached, '*mein Führer*'s here.'

Mrs Macbeth parked her Zimmer in front of the shopping-bag while Mrs McCue translated for me. 'The matron – Mrs Dalzell.'

Mrs Dalzell had an encouraging, Mary Poppins kind of demeanour and indeed she had the same hairstyle as Julie Andrews in *The Sound of Music* (or indeed most of her films) and was progressing rather regally around the graveside, checking on everyone's happiness or lack of it and inviting the relatives back to The Anchorage for 'a small tea'.

Unnoticed by Mrs Dalzell, Janet had escaped her shopping-basket and was now making a beeline for Miss Anderson. Mrs Dalzell's Mary Poppins smile slipped slightly when she saw the dog. 'Whose dog is that?' she barked, looking round enquiringly at her charges. Janet had begun to dig furiously at the side of the grave, trying to cover the coffin with earth. 'It's your dog, isn't it?' Mrs Dalzell said accusingly to Mrs Macbeth. 'It's Janet, isn't it?' She frowned. 'Have you been hiding her somewhere?'

Maisie ran forward and scooped up the muddy, bedraggled body of the gravedigging dog and said, 'She's my dog now. Mrs Macbeth gave her to me.' Maisie pouted in a way that wasn't very fetching and did her impression of a little girl, whereas in reality, as we all knew, she was a seventy-year-old woman trapped in the helpless body of a small child.

Mrs Dalzell didn't look entirely convinced but she started to rally her flock and direct them towards the gates and the waiting minibus.

'First stop Spandau,' Mrs McCue said loudly as Mrs Dalzell snapped at her heels.

I followed them out of the cemetery, while Maisie pirouetted down the path. We were just in time to see Professor Cousins being herded onto the minibus. I shouted to him but he didn't hear and it was Chick who hooked him by his thin elbow and steered him away.

'If he goes in that place he'll probably never get out again,' he said to no-one in particular. Some bizarre sleight-of-hand then proceeded to take place whereby Janet was stuffed back in the shopping-basket and furtively returned to her rightful owner – Mrs McCue and Mrs Macbeth behaving throughout like rather poor amateur actors trying to recreate a Bond movie.

Chick looked at Maisie playing chalkless hopscotch in the rain. 'I suppose you want taking home,' he said gruffly to her, 'whoever you are.'

'Her name's Lucy Lake,' Professor Cousins said helpfully.

We got in the car and set off on the usual narrative detour – betting shops, off-licences, et cetera, even a rather lengthy sojourn for Professor Cousins and Chick in The Galleon Bar of the Tay Centre Hotel which Maisie and I preferred to sit out in the car, playing 'Switch' with Chick's tasteless playing-cards.

Our route to Windsor Place took us past the university, now a hotbed of activity, people coming and going with a restless energy not hitherto witnessed on those premises. A crowd of people had gathered outside the Tower, from the fourth-floor balcony of which a bed

328

sheet had been hung on which, in red paint that looked like blood (but presumably wasn't), someone had written the words THE TIGERS OF WRATH ARE WISER THAN THE HORSES OF DESTRUCTION.

'What the fuck does that mean?' Chick said, slowing down as a group of people spilled into the road. 'Fucking students.' Catching sight of Maisie in the rear-view mirror, he added, 'excuse my French.'

'I've heard worse,' she said phlegmatically. 'Look – there's Dad,' she exclaimed, pointing at a figure standing on the grass outside the Students' Union. 'Dad' turned out to be Roger Lake – fired up, in oratorical mode, shouting and gesticulating for the benefit of a small group of students.

If Maisie carried on much longer with this charade she would forget who she was. 'He's not actually your father,' I reminded her.

'Really?' Professor Cousins said to her. 'And yet you look so much like him.'

Professor Cousins clambered out of the car and snailed towards the Tower. It was at that moment that I noticed an ambulance was parked up ahead, obstructing the road, and adding to a general sense of drama around the environs of the university. Chick started hooting the Cortina's horn impatiently. An ambulanceman glared angrily at him and mouthed something I couldn't understand, although the gesture he made seemed clear enough. He was helping his partner to load their cargo – a seemingly unconscious body, strapped on a stretcher.

329

'Oh look, it's Spotty Dick,' Maisie said excitedly. 'Do you think he's dead?'

I craned my neck to get a better view – she was right, it was Dr Dick on the stretcher. His carcass was wrapped in a red blanket that made him look even paler than usual, did indeed make him look rather dead. I got out of the car and went over to his limp form. 'Are you all right?' I asked him.

'Do you know him?' one of the ambulancemen asked.

'Sort of,' I admitted reluctantly. 'What happened to him? Was he injured in the demonstration?'

'What demonstration?' the ambulanceman said, looking round. He spotted the banner and read out, *'The tigers of wrath are wiser than the horses of destruction* – what does that mean?'

The ambulanceman, although quite short, was young and had sandy hair and kind eyes and the capable manner of all men in uniform.

'What does anything mean?' I said, smiling at him. He smiled back.

'Excuse me,' Dr Dick said, struggling into a sitting position, 'am I going to expire here in the street while you flirt with this . . .' he struggled to find the right word, 'this *girl*?'

The ambulanceman looked at Dr Dick and said mildly, 'You seem lively enough for someone who's expiring.'

'A very professional diagnosis,' Dr Dick said sulkily, flopping back onto the stretcher.

'What happened to you?' I asked him again. 'Were you caught up in the protest?'

Dr Dick squinted at me unattractively. One of the lenses in his little academic spectacles had acquired a crack, giving him an oddly glaikit look. His eyelashes were pale and rather stubbly, like those of a pig. 'Don't be ridiculous,' he said. He seemed reluctant, however, to explain how he had ended up on the stretcher and it was the ambulanceman who finally told me that Dr Dick had slipped on an icy pavement and cracked his ankle bone. He grimaced, although I wasn't sure whether this was from the pain in his ankle or the unheroic nature of his injury.

~ Icy? Nora queries. It was raining a minute ago.

'You're not the only one who can control the weather.'

'Nothing to be ashamed of,' the ambulanceman said. 'Casualty's full of old wifies who've done the same thing.'

'Thanks,' Dr Dick said. He motioned me closer to him and hissed in my ear, 'I think I was pushed. I think someone tried to kill me.'

'Pushed off a pavement?' I repeated incredulously. 'Wouldn't they have pushed you off something higher if they'd wanted to kill you?'

'Hop in,' the ambulanceman said to me. I hesitated.

'Do. Please,' Dr Dick said weakly.

I was trying to think of a good reason (although really I had several) not to go in the ambulance when Chick suddenly drove off in a great crashing of gears, hooting noisily as he overtook the ambulance.

'What a tube,' the ambulanceman said.

Maisie waved cheerfully at me as the car sped by. I recalled the image of the yellow dog being driven away in

331

much the same manner and wondered what the chances were of Maisie arriving home.

'Thank you,' Dr Dick murmured to me, 'you're a good girl.'

In the DRI we took some time at reception, mainly because Dr Dick couldn't think of who to put down as his next-of-kin. It seemed to be a toss-up between his ex-wife Moira and myself and despite my protestations that I wasn't related to him in any way he finally chose me. Also at the reception desk was a Spanish-looking woman with a nail stuck in her hand. When I glanced at the form she was filling in I saw that in the space where it said 'next-of-kin' she was writing 'Jesus'. Perhaps she was a friend of Janice Rand. She gave Jesus a surname (Barcellos) which, to my knowledge, was more than anyone else ever had.

After a long wait, during which I engaged in the most desultory of conversations with Dr Dick – mostly about his childhood ailments (measles, German measles, whooping cough, chickenpox, mumps, glandular fever, plague) – a nurse came and said, 'Dr McCrindle will see you now,' and took Dr Dick into a cubicle to be examined behind garish flowered curtains that must have offended his taste.

A lot of time passed without anything happening. The peeling beige paint on the waiting-room walls was relieved only by a poster encouraging me to brush my teeth after every meal. Dr McCrindle came out of Dr Dick's cubicle and smiled at me wolfishly. More time passed. A student nurse ran down the corridor, shouting, 'Jake, come back.' More time passed. I read my way through a pile of the *People's Friend*, looked through my George Eliot essay, which had got as far as, *James's dislike of George Eliot's stylistic method is rationalized into the strange statement that, 'Its diffuseness . . . makes it too copious a dose of pure fiction'*, which wasn't very far at all and, finally, I wrote some *Hand of Fate* –

'Good morning, Rita,' Lolly Cooper said cheerfully, 'lovely morning, isn't it?' Cooper's was an old-fashioned sort of bakery, the baking still done at the back of the premises by Lolly's husband, Ted. Rumours abounded in Saltsea about Ted's terrible temper. He was a dusty, flour-clad presence, a kind of *éminence blanche*, who whistled all the time in a manner that Madame Astarti found faintly menacing. Lolly, on the other hand, was a frilly sort of woman with fluffy hair who wore Peter Pan collars or big soft kitten bows tied at her neck. Madame Astarti always imagined that Lolly Cooper kept a very neat house with a well-stocked fridge and sets of matching towels, something Madame Astarti herself never expected to achieve.

'What are you after today, Rita?' Lolly said, wringing her hands together like a woman with a dreadful secret even though the expression on her face was one of extreme, almost excessive, cheerfulness.

'Small white farmhouse, please,' Madame Astarti

said and then laughed and said, 'maybe I should go to an estate agent's for that?' but Lolly just looked at her blankly with a fixed smile on her face.

'Never mind,' Madame Astarti sighed.

'And a bit of a treat for elevenses?' Lolly said, and together they conducted the ritual of surveying the trays of iced fancies and cream cakes.

'Jam doughnut?' Lolly said. 'An Eccles cake?' The thin strain of a slightly wobbly whistle could be heard coming from the back. It sounded to Madame Astarti like 'Oh Mein Papa'. She'd never thought of it as a frightening tune before.

'Chelsea bun?' Lolly went on, a mad look on her face. 'Chocolate eclair? Iced teacake? Cream puff?'

I closed my eyes and when I opened them again the woman who had been watching me in Balgay cemetery was standing in front of me. I flinched and stood up too suddenly, making myself dizzy.

'Why are you following me?' I demanded. Close up, I could see the alcoholic's skin, mottled like a reptile, see the lines in her sun-cured face. Her hair looked brassy and green as if she spent too much time in over-chlorinated swimming-pools.

'Excuse me,' she said, her accent hard and tight, South African perhaps, or Rhodesian; 'I wonder if you can help me – I'm looking for my daughter?'

'Who are you?'

'Effie.'

'No, I'm Effie,' I said. I was beginning to feel sick. It was too hot in the hospital, like an overheated greenhouse.

The woman laughed but in a strangled, off-key kind of way and it struck me that she might be insane.

I struggled to make sense of her. 'You're my mother's sister, Effie? You're dead,' I added, rather impolitely.

'No,' she said, 'not her sister.' But then a nurse walked briskly up to me and said, 'You can go in and see your dad now if you like.'

'My dad?' I repeated, bewildered. The woman began to walk away, her too-high heels stabbing the hospital linoleum. 'Wait!' I shouted after her but she had already pushed her way through the swing doors and disappeared.

I felt weak, as if I was going to faint. I was probably the one who ought to be admitted to a ward, not Dr Dick. (But who would I put as my next of kin? My mother is not my mother. Her sister is not her sister. Her father is not her father. My father is not my father. My aunt is not my aunt. Et cetera.)

'Cubicle three,' the nurse said.

Of course I knew it was Dr Dick in cubicle three not my anonymous father choosing a bizarre location in which to come back from the dead, but for just a moment, as my hand went out to draw the curtain back, I felt a little shiver of excitement. If it was my father lying there what would I say to him? More importantly what would he say to me?

Dr Dick was examining the cast on his ankle. 'I'm sure it's not the only thing that's broken,' he complained without even looking at me, 'and they wouldn't listen when I told them I was tachycardic, they could at least have run an ECG. And I banged my head, how do they know I haven't got concussion?'

'Did you tell that nurse you were my father?' I interrupted him.

'Of course I didn't,' Dr Dick said indignantly. 'I'm not even old enough to be your father, although I feel it,' he added, lying back on his pillows. He removed his spectacles and rubbed the bridge of his nose. 'My head hurts,' he said again. I had to admit, he did look exhausted. I felt an unusual twinge of pity for him and reached out and clasped one of his hands in mine. He smelt of Savlon.

'You're a good girl,' he murmured. Like all hypochondriacs, Dr Dick was distressed at finding he actually had something wrong with him and ended up making such a fuss ('Is he often hysterical?') that the junior house officer on duty decided it would be easier to keep him in overnight than it would be to persuade him to go home.

I was shooed away by a nurse with a bedpan who whisked the curtains around the bed with great theatricality as if she was about to perform a disappearing trick on Dr Dick. I hung about for a minute, unsure what to do until the nurse suddenly popped her head through the curtains and said, 'This might take some time. Don't worry,' and then added, with routine cheerfulness, 'we'll take good care of your dad.'

It felt very late, although the clock in reception only said nine o'clock.

'Bye,' the receptionist said indifferently, 'take care now.'

It was snowing outside, big, wet flakes that whirled dramatically in the wind but dissolved as soon as they landed on the ground. They found their way inside the collar of my coat as I trekked along Dudhope Terrace against a strong headwind. A bus sailed by like a ghostly galleon. Dudhope Castle, cloaked in a swirl of snow, seemed to glow eerily as I passed it. The street was deserted and I began to feel anxious. I glanced behind but the snow made phantasmagoric shapes in the dark that made me more nervous so I kept my head down and shuffled on. Where was Chick when you needed him? Or better still Ferdinand, who had been absent from this tale for far too long.

~ Yes, bring Ferdinand back, Nora urges. You left him stranded on a beach, it's time he returned. He's the only remotely sexually attractive male in the entire story.

(You must forgive the eagerness of my mother (who is not my mother). Remember – she is a virgin. Not to mention a murderess and a thief.)

We must pause for a second. We have come to a critical fork in the path. If I had a choice of white knights on chargers come to save me – admittedly only from the weather, but it was very bad weather – which would I prefer, Chick or Ferdinand? A foolish question surely, for there could be only one answer –

337

The snow was beginning to settle thickly and most of the traffic had stopped but I could just make out the yellow headlights of a car, moving slowly towards me along the Lochee Road. The car was almost obscured by the snow as it slewed to a gentle skidding halt on the other side of the road. It was a Wolseley Hornet. The driver's window rolled down and Ferdinand's handsome features resolved themselves out of the white kaleidoscope of snow.

'Hop in,' he said, in a curious echo of the ambulance-man earlier in the evening. Here was excellent good fortune.

The Hornet presented a perfect contrast to Chick's Cortina. Its new-smelling interior was warm and its little engine chugged manfully through what was now a raging blizzard. It even had a tape-deck fitted on which John Martyn's 'Bless The Weather' was, fittingly, playing.

Ferdinand seemed somewhat edgy. He hadn't shaved recently, which made him look older and more danger-ous. His eyes, I was relieved to see, were green and the dark hollows beneath them hinted at sleeplessness and the criminal in him seemed more evident than before. His navy-blue Guernsey, I noticed, was spiked with nee-dles of coarse yellow dog hair. There was sand on the floor of the car and the slight brackish scent of the sea-side that I knew only too well.

'Where do you want to go?' he asked. He sounded hoarse as if he had a sore throat and I offered him a Strepsil, which he declined.

'So?' Ferdinand asked, tapping his hand impatiently on the steering-wheel.

'So?' I repeated absently.

'So where do you want to go?'

'Anywhere.'

He gave me a funny look so I narrowed it down to Terri's address in Cleghorn Street as we were already quite near there and it successfully removed the Bob factor from the me–Bob–Ferdinand equation.

As we drove, Ferdinand kept glancing warily in the rear-view mirror but there were no other vehicles on the road, even the buses had stopped running. I tried to make polite small talk with him although he seemed distinctly taciturn, if not downright moody. He did, however, finally volunteer the information that he was out prowling the streets looking for a dog.

'Yellow mongrel, rather sanguine temperament?' I hazarded.

'How did you know that?' he asked, looking at me in amazement. His eyes narrowed and his face grew menacing. 'You've not been following me, have you?'

'Of course not, Ferdinand,' I said.

'How do you know my name?'

~ I think you should kiss him before he disappears again, my giddy mother (but not – et cetera) interjects.

Personally, I think it better if this kind of thing develops naturally between two people, rather than as a result of intervention. On the other hand, I may never get this opportunity again.

Suddenly, and without any preamble, Ferdinand leant over towards me and placed his hot lips on mine and began to kiss me fiercely.

~ I hope he's parked the car.

Luckily, we were stopped at a lengthy traffic light. Ferdinand's kisses tasted of a combination of things – marijuana and Irn-Bru, turpentine and Tunnock's Teacakes, with a slight undertone of fried onions – a strange brew you could probably have marketed successfully, especially to children. Heaven knows where things might have gone if the traffic light hadn't changed at that moment.

A little further on, Ferdinand parked the car, rather carelessly, outside a shop that was still open on the City Road and said, 'I won't be a minute.'

Another car loomed out of the snow and glided to a silent stop behind the Hornet but no-one got out and the snow was too thick for me to see who was inside it.

I was just nodding off to sleep when Ferdinand came out of the shop, but hardly had he taken a step onto the snowy pavement when two men got out of the car behind and approached him. One of them said something to him that I couldn't hear and then almost immediately the other one punched Ferdinand in the stomach. He doubled up in pain and fell to his knees. I opened the car door although I had no idea what I was going to do, they hardly seemed the type to respond to polite female remonstrance. But before I could make a move to get out of the car one of the men slammed the door shut again. My forehead bounced off the glass of the car window and I could feel a bruise start to form immediately.

The man leant down so that his face was close to the window. He grinned at me, showing rotten, crooked teeth, and then suddenly produced a knife, a huge hunting one that could have felled a bear, curved like a scimitar, with a serrated edge that glinted beneath the street light. He tapped this malevolently against the glass, grinning all the while like a storybook bandit. The message was clear and did not need words.

Then the men yanked Ferdinand to his feet, pulled his arms behind his back and bundled him into their car and drove off in a great flurry of snow, skidding round the corner onto Milnbank Road and disappearing from view.

This wasn't going at all well. I sat for a while waiting for my pulse to slow a little, worried my heart was about to give up. I wasn't sure what to do next – reporting the incident to the police was the first thing that came to mind but I wouldn't get very far if I tried to walk in this weather, and I certainly wouldn't make it as far as the police station in Bell Street without succumbing to hypothermia. The car probably wouldn't make it either, as the whole world had now turned white and anyway I hadn't driven a car since taking lessons in Bob's ill-fated old Riley 1.5 (a tale that still doesn't need telling).

~ What about the shop? Nora says, the shopkeeper will have a phone.

But, no, he won't, because the shop was now in darkness with all the metal grilles and shutters in place.

~ Knock on a stranger's door.

I was about to do that, but before I could even get out of the car the blue flashing lights of a police car appeared from nowhere out of the snow. Hardly had I had time to think to myself what good timing this was on the part of the forces of law and order when I found myself being dragged out of the car, handcuffed and pushed into the back of the panda car, whereupon one of the policemen informed me – in a polite, rather disinterested way – that I was under arrest for being in possession of a stolen vehicle and for being an accessory to a robbery.

'Robbery?'

The policeman nodded towards the shop which was once more brightly lit and open for business. The owner was standing on the doorstep and observing my predicament with satisfaction.

The other policeman looked at his watch and said, 'Night in the cells for you, I'm afraid,' and started up his engine and—

'Flour,' Henry Machin said, looking at the new corpse lying on his slab like a freshly caught fish. The pathologist ran his fingers along the dead woman's skin and studied the trace of dusty white powder on his fingers.

'Flour?' Jack Gannet puzzled. 'Plain or self-raising?'

Or Else

NO, NO, NO, THIS IS RIDICULOUS. I OBVIOUSLY MADE THE wrong choice. Let's try again, even if it means sacrificing the kiss.

~ It exists, it's written down.

But apparently not, for I have no memory of it. If only I could be kissed by him again without having to go through everything else again.

The snow was beginning to settle thickly and most of the traffic had stopped but I could just make out the yellow headlights of a car moving slowly towards me along the Lochee Road. The car was almost obscured by the snow as it slewed to a gentle skidding halt on the other side of the road. It was the Cortina. The driver's window rolled down and Chick's ugly features resolved themselves out of the white kaleidoscope of snow.

'Get in,' he said. 'You can die in weather like this, you know.'

I got in and we battled our way through the snow, the only car on the road. What an heroic beast the Cortina was. How familiar it seemed too, how familiar Chick seemed.

'How come you're always around, Chick, if you're not following me?'

'Maybe I am following you,' he said, lighting a cigarette and offering me one. 'That's a joke,' he added when he saw the expression on my face, 'ha, ha.'

'Did Maisie get home all right?'

'Who?'

The acrid smell of Embassy Regal filled the car and drove out, momentarily, the scent of dead cat.

'Been in the wars?' Chick said. When I asked him what he meant, he pointed to my forehead and said, 'That's a rare bruise you've got.' He turned the rear-view mirror for me to see and there indeed was a blue bump the size of a robin's egg just where the Hornet's door had slammed on me. How curious. For there was no trace of his kiss on my lips.

The Cortina had struggled as far as the junction of Dudhope Terrace with Lochee Road when I remembered something. Chick took some persuading but eventually I managed to get him to turn round and return to the DRI.

'Back so soon?' the receptionist said brightly, but with a rather wary look in her eye at my deranged appearance.

'I forgot something,' I said, searching the waiting-room until I found what I was looking for. My George Eliot was on the floor, under a chair, sandwiched between a *Woman's Journal* and a *Weekly News*.

'You take care as well now,' I said to the receptionist as I left, but she didn't look up.

Chick dropped me off at the end of Cleghorn Street. Even the plucky Cortina wasn't going to make it back downtown on a night like this. The tail-lights of the car quickly disappeared into a wall of whiteness.

Terri had become a homemaker since I last saw her. The dingy flat in Cleghorn Street had been transformed into a cosy little love nest. Patchouli joss sticks burned on the mantelpiece, 'Liege and Lief' played on her Amstrad deck, a fire burned in the grate, church candles illuminated the dark and a *boeuf Bourguignonne* simmered in a well-behaved manner on the stove. Hank, the cause of all this domesticity, was stretched out on the mattress on the floor that served as Terri's bed. The stale sheets on the bed had been replaced with fresh ones and Terri had purchased a piece of red dressmaker's velvet to act as a princely counterpane for her new consort.

'Kinda homey, huh?' Terri said, putting wood that she'd found in a skip in the street onto the fire. She was wearing what looked like a crinoline and smelt of sandalwood soap and meat, an odd, rather unsettling mix that I felt must be for Hank's benefit. She had even made sausage rolls ('Jus-rol, it's easy.'). The sausage rolls were dog bite-size and every so often she would lob one in Hank's direction.

She perched on the edge of the mattress to consult a book called *Cooking for Two*, biting her lip with the effort of reading a recipe.

347

'How about an Apple Betty for dessert?' she asked, although I wasn't sure if this question was addressed to me or to Hank. It wouldn't be long before she was greeting him when he came home from work ('Hi, honey'), waiting at the front door for him with a Martini and a kiss, her hair fixed and her make-up freshened and a big Mary Tyler Moore smile on her face.

I defrosted in front of the fire while we finished what was left of the Don Cortez that Terri had used to make the *boeuf Bourguignonne* and had started on a bottle of Piat d'Or that had been chilling outside on the windowsill. When Terri opened the window to retrieve the wine, flakes of snow flew inside and fell on us like cold confetti tossed by an unseen hand.

While we drank the icy wine, Terri paraded for my benefit the 'dog stuff' she had bought – a Welsh blanket (a woollen honeycomb in pink and green from Draffens) and, from the pet shop on Dock Street, a doeskin collar, a stitched leather lead, and a brown pottery feeding-bowl with DOG stencilled on the side. Perhaps Terri should get a matching one that said GIRL on it. She had also had a tag engraved with Hank's name and address and I noticed that Hank had taken Terri's surname rather than the other way round.

'Hey, sweetie,' she said and stroked the dog's flank, burnished by the candle flame and firelight, as she spoke to him in a low murmur, painting him a picture of their future life together, the visits to the beach at Broughty Ferry, day trips to St Andrews, chasing rabbits in Tentsmuir Forest, the daily walk to Balgay Park and the

348

good times they would have romping amidst the grave-stones of the dead burghers of Dundee. Hank rolled over and groaned at the word 'walk'.

When Terri went through to the scullery to check on supper I tried a low-voiced, experimental 'Buddy?' on Hank. The effect was startling and unwelcome – Hank leapt off the bed, tail wagging, and walked round and round me, sniffing me enthusiastically as if my body carried news from somewhere far away.

'Hey, you guys are getting on great,' Terri said generously when she came back and saw the dog raising a paw in elegant supplication, gazing into my eyes as if waiting for me to tell him something profound. I was just wondering if this was a good time to tell Terri about Hank's other life as Buddy – although obviously there was never going to be a good time – when she dropped to her knees, hung her arms around his neck and said, 'I can't tell you how happy this fella's made me. I haven't felt this good since before Mom died.' Oh dear.

I took advantage of Terri's new personality and got her to help me finish my George Eliot essay. We were rather drunk by now and I think I was beginning to feel slightly delirious but nonetheless I struggled on until I'd finished (which is, after all, the only way to do it) – *The schematic unity and integrity of Eliot's vision must lead us to the conclusion that James's comment that it is 'a treasure house of detail' is a flawed and, ultimately, prejudiced view of the novel and in fact reveals his aversion to the very concept of* Middlemarch.

I was too tired to go home by then and ended up sleeping sardine-style with Terri and Hank. Despite being so tired I had a restless night, finally falling asleep to the sound of a milk-float engine and into a dream where I was trying to persuade a recalcitrant George Eliot to get into the back seat of the Cortina.

When I woke up the sky was the colour of old bone. I was on the cold side of the mattress. Terri was still fast asleep, her arms around her inamorato, nuzzling his neck. I crawled out of bed and wrapped myself in the Welsh blanket. I had a hangover that was mutating into some kind of brain disorder. I would have killed for a cup of tea but the power was off. As long as I lived, I vowed, I would never take electricity for granted again. I got dressed, pulled on my boots and put on my coat and got ready to leave.

Before I could, however, Hank woke up and started pawing at the door to be let out. As Terri looked as if she was having her first good night's sleep in twenty-one years I said, 'OK, Hank, buddy, let's go,' (a compromise form of address), and opened the door of the flat for him while I scrawled a note for Terri saying that I'd taken Hank for a walk because I supposed she would panic if she woke up and found him gone. Then I spent some time rummaging around for Hank's new collar and lead, for George Eliot, as well as my bag, scarf and gloves, before eventually setting off down the stairs – all the leisurely while presuming that the door to the street would be locked as usual. When I got down to the close, however, I discovered the bottom door propped wide open to facilitate a flitting.

I pushed past a couple of removal men hefting a fridge and ran out into the street, treacherous with snow, and managed to catch a glimpse of Hank disappearing round the corner at the top of the street, tail whirling like a helicopter blade. By the time I got to the top of the street he had already crossed the incline of City Road, weaving his way through sliding cars, and was padding up Pentland Avenue, following some mysterious canine map in his head that led to Balgay Park. I trailed him all the way, shouting both his names at random, but he was too delirious with fresh air and open space to pay any attention. By the time I finally caught up with him at the entrance to the park I could hardly breathe, the freezing air in my lungs hurt so much.

Hank raced off before I could collar him, scampering like a puppy along a path leading up to the Mills Observatory. Being a naturally good-mannered animal, he paused every so often to allow me to catch up with him. The cold was raw and chafing, there was no sunshine to make the snow pleasant in any way, only a wintry greyness cast over everything, including the sleeping dead.

I followed Hank up to the Observatory and then down the slopes of the cemetery where the dead of Dundee – the whalers and spinners and shipwrights, the weavers and bonnetmakers, the sea-captains and the engineers – were all waiting patiently under the grass for a day that might never come. Was my father sleeping in a cemetery like this? Perhaps he lay in a pauper's grave somewhere. Perhaps in a shallow grave of leaves and twigs. Picked clean by the little fish at the bottom of the sea. Or mere dust scattered to the wind?

~ Who knows, Nora says.

'So – he might be alive.'

~ Maybe, Nora admits with a sigh.

And my genuine mother as opposed to the fake whose company I keep. 'Dead, I suppose?'

~ Very.

Is there *anyone* in the world that I am related to by blood?

Hank pushed his cold nose impatiently into my gloved hand to encourage me to move. I stroked his lovely velvety pelt and smelt his warm meaty breath.

He led me back to the entrance of the park and sat down patiently for me to put on his collar and lead, but just as I was about to buckle his collar a car drove up and pulled to a halt as if it was being driven by a stunt man and the familiar and over-excited figures of the Sewells clambered out. They were dressed for the weather, Jay in a windbreaker, Martha in Morland boots, an ankle-length sheepskin and a large fur-trimmed hat. Martha spotted the dog and stood rooted to the spot, screaming his name, while Jay ran towards us, skidding and sliding on the icy pavement and finally falling in an undignified heap in front of a very excited Hank and a not so excited me.

Martha hurried towards us as fast as the snow would allow her, taking little baby steps to avoid falling on her skinny derrière, crying out all the time, 'My baby, my baby boy.' Jay hauled himself to his feet and surprised me by catching me in a bear hug, jamming my face into his windbreaker so that I could smell the sweet, almost feminine smell of his aftershave and the breath freshener he was sucking.

'Oh my God,' he said, releasing me, 'how can we ever thank you? Anything you want is yours, Edie.'

'Effie.'

Anything I wanted? A fatted calf? A chest of treasure dredged up from the bottom of the ocean, brimming over with ropes of pearls, opals like bruises and emeralds like dragons' eyes? A father? Ferdinand? A degree? But there was so much strung-out emotion fogging the air that it seemed too cold and calculating to request any of these things. Jay wiped a hand across his eyes and said to Martha, 'Let's get this guy home,' while Martha, who now had tears streaming down her face, said in a rusty voice, 'I don't think I've ever been as happy in my life as I am at this moment.'

Words failed me.

But not for ever.

I stood and watched the happily reunited family drive away, the Sewells' car fishtailing on the icy surface of Pentland Avenue. I still had Hank's collar and lead in my hand and a couple of other hardy dog walkers gave me curious looks as if I was walking an invisible dog. I stood for a long time getting colder and colder, wondering what to do, and finally, because I couldn't think of anything, I took my invisible dog for a walk in the park.

★   ★   ★

Eventually I headed home. I couldn't find the courage to tell Terri that I had lost her dog. What chance was there that I could somehow get hold of another identical Weimaraner before Terri noticed that the original one was missing? Or perhaps I could employ Chick to re-kidnap Hank? Perhaps – most unlikely of all – Martha and Jay Sewell could find it in their hearts to come to some kind of custody arrangement with Terri.

These impossible thoughts were clouding my brain as I ploughed down Blackness Avenue through the icy grey slush that the snow had now become. On the Perth Road I was hailed by Professor Cousins, wearing strange rubbery overshoes and a red scarf tied around his head like a child or someone with an old-fashioned toothache. I could almost imagine that he had mittens on ribbons threaded through his sleeves.

I lent him my arm as he was slipping and sliding all over the pavements in an alarming way.

'No sand on the pavements,' he observed cheerfully, 'that's how accidents happen, you know.' Perhaps Professor Cousins had become magically attached to me in some way – like a mitten on a ribbon – and I would have to spend the rest of my life entertaining him. I supposed there were worse ways to spend a life.

'This is where I live,' I said, steering him into Paton's Lane. 'Ah,' Professor Cousins said, 'home to Dundee's own poetic bard –

'But accidents will happen by land and by sea.
Therefore, to save ourselves from accidents,

354

    we needn't try to flee,
  For whatsoever God has ordained will come to pass;
  For instance, you may be killed by a stone or a
      piece of glass.'

Poor Dundee, surely not doomed for ever to be the town of McGonagall and the *Sunday Post*?

Professor Cousins' creaking bones took some time negotiating their way up to the top floor but they triumphed eventually. 'The air's quite thin up here,' he wheezed, leaning on the door-jamb to recover. I could only guess at what state I would find the flat in when I opened the front door.

I think it's time for some more of the story of my miscreant mother (who is not my mother), don't you? We are huddled inside, in the kitchen, riding out the storm that Nora has stirred up. A fire burns weakly in the grate of the Eagle range. Nora, for reasons best known to her eccentric self, is wearing diamonds around her neck and in her ears.

'Real?' I query.

~ Real, she affirms.

'Stolen?'

~ Sort of.

'Evangeline's?'

~ Maybe.

I sigh with frustration. This is like getting blood out of a stone, drawing teeth from a tiger, wrenching dummies from babies. Has she been in possession of this treasure all through the years of our seaside poverty? Can she explain how she came by them?

What a mystery my mother (but not my mother) is.

I decide on the patient approach of the concerned psychiatrist to pull her tale from her. These are deep waters we are fishing in. 'Tell me your first memory?' I say encouragingly to her. Surely we will find something innocent here, an insight into the childish building-blocks of character. My own first memory, of drowning, is not so innocent, of course. Perhaps it was a kind of afterbirth memory of swimming in amniotic fluid (for we are fish), and yet even as I write I can feel the icy water, filling my nostrils, my ears, my lungs, dragging me down into the depths of forgetfulness.

My second memory isn't much better. We were catching a bus – one in an endless series in my fugitive childhood. A distracted Nora, preoccupied with the amount of baggage she was trying to get on board the bus, forgot all about me and left me sitting on a bench in the bus station and was two miles down the road before she realized that something was missing. The driver had to slam his brakes on when Nora stood up suddenly at the back of the bus and started screaming dramatically, 'My baby! My baby!' so that for one dreadful moment the driver thought he must have crushed Nora's baby under his wheels. By the time he under-stood what she was shouting, Nora had precipitated hysteria in half the passengers and an asthmatic attack in a sensitive young librarian who gave up his calling not long afterwards and set off to travel the world in search of an excitement that could equal that of the wild, red-haired woman at the back of the bus. I'm imagining the librarian obviously.

'And yet I wasn't your baby,' I muse to her, 'was I?' But whose baby am I, for heaven's sake?

~ I thought you wanted my earliest memory?

'Please.'

356

~ I am very small and they are very tall.

'They?'

~ Lachlan and Effie. They must be . . . sixteen and eighteen, maybe a little older. Maybe younger.

'I get the idea.'

~ It's summer and they have taken me down to the loch for a picnic. I've always been their 'pet', their 'plaything'. The trouble is, they treat their pets and playthings very badly. The sun is very hot and the black water is shining in the sun. Insects are dancing and skating on the surface of the water. I can smell rotting weed and heat and hard-boiled eggs –

(If only I had tried the hypnotic recall approach on her years ago.)

~ We're sitting on the little jetty and they're dipping their feet in the water, but my feet won't reach. I've got a splinter in my finger from the rotten planks of wood and I've been stung by a nettle but when I cry Effie says that the giant fish-witch who lives in the loch will come and eat me if I don't stop snivelling.

'Fish-witch?'

~ Fish-witch. Lachlan says he can't eat an egg without salt and hurls it overarm into the water where it splashes like a pebble. He's red in the face from the heat. He says he's bored. She says she's bored. They smoke cigarettes. They make faces at each other.

They begin chasing each other, running around the woods, shrieking with laughter – they are always very childish when they're together. Eventually they grow tired of this and decide to take the little wooden rowing boat out onto the lake. They put me in first, I can feel Effie's arm round me, slick with sweat. Her hair's damp on her neck and the cotton print dress she's wearing is sticking to her body.

Lachlan rows the boat to the middle of the loch and then he jumps in the water and starts pretending to drown. Effie dives in, like a knife in the water, and they start racing each other to the shore. Lachlan does a butterfly stroke, splashing like a water-wheel, but he can't catch Effie, who swims as sleekly as an otter and reaches the bank several lengths ahead of him. They clamber out and shake themselves like dogs. Then they start chasing each other again, screaming and laughing and they run off into the woods.

Then everything falls silent. After a long time of waiting for them to return and an even longer time of realizing they're not going to, I fall asleep in the heat. When I wake up my skin is sore from the heat. The sun has started to sink behind the trees now and it's growing cold. I'm terrified the fish-witch is going to rise out of the water like a leaping black salmon and eat me.

I fall asleep again. When I wake it's dawn – the loch is covered in mist but by the time anyone comes to look for me, the mist has dissolved and the sun is high again. I am the only person ever admitted to the local cottage hospital who is suffering from sun-burn and hypothermia at the same time. Afterwards, they said I had run away from them, but really I think they were trying to get rid of me.

'Why?'

~ Because they were wicked, of course.

'But you learned about boats and swimming from your sister, didn't you?' I puzzle to her. 'Did that come later?'

~ Not *from* her, she never taught me anything. I learned in case she tried to *drown* me.

Chez Bob

I WAS EXPECTING BOB TO BE ASLEEP BUT HE WAS SITTING ON the sofa watching *Playschool*, eating Heinz stewed apples from the jar and speaking conversationally to an invisible person sitting next to him. 'And thus I recognize that the certainty and truth of all knowledge depends on the sole knowledge of a true God, so that before I knew him, I could not know any other thing perfectly. Is Descartes entitled to this conclusion?' He looked up and said, 'Hey,' when he saw us.

'Hey,' Professor Cousins replied amiably.

Bob nodded in the direction of Proteus, companionably sharing the sofa with him and said, rather guiltily, 'I'm only finishing what he didn't want.' Proteus was propped up and bumpered with pillows and cushions. He was covered in food from head to toe, not just the stewed apples but a variety of suspect stains which Bob helpfully mapped – 'Marmite, Ambrosia Creamed Rice, Ready Brek – this thing's a gannet.' Well, it takes one to know one.

Professor Cousins perched himself gingerly on the edge of the only other available seating – a chair on which a pair of Bob's *Dr Who* underpants were un-becomingly draped.

'Why is Proteus here?' I asked Bob, who gave the baby a speculative look and said, 'Is that its name?'

'It's a he. It's Kara's baby, you've seen him lots of times before.'

'Oh, yes,' Professor Cousins said, 'of course, that big girl who always smells of the barnyard. He's a nice little chap, isn't he?'

'But why is he *here*?' I persisted patiently to Bob.

With a long-suffering sigh, Bob tore his eyes away from Big Ted, Little Ted and friends. 'Because that girl left him here.'

'And out of the millions, if not billions, of girls in the world which one would that be?'

'She said she was your friend.'

'Terri?'

'No.'

'Andrea?'

'The lovely one,' Bob said, his features softening as if he was a devout Catholic referring to the Virgin Mary.

'Olivia?'

'She said she had something she had to do and would you look after him.'

Perhaps Proteus has taken on the role of the parcel in Pass the Parcel, or a chain letter that had to be handed on. Perhaps – after bringing good luck and wealth to everyone who dutifully passed him on (and un-fortunate consequences to those who didn't) – he would eventually get back to Kara. If the odds were against him he could pass through the hands of the entire population of the world before returning to his mother. How old would he be then? And how long would it take for a baby to be handed round the world? (That would be an interesting experiment.)

'Wouldn't it be easier just to find his mother and hand him back?' Professor Cousins suggested, unwrapping his head from the red scarf, like a boiled pudding, or even a clootie dumpling.

'What's-her-name said something about Karen being at a women's thingy meeting in Windsor Place,' Bob said.

'You mean Kara?'

'Do I?'

'At a women's liberation group meeting?'

'The round window!' Bob shouted suddenly at the television and Proteus squirmed in terror.

Was Olivia all right? And was an abortion the 'thing' she'd had to do? If I was her friend I wasn't a very good one.

I offered Professor Cousins a cup of tea but at that moment the power went off, much to Bob's distress as he was destined never to know now what was through the round window.

Bob finally recognized Professor Cousins and started enthusiastically explaining to him his idea for his dissertation: 'On *Jekyll and Hyde*, 'cos it deals with like one of the universal myths of western society,' Bob said enthusiastically, waving his arms around like an uncoordinated beetle. 'There's all these ur-stories, ur-plots, ur-myths, right?'

Professor Cousins looked concerned and asked Bob if he always had a stammer.

'The Enemy Within,' Bob said, ignoring the question.

'Stevenson?' Professor Cousins, furrowing his brow in an effort to follow Bob.

'No, *Star Trek*,' Bob said patiently. 'Captain Kirk gets split into two people by a transporter malfunction – the good Kirk and the evil Kirk.'

'Ah, dualistic theories of good and evil,' Professor Cousins said, 'Manicheism, Zoroastrianism.'

'Yeah, yeah,' Bob said, 'the interesting thing is that the good Kirk can't live without the evil Kirk – now what does that tell you?'

'Well . . .'

'Then there's this other episode called "Mirror, Mirror" where all the crew of the *Enterprise* have doubles—'

'And the doubles are all evil?' Professor Cousins guessed.

'Exactly!' Bob said. 'And then Kirk has to use this thing called the Tantalus Field—'

I was distracted from this critical analysis by the sight of Proteus trying to eat the top hat piece from the Monopoly board. I supposed it was lucky that he had chosen that rather than the large lump of Moroccan that had been sitting next to it, nonetheless this was no place for a baby.

'I'll come with you,' Professor Cousins said when I started gathering up Proteus's things, none of which he'd had yesterday.

'Yeah,' Bob said, 'she said she'd had to buy him stuff.'

Olivia had spent a fortune on Proteus. She'd bought nappies and Mothercare Babygros as white as newborn lambs, Tommee-Tippee cups, a Peter Rabbit cereal bowl, a bone china egg coddler, a baby-blue rabbit, Osh-Kosh dungarees in a blue-and-white butcher's apron stripe, a pair of corduroy bootees and enough cleansing, wiping, moisturizing 'stuff' to stock a small branch of Boots.

'His holdall's over there,' Bob said. 'It should have everything you need. His jacket's in the hall. His nappy's been changed and he's due a sleep but if he's hungry there's food in his bag.'

'I'm sorry?' I stared at Bob in amazement.

'What?' He started rolling a joint and in the absence of television opened a 1968 *Blue Peter Annual*.

'Nothing, just for a minute there you sounded like a grown-up person.'

'Not me,' Bob said cheerfully.

I found Professor Cousins in the hall, trying to fold up Proteus's buggy, like someone in a comic film trying to work out a deckchair.

'Where are we going?' he asked as we commenced the tortuous journey down the stairs.

'A women's liberation meeting.'

'Well, that will be a first for me,' he said. 'I do hope I fit in.'

'Wait!' Bob shouted after me, retrieving something from down the side of the sofa. He handed me a well-worn and quite filthy dummy. 'You'll need this,' Bob said. 'It works better than Elastoplast, believe me, I've tried everything.'

What Maisie Didn't Know

'LIKE THE FEEDING OF THE FIVE THOUSAND,' PHILIPPA SAID
cheerfully, making sandwiches from slices of Sunblest
and the remains of the salmon, which had now acquired
a faint tarnish of iridescent green. Even Goneril had lost
interest in it.

In fact there were only eight people at the women's liberation meeting in Windsor Place and four of those –
Andrea, Professor Cousins, Mrs McCue and Mrs Macbeth
– were not members of the group, as Heather took it
upon herself to point out vociferously and at some
length.

'He's a man,' she said indignantly when Professor
Cousins made himself busy slaking Mrs McCue and Mrs
Macbeth's endless need for tea. Professor Cousins tot-
tered around the kitchen table with the teapot, enquiring
about milk and sugar preferences, proffering teaspoons
and murmuring *sotto voce* apologies for the use of tea-
bags. Professor Cousins bought his Darjeeling fresh by
the leafy quarter from Braithwaite's every week and
seemed particularly perturbed by Philippa's oak-coloured
Typhoo.

Mrs McCue sniffed her tea suspiciously as if it might be laced with arsenic.

'She thinks someone's trying to kill her as well,' I explained to Professor Cousins.

'Well, you know what they say, don't you?' he said in a confidential voice to Mrs McCue.

'Just because you're paranoid doesn't mean they're not out to get you?' she said.

'Exactly!' he grinned.

Sheila Lake, smeared with oatmeal and masticated Farley's rusks – and presumably with a baby hidden about her person somewhere – seemed rather charmed by Professor Cousins' geisha qualities, complaining that Roger wouldn't recognize the kettle if it hit him on the head (an attractive idea). She seemed blissfully ignorant of the fact that her husband was planning to move his pregnant (or perhaps no longer pregnant) girlfriend into her sandstone villa in Barnhill.

'No Kara?' I asked. 'No Olivia?' No-one, in fact, who might take Proteus off my hands – Proteus who was currently asleep on the bed in the spare room, the erstwhile place of repose of Ferdinand and Janet. Janet herself was sleeping peacefully under the kitchen table downstairs, but what of Ferdinand, where was he?

'He's taken the dog for a walk,' Philippa said. Duke gave her a questioning look. She frowned at him. 'Not that dog, obviously,' she said, 'because that dog is here and we can't ignore the evidence of our senses because then we would enter the territory of casuistry and un-natural doubt, which is all very well in its place. Of course, some people would argue that the truth of factual statements can only be established inductively from particular experiences. Can perceptions yield knowledge of a mind-independent world? Is such a world ever knowable? Does "being" consist in "being perceived"? Is a dog merely a collection of sense data – the smell of a dog, the sound of a dog, the feel of a dog, the taste of a dog, et cetera?' Philippa paused and, returning Duke's scrutinizing gaze, said rather lamely, 'Another dog, Ferdinand's taken another dog for a walk.'

'The taste of a dog?' Mrs Macbeth puzzled.

The McCue kitchen contained two of the things Andrea feared most in life – food and old people – a fact that was making her rather pale and fidgety. She reported being dragooned by Heather to attend this meeting after being lectured on the ethics of eating an egg from the shared fridge, which she claimed she hadn't even touched – an egg which was marked 'H' in black felt-tip pen, 'Like Humpty-Dumpty,' Andrea said moodily. She was wearing a smocked and ruffled pinafore that would not have looked out of place on a Victorian child.

'I thought property was theft?' I said to Heather.

'Property's property,' she retorted crossly.

'What does that mean?' I said, irritated by this tautologous wisdom, 'like "I'm me", or "a door is a door", "a cat's a cat"?'

'A man's a man for a' that,' Mrs Macbeth said.

'Is this a game?' Professor Cousins asked hopefully.

Mrs McCue was buttering Selkirk bannock. Mrs McCue

and Mrs Macbeth had been busy baking in Philippa's kitchen all morning although, as Mrs McCue confided rather loudly in my ear, not before they had scrubbed everything clean of the McCues' resident germs.

'Bannock, anyone?' Mrs McCue offered, handing round a plate.

'I thought that was a battle,' Andrea said, frowning at the huge slab of calories being thrust under her nose.

'I'm awfie fond of a wee bittie bannock myself,' Mrs Macbeth said conversationally to no-one in particular. She was wearing a wrap-over overall and was lightly dusted with a talcum of flour.

'Oh, me too,' Professor Cousins said enthusiastically. 'I can't think of anything better than tucking into a spread prepared by the deft hands of the fairer sex.'

'Come again?' Heather said waspishly, her face distorting unattractively with disbelief.

'I said,' Professor Cousins began again pleasantly—

'I heard what you said,' Heather said rudely. 'I just couldn't believe you said it.'

'Shouldn't you be at the barricades or something?' I said to her.

'There's no difference between the fight for feminism and the fight for socialism,' she said, inadvertently eating a piece of Irish tea-loaf that Mrs McCue had just buttered. A raisin lodged unattractively between Heather's front teeth but I chose not to tell her about it.

Andrea meanwhile nibbled delicately on a slice of Border tart, looking rather faint, while Mrs Macbeth urged a flapjack on her.

'I like to bake,' she said. 'I like to keep my hand in. Or hands in,' she added, looking down at one of her own midget hands, but then she seemed to grow suddenly confused and hobbled away, patting Andrea's shoulder affectionately as she passed her. Andrea gave a little shudder.

'It's not contagious,' I reassured her. 'It's not like leprosy, you can't catch old age by touching them.'

'She seems so very *small*,' Andrea whispered to me, nodding in the direction of Mrs Macbeth's retreating back. 'Was she small to begin with? Or do we all end up like that?'

'What?' Mrs McCue said. 'It's rude to whisper, you know.'

'I said,' Andrea said more loudly, 'that she seems very small.'

'Who? Who seems very small?' Philippa asked.

'That . . . small woman,' Andrea said helplessly, for Mrs Macbeth was now out of sight.

'She means Mrs Macbeth,' Mrs McCue said, buttering everything she could get her hands on.

'Mrs Macbeth?' Andrea repeated doubtfully.

'It's a perfectly good name,' Mrs McCue said. 'People are called it.'

'Well, they're not called "*it*",' Professor Cousins said and laughed.

'Look,' Heather said crossly, 'this isn't the WI; we're supposed to be having a serious meeting about wages for housework.'

Mrs McCue took out a familiar piece of knitting and

373

frowned. 'Wages for housework? But who would pay them?'

'The wages of sin,' Professor Cousins said vaguely. 'You don't seem to have a hot-water jug,' he added to Philippa.

'What would I want a hot-water jug for?' she puzzled.

'For hot water, of course,' Mrs McCue said. Before this conversation could carry on ('What would I want hot water for?' et cetera), Maisie burst into the kitchen, Lucy Lake trailing on her heels.

'Hello, Emily,' Sheila said carelessly, when she saw Lucy.

'Lucy,' Lucy corrected her. Sheila peered at her eldest more closely and still didn't seem convinced.

'Salmon sandwich?' Philippa coaxed, pushing the plate towards Lucy and Maisie. No-one had so far touched one. Mrs Macbeth wandered back into the room and looked startled, as if she had been expecting to enter a quite different room in a quite different house (and perhaps at a quite different point in the century).

Professor Cousins cranked his skinny cat hams up from his chair and pulled another one out for Mrs Macbeth and said, 'Do take a seat, Mrs Macbeth,' so that Heather looked fit to explode at this further affront to her egalitarian sensibilities.

The sight of Maisie reminded me that the last time I saw her I had recklessly abandoned her to Chick's dubious guardianship.

'You got home all right then last night?' I asked her.

She rolled her eyes ('Oh, don't,' Professor Cousins said faintly). 'It depends what you mean by "all right",' she mumbled through a mouthful of bannock.

'She was late, I know that,' Philippa said.

'I had recorder practice,' Maisie lied artlessly, but then a muffled squealing noise announced that Proteus had woken up. I hoped he hadn't fallen off the bed.

I had moved Archie's manuscript from beneath the guest bed before putting Proteus down. He was too young to be exposed to the corrupting influence of J and his cohorts. The latest chapter to be added was particularly nasty. J – or J's doppelgänger, for he appeared to have acquired at least one recently – was being tortured by a particularly sadistic woman wearing nothing but high-heeled leather boots. More bizarrely still, *The Expanding Prism of J* had been joined in the spare room by *The Wards of Love*, like a matching pair of His 'n' Hers imaginations. I dreaded to think what would happen if the two got mixed up. Before she knew where she was, Flick would be wearing *Avengers* boots and running up and down end-less stairs in European apartment blocks being chased by the vile beasts of the imagination (Paranoia and Melancholia).

I changed Proteus's nappy, bundling him anyhow into the awkward terry square but pinning it very cautiously in case I pierced his fragile baby flesh. I wondered what I was going to do when I came to the end of Olivia's supply of nappies. Perhaps I'd have to start washing them. (What a thought.) I jiggled Proteus around on my hip for a while and showed him the view from the window. He held out one fat arm and tried to catch a seagull flying low. Today the Tay was the colour of infinity and made me feel suddenly depressed. Nothing good ever seemed to happen to me. And I was stuck with a madwoman with the same name as me stalking me, and someone else's baby and Bob for a boyfriend and some horrible virus that had got into my blood and was taking over my body like the alien being that it was.

If only Ferdinand were here right at that very moment he could take me masterfully in his arms and I could wilt under the smouldering gaze of his soulful, troubled eyes. He could trace the outline of my face with his surprisingly gentle fingers – perhaps smile wolfishly – and bury his face in my hair and say in a smoky voice, 'No woman until now, Effie, has—' Proteus started to go purple in the face and I realized he was choking on something. I patted him on the back as hard as I dared but he still couldn't breathe.

In desperation I held him upside down by his ankles and shook him. Thankfully, this extreme measure succeeded in dislodging a wad of paper like an owl pellet and Proteus gave a reassuringly hearty roar of distress. When he'd calmed down I unwound the pellet and discovered a particularly delirious page of Philippa's dialogue. *The Wards of Love* really ought to carry a health warning.

When I took Proteus back downstairs I discovered that Professor Cousins was trying to get everyone to play 'a word game' which seemed to owe quite a lot to Martha Sewell. He caught sight of me and said, 'Not The And – you know that game, don't you, dear?'

The thought of Martha made me feel suddenly stricken with guilt about Terri. By Philippa's kitchen clock it was now a quarter past one. Terri must surely be awake by now (although perhaps not) and wondering if Hank *aka* Buddy had gone AWOL.

'You take three words,' Professor Cousins was explaining, 'and you try and make a sentence from them. For example *fish*,' he bowed courteously at the ruins of the salmon, '*table* and, um, let me see, *erythrophobia*.'

'Erythrophobia?' Mrs Macbeth said tentatively.

'Fear of blushing,' Philippa declared.

'I didn't know that,' Maisie said.

'So . . .' Sheila Lake said doubtfully, 'the salmon on the table had erythrophobia. Is that right?'

'Exactly!' Professor Cousins said enthusiastically.

'What a stupid game,' Lucy Lake remarked.

'Can we stop this?' Heather sulked, but was ignored by everyone.

'Another one,' Mrs McCue demanded.

'Well . . . cat,' Professor Cousins said, catching sight of Goneril slinking into the kitchen, 'beetroot and . . . kazoo.'

'Well, that's more of a challenge,' Philippa admitted, but then Mrs Macbeth gave a little screech of alarm as Goneril jumped up on the table and deposited a limp McFluffy in front of her.

'Jings, crivens and help me Boab,' Mrs Macbeth exclaimed.

Some drama ensued – Maisie administering mouth-to-mouth resuscitation, Mrs McCue producing a bottle of

377

Macintosh's smelling salts, and so on, but in the end the unfortunate creature was pronounced dead.

'There's no keeping them,' Philippa sighed. 'They're as bad as lemmings.'

Maisie was sanguine about the sudden demise of the latest McFluffy and had already started explaining to Professor Cousins the complexities of hamster heaven, which was a branch of rodent heaven (rather full thanks mainly to the McCue household), itself a division of small mammal heaven, and so on.

'And hamster heaven,' Professor Cousins asked, absent-mindedly stroking the silken fur of the little corpse, 'does that have further sub-divisions – Russian, Golden, Dwarf, and so on?'

'Dwarf?' Mrs Macbeth queried quietly but Professor Cousins had already embarked on another game. 'You take a word of five letters,' he beamed, '"novel", for example, and then you must find something beginning with each letter – n-o-v-e-l – in each of the following categories – a town, a river, a flower, a writer and a composer. For example – Nottingham, the Nile, nasturtium, Nabokov and, um, let me see – a composer beginning with "N"?'

'Luigi Nono,' Philippa said.

'Who?'

'He wrote *Il canto sospeso*,' Philippa said, 'a spare, rather enigmatic work, in 1955, followed by *Intolleranza* in 1960. Quite controversial, interested in social issues, influenced by Webern.'

'How about Ivor Novello?' Mrs McCue suggested.

'Much better,' Professor Cousins agreed. 'So – let's see, a five-letter word, what about "basil"? The herb rather than the man—'

'What man?' Sheila asked.

'Well, any man,' Professor Cousins said. 'Any man called Basil. Effie – that *is* your name, isn't it?' I nodded. 'Why don't you start?'

'Me?'

'Start with "B",' he said encouragingly.

'Why not "A"?' Mrs McCue puzzled.

I sighed. 'B . . .'

'Town, river, flower, writer, composer,' Professor Cousins coaxed.

'Birmingham, bluebell, Barthelme, Berlioz.'

'You missed out the river,' Lucy Lake said. But no-one could think of a river beginning with B and, before they could, Professor Cousins suddenly gasped, *'The Duchess of Malfi*!' So I presumed he was meant to be teaching it – or thought he was supposed to be teaching it.

'Roger and I went there on honeymoon,' Sheila said vaguely, 'the Malfi Coast, the Neapolitan Riviera.'

'No, no, no,' Professor Cousins corrected her gently, 'that's the *Amalfi* coast.'

'The Neapolitan Riviera,' Mrs Macbeth said; 'it sounds like an ice-cream.'

'I've been to the Riviera,' Mrs McCue said unexpectedly, 'the French Riviera. A long time ago, before I was married, before Archie was born. With a man called Frankie.' She sighed. 'He was rich. Very romantic, it was – walking under foreign moonlight, smoking those French cigarettes. We drove there in Frankie's cream Bristol—'

'A Bristol cream?' Professor Cousins said, looking round hopefully.

'No, a cream Bristol, it's a car.'

'I've never been further than Blairgowrie for the berries,' Mrs Macbeth said sadly.

'*La Terrazza dell'Infinità*,' Professor Cousins said dreamily. 'The Terrace of Infinity – that's on the Amalfi Coast, you know, near somewhere I can't remember. I had the most charming experience there once.'

'Really?' the romantic novelist in Philippa asked.

'Cover her face,' Professor Cousins murmured.

'Whose?' Mrs Macbeth asked, looking askance. I thought it would be as well to introduce some other topic of conversation and I asked Andrea – who had now finished the entire Border tart and looked as if she was about to throw it all back up again any minute – how her spells were coming along. I was wondering if she could magic up another Weimaraner for me.

'Do you have dizzy spells too?' Professor Cousins asked her, full of concern.

'Magic spells,' I explained to him.

'Oh, how thrilling for you,' Professor Cousins said, clasping his hands over his heart.

'Well?' I prompted Andrea, who was looking at Professor Cousins as if he was insane.

'What exactly were you looking for?' she asked doubtfully.

'How about replicating something?'

'Replicating? Replicating what?'

'A dog.' What a lot of problems it would solve if there could be a Hank *and* a Buddy.

'Cloning,' Philippa snorted dismissively, 'they'll never achieve that, not in Scotland anyway, and think of the ethical problems.'

'No, this would *solve* ethical problems,' I said. Why was I even having this ridiculous conversation, I wondered.

'Magic,' Professor Cousins said wistfully, 'do you believe in it?'

No I didn't. But I wished I did.

The front door slammed vigorously and Archie entered the kitchen on a great draught of cold outdoor air. He looked perturbed at the sight of not only Professor Cousins but also Mrs McCue and Mrs Macbeth, cosily ensconced at his kitchen table.

'It's like a nursing home in here,' he complained, glaring at his mother who pulled out a chair and said, 'Take the weight off your feet, son.'

'You'll be late for school,' Philippa said to no-one in particular so that everyone glanced nervously at their watches, everyone except Maisie and Lucy Lake.

'An education's everything,' Mrs McCue said encouragingly to them.

'Well, not everything,' Mrs Macbeth protested. 'It's not meat and milk, or weather, or tea or—'

'Or sheep,' Maisie offered.

'Sheep?' Philippa frowned.

'Or roof tiles,' Professor Cousins contributed, getting into the spirit of things, 'or cushion covers or—'

'Stop it now,' a very vexed Heather said, clapping her hands like a nursery school teacher; 'this is absolute, gratuitous nonsense.'

And so it was.

Is Achieving a Transcendentally Coherent
View of the World Still a Good Thing?

I LEFT THE MCCUE HOUSE AND PUSHED PROTEUS IN HIS BUGGY along Magdalen Yard Green and down onto Riverside. I wondered if Proteus was my baby now, his mother having apparently lost all interest in him. I parked him by a bench and sat down to consider all the adjustments I would have to make to my life if I was stuck with a baby for the rest of it. Proteus dozed off, ignorant of his dubious future in my hands.

A weak sun had managed to dissolve the last of the snow and it had polished up the Tay to a gleaming silver. A faint aroma of sewage perfumed the air. The bridge was empty of trains but in the distance, on the sandbanks in the middle of the river, seals were sunning themselves. From here they looked like amorphous lumps of sluggish rock but I knew that if I was close to them I would see that they were freckled and speckled like birds' eggs. A heron lifted itself delicately off a sewage pipe and flew away.

I closed my eyes and felt the sun on my face. Suddenly (and quite illogically as far as I could see), I felt my spirits lift. I was aware of the strange feeling I'd experienced at the standing stones in Balniddrie – a kind of bubbling in the blood and an aerating of the brain – as if I was on the verge of something numinous and profound and in one more second the universe was going to crack open and arcana would rain down on my head like grace and all the cosmic mysteries were going to be revealed, perhaps the meaning of life itself and – but no, it was not to be, for at that moment a dark shadow fell across the world.

The icy interstellar winds whipped rubbish along the footpath and caused a great tsunami to travel up the Tay, overwhelming the road bridge and sweeping the rail bridge away. Volcanic ash rose into the air and encircled the earth, choking out all the air and blotting out all the light. The terrible figure that was the cause of this stood before me. Dressed in widow's weeds like an unravelling shroud, this daughter of Nemesis was gnashing her teeth and wringing her hands and rending the air with lamentation and woe. Black smoke rose from the top of her head and her aura was composed of nothing but scum and scoria. Yes, it was Terri.

She was waving a black ostrich-feather fan in an agitated manner and wearing long black gloves and jet earrings as befits a woman in mourning, for she had discovered the fate of her beloved – encountering the Sewells in the street, in the company of a docile Hank/Buddy trotting along on a lead, and had engaged in a vigorous wrestling match with Jay's six-foot-two inches of jogger's flesh from which he was lucky to emerge the winner and only did so because Martha threw her dignity to the winds and started brawling and scrapping like a streetfighter.

'I've lost him,' Terri said forlornly, sinking onto the bench and lighting a cigarette. 'So now we have to get him back,' she added, glaring at Fife in the distance.

'*Kidnap* Hank, you mean? It didn't work with the goat, did it?' I reminded her.

'All the more reason to make it work with the dog, then.' Terri threw the stub of her cigarette away and stood up. 'So – do you know how to break into a house?'

'No,' I said wearily, 'but I bet I know someone who does.' We had walked all the way up Roseangle before Terri wrinkled her nose as if smelling something bad and said, 'Where did that baby come from?'

We still had Chick's grubby card – *Premier Investigations – all work undertaken, no questions asked*. The address for his office was up a close, off a cobbled side street, in the jumble of small side streets around the skirts of the Coffin Mill, whose sad ghosts were lying low today. 'Kinloch House' a sign on the door said. You could imagine that the building once housed large mysterious machinery – saw-toothed cog-wheels and hammering piston shafts. Now the place was a warren of dilapidated business premises, all of them dingy and most of them abandoned or acting as dubious registered offices for even more dubious-sounding businesses.

We had acquired Andrea on the way, fleeing the madness of the McCue house. She was wary about the whole kidnapping enterprise, her father being a Malton

387

magistrate, and was only persuaded into it by the argument that it would be good experience for her as a writer – *Anthea Goes Kidnapping* kind of thing. I was thinking she could be some help on the babysitting front as it's quite hard to be a criminal when hampered by a large, fat baby, but I realized I'd probably made a mistake when she grew green at the sight of Proteus covered in food, even when I explained it was only Robinson's chocolate pudding.

On the very top floor we found one of Chick's *Premier Investigations* cards stuck on a door with a piece of chewing-gum. The door was locked and the glass in the door covered by a blind made of waxy blackout material. Terri hammered on the door and after a considerable interval Chick, looking even more seedy, if that was possible, opened it cautiously.

'Oh, it's you,' he said.

He seemed to be in the middle of manoeuvring an old filing-cabinet across the frayed linoleum of the floor, panting with the effort, droplets of sweat exuding from his balding head. He looked as if he was on the verge of a cardiac arrest – pasty and damp – but that was how he looked every time I saw him.

'What do you want anyway?' he asked gloomily. 'Not money, I hope, the cow's cleaned me out. Well, don't just stand there,' he added, 'give me a hand.'

The filing-cabinet turned out to be lighter than it looked because it was empty.

'I thought I'd get a woman,' Chick said, contemplating the filing-cabinet as if he was thinking of actually keeping a woman in it, 'to file and type,' he said, 'that sort of . . . stuff.'

I thought about recommending Andrea's typing skills to him but she'd just finished carrying Proteus up four flights of stairs and was lying on the floor, panting, with her eyes shut.

'Make yourself at home, why don't you?' Chick said to her, stepping over her prone form to reach a poke of chips in the in-tray on his battered desk. 'I didn't know you had a kid,' he remarked to me, offering a cold chip to Proteus.

'He's not mine.'

'You should be careful,' Chick said. 'Kidnapping's a crime.'

'Yeah, well,' Terri said, 'it's funny you should mention that.'

The Sewells rented a big semi-detached house called 'Birnham', perched halfway up the slopes of the Law. Getting in was no problem; Chick had picked the lock on the back door before we'd even got Proteus out of the car. I wondered how noticeable four adults and a baby would be breaking into a house on a quiet street. Very noticeable, probably.

'And you're sure they're not here?' Andrea hissed for the hundredth time.

'No, I told you,' Terri said impatiently. 'I heard them say they were going to Edinburgh. And they were leaving the dog.'

~ How convenient for the plot, Nora murmurs. If you can call it plot.

389

Andrea had been in favour of taking the role of getaway driver and staying outside in the Cortina, but eventually had to admit, under Chick's relentless interrogation, that she had no idea how to drive.

Inside Birnham, we entered each room cautiously, speaking in the hushed whispers of church-goers (or burglars).

'This feels so . . . illegal,' Andrea said.

'That's because it fucking is,' Chick said, 'and if I go down for stealing a dog that doesn't even run for money, someone's going to pay, I tell you.' This last remark seemed to be addressed to me but I ignored him.

'His bark's worse than his bite,' I reassured Andrea, who was regarding Chick with horror, never having been exposed to him before. Terri was sniffing the room for musk and spoor of dog. 'He's definitely here,' she said with the conviction of a medium.

I had never been in such a clean house, it was like being in a showhouse or the home of a robot. All the décor was in muted shades of magnolia and there wasn't a single thing out of place, not a cup unwashed or a cushion unplumped. We tiptoed around the place like cat-burglars – or, to be more accurate – dog-burglars.

In the bedroom the Sewells' night clothes were lying neatly on the end of the bed, maroon pyjamas for him, a lacy honeymoon-type garment for her. I placed Proteus on the eiderdown – a thick quilted-satin affair that was asking to be reclined on, and I couldn't overcome an irresistible urge to lie down on it next to where Proteus was drowsily sucking his thumb. I would undoubtedly have fallen asleep if Hank/Buddy hadn't suddenly bounded out from nowhere in a paroxysm of barking and bared teeth, like a hound from hell.

Chick and Proteus both started screaming while Andrea tried to faint, but Terri dropped to her knees and held her arms open like a beseeching martyr so that I was convinced she was going to be torn to pieces; but luckily at that moment Hank/Buddy recognized her and fell into her arms. (A girl in love is a frightening sight.)

'Ah, true love,' Chick said sarcastically. 'Right, mission accomplished, can we go?' he said, hustling everyone out onto the landing, just in time for us to hear the most unwelcome sound imaginable – the noise of the key turning in the lock downstairs.

'Fuck, fuck, fuck, fuck,' Chick said expressively.

'Maybe it's burglars,' Andrea whispered. I didn't bother pointing out the odds against two sets of burglars breaking into a house at the same time and instead, trying to stay in the shadows, I peered tentatively over the banister rail into the stairwell below, where Martha and Jay were depositing piles of Jenners' carrier bags on the terrazzo and looking around for the sight of their dog running to greet them. Which he was unable to do because Terri had him pinned to the ground with her entire body.

'Where's Mummy's little pooch?' Martha cried and Jay shouted, 'Buddy boy, where are you, boy?' to no avail as Terri had wrapped her hands round Mummy's little pooch's muzzle so that the only bit of his anatomy able to greet his owners was a mute tail. Jay suddenly bounded up the stairs – too quickly for any of us to react

– and stopped in surprise when he reached the top stair and saw the little party waiting to greet him. He frowned, trying to make sense of it.

'Aren't you all Martha's students?' he puzzled. 'Is this some kind of college prank?' He caught sight of Chick – clearly not a prankster of any kind – and looked alarmed. At that moment Hank/Buddy escaped Terri's stranglehold and leapt towards Jay Sewell to greet him. Terri leapt as well, in an attempt to hang onto the dog, resulting in both dog and girl lunging into Jay at the same time. Which is *exactly* how accidents happen.

I suppose the laws of physics could explain what occurred next – pivots and fulcrums, et cetera; the way that there was more of Jay's body above the banister than below it; the ratio of the Hank/Buddy/Terri combination to the singular Jay Sewell – but however you explain it, the effect was that Jay went cartwheeling over the banister rail and plummeted down into the stairwell – so quickly that not even a single cry escaped his lips. We all stared at each other in dumb amazement, all except for Proteus in my arms, who had fallen asleep with his head on my shoulder.

I rushed to look over the banister. Jay was spread-eagled on the floor below, blood pooling around his head and freckling the terrazzo. His eyes were open, giving him an air of, if anything, surprise.

'Dead as a doorknob,' Chick muttered to himself.

'I think that's as dead as a door*nail*,' Andrea murmured, gazing at the blood-glazed tiles. In the profound silence that had befallen us – broken only by a faithful whine on the part of Hank/Buddy – I could hear Martha in the kitchen chatting blithely on about cashmere sweaters and the 'cultural oasis' that was Edinburgh. Any second now she was going to come out into the hall and discover her previously healthy husband as deceased (which is a longer form of dead) as an item of door furniture.

'If you're ever going to succeed at magic,' I whispered to Andrea, 'then now would be a good time to begin.'

Proteus woke up with a start and began to cry, breaking the trance that we'd been plunged into. I rifled desperately through my pockets for his dummy but all I could find was a torn piece of paper, the stray page of *The Expanding Prism of J* in which J plunges over the banisters and dies.

A sudden horrendous scream rent the suburban air, indicating that Martha had discovered her spouse's unexpected demise.

'Give me your lighter,' I whispered urgently to Chick. He raised an eyebrow at me as if this was no time to take up smoking (although if not now, then when?) and passed me his lighter – a lurid affair displaying a naked female on its casing. I grabbed it off him and set the flame to the piece of paper in my hand. (Well, it was worth a try.) *The Expanding Prism of J* flared up with a malevolent hiss in a greeny-blue flame – perhaps cyan, who knows? – and turned into a thin charcoal skin that floated up and hovered over the stairwell before disintegrating into a little shower of carbonized fragments like black snow.

'Fucking hell,' Chick said, looking down at the hall,

'where's he gone?' For there was indeed no sign of a blood-boltered Jay, no screaming Martha, no sign of life or death. It was as if we had suffered a mass hallucination.

'This is *so* freaky,' Andrea said quietly.

'Let's get the fuck out of here now,' Chick said, a sentiment we all agreed with heartily, and we ran out of the house and piled into the car anyhow so that for a brief and surreal moment Hank/Buddy was sitting behind the Cortina's steering-wheel. Chick and the dog finally sorted themselves out and as we pulled away from Birnham with Chick in the driver's seat we saw the Sewells' car rounding the corner and drawing to a halt outside their home. I was glad to see that Jay was not only driving the car but was also in possession of a fully intact skull. Martha caught sight of us and her features contorted in a little grimace of recognition. She didn't espy Terri or her erstwhile dog, as they were lying on the floor of the car.

'So he was dead,' Andrea puzzled, 'and now he's . . . not dead?'

'Apparently,' I said.

'Now *that's* magic realism,' I say to Nora.

Terri asked Chick to drop her off at the bus station. I presumed she was going somewhere like Balniddrie to lie low for a while – it was obvious the Sewells would realize who had abducted their dog.

'You don't need to wait to see me off,' she said to me and made a move to kiss me then thought better of it. Hank (as he would now be for ever more, I supposed) licked the back of her hand while he sat waiting patiently by her side.

'We're outlaws now,' Terri said dreamily; 'we have to go where desperadoes go.'

'Where's that?' Chick asked. 'Glasgow?' and Terri said, 'No, but it rhymes with that.'

'Where?' I said. 'Aleppo? Cairo? Truro? Fargo? Oporto? Quito? Jericho? Soho? Puerto Rico? Kyoto? Chicago? Bilbao? Rio de Janeiro? Io? El Dorado? Kelso?'

'Who would have thought,' Andrea said wearily, 'that so many places rhymed with Glasgow?'

'There's more if you're interested.'

'Where's Io?' Chick asked.

We got back in the Cortina, which seemed strangely empty now. In the absence of alcohol, Chick took a swig of Proteus's gripe water. Proteus himself hadn't stayed awake to watch Hank and Terri go. He was sitting on my knee, his head lolling uncomfortably. He was beginning to smell overripe.

'I wish I could find Kara and give him back,' I said to Andrea. Now that I had embarked on a life of crime it didn't seem right to have an innocent infant in my care. (Although such ethical reservations never stopped Nora.)

'She's going to that party tonight,' Andrea said, 'the one in Broughty Ferry.'

'Why didn't you say that before?'

'I didn't know whose baby it was,' she said huffily; 'they all look alike to me.'

*   *   *

Broughty Ferry, once a fishing village now the closest thing Dundee had to a bourgeois suburb – the party was in a huge house that looked more like a small castle than a normal home. It was a red sandstone confection in the Scottish fantasy style – hotching with corbels and crow-stepped gables and fanciful little turrets with arrow-slit windows, like the result of a Victorian architect's fevered dream.

'Forres,' Robin informed us, built for a nineteenth-century jute baron, but currently home to a disreputable gaggle of dental students and medics. Robin and Bob were the first people we saw as we staggered off the bus with Proteus and headed for the house. 'Remind me never to have children,' Andrea muttered.

Bob was excitedly explaining to Robin what had happened in the concluding part of Dr Who's latest adventure, *The Curse of Peladon*, which he had just viewed. 'And then this evil alien ambassador, who's just a brain on wheels basically –'

'Where do you suppose Shug is?' Andrea said, interrupting this sophisticated critique and speaking to Bob as if he was a slightly retarded chimpanzee.

'Dunno,' Bob said.

'Did he say anything to you?' Andrea persisted, 'about me, for instance?'

'He said . . .' Bob closed his eyes.

'He's thinking,' I explained to Andrea.

'He said – "Don't forget to bring the Thai sticks."'

Andrea sniffed the air and set off, following her moon-struck nose. Bob followed her, leaving me with Robin in the kitchen of the house which was dimly illuminated by one yellow lightbulb. A trail of people were coming and going, all in a desultory state of drug overload – the doctors and dentists of tomorrow presumably. On offer was the usual student party fare – a couple of large pan loaves and a block of red Scottish Cheddar, cheap wine and a metal keg of gassy lager squatting in the walk-in pantry, the floor of which was swilling with spilt drink. The bottles of wine on the table were almost all empty by now, although a milk crate of Balniddrian elderflower champagne remained untouched.

Robin poured the remains of a massive bottle of Hirondelle into a couple of plastic cups and gave one to me. Miranda, the dopey goat executioner, wandered into the kitchen, an almost visible aura of torpor about her, and started knocking back Tiger's Milk from the bottle. She caught sight of Robin and gave him a lethargic 'Hi.' I don't think she recognized me. Was she a fit person for me to hand Proteus on to, I wondered. Hardly. I asked her if she'd seen Kara and she made a vague gesture towards the door before slumping onto a chair and apparently passing out.

I pushed my way out of the kitchen, past a crush of people in a hallway and up a staircase, Robin trailing on my heels. We came upon what appeared to be a small ballroom – a space that was like a cross between a railway station and a bordello. There was a fireplace at either end of the room in that red-and-white marble that looks like uncooked beef and huge mirrors fixed to the wall, set in ornate ormolu frames. A massive milk-glass chandelier shaped like a palm-tree hung from the middle of the ceiling and smaller versions sprouted from the walls. I could almost imagine myself being waltzed off by a dashing cavalry officer, my *mousseline de soie* skirts swirling, a dance card dangling from my wrist.

'Really?' Robin said, apparently quite aroused by this vision. Something rather slimy, like a snail's silver trail, had dribbled down his beard.

'No, not really.'

Sadly the chandelier was unlit and the only light was provided by candles from Balniddrie, which were dotted perilously around the room, just waiting to be knocked over and catch on the drooping tattered curtains.

There was no furniture apart from two incongruous *chaises-longues*, covered in a red velvet that had frayed to almost nothing, and on which people were slumped like wet sandbags. Around the edges of the floor, where there must have once been elegant little gold chairs for the fairer sex to rest on, there were now heaps of old, stained mattresses. On one of these, on the far side of the room, I spotted Bob already wired up to a hookah.

The ballroom was still fulfilling its original function, to some degree anyway, as someone had set up a primitive disco with red, green and blue flashing lights and the occasional unnerving strobe. Quite a few people were dancing, if it can be called that. Andrea, still Shug-less, was one of them. Andrea had refined her rather abstract terpsichoreal style at the Isle of Wight Festival so that she now danced like a four-legged octopus in extreme pain.

To my surprise a few of the supposedly more voguish

members of staff were present, although that adjective hardly applied to Dr Dick, loitering palely in a corner of the room and deep in conversation with his arch adversary, Archie. I think Dr Dick might have been drunk but Dr Dick drunk and Dr Dick sober was pretty much the same thing.

Andrea danced up to us and Robin said to her, 'Do you want to dance?' more in fear than hope, but I said, 'No, she doesn't,' and thrust Proteus into her arms. 'Just while I try and find Kara,' I said, when she tried to run away. Before I could say anything else to her she was swallowed up by a mob of people and disappeared.

Robin was now dancing to 'Spirit In The Sky' with his eyes closed and moving like a Woodentop, jerky uncoordinated movements that at first made me think he was having a fit. The music changed to 'Whiter Shade Of Pale' and Robin opened his eyes and grabbed me and pulled me to his thin bird breast. His granddad T-shirt smelt of cheap joss sticks and sweat.

I was beginning to feel nauseous and oddly disassociated. I wondered if I'd accidentally eaten brownies again without noticing. There was a buzzing in my ears that I couldn't shake out and I almost welcomed the support of Robin's body. He started trying to kiss me but his general ineptitude, coupled with beard and droopy moustache, proved something of a hindrance, thank goodness. My head was beginning to feel very strange, as if my brain had been replaced with a skullful of wheat grains. If I tilted my head to one side all the grains of wheat seemed to roll in that direction.

'I've been thinking a lot recently,' Robin said softly, so close to my ear that I could feel how damp his lips were, 'about *Life Sentence*. About the dynamic interplay between character and theme in the play. You see, Kenny's the eternal outsider—'

'I thought that was Rick.' Oh no, I mustn't enter into this conversation. 'I've got to find Kara,' I mumbled.

Robin started fumbling with my clothes. I was wearing so many that it would have taken him hours to get down to skin. I appealed to the estate agent's son in him. 'I think I need another drink, Robin.'

'Right, I'll get you one,' he said, setting off eagerly across a dance floor that was now strewn with discarded plastic cups and the dog-ends of cigarettes and joints. The room was pitching and bucking like an ocean-going liner in distress and a strange centrifugal force affecting my body made sitting down a sudden imperative and I subsided quietly onto the spare corner of a filthy-looking mattress.

The rest of the mattress, I suddenly realized, was occupied by Roger Lake, locked on like a lamprey to a first-year girl less than half his age. I would have asked him how his wife and his mistress were but I couldn't really speak; my tongue had grown too big for my mouth and the centrifugal force was trying to drag me down a black hole. My head had the gravity of a small planet. My mouth felt dry and clinkerish and I reached for an opened can of Export on the floor and swallowed a great draught of it before gagging it all out again, along with its flotsam of ash and butts. Someone loomed in front of me

400

and asked me if I was all right. It was Heather, wriggling unrhythmically to 'Go Ask Alice', her nipples jumping in my face. Her voice boomed and ebbed in a distorted way as if we were underwater. Eventually she got fed up with getting no response from me and started talking to Roger in a familiar way which confirmed that they had previously shared more than an interest in Marxian economic theory or a copy of Cairncross.

I decided to try and make it across the floor to Bob, although it was unlikely that he would be able to do anything to make me feel better. I had once fainted in the Ladywell Bar in Bob's company and, at a loss as to what to do, he had simply lain down on the floor next to me. An action which resulted in our both being thrown out. I could see him, without the hookah now but with the *Finnegans Wake* girl, who looked to be sprawled across his lap in uncharacteristic hedonistic abandon.

I stood up and the room immediately broke up into thousands of little dots, as if I'd suddenly stepped inside a pointillist painting. I couldn't be sure, but I could have sworn I saw the elusive shape of the yellow dog on the far side of the room. I wondered if it was an hallucination or a mirage? And was the yellow dog now my quest since Terri had gone to hide in a place rhyming with Glasgow? Perhaps, Lassie-like, it was trying to show me the way to Kara.

I struggled heroically across the wasteland of the ballroom floor, occupied now by a frenzy of people dancing to Santana, only to find when I arrived on the other side that there was no sign of Bob anywhere, or of the yellow dog. It was very hot and airless by now and a herd of people milled around aimlessly, amplified and distorted by the candlelit mirrors and my dappled vision. My blood pressure was low and falling and there was a blackness closing in around me and I knew I had to get out of that room or I was going to pass out, and the last thing I wanted was attention from any of the drug-fuelled medical students in Forres.

I finally managed to fight my way out of the room, passing Davina on the way –

'There,' I say to Nora, 'you owe me a pound.'

– and entered what must have once been the billiards room, where the air was slightly fresher. No-one was wielding a cue and the green baize of the large billiards table was currently occupied by the apparently unconscious body of Gilbert, splayed out over a Scalectrix set, much to the annoyance of the people who wanted to play with it. Around him, small groups of people, without exception male, were sitting on the floor playing Risk and Diplomacy, Mah-jong and – naturally – Go. If only they would. The atmosphere in the room was so boring it could have caused living flesh to petrify and I hurried away, pausing only to heave Gilbert's prostrate form into the recovery position.

I tried a door at the far end of the billiards room and found it opened into a small room that was entirely dark, save for the light coming from a television set that was showing *Dad's Army*. In the doorway I bumped into Shug, who said, 'Out on the ran-dan, eh, hen?' and put his arms around me. He was very drunk and said, 'So how about

402

it – you and me?' and I had to push him away and remind him that he was 'Bob's pal' and therefore couldn't shag me. Where *was* Bob? Shug shrugged (as he had to do sooner or later). 'Dunno.'

I lurched on, up a small servants' staircase to the mysterious upper regions of the house where, in a cold bedroom heated to no effect by an oil-filled radiator, Kara and Jill were sitting cross-legged on the floor. Deposited on the cold candlewick of the double bed was Jill's child with the unpronounceable name, two more sleeping infants of indeterminate age and – to my extreme relief – Proteus.

'Welcome to the nursery,' Kara said, lighting up a joint.

'You got him back OK, then?' I said, looking at Proteus's peaceful sleeping face.

'Are you all right?' she said to me. 'You look a bit pale.'

'I feel a bit pale.'

Kara reached out and grabbed my wrist and took my pulse in a professional sort of way. 'I've got a St Andrew's Ambulance Brigade certificate,' she said, but then she let go of my wrist and said indifferently, 'You're dead.'

'Do you want to stay here and babysit for us?' Jill asked. *Dead Babysitter*, now that would be a good title for something. I made a vague mental note to tell Robin.

I moved on, back down another small staircase, and tried other rooms, unsure now whether I was looking for something or not. Perhaps like Professor Cousins I would recognize it when I found it. In a small back room I found a solitary boy, alone with a bong and an overwhelming

403

scent of burning sage that drove me straight out again into a room with another television – an old Philips portable sitting in the middle of the floor. There was no audience for the country being burned on screen and I felt I had a duty to stay and watch for a few minutes but then I started to feel ravenously hungry and wondered if I could find my way back to the kitchen.

Instead, I found what seemed to be a quite separate wing of the house. Forres must have been designed by Borges and constructed by Escher, I had no idea if I was facing north, south, east or west, or even which floor I was now on. I peered cautiously into a room that might once have been a grand upstairs drawing-room but was now a dystopian vision of carnal debauchery as, by the light of several smoky candles, naked bodies writhed in a tapsie-teerie abandonment worthy of Bosch.

'Do you mind?' a disembodied voice said. 'This is a serious massage class.'

I hurried away; nothing would have induced me to stay. I went, instead, into the bathroom, a place of glacial chilliness boasting all its original fittings – complicated brass pipework and florid tiles that would have looked more at home in the Speedwell Bar. An ancient bath, like an ornate catafalque, stood in the centre of the room, its enamel pitted and chipped. Empty of water, it was tenanted by a fully dressed boy wearing a top hat. On the edge of the bath was perched another, very thin, boy in a Black Watch dress jacket. He was clutching a copy of *Sgt. Pepper* and explaining to the boy in the bath how depressed he felt in a conversation that seemed to have been scripted by Robin: 'Like really down. I mean what's the point of it all?'

The boy in the bath nodded sympathetically. 'I know – the meaning of Liff and everything.'

A girl on her knees, as if in prayer in front of the filthy toilet, was moaning quietly. It was the first-year student I had lately seen in Roger Lake's arms. She lay down on the floor, her forehead pressed against the cold stained tiles. I put her in the recovery position (maybe this was all I was good for in the world) and told the *Sgt. Pepper* boy to keep an eye on her, but I doubted that he would.

I had to get some fresh air. By mere accident, I discovered the main staircase of the house, a great wooden mock-Jacobean flight of the imagination, carved with thistles and emblazoned with gryphons and strange armorial devices. The tall banister finials at the foot of the staircase were in the form of aggressive wyverns, poised to leap on the unsuspecting passer-by. I scurried past them rather fearfully and into a square hallway that was large enough to merit its own fireplace – black iron, cast in the shape of a scallop shell, with a padded red velvet fender seat on which I sat down gingerly next to Kevin, who was drinking from a large bottle of Irn-Bru.

'Parties are such crap,' he said disconsolately.

'I really don't feel well, Kevin. I think I need a doctor.'

'In Edrakonia,' he said, 'the physicians are also alchemists, transmuting base metal into gold and so on.

405

Of course since the Murk fell all kinds of strange diseases have arisen, the fading disease, for example.'

'The fading disease?'

'Self-explanatory.'

Maybe that was what happened to The Boy With No Name. Maybe that was what was happening to me. I was relieved when Gilbert joined us, remarkably fresh for one who was unconscious so recently.

'Good party, isn't it?' he said cheerfully.

'Or the falling disease,' Kevin continued relentlessly.

'Have you seen a yellow dog?' I asked Gilbert, ignoring Kevin.

'A *yellow* dog?' Gilbert repeated. 'I didn't know you got *yellow* dogs. No, sorry.'

I pushed my way outside. A bonfire had been built out on the back lawn and was now blazing fiercely. The air was ringing with frost, sparks rose like tiny barbs of light into the night sky, a sky that was swimming with stars. Some people were dragging old furniture out of the house to keep the conflagration going. I saw one of the ballroom curtains go up in a roar of dust and flame. Other people were dancing round the bonfire like members of a lunatic coven. Andrea was one of them. She spotted me and danced over.

'It's like a planetarium,' a stargazing Andrea said, looking at the heavens in open-mouthed awe, 'a kind of . . . open-air planetarium.' I told her Shug was upstairs and she danced off eagerly. I felt suddenly cold and sick. I looked around for Kevin or Gilbert but couldn't see them any more. A threatening figure suddenly appeared in front of me. It was a nightmarish Archie, dressed in a daring pair of youthful flares that were an uncomfortable size too small for him.

'You,' he said, obviously very drunk.

'Yes,' I agreed, 'me.'

'Have you seen Dickhead?' Archie asked, casting his eyes vaguely around the garden. (I was glad Professor Cousins wasn't there to witness this.)

'Who?'

'Dr Dick,' Archie said irritably, 'he's—' but just then a tremendous explosion drowned out whatever it was he'd been going to say.

~ Is this a denouement?

'No.'

I thought Forres must have been blown up by a bomb or a gas leak, but the boy with the top hat who had been in the bath ran by and said breathlessly, 'Elderflower champagne,' by way of explanation.

'The protesters are using elderflower champagne? How does that work?' Archie puzzled to me but I didn't hang about to explain. I felt claustrophobic, even though I was in the open air, and started trying to find a way out of the garden that didn't involve going back through the house. I could feel myself falling. Fading and falling – and then a pair of arms encircled my waist from behind and held me up. In my fevered brain I thought I smelt Ferdinand's masculine scent. 'Time to get you to bed, young lady,' a familiar voice said.

'Ferdinand,' I murmured and rested my head gratefully on his shoulder before finally fading right away.

I woke up slowly to the steady sound of rain. Something as cool and smooth as soapstone was spooning my naked body. I rolled over and saw –

Dr Dick.

I propped myself up on one elbow and looked at him in horror. His eyes opened slowly and I was able to observe his brain catching up with them.

'Effie,' he said, yawning and fondling the pale stalk of his penis in a boyish, asexual way. Had we been having an extra-curricular tutorial of some kind? And would it result in better marks for me? Or worse?

'What have we been doing exactly, Dr Dick?' I asked tentatively.

He groped on the bedside table for his little spectacles and put them on and said, 'I think we're on first-name terms now, don't you? Call me Richard, why don't you?'

I tried to comfort myself with the thought that worse things could happen to me but just then I really couldn't think of any.

A wretched cold fog was coming in from the sea and crawling over the city. The melancholy sound of the foghorn boomed at regular intervals and set up a strange melancholic echo in my bones.

~ Can you have fog and rain at the same time?

'If I want.'

'Tea?' Dr Dick offered, gesturing vaguely in the direction of his kitchen. 'There's no electricity,' he added, in case I was thinking of saying yes. Dr Dick was helpless without the Monopoly board utilities. I glanced at the clock.

'No, thank you,' I said. 'I really have to go, I have to hand in an essay.'

But first I had to see Bob. Because the last time I caught sight of him was in the massage room in Forres in the oily hands of the *Finnegans Wake* girl and I wondered if he could give me an adequate explanation of his behaviour. I doubted it somehow. Was he going to leave me before I could leave him?

Nora is walking on the strand – a place that is neither sea nor land and which she says is one of the doorways to the other world. She is careless of the surf washing around her wellingtons. Occasionally she picks up a pebble or a shell and stuffs it into one of the pockets of the large man's overcoat she is wearing. I suspect she is still wearing the diamonds under her woollen scarf. She keeps looking out to sea with the eagerness of a mariner looking for landfall. She smells the wind.

~ It's coming, she says.

'What is?'

~ The end.

She walks off, her pockets bulging with stones. I run after her, battling the wind.

'So . . . elaborate on the marriage, divorce, death bit.'

Nora sighs and recommences her tale with almost theatrical reluctance:

~ Effie was packed off to London to some distant Stuart-Murray relation, to be 'finished' in some way. It was a shame she wasn't just finished off. Lachlan went to study law in Edinburgh and when the war started he joined the army and Effie came home to Glenkittrie, where she hung around all day saying she

409

was 'bored out of her skull' and there was nothing worse than Effie when she was bored. I used to look forward to going to school every morning – I attended the local primary – just to get away from her. I was 'the brat', 'the kid'. She was supposed to look after me because Marjorie was ill but she never did. There were no nannies or anything by then – the London house had been sold long ago, the Edinburgh house rented out to a property company, there was always a large, but invisible, drain on the Stuart-Murray finances.

~ Kirkton of Craigie was a tiny school; most children came from the farms round about. I spent a lot of time with them outside of school as well –

Nora pauses and looks pensive. I suppose it's disturbing for her to go back to a time when she had a normal life, when she had friends, when her future was still full of possibilities.

~ I used to think I must be a wicked child because I felt no love for either Donald or Marjorie. I worried that it meant I would grow up like Effie – incapable of caring about anyone but myself. But it wasn't my fault if Donald was a foul-tempered bore, Marjorie a drunkard. They barely spoke to me, even less to each other. They were like people who had lost their souls.

(What a metaphysical turn of mind my mother (not) has.)

~ Then the army started up a camp nearby and Effie wasn't bored any more. I remember a time when she came home while we were eating breakfast. Her make-up was smudged, her hair was a mess and she smelt of drink and cigarettes and something more rank and vulgar. She used to think that she was so beautiful but sometimes she was the ugliest creature imaginable.

Donald started shouting at her, calling her a disgraceful whore, a little bitch in heat and so on. Did she want another little bastard? he yelled at her.

And Effie replied, 'Not if it turns out as dull as the first one.'

'Is that a clue?'

Nora ignores me.

~ Anyway, eventually she fell pregnant – there was a whole regiment that could have fathered the child but she managed to net an officer and got married.

Then the war ended—

'How fast time goes in this tale, and you're leaving out all the details.'

~ There's not enough time for details. Effie's husband – I think he was called Derek, but I can't be sure, he made very little impression on anyone, least of all Effie – was demobbed – I think he was a chartered surveyor. Derek, as we'll call him, even if that isn't his name, started talking about buying a nice house in a garden city down south and starting a family. I don't think it had ever occurred to Effie that he might have a life beyond the war. She left him as soon as she saw him in his demob suit.

Marjorie was dying by then. Donald had had his first stroke. I'd been sent away to school – to St Leonard's – where all the teachers were suspicious of me because I was 'Euphemia's sister' and I had to work very hard to reassure them I wasn't like her.

Lachlan was working in a law firm in Edinburgh. He had a squalid little basement flat in Cumberland Street, in the street next to the family's old New Town house, now home to an insurance office – that's a detail since you're so keen –

Effie used to go and stay with him there for days on end after her divorce. They made quite a seedy couple. I have no idea what she did all day when he was at work.

I had to go and stay there once, just before Marjorie died. I must have been thirteen or so. I slept on the couch and Effie said, 'Oh, no, no room for me, I'll have to sleep with *you*, Lachlan,' and laughed. They both seemed to think this was hilarious. It never seemed to occur to them that Lachlan could sleep on the couch and Effie and I could share a bed.

It was a weekend and they stayed in with the curtains closed and drank and smoked the whole time. I'd hoped that they might at least have taken me to the Castle. In the end I went out on my own, roamed around Edinburgh for hours and ended up getting lost. A policeman had to show me the way home. It was a shame he didn't come in with me. I might have been taken away by a welfare officer and had a normal life. The flat was a wreck – bottles and ash-trays, dirty plates, even underwear. Lachlan had passed out on the couch and Effie could barely speak she was so drunk.

When I came home I found that Marjorie had died in the local cottage hospital and without a single living soul to see her off, the nurse by her bedside having slipped outside for a cigarette.

Lachlan, who had turned out in adulthood to be as vain, weak and selfish as his childhood character predicted, decided it was time he acquired a wife and got engaged to the highly strung daughter of a judge. Effie was furious, jealous as a cat, and immediately got married again herself to a man she met on a train. It was to spite Lachlan, I suppose. This new husband of Effie's – let's call him Edmund – was rich – he owned a business

412

– war-profiteering of some kind, although Lachlan always referred to him as a car salesman because he'd offered to sell him his old Bentley 'at a good price'.

Lachlan's own wife, Gertrude, proved a disappointment. Chosen to be a brood mare for the Stuart-Murray blood, she turned out to be incapable of bearing children.

Donald had another stroke and became bedridden. Whenever I came home from school it was to the smell of the sick-room. The house was full of nurses coming and going, mainly going – Donald was a terrible patient, most of his nurses only stayed a few weeks; one only lasted a night after Donald threw a full urinal at her head.

Then Mabel Orchard came.

'And?'

~ And everything.

Brian twirled his cane and his false moustache for Madame Astarti's benefit.

'Can you get my fags from the dressing-room?' Sandra asked her. They were waiting in the wings (a place Madame Astarti felt she'd spent her whole life), waiting for their cue to go on stage and start sawing and vanishing.

There was something melancholic about an empty dressing-room, Madame Astarti thought, even threatening in a funny way. It reminded her of *Stage Fright* or clowns. Madame Astarti had always found clowns frightening. They were so . . . unfunny.

There was no sign of a packet of cigarettes

413

anywhere, but there were clothes hanging on a
rail and a coat on a hanger on the back of a
door and Madame Astarti went through the pockets of all of them, gingerly, because you never
knew what you would find in a strange pocket,
but she found nothing. She tried the cupboard.
The door handle was stiff and she had to pull
hard on it. She nearly fell over backwards when
it suddenly responded—

Chez Bob

I COULD HEAR BOB TALKING IN THE BEDROOM AS I CAME INTO
the flat. At first I thought it must be his usual sleep
gibberish, but gradually it resolved itself into (a kind of)
Logic –

> *'Symbolize the following propositions in the symbolism
> of Predicate Logic:*
> *a) The miners have a special case.*
> *b) University teachers don't have a special case.*
> *c) The miners work harder than the university teachers.*
> *d) The miners will get a bigger rise than the university
> teachers.*
> *e) No group will get a bigger rise than the miners.*
> *f) If one group works harder than another group, it will
> get a bigger rise.*
> *g) A group will get a bigger rise than another group
> only if it has a special case and the other group doesn't.*

And that,' Bob said in an exasperated voice, 'isn't even the
difficult bit – right?'

'Right,' another voice said, sounding rather tired, as if
it might have been listening to Bob for some time.
Interestingly, the voice was female. I crept as silently as a

417

dog-burglar across the carpet towards the bedroom door.

'"M",' Bob continued 'is "the miners", "u" is "the university teachers", "sx" is "x has a special case", "hxy" is "x works harder than y", "bxy" is "x will get a bigger rise than y", Universe of Discourse is groups of workers. Show by constructing a formal derivation that (c), (f) and (g) together imply (b). You don't know how to do this stuff by any chance, do you?' he asked this anonymous female hopefully. 'My girlfriend thinks I have no brain.'

'And is she right?'

'Ha, ha,' Bob said. 'You're quite witty, aren't you?'

The door to the bedroom was ajar and I gave it a nudge so that it opened just wide enough for me to catch a glimpse of Bob lazing naked amongst a tumble of empurpled sheets.

'Brain and brain, what is brain?' Bob said in a ridiculous voice. I nudged the door a little further until I could see the *Finnegans Wake* girl lying with the sheet pulled decorously up over her torso but nonetheless presumably naked also.

'What are you *talking* about?' she said in an exasperated tone.

I pushed the door wide open.

'Arse,' Bob said eloquently when he saw me. The *Finnegans Wake* girl screamed realistically.

'It's *Star Trek*,' I said helpfully to her, 'an episode called "Spock's Brain", from the third series.' I shut the bedroom door. I couldn't think of anything else to do.

I was about to leave when the phone rang. I picked it

up and listened in silence to the voice at the other end. Finally, I said, 'Right, I'll tell him then.'

When I opened the door to the bedroom Bob put his hands up as if he was expecting to be shot.

'Bob,' I said with a heavy heart, 'Bob, I'm afraid I've got some bad news for you.'

'The power's off?' he guessed. 'We're out of tea? You're leaving me?' he added rather dejectedly.

I sighed. 'No, none of those things. Your father's dead.'

Poor Bob Senior, a man I hardly knew really apart from the odd conversation over the tea-table about the state of the garden or the politics of state. Nonetheless, it was I who had the tears running down my face, while Bob stared helplessly at the *Finnegans Wake* girl, already pulling her clothes on and heading for the door.

What a particularly bad twenty-four hours it had been.

'Buggery rats,' Madame Astarti exclaimed as the body fell out of the cupboard on top of her.

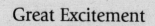

Great Excitement

Madame Astarti had opened up early and was sitting in her booth, drinking tea and idly
shuffling her Tarot pack whilst wondering
whether to eat all of her Kit-Kat now or save
two fingers for later, when she heard a strange
ticking noise. She left the booth and went and
scrutinized the war memorial suspiciously. The
deactivated torpedo was definitely ticking like
an alarm clock ready to go off. Madame Astarti
looked around; no-one else seemed to have
noticed it. Frank the fishman was unlocking his
stall, fiddling with an awkward padlock.

At that moment Madame Astarti became aware of
another noise, this one like the droning of a
large, angry insect. 'Look!' she shouted to
Frank, pointing in amazement to the blue sky
where a small light aircraft was circling lower
and lower, smoke trailing from one of its
engines.

Frank finally managed to yank open the shutters of his stall just as the little aircraft

423

plunged into the sea with a kind of plopping noise. A few minutes later a woman struggled out of the water and waded ashore. Not often you saw that, Madame Astarti thought.

Frank was indifferent to the woman walking out of the water, instead he was screaming at what he had found inside his stall. Where his plaice and haddock and tubs of whelks were usually displayed was an altogether more sinister cold water fish - the body of a dead woman lay on the slab, with a lemon stuck in her mouth and a few sprigs of parsley for garnish.

~ Mabel Orchard was thirty-four years old when she arrived in the glen to nurse Donald and was as passive as a piece of furniture and as placid as a bowling-green.

(How fanciful are my mother-not-my-mother's figures of speech.)

Mabel was very religious; she claimed she'd had visions as a child, something which hadn't gone down very well with the strict and obscure Christian sect that her parents were members of, who branded her a fanciful and heretical child, one teetering dangerously on the brink of papism and idolatry. Now Mabel no longer bothered with the edifices and ritual of the Church but claimed, like Joan of Arc before her, that God spoke to her in person all the time, although sometimes he sent his Son to have a word and very occasionally she was blessed with a *tête-à-tête* with the Holy Ghost Himself. Like Joan of Arc, she was also

424

engaged in a one-woman battle with the enemy, but in the case of Mabel it was the forces of Satan rather than the English (which is not the same thing, despite what some may say).

Mabel was herself English, born in Bristol to a family that, despite its earthbound name, had been seafaring for centuries, manning men-o'-wars, submersing in submarines and ferrying cargoes of slaves across the great wide ocean. The last male in the Orchard line – Mabel's brother – had been torpedoed on the China Seas and there was a general sense of disappointment in the family that the nautical genes were going to die out with Mabel, who had decided to remain as chaste as a nun.

Although she had spent her whole childhood wishing for children of her own, Mabel had forsaken personal happiness and all thought of marriage and married love after her fiancé – Dudley – was shot through the heart at Tobruk, this in spite of the little Bible Mabel had given him as a parting gift and which had nestled snugly in the pocket of his uniform waiting to catch bullets and save his life – in the manner of a story she had read in a magazine. After it fatally failed to fulfil this function, Mabel was uncertain as to whether she should stop believing in God or in fiction. She chose the latter and never opened a magazine – or even a newspaper – from that day forward. After Dudley died Mabel trained as a nurse. If he had lived she had planned to fill her arms with so many babies that when they grew up there would be enough Orchards to crew the entire British naval fleet if necessary.

Mabel wore a plain gold crucifix around her neck, given to her by Dudley on his last leave, and the chain was so thin that it was beginning to disappear into the folds and rolls of flesh around her chin. For Mabel was fat. There was no politer word for it. Her personal God put no restrictions on appetite or intake, indeed, Mabel had a feeling that he actively encouraged her to eat. And her body, she reasoned, was made by Him, so what better way to praise His works than to develop more of it. It was God, after all, who had put all this bounty on earth – even lardy cakes and black bun – who was she to shun it? Lachlan, when he first met her, called her 'the cow' and she did possess a strange passing resemblance to a Jersey in the colour of her hair, the length of her lashes, the flesh on her ample fallow flank. Yet she was stately, almost majestic, in her bulk – more like a great tribal queen than a milch-cow and when she ate – which was often – she was as delicate as a cat.

'Well-upholstered,' mumbled Donald – who still had the power of speech, if little else, and had taken an uncharacteristic 'shine' to his new caretaker. Mabel was so relentlessly nice to him with her 'God bless you's and 'Jesus loves you's that he began to believe this propaganda and the idea that God might still love him, despite his flaws, wrought a strange change in his character and made him almost bearable. And, although now in his seventies, Donald was still capable of appreciating a female bosom and took considerable, albeit heathen, pleasure in trying to catch sight of Mabel's butterfat breasts through her cheap blouses, as she bent over him to attend to some intimate bodily function or other of his.

Unfortunately for Donald, he was now paralysed down his left side and could not really put his thoughts into action.

Such servants as there were had now all departed. They had either been driven away by Donald (before he was blessed by God) or they had got tired of not receiving any wages (the Stuart-

426

Murrays had always had a tendency to resent the idea that servants were supposed to be paid), and Mabel cheerfully took on all the work of the house. Her big dumpling-fleshed arms washed and wrung out any number of soiled bedsheets and stained clothes; she swept and scrubbed and shined and even found time to cook the kind of hearty food that her mother had cooked for her when she lived at home – suet puddings, boiled brisket and shin-beef stews, rissoles and scrag-end hot-pots, jam roly-poly and bread-and-butter pudding. Donald discovered that he rather liked this food and wished he'd met Mabel when he was younger; she would have surely have produced more wholesome and longer-lived heirs than either Evangeline or Marjorie had managed (although Evangeline could hardly be blamed for the First World War).

God's favoured time for a little chat with Mabel was in the afternoons, so once lunch was done with and the pots cleared, Mabel would sit in the ladder-back chair in the corner of the kitchen, hands folded quietly in her lap as if in a private church and wait for God to find her. Naturally, God could, if necessary, communicate at any time, even, Mabel once shyly revealed to me, when she was 'on the WC', which was a natural act created by God Himself. But the afternoons were the best as far as both Mabel and God were concerned, after a nice lunch – boiled bacon and salad and new potatoes and a slice of apple pie with cheese was a favourite mid-day repast (of Mabel, not God).

Listening out for God was the only time her hands were idle; the rest of the time they were the busiest hands He ever fashioned. Mabel was particularly fond of knitting; sometimes she unravelled things on purpose just so that she would have something to knit back up again.

427

When I first met her, in the school summer holidays when I was nearly sixteen, Mabel had already been ensconced in the house for three months. The atmosphere in Woodhaven was quite changed. Everything was clean and orderly and, possibly for the first time ever in that household, everything was peaceful – but then Effie wasn't there and peace and Effie never lived in the same room together.

Mabel was so kind to me, always asking, Was I all right? Was I warm enough? Did I need anything knitted? Would I like something to eat? To drink? Did I want to walk? Talk? Listen to the radio? It made me realize what a cold childhood I had had, how mean-spirited my mother had been, how distant my father, and last, but not least, how peculiar and perverse my siblings.

Effie had been living in London with Edmund, the businessman, all this while and had hardly ever visited the glen or taken an interest in its goings on, so it was quite a surprise for her when she came home, wild-eyed and teetering on the brink of an unsavoury divorce, to be greeted on the doorstep of Woodhaven by Mabel Orchard proudly (yet humbly) displaying a wedding-ring and introducing herself to Effie as 'Mrs Donald Stuart-Murray'.

Silence.

'And?'

~And I'm going to bed. Goodnight.

I saw Bob onto the train. It seemed the least I could do, in the circumstances. I walked down to Riverside to watch the London-bound train passing over the Tay but the fog was so thick that I could hardly make out the bridge, let alone the train. The river, what I could see of it, was a cold

428

gunmetal colour. I could have sat down by the banks of the Tay and wept (although for myself rather than Bob), but I didn't because I had a deadline to meet.

I had to fight my way into the English department. The Tower extension was under siege from protesters, a motley crew now as it seemed anyone with any kind of grievance had begun to attach themselves to the uprising to demand a new world order – students wanting free condoms or the tied-book loan period extending, anti-vivisectionists, diggers and levellers, even a sprinkling of Christians – I spotted Janice Rand and her balding friend holding a hand-made sign that said 'Overthrow sin – let Jesus into your life'. I doubted that there would be enough room.

The lift to the extension was out of order, jammed open with a mop and guarded by a boy reading *Culture and Anarchy* who took the time to ask me if I'd done an Emily Brontë essay and if so could he borrow it? I ignored him and hurried up the stairs where I found the English department being stoutly defended by the redoubtable Joan, standing like a guard dog at the top of the stairs and murmuring something about boiling oil. 'I think they've got Professor Cousins,' she said, looking rather pleased at the idea.

There was no sign of Maggie Mackenzie in her room and Joan seemed unsure of her whereabouts. This was very disappointing. I had gone to great lengths to hand in George Eliot on time and now Maggie Mackenzie wasn't even there to receive her.

The door to Dr Dick's room was closed, of course. I knew only too well why he wasn't behind it. (Had I had sex with him? And wouldn't I be able to tell if I had?)

Watson Grant's door, on the other hand, was open to reveal a group of bored students to whom he was dictating like an old-fashioned dominie. He was sitting on the wide windowsill surrounded on all sides by books, and frowned when he saw me.

The door to Archie's room was also open and I could hear his voice drifting out into the corridor –

'Kierkegaardian dread . . . The identity of essence and phenomenon "demanded" by truth is put into effect . . .'

I tried to tiptoe past unnoticed but Archie caught sight of me and shouted, 'What are you doing skulking about out there? Come and sit down!' My protestations went unheeded and he almost dragged me into his room and pushed me into one of the uncomfortable plastic chairs.

'What Heidegger might call "an empty squabble over words" . . .'

I could see why he needed me, the only other person present was Kevin – looking distressed, like an animal tracked and hunted down by Archie's relentless verbosity. No Shug, no Andrea, no Olivia, no Terri (well on her way now, presumably, to Fresno or Sorrento).

'The use of the fragmentary and contingent to express the dissonant . . . as Pierre Machery says . . . the line of the text can be traversed in more than one direction . . .'

Was it really a week since I had last endured this? Archie bored on:

*'. . . the line of its discourse is multiple . . . the beginning
and the end are inextricably mingled . . .'*

I felt hot and cold at the same time, there were bees (or
maybe Bs) in my head and my brain seemed to be in
spasm. Was it my imagination or had the fog outside
started to creep inside the room?

I began to shiver. I stood up and the room tilted. The
fog was everywhere, I pushed my way through it.

'Wait!' Archie shouted after me, but I really couldn't. I
ran past Watson Grant's room and saw him struggling to
open his window. To let the fog out, I supposed.

I hurried on and, as the lift was out of order, thanks to
the *Culture and Anarchy* boy, I barged past Joan and stum-
bled down the stairs.

As I ran outside into the chilly air I nearly collided with
Maggie Mackenzie – in the middle of berating a rather
cowed-looking Professor Cousins over some perceived
administrative oversight.

'I've been looking for you,' I said weakly to her. 'I've got
the essay for you.'

'What essay?' she said, looking at me as if I had grown
even more stupid than usual. I raked through my bag for
the essay, finally retrieving the tattered pages of my
George Eliot.

'What is this?' Maggie Mackenzie asked, holding up the
proffered essay between the tips of two fingers as if it was
contaminated. I regarded it with horror – the pages were
torn and ragged, the front cover almost shredded. There
were filthy marks all over the paper as well as stains and

blotches, as though someone had cried all over it. I peered at it more closely – the filthy marks seemed to be paw prints and the stains produced by dog slobber.

'I'm sorry,' I mumbled to Maggie Mackenzie. 'I think a dog ate my essay.'

An alarm bell sounded shrilly. At first I thought it was in my head, so odd was I feeling, but then people began to stream out of the building.

'Oh, my lord,' Professor Cousins said, 'I do believe the place is on fire.' I could see the fog escaping from the windows of the extension and suddenly realized that it wasn't fog at all – it was thick smoke that was pouring out of the building.

Above our heads the sound of muffled shouting and banging grew more insistent. I looked up and saw Grant Watson hammering on the window of his room, pushing and pulling at the handle as if he was trapped inside. Then the window flew open suddenly and in doing so it sent flying all the books that had been piled up on the sill. Watson Grant shouted a warning but it was too late – the books rained down slowly like books in a dream and I looked on with paralysed interest as first one volume of the *Shorter Oxford Dictionary* (*A to Markworthy*) and then the second (*Marl to Z*) fell like slabs of Old Testament stone onto Maggie Mackenzie's head. A strange *Splat!* sound that could have belonged in a cartoon speech bubble was made by her body as it hit the ground.

Things weren't quite as bad as they seemed. Everyone escaped the building and the fire brigade doused the flames (feeding on the university's abundant supply of flammable grey plastic) before they could do any real harm.

Professor Cousins and I rode (reluctantly) with Maggie Mackenzie in the ambulance. The ambulanceman who had ferried Dr Dick to hospital smiled at me and said, 'You again.' Unfortunately, Maggie Mackenzie wasn't unconscious and, if anything, rather garrulous, as if being hit on the head by so many words had stimulated the vocabulary department of her brain.

When we got to the DRI we had to wait while she was seen and Professor Cousins suggested we go and visit Christopher Pike, former front-runner for head of department, 'and perhaps Dr Dick's still here?' he mused to himself. I assured him that he wasn't.

After some detective work, we eventually located Christopher Pike in a two-bed side bay of the men's surgical ward. He was still trapped in his web of ropes and pulleys although now only recognizable by a name pinned up above his bed. The rest of him was swaddled in bandages from head to foot, like the Invisible Man, so that it could have been anyone pupating inside the crêpe-bandage chrysalis. Tubes came in and out of the bandages, all of them carrying liquids of a yellowish hue.

'Poor old Pike,' Professor Cousins said quietly to me. 'I'm afraid he had another accident while he was in here.'

On Christopher Pike's bedside locker there was a glass of sticky-looking orange squash and a bunch of yellow

Muscat grapes, proving that somewhere else in the world there must be heat and light.

'I don't know,' Professor Cousins said, making a great performance of chewing on a grape. 'I may as well transfer the English department to the DRI.' Christopher Pike gurgled something incomprehensible from inside his mummy suit.

'You'll soon be back on your feet, dear chap!' Professor Cousins shouted at him.

'He's not deaf,' the patient in the neighbouring bed remarked, without taking his eyes off the *Courier* he was reading. Christopher Pike made some more incomprehensible noises and his neighbour put down his newspaper and inclined his head towards him like a rather poor ventriloquist to translate the gurgling but then frowned and shrugged and said, 'Poor bastard.'

The ward sister swept in ahead of a consultant who in turn was followed by a group of medical students like a gaggle of goslings. I recognized a couple of them from the Union bar.

'Out,' the sister said peremptorily to us.

We found Maggie Mackenzie restrained by the tight tourniquet of starched white sheet and baby-blue coverlet. Her hair was a knotted mass of grips and snakes and plaits on the pillow. Her face bore a vague resemblance to corned beef and a deep blue bruise had bloomed on her forehead. I touched my own bruise to see if it was still there. It was.

Professor Cousins offered Maggie Mackenzie a

Nuttall's Minto. She ignored him and said, in an even more crotchety way than usual, 'I'm lucky I'm not dead. They're keeping me in for a day or two, I'm concussed apparently.'

'I was concussed once,' Professor Cousins said, but before he could embark on this familiar tale, a bell rang to signal the end of visiting-time – although for a moment Professor Cousins was under the impression that the hospital was on fire.

'Well, goodbye,' I said awkwardly to Maggie Mackenzie and, uncertain what was appropriate in the circumstances, I patted one of her washerwoman's hands that lay atop the coverlet. Her skin felt like an amphibian's.

As we made our way out through the overheated corridors of the DRI, Professor Cousins cast a nervous glance over his shoulder. 'They're trying to kill me, you know,' he said conversationally.

'Who?' I asked, rather impatiently. '*Who* is it exactly that's trying to kill you?'

'The forces of darkness,' he said conspiratorially.

'The . . . ?'

'Forces of darkness,' he repeated. 'They're all around us and they're trying to destroy us. We should get out of here,' he added, 'before they spot us.'

~ No-one's trying to kill him at all. He's just paranoid, isn't he? Nora says irritably. He's just a red herring. And the old people – I bet they're just paranoid as well.

'Ah, yes, but that doesn't mean that someone's not out to get them.'

~ You'll never make a crime writer.

'This isn't a crime story. This is a comic novel.'

I abandoned Professor Cousins to the forces of darkness and made my way home, taking a mazy route through the back streets of Blackness until finally pitching up on the Perth Road. There was an ambulance on the street, blue lights flashing, and with a sense of alarm I realized it was parked outside Olivia's flat. Olivia herself appeared – pale and unconscious and strapped on a stretcher, rather like Dr Dick before her. The same ambulanceman was there, as if there was only one crew in the whole city. When he caught sight of me this time he gave me a suspicious scowl of recognition. I suppose I did seem to be in attendance at rather a lot of mishaps.

A distraught Kevin appeared as if out of nowhere, along with all three of Olivia's flatmates. 'An overdose,' one of them whispered to me.

'I found her,' Kevin said when he saw me. He was sweating uncomfortably and a wheeze like that of Mrs Macbeth's old dog was coming from his chest. 'I came to ask her if I could borrow her George Eliot essay,' he said.

'She did Charlotte Brontë,' I said flatly.

'She had an abortion yesterday,' one of her flatmates said to me as we watched Olivia being loaded into the back of the ambulance. 'It's a shame, she loved babies.'

'Loved?' It was only then that I realized that Olivia wasn't unconscious – Olivia was dead.

~ No, no, no, no, *no*, Nora says, very agitated, you said this was a comic novel – you can't *kill* people.

436

'People are already dead.'

~ Who?

'Miss Anderson, poor Senga.' (Not to mention most of Nora's family, but I suppose it's tactless to mention that.)

~ They don't count, we didn't know them. Don't kill Olivia. I shall stop listening to you, I shall leave, I shall . . .

She searches for the biggest threat she can think of. And finds it –

~ I shall *erase*.

'Oh, all *right*, calm down.'

Maggie Mackenzie was diagnosed with concussion and Professor Cousins went reluctantly with her in the ambulance. The ambulanceman who had ferried Dr Dick to hospital smiled at me and said, 'You again.'

I elected not to go to the hospital, making the excuse that I had to redo my essay, and set off, taking a mazy route through the back streets of Blackness until finally pitching up on the Perth Road, where I bumped into Miranda, substantially the worse for wear but a medic nonetheless, and I grabbed hold of her limp form and hung onto it while I repeatedly rang the bell on Olivia's front door.

After an agony of waiting the heavy door swung open and I dashed – as well as one can dash when hampered by a raging fever and a recalcitrant girl – up the stairs to her flat. One of Olivia's flatmates was in the process of letting Kevin in. He was stammering on about George Eliot as I barged into him, sending him flying into the flat.

'Olivia!' I gasped to one of her flatmates.

437

'She's in her room, what's the—'

Olivia's door was locked. I told Kevin this was a matter of life and death, Olivia's to be more precise, and he responded as heroically as Thar-Vint might have done by throwing his soft body repeatedly against the solid door until it gave in to his chivalrous bulk and opened with a splitting of wood.

Olivia was lying on her bed. An empty bottle of tablets and the remains of a glass of whisky were tumbled on the carpet. Her eyes were half open and she whispered to me, 'Is Proteus OK?' – which proved, if proof were necessary, what a charitable and altruistic person Olivia was. He was in good hands, I reported, and quite well – a sentence which contained one truth and one lie, which is a good balance in my opinion.

I pushed Miranda forward and said sternly, 'Right – do something.'

'Like ring for an ambulance?' she said vaguely.

'I've done that,' Kevin said, dropping to his knees by Olivia's bedside. Olivia's lovely lip started to tremble and she began to weep – because beautiful girls weep where ordinary ones merely cry and grow blotchy (although Terri had a tendency to howl) – and I put my arms around her and stroked her hair and then burst into tears myself (because that was more the kind of girl I was).

'For God's sake,' Miranda said crankily, 'get some black coffee and start walking her round the room.'

I didn't go in this ambulance either. The ambulancemen, different ones thank goodness, said Olivia was going to

438

have to have her stomach pumped but would be fine.

'Can I go now?' Miranda said, once we'd watched the ambulance drive away.

'Please do,' I said faintly. My throat was swollen and my skin felt as hot and dry as desert sand, even though I had cold gooseflesh. I walked off quickly although I was having terrible difficulty co-ordinating my arms and legs. My legs felt weightless, as if I was on the moon, and I was worried that they might just float away. Other parts of me – my hands and my head most noticeably – felt as if they were being subjected to tremendous G-forces. Perhaps I should have consulted Miranda after all and explained to her that I was in the grip of the fading, falling disease.

I walked through town, not going anywhere in particular as long as it wasn't home. I walked down Seagate, thought about going to the cinema but didn't. The sickly smell of whisky drifted from a bonded warehouse and made me feel sick to my stomach. I carried on, down Candle Lane to Marketgait, across Marketgait to the Victoria Dock, where the ancient frigate *Unicorn* had found her final berth. Further off, a huge Scandinavian freighter was unloading wood and the smell of pine was carried through the foggy air. The water in the dock was brown and filmy and did not smell good, but I threw in a silver coin and wished for happiness and stepped back from the edge because the pull of water is a powerful thing and I expect many people have accidentally drowned on account of it.

Someone was standing next to me, a shadow on my vision, and laid a claw of a hand on my arm. I recoiled from the touch. It was the water-baby. The bad girl. The woman who is not the sister of the woman who is not my mother. (Not surprisingly) I didn't have a full understanding of these tangled family ties and I asked her, rather tentatively in case the answer was in the affirmative, 'You're not my mother, are you?'

She made a face as if the idea was distasteful, though I think it was probably caused by some kind of alcoholic palsy. Her bony hand was still gripping my arm. When she spoke it was a sibilant, 'Listen.'

~ No, don't, Nora says, looking uncomfortable. Don't listen to anything she says. She was born a liar, she'll die a liar.

'I was always misunderstood,' Effie said. 'Just because I liked to have a good time. If it was nowadays I'd be called "liberated". I didn't do anything wrong.'

~ Oh, but she did, she did, Nora says. She did nothing but wrong.

Effie lit a cigarette and stared into the fog.

'Eleanora,' she said and sucked through her teeth as if she was smoking a joint, 'or Nora, as she calls herself, is a murderer.'

'Murderess,' I corrected her weakly.

'She killed my father, she poisoned her stepmother, she tried to drown me, and very nearly succeeded I might tell you. It was sheer chance I didn't die.'

'Killed her father?' I echoed vaguely.

'Not her father,' Effie said, her harsh accent making her sound impatient, 'my father, not her father. Her father was a wonderful man. The world never appreciated Lachlan for what he was.'

I was very confused. Perhaps the fever was making me delirious. 'Lachlan was Nora's father? I don't understand, I thought Donald was her father?'

~ I've changed my mind, Nora interrupts, I think exposition is a bad thing in a story, some things should not be revealed.

Effie turned to look at me. Her dull eyes glittered for a moment and then clouded. Her voice continued but I could no longer really make out the words. Waves of nausea were washing over me and I couldn't focus on anything; the *Unicorn* looked like a ghost ship appearing out of the mists of time. The fog was everywhere, inside my head and out.

'Are you OK?' a voice asked in my ear. The voice sounded tiny, as if it belonged to a gnat or someone far away, but it had Effie's accent. I tried to say something but my tongue was too big in my mouth. My ears were filling up with fog. I felt my legs going from under me and held out my hands to ward off the ground when I fell – but there was no ground to fall onto, only space and air and then, finally, foul-smelling freezing-cold dock water.

I was plunged down to the bottom as if liquid lead ran in my veins, as if I was the bob on the end of a fathom-line, sent to measure the watery Murk. There was a taste of oil and sewage, there was darkness and there was bemusement too, for it seemed I had forgotten how to swim, despite having been carefully taught by Nora when I was small in a variety of municipal swimming baths up and down the coast.

But suddenly, without any effort on my part, I was shooting up to the surface, choking and coughing and

441

fighting desperately to get a breath. I could see the *Unicorn*'s wooden hull looming out of the fog and caught a glimpse of Effie's impassive features as she stood on the dock, but before I could shout to her for help I found myself being pulled back down to the bottom. The water was colder and darker this time and I was surprised when I popped back up to the surface again like a stopper out of a bottle of elderflower champagne. I had barely got a breath when the waters closed over my head a third time – which we all know must be the last.

The water no longer felt so cold, nor, strangely, so dark, and I was able to look around me a little and see that it was teeming with fish. They were not the kind of fish one might have expected to find in the sludgy waters of the Dundee docks – there were blue carp and shining golden orfs and the king of the fish, the great silver salmon. And then the most unexpected thing yet occurred – a mermaid pushed her way through a curtain of weedy fronds and swam into view. She had a huge fishscaled tail and her long hair trailed behind her like ribbons of seaweed. She lifted me in her strong arms and held me to her woman's breast as we swam up through the water, through a trail of silver bubbles, up, up and up until we were finally once more in our natural element, which is to say, air, and I caught a glimpse of the mermaid's face and it was Effie. The water-baby.

I was landed on the dock by invisible hands, but was not weighed and measured as a record catch. Instead I felt my chest being pummelled by one of the dockers who had been unloading the timber freighter, so that the first breath I took was scented with the pine of northern forests. When I finally opened my eyes, it was to the friendly face of the yellow dog. It thumped its tail on the pavement in recognition and grinned at me. Then I passed out.

We are braving the great outdoors. We shall most likely be blown away. The grey seas are mountainous, the white horses wild and the clouds are whipped across the sky by an invisible hand.

'Go on.'

~ The summer holidays before my final year at school. I spent most of my time studying, I was hoping to go to Edinburgh University to read science.

'Really?'

I've never thought of Nora as having a scientific kind of mind, never think of her having any left-brain at all.

~ Yes, really, she says. I remember that it did nothing but rain that summer. That was nothing unusual, of course, but it was so warm as well and often the air had a heavy, tropical feel to it as if we were in the middle of some great climatic change. It was the strangest weather – purple, stormladen skies, air humming with static. I saw hornets for the first time, droning through the air as if they could hardly lift their own weight. And we were plagued all summer by wasps, one bike after another turning up, under the eaves, in the attics, in the lilacs overhanging the lawn. Mabel bought cyanide to poison them but apparently she'd bought the wrong kind – powder instead of gas – and we didn't get rid of the wasps until the first frost of winter.

Then Effie came to stay, trying to avoid the sordid details of

443

the divorce courts and the relentless pursuit of a *Daily Express* reporter intent on a photograph to reveal the face of the notorious co-respondent to the public. Apparently, the divorce courts had been shown photographs of every part of her anatomy *except* her face.

Effie was continually loathsome the whole time, hanging about the house, listless and boréd, muttering vile things about Mabel – her size, the common food she cooked, her dubious morals. Mabel smiled at Effie and told her God loved her.

'No he fucking doesn't,' she spat back. Effie was convinced Mabel was nothing more than a gold-digger and was terrified that she was going to lose whatever inheritance was left (which was very little and mostly composed of Evangeline's diamonds, which Mabel had never worn), and although she hated sick-rooms she spent a lot of time sitting by Donald's bed trying to find out details of his will.

She considered her father to be completely 'ga-ga' and had consulted her solicitor – Effie spent half her time with solicitors now – about getting the marriage declared null and void. I kept out of her way, she never had a good word for me. 'Every time I look at you,' she said, 'I see myself getting older.'

Effie spent a lot of time on the telephone to Lachlan, who was still living in Edinburgh, trying to persuade him to visit, which he did eventually, in August. He brought his neurasthenic wife, the judge's barren daughter—

'Oh, give her a name, for heaven's sake.'

~ Sure?

'Yes.'

~ Pamela.

'Thank you.'

444

~ His neurasthenic wife, Pamela, city born and bred and highly averse to the country. Pamela took to her bed almost immediately, complaining of headaches and humidity. Mabel spent her time ferrying iced tea and aspirin and arrowroot biscuits up the stairs and reassuring Pamela that despite all signs to the contrary, God loved her very much. An ungrateful Pamela complained that Mabel smelt of bacon fat, which wasn't true – she smelt of Yardley's freesia talcum powder and jam, for it was jam-making season and Mabel spent hours at a time stirring the boiling fruit and sugar in Woodhaven's old copper jeely-pans that she had burnished up again with lemon juice and elbow grease. Jam-making was a dangerous activity because of the plague of wasps, so that before she began her task Mabel had to seal up the kitchen windows and warn no-one to trespass over the threshold of the kitchen.

She must have been making the jam for herself, for no more than two pots a year were consumed in that house. Effie was too bitter to have a sweet tooth and Donald certainly didn't eat any jam, he was now living off sops and milk soup. He had recently begun to suffer dreadful pains in his stomach. The local doctor, who was surprised Donald was still alive anyway – a fact that was probably due to Mabel's careful nursing – guessed at ulcers and prescribed Milk of Magnesia.

Lachlan and Effie spent all their time together, usually out of the house, driving or walking in the hills, sometimes swimming in the loch, in the rain, always plotting how to get rid of Mabel. Mabel herself was serenely indifferent to them, humming happily to herself as she went about her lowly tasks. She seemed like a woman keeping a secret to herself, and I was surprised that Effie – who had so many secrets of her own – didn't try to prise it out of her.

The whole week that Effie and Lachlan were visiting, the short summer nights were rent by Donald's roars of pain, nights already disturbed by the beastly moans of the cattle, newly deprived of their little calves, and the bleating of the sheep torn from their lambs.

'So much for pastoral innocence.'

~ There's no such thing as innocence, unless it is in the beating heart of a tiny bird—

—but then Nora is dive-bombed by an angry seagull, which serves her right for being so fanciful.

'Go on.' (How tiring all this encouragement is.)

~ No.

When I came round I found myself dry and tucked neatly into the spare bed in the McCue house. Mrs McCue and Mrs Macbeth were sitting either side of me, both of them knitting like enthusiastic *tricoteuses*.

'Flu,' Mrs McCue said, nodding and smiling at me.

'Very bad flu,' Mrs Macbeth added.

'Is that all?' I asked.

'You want something worse?' Mrs McCue puzzled. 'You nearly drowned, you know,' she added. 'Ferdinand saved your life. He's a good boy,' she added defensively; 'they should have given him bail.'

'He's back in jail?'

No, this mustn't happen, we mustn't start to rhyme. I tried again, 'How did Ferdinand save my life?'

'He'd just got a job working down at the docks,' Mrs McCue explained proudly. 'He did a lifesaving course while he was in jail, so he knew what to do.'

446

'But who pulled me out of the water?'

'Don't know,' Mrs McCue said. 'Some woman.'

It is the dead of darkness, and the world outside our window is in confusion and uproar. Waves pound the rocks, the heavens roar and quarrel with the sea. The dark skies are torn by lightning so that if we were to look out of the storm-proofed windows of the big house we might see the hapless victims of this night's havoc – the tempest-tossed seabirds, the shipwrecked sailors, the exhausted mermaids and disorientated narratees and the poor fish hiding in the watery chasms of the deep.

~ The night that Mabel's baby was born—

'Baby? What baby?'

~ It was a secret that only I shared. Donald had another stroke – one that robbed him of the power of speech – so he had no way of expressing his astonishment when his wife became miraculously pregnant. Not that I think for a minute that she told him, for she had told no-one else. Donald's sick-bed had never been a marriage-bed and Mabel remained a virgin, untouched by first Dudley and then Donald. Yet somehow an immaculate conception seemed more likely than Mabel succumbing to the temptations of the flesh. Not that for a moment I thought God – in whom I did not believe – had chosen Mabel as His vehicle for the second coming.

Nor, clearly, did Mabel, for God was now punishing her in the most malign way he could – He no longer spoke to her. Mabel could sit all afternoon in her ladder-back chair in the kitchen after any number of pleasant lunches of cold chops, pork pies and

447

home-pressed tongue sandwiches and not a word would fall from His lips.

No-one noticed that Mabel was pregnant. A few extra pounds of baby seemed to make no difference to her size. She never spoke about the father of her child and I didn't understand what she planned to do once the baby was born. You can hardly keep a baby hidden.

'Although you can keep its origins hidden.'

~ Not for ever. Mabel told me about the baby when I was home for the Christmas holidays. She was looking after it well already – dosing herself with cod liver oil, avoiding bad thoughts and spiders and drinking gallons of milk. 'I'll turn into milk,' she laughed, but sadly. And knitting like a demon, of course, the drawers were full of little white lacy garments.

Effie had been in London, trying to rescue some money from the divorce. Unfortunately, she returned after Hogmanay and discovered a set of tiny woollen mittens, the purpose of which even a fool could have guessed at. Effie was like a cat in a box, I thought she was going to rip the baby out of Mabel's stomach right then and there, and Mabel didn't make things any better by telling Effie that God loved her when it was clear to everyone that not even God could have loved Effie.

So. The night that Mabel's baby was born I had been at a ceilidh in the village hall in Kirkton of Craigie. It was Easter and my final school exams were in a few weeks' time, I hadn't done anything but study for months. Effie was away for the weekend with some man, I expect.

I'd had such a fine evening at the ceilidh, hurling and birling and falling in love with a strapping farmer's son. We'd known each other for years, we'd been at the primary school together, but that was the first time he'd ever noticed I was female. I was wearing one of Effie's cast-offs – a green taffeta dress with a huge skirt – New Look, certainly a new look for me.

I got a lift home on the back of the farmer's son's tractor and walked the last few hundred yards home. I was still hot from the dancing and the falling in love and so on, and didn't feel the cold at all. It was past one in the morhing but there was a full moon – a fat, cheesy moon, more suited to a harvest than a cold spring night. The cattle in the fields were all due to calve and I could hear their restless shuffling and puffing, but other than that it was so quiet. I felt as though I was standing on the edge of something high and glorious, flexing my wings and getting ready to fly.

(A girl in love is a frightening sight.)

The house was quiet too, more than usual, for Donald had recently subsided into a ghastly kind of darkness where pain was the only thing that seemed to get through to his mind. His doctor, making a more sophisticated diagnosis this time, declared it to be cancer of the stomach and prescribed morphine. I think he was hoping that Mabel would quietly overdose her husband and hasten his inevitable end, but Mabel didn't believe in taking life – unless it was to end up on the kitchen table and be eaten – and thought that God should be left to do His business in His own good time. For she still believed in God, even though He no longer believed in her.

There was a kettle still hot on the range when I came into the kitchen and I made tea with it and sat at the kitchen table to drink it and plan my future with the farmer's son. Would he wait four years while I did my degree? What would our children look like? What would it be like to be kissed by him?

'You hadn't kissed him?' (How hard it seems to be to get a

449

kiss off the man of one's dreams. Has Nora ever been kissed?)

~ No, she says regretfully – as you would if you were thirty-eight and had never been kissed, but then I am nearly twenty-one and have been kissed many times and all of them put together aren't worth an imaginary kiss with Ferdinand.

The weather is getting worse if that is possible. The welkin rings with the wind, the sky is cleft by fissures of lightning, the wind threatens to set the little island to sail on the wild waters. Outside, the Siamese cats are slinking along the walls of the house for shelter. We're afraid that if we let them in they might eat us but eventually we cannot bear their noise any more and relent. They prowl around the house suspiciously as if we might have set traps for them.

'Go on.'

~ Then, finally, I went upstairs. First I looked in on Donald – usually if you couldn't hear him moaning with pain you could hear him snoring but tonight he was very quiet. It struck me that despite her objections Mabel might have put him out of his misery. The moon was shining through a high windowpane, illuminating Donald – as still as any corpse – in his bed. The covers didn't rise and fall with a breath and his arms were crossed over his chest as if he had gone to sleep expecting never to wake. I called out, 'Father,' and pinched his hand; his flesh was still warm but he was gone. I picked up the bottle that contained his morphine tablets from the bedside table and could feel its emptiness without looking inside. I felt nothing for the passing of Donald, except perhaps relief.

I hurried to Mabel's room and as I neared I heard a fretful mewling sound. I thought it was a cat – I'd never heard a newborn baby cry before. I knocked on her door and opened it.

(Our own cats – although we hardly own them – are wandering around our feet, crying like banshees, not babies.)

Mabel was propped up in bed, a bed on which the sheets were in mangled and bloody disorder. She looked so dreadful that for a moment I thought she must have had some terrible accident – she had black shadows under her eyes, her hair was plastered to her head with sweat and the terrible look on her face suggested she had stared into the maw of hell. She was holding a baby in her arms – a red, prune-skinned infant. The baby was dressed in a great assortment of the clothes that she had been knitting all winter – leggings and a little coat, bootees, mittens and a beribboned hat. It looked like a baby that was ready to go on a long journey.

Mabel held the baby out to me without a word. It was sleeping and bore no resemblance to anyone. The question of its paternity wasn't answered by its looks. It half opened its eyes and I took it over to the window and showed it the moon and, not knowing what else to do in these strange circumstances, I began speaking the kind of nonsense to it that you speak to babies.

Then the quiet night was disturbed by the noise of an approaching car engine. I heard the car turn into the drive and recognized Effie's brutal driving. I looked to Mabel to warn her of Effie's imminent arrival and saw her stirring a white powder into a glass of milk on her bedside table. I thought it must be a Beecham's Powder – although that seemed a strange antidote to childbirth – but then I smelled the faint almond-smell of it and recognized the little paper packet that had held the poison for the wasps last summer.

I cried out and put the baby down on a chair and rushed over

451

to Mabel and grabbed the paper packet off her, but it was too late, she had already swallowed the cyanide-flavoured milk. She wore a surprised expression on her face as if she couldn't believe what was happening and then—

Nora pauses, not for effect, for she is taking no delight in her storytelling.

~ Have you ever seen anyone dying from poison?

'Obviously not.'

~ Well, I don't want to describe it, thank you. I think we should leave a space and imagine it, if we have the stomach—

'That's called cheating. And then?'

~ And then she was dead – what else? She'd had to wait until she'd delivered the baby before she could kill herself; it would have gone against everything she believed in to have killed the child inside her. She must have planned to do it all along. And I suppose she thought that, as she was going to hell anyway, she might as well release Donald from his suffering. She did speak before she died. She said, 'God will talk to me again.' She was in despair, which is a forsaken place to be, and I wish I had realized, for then I might have prevented what happened.

I was feeling for a pulse, thinking something might still be done to save her, when Effie came in. Naturally, she was stopped in her tracks at the sight of Mabel. Effie stank of alcohol and she had a bite-mark on her neck. She seemed quite deranged. Then she noticed the baby lying on the chair and pounced on it, saying it wasn't going to end up with what was hers. I've never seen such hate on anyone's face, not even Effie's. I would have tried to wrest the baby off her but I knew she wouldn't care if she hurt it. She was screaming, all kinds of filth and obscenities about

452

Mabel and the baby, about money, about solicitors. I thought someone would hear and come and help me but there was no-one there to come.

Effie darted out of the room and ran downstairs with the baby. I chased after her, across the lawn, through the gate in the fence and down to the river. The river was swollen and icy with the snow that had melted on the hills, but Effie waded into it as far as she could go. For a moment I thought perhaps she was going to kill herself too – my head was still so full of Mabel – and it was only when she shouted to me, 'What do they do with kittens on the farm, Eleanora?' that I realized she meant to drown the baby. She was quite mad, of course.

I waded in after her. The water was unimaginably cold and the current much stronger than I'd thought. The stones on the riverbed were slippery so that I had difficulty keeping my footing. The green dress, heavy with water, was dragging me down. I tried to snatch the baby out of Effie's arms, but as I lunged for it I slipped and fell towards her. I caught her off balance and we both fell into the water. I caught a glimpse of the baby being carried away by the river, like a basketless Moses.

Effie and I clung on to each other as we were swept downstream. We fetched up close to the river bank, entangled in the branches of a tree that had fallen in the water. And then suddenly, without even thinking about it, I clutched a handful of her long hair in my hand and pushed her head under the water. I wanted her to die. I wanted her dead. She fought her way back up, clawing at me like a cat from hell. I had the advantage, though, for she'd been drinking and I had been toughened by years on the playing fields of St Leonard's, which is a better training than a marine gets. She could hardly speak from the cold but

453

she managed to plead with me, stuttering out the words that I'd been waiting for her to say for a long time.

Silence.

'The words, what words?'

~ 'Don't kill me,' she begged, 'I'm your mother.' And then I pushed her head under the water and held it there. When I let her go, she didn't come back up.

~ On the whole, Nora says thoughtfully, I think I prefer *your* story.

'Let me get this straight – Effie and Lachlan were your *parents*?'

~ Of course. Surely you'd guessed? Effie had me when she was fourteen. She didn't tell anyone until it was too late to do anything about it, I suppose she hoped it would just go away. That I would just go away. She was still running up and down St Leonard's lacrosse field when she was eight months pregnant, probably keeping it hidden by willpower, knowing her.

She gave birth in her own bed at home during the summer holidays and the easiest way to conceal the truth was to say the baby was Marjorie's, although God knows by that time Marjorie wasn't fit to look after an infant. Effie wasn't even late returning to school, leaving Marjorie and a completely disreputable nanny to bring me up. They thought I would be defective, being in-bred. They always treated me as if I was, even when I proved not to be. Lachlan was given a thrashing the next time he was home from Glenalmond and told not to do it again. That's the ruling classes for you.

(This is all a little melodramatic, is it not? Grand Guignol with a pinch of Greek tragedy.)

~ I warned you, I told you right at the beginning that it would

454

be a tale so strange and tragic that you would think it wrought from a lurid and overactive imagination rather than a real life.

'And what of the baby? Is it dead?' I ask.

~ You are so *slow*, Nora laughs fondly.

I am that red, prune-skinned infant. I am that baby in the water. My mother is not my mother, her mother is not her mother, her father is not her father, her sister is not her sister, her brother is not her brother. Lo, we are as jumbled as the most jumbled box of biscuits that ever graced a grocer's shelf.

'Buggery rats!' Madame Astarti exclaimed as the torpedo on the prom exploded.

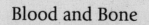
Blood and Bone

AGAINST ALL THE ODDS, DAYLIGHT HAS COME AGAIN AND WE HAVE survived the tempestuous night. We are lucky we haven't woken up and found ourselves over the rainbow. Although there is no rainbow to be seen and the skies are ashen and Nora's eyes are the colour of dead doves. The cats, offended at our lack of milk and fish and meat, have returned to their weather-beaten abodes.

We breakfast in the dining-room of the house, a room we are never usually in. The furniture – table, chairs, a huge dresser – is all dark and heavy in some mock-Elizabethan style that depresses the spirit. We might be in a hotel, the way the table is placed in the window to give us a sea view while we eat, although one would hope that a hotel would provide better fare than our meagre repast of oatmeal and milkless tea. When we finish we remain at the table. We seem to be waiting for something.

'Are we waiting for something?'

Nora doesn't answer. She is paying even more attention than usual to the sea. I hand her dead Douglas's binoculars that have been sitting on the sideboard.

~ Thank you.

There is a dot on the horizon – a little black speck of nothing on the edge of infinity. We wait. The dot grows bigger. And bigger. And eventually the dot declares itself to be the fishing-boat that first dropped me off here. It lurches up and down with the waves and it makes me feel sick just to look at it. The boat is ferrying a passenger to us, though his figure is indistinct and not yet known to us. My heart tips like the waves – perhaps Ferdinand has broken out of prison and come to find me.

~ Unlikely, says my unromantic unmother.

We grab our outdoor clothes and scramble eagerly down the cliff-path to the shore to welcome our anonymous visitor. The fisherman waves to Nora and she waves back. This is probably as close as she gets to a social life. The fisherman helps his cargo – a rather shabby middle-aged man, bundled up in clothing that would do for a trip to the Arctic – into a little boat, as frail as a nutshell, and rows him as close to the shore as he can.

The man staggers through the waves and onto the clattering pebbles of the beach.

Nora puts out a hand in greeting and says,

~ Hello, Mr Petrie. I've waited such a long time to meet you again.

And Chick – for it is indeed he – says, 'Watch it, I'm away to boak again,' and is true to his word.

We sit in the kitchen with a poor fire in the grate. The fishing-boat dropped off provisions and we are enjoying a feast worthy of Joppa, comprising tinned soup, oatcakes and cheese, Abernethy biscuits and a Lyons' Battenberg.

~ I've been telling her, Nora says to Chick.

'Everything?' he asks warily, lighting up a cigarette. He offers one to Nora, which she takes and then, squinting through the cigarette smoke at him, she says –

~ Not everything. I've left room for your story.

There is much to be explained – why is Chick here? How do Chick and Nora know each other? How infuriatingly enigmatic this pair are.

~ Constable Charles Petrie, Nora says. You had that nippit wife, Moira, wasn't it? I bet she ended up leaving you.

Of course, now I remember – when Chick gave me a lift home on the road from Balniddrie to Dundee that night, he had mentioned working on the 'Glenkittrie case' when he was a village policeman in 'heuchter-teuchter land'.

'It was me that found the bodies,' Chick explains to me. 'The old guy was dead with a huge morphine overdose. His wife poisoned. She'd obviously given birth. Elder daughter was never found but her dress turned up in the river – identified by a man that she'd had it off with the day before the murder, so presumed drowned. The younger daughter . . .' Chick pauses and looks at Nora '. . . was missing, along with the bairn, the car, the diamonds. The only thing that wasn't missing were your fingerprints on the poison and the morphine. Heid-yins were called in from Dundee,' Chick says glumly. 'Soon every police force in the country was looking for one Eleanora Stuart-Murray. Big case,' Chick says, 'big case, famous in its day.'

'I never thought you did it,' Chick says to Nora. 'You seemed like a nice lassie. I'd seen you at that ceilidh, dancing with that big farmer's laddie, what was his name?'

'He doesn't have one,' I tell Chick.

~ Robert, Nora says sadly, he was called Robert.

'The evidence was against you,' Chick says to her. 'I'd have done the same in your shoes, I'd have legged it. Any more tea in that pot?'

~ I ran to save the child, Nora says.

'From what?' the 'child' asks.

~ From Lachlan, from your self, from the past you didn't know about yet.

I have no mother, no brother, no sister, no father. I do not want to be a person who opened their eyes on the world for the first time and saw their mother dead. I don't want to be a person who set foot on earth only to be tossed back into water, like a fallen leaf, an abandoned sweet wrapper.

~ The first thing you saw was the moon, Nora corrects me.

'And that makes it all right?'

I would like my self to be given back to me. I would like a mother, father, brother, sister, aunt. I would like a family dog and a family car. I would like to live in a traditional thirties semi with a swing in the garden and I would like to eat lamb chops for my tea, with potatoes and peas and afterwards a Victoria sandwich cake made by the hand of a genuine mother.

'Jam and buttercream?' Chick says, wiping his nose with the back of his hand.

~ Well, I can't give you *that*, Nora says, but I can tell you what happened afterwards and of how you came to dry land. For I was not the only thing to snag on the fallen tree in the river. As I was trying to drag myself out of the water I noticed something caught by a branch. I heard its cry –

'Its?'

~ Yours. I heard your cry even above the noise of the rushing water. The lacy matinée coat had hooked itself onto a branch and

462

you were bobbing around like a baby made of cork rather than flesh.

I managed to get both of us out of the water and back to the house where I warmed you up as well as possible. I was sure you were going to die. There were plenty of clothes for you. Mabel had knitted a layette that would have done for quadruplets. When I took off your soaking things I found her little crucifix around your neck, it was a wonder it hadn't strangled you.

'And I suppose you are going to hand it to me now,' I say to her, 'as one does in all good stories, so that I will have a treasured memento of the mother I never knew.'

~ Well I lost it actually, she says carelessly. On a train. Or a bus. Who knows? Pass me an Abernethy.

So. Then I took what money I could find in the house, took the diamonds, sitting carelessly in the sideboard drawer – I was very calm – I was thinking that I could sell them when we ran out of money. Of course, I never did for fear I would be discovered. I packed baby clothes and made sandwiches, I even took a Thermos of tea. It was almost as if we were setting off on a great adventure. Then I drove away in Effie's car – I had a vague idea how to drive it, I'd sat next to her a few times and there was no traffic around. I stopped in a passing-place to feed the baby, put her to my breast and milk came. It seemed like a miracle, a sign, but I've read of such things since.

'So, you were a seventeen-year-old schoolgirl who'd just killed her sister who was really her mother and you were breastfeeding a baby who wasn't yours on a deserted Highland road in the middle of the night.' I wonder if there are any words that can adequately cover this situation. The ones that spring to mind – absurd, surreal, grotesque – don't really do, somehow.

463

~ Then I drove to a station and waited on the platform with the milk churns and caught an early train over the border. We went to London where we were anonymous and then to Brighton. I saw the name 'Andrews' above a butcher's shop and thought it ordinary enough and – well, you know the rest.

I kept track of things in the newspapers – I could hardly go to a police station and protest my innocence over two murders when I was guilty of the third – they still hanged people then. So I went on the run.

And now, Nora says, Effie turns up alive after all these years. It makes no difference, of course – for I *meant* to murder my mother and intention is everything. Another slice of Battenberg, Mr Petrie? she asks, as regal as a duchess.

'Call me Chick,' Chick says, 'and yes it was Moira, and yes, she did leave me.'

~ What a cow, Nora says cheerfully and Chick says, 'How did you know?'

I know what happened to Effie because she told me, just before I fell off the quay of the Victoria Dock. I didn't understand then what she was saying, but I do now.

Further down the bank a man had spotted her being swept down river. He had parked his car next to the water in preparation for running a length of hose pipe from his exhaust to the inside of the car and removing himself from the planet for good. He was a rep from Peterborough – ladies' shoes – and was married to a woman he hated but felt he couldn't get divorced from because they had three small children and a huge overdraft. He was a coward and thought it was just easier to die than cope with his wife's wrath, although he didn't feel very cowardly, having his last cigarette and contemplating the Highland scenery by night, he felt downright brave when he thought of what he was about to do. At that moment, as if to call on the hero hiding inside him, he saw something drifting down the river and with some difficulty, and not without getting his trousers soaked, he managed to haul in his salvaged naiad – Effie. Still alive (and enticingly naked), she was a water-baby, after all, and once she was on the bank she coughed up a great deal of river water, some pond weed and a couple of small fishes –

~ Really?

'No. And so she came back to life. And he drove off with her – blah, blah, blah.'

~ Blah, blah, blah?

'It was like a sign for both of them. A fresh start. A re-birth. They went to Rhodesia together, set up a business which was very successful, he died a year ago and she came back to lay things to rest. Atonement, maybe. And she saved me from drowning so perhaps in the grand cosmic design of things that cancels out trying to drown me in the beginning.'

~ I doubt it.

'And she *was* looking for you. So perhaps she wanted to make amends.'

~ So where is she now?

'Wouldn't she have gone to see Lachlan?' I ask. 'And what happened to him anyway?'

'Dead,' Chick says, 'a few weeks ago.'

~ I hope it was a prolonged and painful death, Nora says, taking another of Chick's cigarettes.

'Aye, I believe it was,' Chick says. 'I was working for him,' he explains to me –

'Is everything to be tidied up and explained in this part of the story?'

~ Yes.

'He employed me,' Chick continues, 'to find his daughter. You,' he adds to Nora in case she's forgotten, which is highly unlikely. 'And the bairn,' he says, looking at me in an odd way. 'Maybe his conscience got to him, but I think he wanted to make sure his money was kept in the family. No other heirs,' he says to Nora, 'just you and the bairn. It was coincidence that he picked my name out of the Yellow Pages.'

~ There's no such thing as coincidence, says my airy-fairy non-mother, draining her cup and glancing at her leftover tea leaves.

'So you *were* following me?'

'Maybe,' he says with just a hint of contrition in his voice.

This has been as strange a maze as ever man trod but thankfully we are approaching the promised end. We are done with Effie and Lachlan; they belong in a whole book of their own and there is no more room for them here.

'Well,' Chick says, 'there's one wee thing.' He takes a cutting from the *Courier* out of his pocket. He has circled a small article with a sub-headline that said 'Mystery Woman', which he proceeds to read in his own fashion '. . . a certain William Scrymegour . . . no direct relation to the famous prohibitionist, Neddie Scrymegour nor to the great Alexander Scrymegour wha' bled wi' Wallace, blah, blah, blah . . . an elderly gentleman who fought with the famous Fourth Battalion Black Watch . . . Battle of Loos . . . wiped out, blah, blah, blah . . . rented a flat . . . Magdalen Yard Green . . . poor sleeper . . . amused himself . . .

466

early morning hours . . . Tay through his binoculars . . . the weather this particular morning . . . damp and foggy, blah, blah, blah . . . morning train from Edinburgh due over the bridge in seven minutes . . . knew the timetables off by heart . . . raised his binoculars . . . struck by extraordinary and unexpected sight of a woman walking out along the rail bridge . . . wearing a red coat of some kind . . . well on her way to Fife . . . reached the high girders . . . climbed up onto the edge of the parapet . . . perched like a bird . . . stood up . . . on the edge . . . executed a magnificent dive into the water, blah, blah, blah, didn't re-emerge. The Edinburgh train whistled and appeared out of the mist . . . on time, Mr Scrymegour noticed . . . extensive search of the Tay . . . no body found . . . no-one had reported a friend or loved one missing and the case had been closed, blahdy, blahdy, blah. End of story.

'Of course, the interesting thing,' he says when we have all digested his strangely cooked story, 'is that the day the "mystery woman" dived off the bridge was the day *before* you fell in the dock.'

~ Oh, no ghost stories, Nora says with a shiver, I really can't abide them.

~ We still have another loose end, Nora says, and who better to tie it up than our detective.

'Me?' Chick says.

~ Yes, Chick, Nora says, and to do that you must tell us *your* story.

'How?' Chick asks, looking suddenly worried. 'I've told mine, remember – *I found the bodies. The old guy was dead* – and so on.'

467

~ I know everything, Chick, Nora says softly, and I mean everything.

Chick sighs, like a man who knows he's up a blind alley with his back against the wall and a knife at his throat.

'Well. I'm not used to this kind of thing,' he says, staring at his feet.

'Begin at the beginning,' I tell him, remembering Mrs Macbeth's dictum (which she may well have stolen off someone), 'and carry on until you've finished.'

'Hm.'

~ Start with the weather, I always like to do that.

'It was *weird* weather,' Chick says. 'Warm but rainy, like a monsoon or something. Thunderstorms. And animals appearing that didn't belong. A puma was found wandering the hills in the glen. I had to get a bloody zoo keeper up from Edinburgh.'

~ Oh, I'd forgotten that, Nora says. The hunters were all stalking it, they said there was no closed season on cats.

'And fish,' Chick said, 'there was an angler claimed to have caught an angelfish. Another one said he netted a mermaid. People were aff their heid with the weather. And those bloody wasps, they were everywhere, in people's hair, in their beds, in their baffies, their biscuit tins. Mind that woman over at Kembie,' he says, turning to Nora, 'got stung when she was hanging out her washing and dropped down deid. And it was jam-making time so the women were aff their heid, the wasps were aff their heid. Everyone was aff their heid.

'Raspberry,' he says, suddenly, unexpectedly wistful, 'raspberry was the sweetest.'

Who would have thought Chick a jam-connoisseur?

'She made such a lot of it,' he continues, 'forever stirring that jeely-pan. I dropped in one morning to warn her about a Geordie gang that were raiding over the border – stealing stuff out of folk's houses. No-one kept their doors locked thereabouts.

'It was like a Turkish bath in that kitchen. She gave me a bit of mutton pie and some green beans, leftover rice pudding, a cup of tea.'

(The way to Chick's heart is clearly the traditional route.)

'It just went on from there.' Chick shrugs. 'She was lonely, I was lonely. She'd never had a man, never had her furrow ploughed –'

~ Charming.

'She was married to that dried-up old crippled stick. She was such a nice woman, she started off telling me that God loved me, but I think she'd changed her mind by the end. We'd knocked over a few jam pots in the heat of things. The stuff was everywhere. Wasps were throwing themselves against the window –'

Realization has been dawning slowly, very slowly, on me.

'Oh my God,' I say to Chick. '*You're* my father?'

So I have gained my inheritance, which is to say, my blood. My mother was my mother, my father is my father.

On the last day of winter, which is the very next day, we go down to the shore and Nora takes the – rather gratuitous – diamonds from her overcoat pocket and flings them into the grey ocean where they disappear into the waters with a steaming hiss.

'Aff her heid,' Chick says to me and I can only agree.

~ There, Nora says, that's the end of that.

469

'You promised madwomen in the attics.'

~ One madwoman, I only promised one madwoman and there wasn't enough room for her.

I suppose Effie will do well enough for our story's madwoman.

'Aye,' Chick says. 'Aff her heid, that one.'

~ I could put an attic in if you really wanted, Nora offers, in an agreeable mood now she is rid of her tale.

But I think we will leave it at that.

~ No attic?

'No attic.'

1999

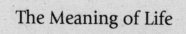

The Meaning of Life

IT IS ALL ENDINGS NOW.

Lachlan left nothing but debts after all, and the diamonds that were at the bottom of the sea were all that was left of the Stuart-Murrays' wealth. No body was ever found in the Tay but nor was there any more word from Effie.

I never took my degree. Instead my new, unlooked-for father took me back to Dundee to collect my belongings – Bob was sitting the last paper of his finals at the time (he got a third-class degree, but didn't understand how), but I didn't hang around to see him.

I stayed with Chick for a while – he had a sort of hovel in Peddie Street, we had to climb out of the downstairs window to get to the outside toilet – and he made a great effort to be paternal, which mostly meant buying me fish and chips and offering me cigarettes every time he lit up. It wasn't long before I left Dundee – leaving the north for ever to find my fortune elsewhere – but I kept in close touch with Chick as well as 'the mingin' little bastards', who were my half-siblings, of course (much to Moira's fury). Chick died a few years ago but I think of him fondly.

It was Chick who persuaded Nora that it was safe for her to return to the land of the living and she took things up much where she had left off, becoming a mature student and taking a degree in marine biology. She married a diver – a handsome one, you will be pleased to know – and he knows the story of her life as a murderess and a fugitive. They have a little boat called *Sea-Adventure II* that they more or less live on and they wander around the warmer parts of the world like a pair of sea-gypsies. So, there's a happy ending. I don't see Nora often but that's all right. She will always be my mother, as far as I'm concerned.

I have been back to Dundee very recently, crossing over the rail bridge under a sky of saltire blue. I saw the stumps of Thomas Bouch's disastrous bridge, the seals – as freckled and speckled as mistle thrushes – sunning themselves on the sandbanks in the middle of a Tay that was the colour of the sea on the Neapolitan Riviera. Dundee had changed and yet hadn't changed. There were new buildings – a contemporary arts centre, a big blue medical research building – and old ones had disappeared – the Overgate, the Wellgate Steps and the flat in Paton's Lane where I had once lived with Bob. The headline on the newspaper stand was 'Dundee reptile saved', proving that the local press remained as Dundeecentric as ever.

I had lunch in the new arts centre, overlooking the Tay. I visited the Howff graveyard and I bought tea in

Braithwaites' and fern cakes from Goodfellow and Steven. I wandered round the university. Watson Grant was no longer there, of course. Aileen left him in 1973 to live with her lover – a dashing pilot stationed at RAF Leuchars. Grant Watson declared personal bankruptcy a year later, lost his tenure, got taken into Liff for a while. Now he lives quietly in Devon and works as a bookbinder.

Dr Dick was no longer there either – he moved to Lancaster University – and Maggie Mackenzie died of a blood clot on the brain a few minutes after I patted her hand and said goodbye to her in the DRI. Professor Cousins died years ago after handing over the reins of the English department to Christopher Pike, who had undergone a miraculous recovery.

To my astonishment, I saw Bob again. The reason I was in Dundee was because I was on a book tour, of sorts. To everyone's surprise, but mostly mine, I had eventually become a writer of detective fiction – the genteel kind for nervous people who like their crime free of anything to do with urban decay, computers or sex, and for foreigners who like their English detectives to be quaint and colourful.

I was giving a reading, to a modest audience, in James Thin's bookshop in the High Street. Halfway through, I looked up and saw a figure staring in through the plate glass of the window like a curious fish in a tank.

I thought he was another madman and returned to reading. A few minutes later the madman came into the shop and hovered annoyingly behind the rest of the

477

audience. Only after the usual questions were done with did the madman – overweight, balding, a rather sleazy air – speak.

'Is it really you?' he said, his natural nasal Essex returned.

It really was me but could it really be him? Yes, it seemed.

We went for coffee the next day in a little café on the Perth Road. Bob was now a Modern Studies teacher at the Morgan Academy. Two children, divorced, a new girlfriend – this latter said shyly. Middle-aged, middling happy, a droop to the shoulders. 'What more is there to say?' Bob shrugged. 'Drink too much, smoke too much, try not to think too much,' he laughed.

We chatted about Kevin – for Kevin Riley is now, of course, the second most famous writer of fantasy in Britain. His latest book, *The Balniddrian Conspiracy* – the most recent in the seemingly endless *Chronicles of Edrakonia* – was at the top of the paperback bestseller list.

I told Bob how once, browsing in a second-hand bookshop in Suffolk, I discovered a long out of print book entitled *The Invasion of the Tara-Zanthians* which was indeed about a group of alien invaders who introduce a currency based on the domestic cat and dog. It had not been written by 'The Boy With No Name' but by someone called 'Colin Hardy'. So that was one mystery cleared up.

We talked, too, of Janice Rand, who dropped out of university and became a geriatric nurse. Three years later she was convicted of murdering her charges (she was

478

'sending them home to God', her barrister said) and sent to a high-security mental hospital. It was Chick who, after doggedly pursuing her all that time on behalf of poor Aunt Senga's relatives, managed to secure filmed evidence that convicted her.

I visited Ferdinand in prison once or twice but he seemed to have a rather two-dimensional character and I gave up on him after a while. He disappeared a few years ago and Maisie – now a maths lecturer in Cambridge – thinks that he might have been killed over a drug deal that went wrong.

As for the yellow dog, I have no idea what happened to him but I like to imagine him living on, even if only in a book somewhere.

So that's it.

Bob had to go – he was meeting Robin, now a social worker, for a drink in the Tay Bridge Bar. I declined his offer to join them.

I wondered if Bob's life would have turned out differently if I hadn't stolen the meaning of life from him.

Bob discovered the meaning of life one grey day shortly before this story began. When Bob experienced his epiphany he was lying on the gritty carpet, mindlessly practising the Vulcan death grip on Shug. Shug persevered manfully with rolling a joint on the cover of Bob's *Electric Ladyland* album. On the television, which no-one was watching, there was news footage of a far-away country that we knew nothing about being bombed.

Bob changed the television channel. *'Dr Who,'* he explained to Shug, *'the second episode of "The Curse of Peladon". The Ice Warriors are in it, they're at this alien gathering thing . . .'* I left the room for a minute and when I came back I found the pair of them in the grip of a strange kind of metaphysical hysteria, flopping around on the carpet like newly caught fish.

'Wow,' Bob kept repeating, 'the meaning of life, that's like . . . *big* stuff.'

'The meaning of Liff,' Shug said with a grandiose gesture that knocked his tin of tobacco flying across the room.

Unfortunately, Bob and Shug were too wasted to elucidate their momentous findings to me. Bob had become distracted by a pan sitting in the middle of the carpet. The pan contained the remains of a spaghetti Bolognese which, in Bob's acid-etched brain, had just turned into a pit of writhing snakes. By the time he had recovered from this delusion and stopped screaming, both he and Shug had forgotten their great, arcane secret.

'Arse,' Bob said and struggled to his feet to wander helplessly around the room, looking in drawers and under pillows as if the meaning of life was part of the stuff of the material world.

Luckily, at that moment, he tripped over his bootlace and the meaning of life was restored to him. Distressed at finding how easy it was to forget something so important, Bob and Shug spent some time discussing how they could preserve it for posterity. Eventually, I took pity on them and suggested they write it down.

'Write it down!' Bob shouted, gripping Shug's arm to stay upright as he was in danger of falling over from excitement. They both thought that writing it down was a brilliant idea, almost as brilliant as the meaning of life itself, and, after much searching, Bob found a scrap of ruled paper and wrote, although with some difficulty, because every time he wrote a letter it turned into a little cartoon stick-man and ran away. Finally, he managed to tame the little men into a semblance of literacy and after much discussion it was decided to place this precious piece of paper in an envelope in the drawer of the living-room sideboard.

Once the meaning of life was safe, Shug and Bob drank a toast to it, in cans of Tennent's lager, the ones with the pictures of girls on them – Tracy was Bob's favourite.

'Here's to us, then,' Shug said with an effort. 'Wha's like us?'

Rejecting the appropriate answer – 'Gey few and they're a' deid' – Bob struggled for his own benediction. He furrowed his brow, he thought hard and visibly and finally declared, with great solemnity, 'Live long and prosper.'

I found the envelope a few days later when I was looking for my matriculation card. I have kept the piece of paper – it sits now in the drawer of my own sideboard in my

Breton home – and I look at it occasionally just to remind myself what the meaning of life really is.

This is what Bob had written. Guard it well for it is the meaning of life:

> *'When you stand on the table you can touch*
> *the ceiling.'*

The Hand of Fate
by
Effie Andrews

Originally published twenty-six years ago, we are pleased to be issuing this special edition of Effie Andrews' very first 'Madame Astarti' novel, *The Hand of Fate*, to coincide with a major new television adaptation of the series.

What the critics say about Effie Andrews:

'A Miss Marple for the Millennium' *Woman's Realm*
'She improves a little with every book' *Yorkshire Post*
'Fascinating' *Whitby Gazette*

Other 'Madame Astarti' novels include:

The Wheel of Fortune
Mermaids Ahoy!
The Finger of Fate
And the prize-winning *Pick a Card, Any Card*

Effie Andrews was born in Scotland in 1951. She
now lives in France.

In this work of fiction, the characters, places
and events are either the product of the
author's imagination or they are used entirely
fictionally.

Chapter One
Lady Luck

A lone fisherman up early looking for sea trout
found the first body. The fisherman was thinking
what a beautiful day it was going to be. The pink-
gold rays of a cinematic dawn were gleaming on the
dark metallic surface of the sea when he netted the
unwanted catch on his little boat, the *Lucky Lady*.
He was not a man given to superstition and yet in
the semi-dark he thought he saw silver scales and
seaweed hair and believed for one wild, terrible
moment that he had caught a mermaid. When he hooked
her and pulled her towards the boat, however, he saw
it was no mermaid but the bloated body of a woman,
draped in what remained of a silver-lamé evening
dress. Seaweed was entangled in long hair which
looked dark, but by the time he had got her to shore
was already drying to a bleached-out blond.

He grabbed hold of her hand to help her on board
the *Lucky Lady* but her skin peeled off her arm
like a long satin glove. The fisherman had to
leave her in the water a little longer while he
retched over the side of his boat. She drifted

lazily off, she was in no hurry, she had been dead five days now and was getting used to her watery element. She was already beginning to suffer a sea-change, her bones were not yet coral but her one remaining eye was an opaque pearl and flat strands of seaweed, crimped at the edges like ribbons, adorned her long tendrils of hair. A whole flotilla of tiny, greedy sea-creatures had seen the early-morning mermaid into safe harbour.

2

The woman was finally brought to shore and logged by a pale Constable Collins at 6.32 a.m. precisely. After an undignified struggle to get her out of the boat, the policeman finally lifted her dead-weighted body ashore in his arms. He thought of the warm body of his wife still asleep in their bed in their little modern house and his sky-blue eyes clouded over. What had she meant last night when she'd rolled over in bed and stared at him unpleasantly and said she was dying of boredom? One thing was certain: it couldn't be worse than death by drowning.

Flashing blue lights guided Inspector Gannet down to the harbour where a crowd of holiday-makers were craning their necks to try and get a view of the excitement. So, yes, Jack Gannet thought, this is how it begins . . .

Last Words

'Perhaps,' J agreed cautiously with the man who would forever be an enemy to him, 'but on the other hand, perhaps not.'

Kenny There's nothing. Nothing. Do you hear me?
Dod   I know.
Jed   Perhaps Rick was right after all.

'Yes, of course l will,' Flick murmured happily as Jake pulled her into his arms and began to kiss her with fierce abandonment.

'Well, well,' Madame Astarti said. 'Whoever would have thought that you were the murderer all along.'

Duke Thar-Vint mounted his steed Demaal and saluted farewell to his trusty steward Lart. He turned to the Lady Agaruitha riding beside him and said, 'One chapter may have closed, but the fight for justice will go on for ever.'

And the winner of the Booker Prize for the year 2001 is
. . . Andrea Garnett for her novel *Anthea's Anguish*.

Whatever we fondly call our own
Belongs to heaven's great Lord
The blessings lent us for a day
Are soon to be restored

(Carved on a tombstone in the Howff, Dundee, and used by Terri as an inscription on the tasteful stone arches which form the entrance to all of the pet cemeteries in the hugely successful chain which she started in San Francisco in 1976.)

BEHIND THE SCENES AT THE MUSEUM

Kate Atkinson

'An astounding book . . . without doubt
one of the finest novels I have read for years'
The Times

Ruby Lennox was conceived grudgingly by Bunty and born while her
father, George, was in the Dog and Hare in Doncaster telling a woman
in an emerald dress and a D-cup that he wasn't married. Bunty had
never wanted to marry George, but here she was, stuck in a flat above
the pet shop in an ancient street beneath York Minster, with sensible
and sardonic Patricia aged five, greedy cross-patch Gillian who
refused to be ignored, and Ruby . . .

Ruby tells the story of The Family, from the day at the end of the
nineteenth century when a travelling French photographer catches frail,
beautiful Alice and her children, like flowers in amber, to the
startling, witty and memorable events of Ruby's own life.

'Little short of a masterpiece . . . fizzing with wit and energy, Kate
Atkinson's hilarious novel made me laugh and cry'
Daily Mail

'Enchanting. It hops with sprightly omniscience from past to future
and back again . . . takes in tragedy, history, mystery and comedy
through the sarky, perky, pessimistic voice of Ruby Lennox'
Sunday Times

CASE HISTORIES

Kate Atkinson

'Not just the best novel I read this year
but the best mystery of the decade'
Stephen King

Cambridge is sweltering, during an unusually hot summer. To
Jackson Brodie, former police inspector turned private investigator,
the world consists of one accounting sheet – Lost on the left,
Found on the right – and the two never seem to balance.

Jackson has never felt at home in Cambridge, and has a failed
marriage to prove it. Surrounded by death, intrigue and misfortune,
his own life haunted by a family tragedy, he attempts to unravel
three disparate case histories and begins to realize that in spite
of apparent diversity, everything is connected . . .

'An astonishingly complex and moving literary detective
story . . . the sort of novel you have to start re-reading
the minute you've finished it'
Guardian

'Triumphant . . . her best book yet . . . a tragi-comedy
for our times'
Sunday Telegraph

'Part complex family drama, part mystery, it winds up having
more depth and vividness than ordinary thrillers and more thrills
than ordinary fiction . . . a wonderfully tricky book'
New York Times

LIFE AFTER LIFE
Kate Atkinson

'If you wish to be moved and astonished, read it'
Hilary Mantel

What if you had the chance to live your life again and again, until you finally got it right?

During a snowstorm in England in 1910, a baby is born and dies before she can take her first breath.

During a snowstorm in England in 1910, the same baby is born and lives to tell the tale.

What if there were second chances? And third chances? In fact an infinite number of chances to live your life? Would you eventually be able to save the world from its own inevitable destiny? And would you even want to?

'Truly brilliant'
The Times

'Her most ambitious and most gripping work'
Guardian

'A dizzying and dazzling tour de force'
Daily Mail

'Deliriously inventive . . . magnificently tender and humane'
Observer